1

1

Cyril stood in one corner of the Boys' playground, watching a battle. All he could hear was the headmaster's frustrated shouting; otherwise this was a silent conflict. One little boy had put his gas mask on as soon as he left the classroom, others followed suit and by the time they reached the playground a series of skirmishes had begun. When this little war was over, Cyril would make it clear that gas masks were not playthings. One day they may save the lives of these children, who represented the future of the valley he loved so much.

Cyril and Bertha Thomas founded Colesclough Air Raid Precautions section in 1940, soon after war broke out. He had recently retired from his job as Spinning Manager at Harrison's cotton mills and was a man of some consequence in the Coll Valley. He survived the Battle of the Somme and then Passchendaele, at which he had been awarded the Military Medal. So far his ARP section had seen only a few enemy bombers cross its territory and had not yet been called into action, but he and Bertha regularly gave lectures to local societies and schools. Today they were at Rossendale Road Infants School to alert the pupils to the dangers of poison gas.

Meanwhile, the girls had marched into the adjoining playground in pairs, holding hands. They quietly formed a circle around the elderly woman. Their teacher introduced Mrs Thomas. Bertha noticed that one of the girls carried her gas mask in a waterproof shoulder bag. She thought the cardboard boxes in which the respirators had been issued would be quite inadequate to withstand the regular rain with which East Lancashire was blessed. She and Cyril, although they avoided making it public, believed that this war

2

could be a long one. 'Happen longer than *our* war' was how he put it.

'Right my dears', Mrs Thomas began, 'I do hope as you've all tried on your gas masks at home, because after I've given my little talk me and Miss Hothersall will be checking that you know how to put them on right. But first, I want that little girl with the dark-hair to join me. Yes, that's right, *you* dear. You're Jane Clarke aren't you, Agnes's daughter?'

'Yes Miss,' said Jenny, stepping forward.

'Yes Ma'am,' the teacher corrected her.

'Sorry Ma'am, but they call me Jenny, please.'

'All right then Jenny, I want you to show these other girls that lovely bag you've brought your gas mask in. Did your mummy make it for you?'

'Yes Ma'am. There was a pattern in *Woman's Weekly*. She used my old pram sheet.'

Mrs Thomas positively beamed. 'Did you hear that, girls? Waste not, want not, that's how we're going to beat Mr Hitler and his nasty chums --- so when you all get home I want you to tell your mummies that you want a gas mask bag like Jenny's just shown you. Waterproof, we call it. Why would we want a waterproof bag, do you suppose?'

Jenny knew the answer, but could not risk further attention. What Mrs Thomas had just said would have incensed the two second-year girls who had been picking on her since she started school, just over a month ago. On the first day she had burst into tears as her Mum was leaving. Now they called her 'cry baby'.

3

'Because it rains a lot round here,' said a girl called Alice Foster, 'and if...'

'Well done, love,' Mrs Thomas intervened. 'The cardboard would get all soggy and we wouldn't have anything to carry our new gas masks around in, would we? Now, please listen carefully to what I have to tell you.'

Jenny wasn't able to pay close attention. Her mind was on whether she could get back to the girls' cloakroom in time to put the bag on her hook before her two enemies could get to her; also she wanted to wee.

Miss Hothersall told them to put their gas masks on and she and Bertha went to check that they fitted properly and were in good order. When Jenny had passed inspection she hurried to the Girls cloakroom, only to find her adversaries already there.

'Think you're summat special then, do you?' the fat girl said. 'Gimme that bag.'

'Don't bother with it Maisie,' said the tall one. 'Who'd want a soppy bag like that? My Mum'll make me a *proper* one out of *proper* stuff, not a smelly old pram sheet.'

Jenny had no intention of giving way and was planning a route around them. They mistook her indecision.

'I reckon she's scared, don't you, Maisie?' the tall one said.

'Yeah, she's wettin' herself. She's a pissy-knickers!' This greatly amused the girls but heightened Jenny's determination.

4

'And why they call her pretty I just don't know, said Heather. 'I'd call her ugly, wouldn't you? Don't suppose she'll ever get a boyfriend.'

'My boyfriend showed me his thingummy,' Maisie boasted.

She knew what they were talking about, having watched her next-door neighbour bathing little Kevin. Granny Entwistle had taught her that such remarks were unladylike and should be ignored. Her maternal grandmother was Jenny's mentor on etiquette. Before she married she worked at the Town Hall and had once spoken to Queen Alexandra.

Jenny decided it was time for action and got up onto the bench which ran the length of the entrance corridor.

'Excuse me please,' she said, using her 'posh' voice, which had the desired effect on the two girls, who obediently stood back to let her reach her hook. From this dominant position she went on to say, 'I think you two are very rude and it's time you stopped pestering me.' Then, against her better judgement, she responded to their taunts.

'And you're quite wrong because there *is* a boy who is in love with me and his name is Kenneth. So there!'

She jumped down and ran to the lavatories.

2

Jenny lived at 48 Bright Street and belonged to a gang called 'The Top Lot', whose membership was restricted to children from the upper half of the mill rows. That was probably one reason these two girls disliked her; they both came from the bottom end of Harrison Street. The acknowledged leader of the gang, an eight-year old lad named Harry Parker, told her that allowing a girl to join was a wartime concession. His eldest sister had persuaded him that, if women were good enough to serve in the ATS or the WAAF, then girls ought to be able to become members of the Top Lot. After Jenny informed them that Granny and Grandpa Entwistle had bought her a first-aid book and nurses outfit for her birthday the gang decided that Jenny could become their medical officer. For some time she was the only female member but eventually Doris Parkinson and a few of Jenny's other nominees were co-opted.

It was at this early age that she decided she would stand no nonsense from boys.

Her first move was to insist that members of the gang contribute to her 'Hospital Fund', donating a halfpenny each Friday, this being the day when parents paid pocket money. For several boys Jenny's impost represented a significant slice of their weekly income, but Harry decided that anyone not contributing would face expulsion. When some of the parents learned of Jenny's initiative they made extra contributions, so after a few months she found she had collected enough to visit Boots the Chemist to purchase essential supplies such as disinfectant, sticking plasters, cotton wadding and bandages. As an afterthought she went into the Co-op drapery department and said she would like to buy some cheap material to make slings, in case any members of the Junior Home Guard section of the gang suffered an injury while searching for German parachutists on Daisy Hill.

The lady assistant listened to her request and smiled, which rather annoyed Jenny, who had hoped to persuade the woman that this was a serious request, vital to the war effort.

The manager was summoned and the lady insisted that Jenny repeat her story to him. He too smiled, but the end result was that Jenny was given a bolt of mildewed curtain lining without charge. It was far too heavy for her to carry, so she arranged to return on the following Saturday morning with one of the older gang members as her porter.

Jenny made it clear that she would not treat football injuries. Grazed knees were a common hazard in those days, when every boy under the age of fourteen wore short trousers, but unless the damage was sustained on official gang business she referred the complainant to his mother.

Her success as medical officer earned Jenny considerable respect among her male colleagues but she nevertheless reached the conclusion that boys in general did not like girls; some of the gang members whom she rather fancied seemed immune to her charms. Only because her two adversaries at the infant school had riled her, did she name Kenneth as her boyfriend. The extent of their intimacy was that he and she sometimes held hands as they walked to school together. His had been the only name she could think of on the spur of the moment.

*

Jenny was proud of the fact that her father joined up as soon as war was declared and that within a short time he was made a lance-corporal. Originally he was posted to Preston, only a thirty-minutes bus ride from Colesclough, which meant he often came home to see them, but after what he called 'basic training' his regiment was sent out to France.

Kenneth explained that his dad was not called up because he had the wrong sort of feet. Jenny studied Mr Thistlethwaite's feet as he set off on his rounds as an insurance collector but failed to see how they disqualified him from war service. Although she did not say so to Kenneth, she believed that he could have joined the air force or the navy, where she assumed there was not a great deal of marching involved. She herself planned to join the WRNS as soon as she was old enough: they had the nicest uniforms.

No bombs had so far fallen anywhere in the Coll valley, though the air raid siren sounded regularly. Jenny and her mum, Agnes, could hear the drone of enemy planes passing overhead on their way to Manchester or Liverpool. At first they used to go down into the cellar each night as soon as the siren sounded but after a few weeks Agnes decided it was safe for them to stay in the living room.

Jenny was thrilled by the sound of anti-aircraft fire, which seemed to come from the direction of Blackburn. They would wait for the all clear to sound before venturing out into Bright Street and would often see a red glow in the sky as one or other of the cities illuminated the horizon. To Jenny this was exciting to watch; she did not then know what destruction and loss of life was involved.

They listened avidly to war reports on the wireless to see whether there was any mention of the Lancashire Fusiliers, but there never was. They received the occasional letter from France. Her mother read out only extracts, though Jenny was by then good at interpreting joined-up writing. She guessed that her Mum didn't want her to see what Kenneth called the 'lovey-dovey bits'. It was not long before Mr Clarke was made a full corporal and when he returned on a short leave after the fall of Dunkirk he had three stripes on his arm. Then he went to Africa.

A few weeks after his leave her mother told Jenny that she was going to have a brother or a sister. She hoped it would be a brother. Kenneth said it was likely to be a sister because ladies usually had either girls or boys, but she did not believe him. The issue was never resolved, because a few weeks later she found her mother crying after a visit to the doctor and was told that it was a 'false alarm'. When she asked what that meant, her mum said that there was not going to be another baby. Probably ever.

3

More than half the children who attended her Infants school came from the 'mill rows', which was how people in Colesclough still referred to the four streets on Daisy Hill, though few of the residents nowadays worked at Isaac Harrison's cotton mill.

In 1862 the original Mr Harrison persuaded a group of local businessmen to finance him in buying about four hundred and fifty acres of the western slope of the hill which dominates the town. For many decades there had been a tradition of home spinning and hand-loom weaving in the area and the Coll valley was then enjoying a period of prosperity, its damp climate being ideal for the manufacture of cotton textiles. Nowadays there would be an outcry against building a large factory on such a lovely site as Daisy Hill, but when Isaac began construction in 1864 it was a source of pride to the citizens of the small town that they were to have as fine a factory as any found in Burnley or Blackburn.

While Daisy Mill was being built, Mr Harrison also decided to have two streets of terraced houses erected. He named them Peel Street and Cobden Street. The houses were within easy walking distance of the factory and were offered to his workers for a token rent, or they could be purchased through instalment payments. At the time, these properties were considered to be too good for mere mill hands, but Isaac had a strong benevolent streak, stemming from his attachment to Methodism. He added another two rows of houses five years later while he was building Buttercup Mill. Those he named Bright Street and Harrison Street. It was his intention that there should be a complete new village on the site but he died before his dream could be fulfilled.

Wesley Harrison did not inherit his father's benevolence, so apart from the two mills, which by the 1940's provided employment to around nine hundred people, Isaac's generous legacy to the town of Colesclough comprised the four streets on Daisy Hill, Broadholme chapel, the public library and a tract of land alongside the River Coll which later became Harrison Park.

The mill rows ran parallel, up a steep incline from Blackburn Old Road towards the summit of Daisy Hill. Kenneth was born in Cobden Street, which shared a back ginnell with Bright Street. Despite their grimy stonework the four streets were superior to much of the property in the town below. Householders took pride in maintaining a bit of garden in the small space between the railings and their front doors; there was a lamp standard at the corner of each block and larch trees grew at intervals in the pavements of the four streets: a more pretentious man than Isaac would have called them 'avenues'. The houses had gas lighting installed from the outset, since Isaac was a director of the Coll Valley Gas and Coke Company, and when electricity came to Colesclough the mill rows were among the first to be connected.

The Clarkes lived in one of the two top properties in Bright Street. These houses had an extra yard, which faced open hillside over a low stone wall. There had been an iron gate

10

in the wall of number 48, but in 1940 it was removed to help the war effort. Jenny asked her mother how their gate was going to help the allies and was told that it would soon be part of a Spitfire, which some of her gang did not believe. Agnes had it replaced with a wooden one after some sheep came down from Daisy Hill one night and ate most of the Brussels sprouts she had planted. All the houses had a wash-place and a long-drop privy in the back yard, but part of the large bedroom of number 48 had been converted into a bathroom. Jenny considered hers to be far the best house in Bright Street, though she was aware that people turned up their noses when you said you came from the mill rows.

She used to doubt that anybody would consider her street to be 'bright,' for the stonework of the terraces was ingrained with grime from almost a century of smoke drifting from the two mill chimneys less than half a mile away. Yet once the Harrison chimneys were fully fired and the breeze was in the right direction, Daisy Hill would isolate itself from the rest of Colesclough. The pall of smoke hanging over the town below her made the mill rows seem to be their own little kingdom, and Jenny felt proud to be part of it.

In the fourth form at grammar school, when her history teacher explained the background to the formation of the Anti-Corn Law League, she had even more pride in her streets, knowing that three of them took their names from the great reformers, Robert Peel, John Bright and Richard Cobden. She also formed the opinion that old Isaac had taken a bit of a liberty in giving his own name to the fourth.

It was Jenny's maternal grandparents the Entwistles, who originally bought number 48 from a man who worked at the mill. They named their firstborn Agnes, giving her just the one name because they planned a large family and wanted to reserve their options, but fate decreed that Agnes should

11

be their only child. Being a frugal couple they eventually saved enough to buy another house at the bottom of the street. They bought it purely as an investment, but Granny Entwistle developed arthritis in both knees while she was still in her forties. So, when Agnes became engaged to Tommy Clarke, they sold number 48 to the young couple for the discounted sum of £160, to be paid off over three years. Jenny's grandparents then moved down to live at number 7, in order that Mrs Entwistle should be spared the long climb up the hill.

Jenny had never known either of her father's parents. Grandpa Clarke was killed in the Great War and her other granny died before she was born, so she greatly cherished Grandpa and Granny Entwistle. She used to stop at their house every day after school until her mother had finished work, and after Grandpa died she took charge of Gran's ration book and did the shopping for her. Eventually Mrs Entwistle became housebound and suffered great pain, so it was considered a 'blessed release' when she passed away in 1952. Number 7 was then rented to a newly-arrived Pakistani family.

4

Kenneth and Jane were inseparable. They were born in the same week and had been playmates for as long as either could remember. When the time came for them to go to school they walked together to Rossendale Road Infants, then to Saint Peter's C of E, and after they both won scholarships to Colesclough Grammar they walked down Bright Street to catch the school bus on Blackburn Old Road. He grew to be just an inch shorter than her, slim, verging upon willowy, with hair somewhere between blond and sandy.

Ken obviously knew it was his best feature and he spent a lot of time combing it. After he changed his National Health glasses for a pair of rimless ones, Jenny decided he was quite handsome.

Her closeness to Kenneth meant that she never had any other boyfriend. Yet, although she never seriously contemplated marrying anyone but him, the relationship was not what she would call romantic. She did not derive from him the thrill she used to get from poring over her collection of photographs of film actors which she kept under the lining of her underwear drawer. Her fantasy relationship with these handsome men was more potent than the real thing with Kenneth. When she first kissed Kenneth there was never quite the excitement that film close-ups had led her to expect.

Her first intense sexual thrill came when he called round with his Higher School Certificate results. The Deputy Head had made them all fill in stamped addressed postcards with their subjects listed, so that the school secretary could easily complete and post them when the examination results were announced. Jenny was still in bed when the mail arrived that morning, because it was Saturday. She heard her father shout.

'You'd better come down young lady. There's a postcard here that you might be interested in.' She slipped her dressing gown on and almost fell downstairs. 'Is it awful?' she asked. 'Tell me, I can't bear to look.'

'All right then, let's have a see.' He paused, and said teasingly, 'By the way, a Distinction is good, is it?'

'Of course it is Dad; you know very well that's the best grade. Have I got a distinction? Which subject?'

13

'Well love, it's all a bit boring really. You see, you've got four distinctions --- English Literature, History, French and German. Is that the sort of result you'd call awful?'

Mr Clarke held out his arms. 'Come here lass and let your old Dad give you a kiss.' Jenny never liked to kiss him in the morning because he always smelt of stale beer.

Within a few minutes Kenneth was round, displaying his own postcard with obvious pride.

'A very good day to you my dear neighbours,' he said pompously. 'I would like you to meet Manchester University's most promising new undergraduate.' He deliberately held them in suspense.

'Come on then,' Jane prompted.

'OK, listen to this. Distinctions in Maths and Chemistry and Credits in Biology and Physics. What about that then?'

'Congratulations lad,' said Mr Clarke. 'Seems like the mill rows have turned out a couple of geniuses. Show him, Jenny.'

After he saw her results, Kenneth gave her a big hug and a long kiss on the lips. She only wore her nightie under the dressing gown and this kiss made a wonderful shiver run down her spine. She decided that there might be more to Kenneth Thistlethwaite than she had previously realised. But then his expression changed to something less than delight.

'Oh heck,' he said, 'old Hoppy got you put down for Oxford, didn't he?'

'That's right,' her father said. 'You did well at the interview didn't you love? Saint Hilda's College should give her a place with these results.'

'Then it looks like we'll be saying goodbye to your lovely daughter, Mr Clarke.'

Two weeks later Jenny's father drowned himself in the River Coll. He chose the place where it is deepest, a few yards beyond where the old mill race meets the effluent drain of Harrisons' bleach house. By the following afternoon his creditors had started to call at 48 Bright Street.

5

Geoffrey Harrison was a dutiful son. He loved and respected his parents, who had brought him up to accept the responsibilities which accompanied the privileged position to which he was born, but he often wished that he could take a job outside the family firm and make his own way in the world, not dependent on what outsiders doubtless regarded as nepotism. Yet he knew that it was up to him to try to keep the family business alive for the next generation.

It was on the subject of 'generation' that he had begun to resent what were considered to be his responsibilities. The wealth of many East Lancashire manufacturing families was enhanced by a judicious choice of partners for their offspring; indeed, there had been so much intermarriage among the Coll valley slipper manufacturers that babies were said to have been born with tiny bootees on their feet. Geoffrey knew that his parents had married for love and that his mother had brought no money to the match, but she remained adamant that he must choose his life's partner from among the business elite of Lancashire or, if all else failed, Yorkshire.

He imagined what his mother might say if she ever discovered that he had fallen in love with Jane Clarke. *Quite unacceptable Geoffrey dear. She is a pretty girl I grant you, but it's a long way from Bright Street to The Little Lodge*, or words to that effect. She would be speaking figuratively of course, in terms of mileage Sabden was not all that far from Colesclough. Geoffrey had clocked it at under twenty-five minutes in his MG; his father's chauffeur-driven Lagonda took a more sober three-quarters of an hour. Nevertheless, *The Little Lodge* was indeed a world apart from number 48 Bright Street.

Alice Harrison (born Schofield) knew that only too well, for she had made such a transition, from a two-up two-down terraced house in East Colesclough to a mansion on the outskirts of the Ribble valley. But Alice had long since expunged from her memory the surroundings in which she had been born. A course of elocution lessons and the skilful attentions of the couture salon of Kendal Milne's department store in Manchester had wrought such change in Alice that few would now recognise her as the naïve girl who had once been a trimmer at the Crown slipper works.

She used to embarrass Geoffrey when she came up to see him at his boarding school, Castleberg. Alice judged his friends by what she called their "background and breeding", but which he knew had more to do with the size of their parents' bank balances. His best friend at school was the son of a Baptist minister, which rather flummoxed Mrs Harrison. 'One has to respect anyone who has opted for such a career,' she once said on a visit to the school, 'though how he can afford to send Simon here quite baffles me. There must be private money.' To Mrs Harrison, "private money" excused most failings.

For her children's birthday parties there was a carefully prepared list drawn up of those who might be acceptable as guests, not dissimilar to that of selection for a royal garden party. The candidates were chosen only after interrogation by Alice of her long-suffering husband Harold as to the financial status of each young person's family. Girls were vetted with special care. "Relationships can be forged at a very early age", she used to say, "One can never be too careful."

The elder son, Roger, fled the nest by staying on in the army after National Service and was currently serving with BAOR in Germany. On the grand piano in the morning room was a silver-framed photograph of Roger in the uniform of a Royal Artillery captain, which Alice showed to visitors with the pride of a mother who has spawned a war hero.

When Geoffrey left Castleberg he expressed a wish to read for a law degree at Cambridge, after he had done his National Service. His father reacted almost with disappointment. Harold made it clear that he would allow this indulgence in view of the hard work that the lad had obviously put in at school, but there must be no doubting that when the interlude was over he would come back north to take up his duties as the heir to Isaac Harrison Limited. As Harold once put it, "We couldn't expect our Harriet to take over, could we?"

Their youngest child had only one ambition in life --- to become the three-day event champion of Great Britain.

*

The Little Lodge was built in 1910 by Wesley Harrison in a style which became known to its critics as mill-owners' Gothic. There are fine examples of the genre still to be seen on the outskirts of towns such as Oldham or Bolton but *The Little Lodge* was unique in the Sabden area. The understated name was thought to have been recommended by the architect, no doubt to disguise the fact that such an edifice was not entirely in keeping with the leafy countryside among which it sat, for it was neither a lodge nor was it little.

When Harold Harrison first introduced Alice Schofield to his recently-widowed mother as his chosen consort, she was given a frosty reception. Alice was overawed by the surroundings. Before she and Harold were to be married he had difficulty in persuading her that it was their duty to go to live at the Sabden house in order to look after his mother. Even after Alice had produced a son and heir it took some time for her to overcome her mother-in-law's antipathy. The fact that the old lady continued to live with them could not but remind Alice that she was very much the junior Mrs Harrison. The Little Lodge remained a somewhat forbidding place to her until she finally became its mistress.

When Harold's mother died, in 1946, Alice took the place in hand. A seven-bedroomed mansion with one bathroom was converted into a comfortable family home with five bedrooms and three bathrooms. The spacious kitchen was gutted and refitted with the most up-to-date equipment. A utility annexe was added, a four-car garage replaced the original wooden structure built to house Wesley Harrison's Daimler and stables were erected behind the tennis courts for little Harriet's horses. *House and Garden* featured the refurbishment in its November 1949 edition.

What continued to annoy Alice was the name of the house. She wanted it changed to *Harrison Hall* but Harold refused. Still it was satisfactory not to have to add a street name to the address. *The Little Lodge, Sabden, Lancs* remained embossed on their white wove notepaper.

6

The tacklers' cabin was a haven of comparative quiet, reached from the weaving shed by a flight of iron steps and protected by a triple-glazed window from the constant clatter of three hundred looms.

Jenny could see Abram Pickup enjoying his tea break with the other tacklers, seated, like the disciples, at their long table overlooking the shed. Even during their break time one was supposed to keep watch, in case any weaver needed help, but there was no response to her waving. She walked along to the end loom of her set and pressed a bell-push which would ring in the cabin to summon Abram. Within a couple of minutes he was down, not at all angry at being disturbed, since a stopped loom meant lost money for both of them. She had not yet learned lip-reading so he yelled directly into her ear. ' What's up, Jenny?'

She had to mouth her reply because Abram could lip-read better than he could hear; having worked in Harrisons' weaving sheds for thirty-five years he had become quite deaf.

'There's a slack warp on number seventy-two,' she told him. 'Either the pick wheel's damaged or the take-up motion needs tightening. We could have a smash.'

'Good lass,' he said. 'Well spotted. Weaving's in your blood, isn't it?'

Of course that was nonsense. Abram had been her mother's tackler before Agnes gave up her job as a weaver to marry Tommy Clarke. She went back to work in the mill after Tommy joined up, though she had to stop in 1942 because of some trouble with her inner ear. Abram liked to think that young Jenny had somehow inherited what he had taught Agnes Entwistle, but of course she had to learn the job just like everyone else.

Agnes had talked of going back into weaving when Tommy died. Jenny insisted she get their doctor's advice. He told her she would be at great risk of losing her balance and falling into machinery if she were again exposed to such excessive noise. Other jobs Agnes applied for paid hardly enough to make it worthwhile leaving the house, certainly insufficient to help support her daughter at college, be it Oxford or Manchester. So Jenny decided that it was up to her to look for a job. Harrisons seemed the obvious choice.

It was a hard decision. Her modern languages teacher had given her special coaching and was justifiably angry when she told him she would have to forgo a place at university.

'For God's sake reconsider, Jane,' Mr Hopkinson said. 'You have the State Scholarship. The days have gone when girls like you had to sacrifice an academic career to look after their families. Dammit, we have a Welfare State now. Your mother shouldn't need to find a penny.'

'With respect, sir, you don't understand. We have debts to pay.'

'But surely you and your mother can't be held responsible? I'll see a solicitor about it if you like. Manchester have confirmed a place, and with these results the Head has high hopes of you getting an exhibition from Saint Hilda's. Oxbridge colleges are keen to get more grammar school pupils these days. Do you realise you would be our first female pupil to reach Oxford or Cambridge? Let me have a talk with your mother.'

'No need for that, sir', she said. 'We've already seen a solicitor and he agrees with you. Mum agrees with you too; she's just as cross as you are that I'm not going to university, but it's my decision and I'm sticking to it.'

Nevertheless, Mr Hopkinson did visit Agnes, who then tried a different form of persuasion on her daughter. 'It's not right that a girl with your education should end up in the mill. It makes me feel we've failed you. You could easily get a nice office job.'

'None of this is your fault, Mum,' Jenny replied. 'Blame Dad by all means, but the fact is we just can't afford for me to go to university, and if I do get a job it might as well be the best paid one. There's no shame in being a weaver.'

'I know that, but don't give up on Oxford, love', she pleaded. 'Mr Hopkinson said you're sure to get a grant from the college on top of your scholarship.'

'It'll still be nowhere near enough, Mum.'

'I could manage. There's the rent from number 7, don't forget.'

'Do be sensible. How far does thirty shillings a week stretch these days? And even if you sell it ... '

21

'I can't, not at present. The Quereshi family have four years left on their lease.'

'There you are, then. To be honest Mum, I'm not sure I want to go to Oxford. Not with all those la-di-da girls I met when I had the interview --- they're not our sort. And even if I went to Manchester there'd be bus fares, books and all sorts of expenses. Kenneth's having second thoughts about university too. No, I've thought long and hard about it and I've decided I'm going to put us back on our feet. Harrisons' weaving shed is where the best money is.'

So Mr Hopkinson's ambitions for his star pupil were frustrated and Harrisons recruited the best educated weaver they had ever had.

7

Jenny started as a ring frame operator in the spinning mill because there were no vacancies in weaving, but after six months one of the weavers left to have a baby and Jenny got her job. This was in Buttercup Mill, where they still had the original Lancashire looms. The machines had drop-boxes and four shuttles, so she had to watch carefully to see when the weft was about to run out, then stop the loom and change the shuttle. She soon got the hang of it but the work was both tiring and tedious.

When Daisy Mill went onto two shifts she applied to move to the Northrop looms which more or less ran themselves. They only had one shuttle and the pin changed automatically. All she had to do was make sure the warp threads were in order and keep the weft batteries full. She found the job much easier, despite being given more looms than she had in Buttercup Mill. She was allocated ten machines to start with, but within four months she had built up to a set of thirty.

Jenny and Abram regularly topped the efficiency ratings, which meant that, with piece work bonuses, she sometimes earned as much as fifteen pounds a week. She used to give her mother six pounds every Friday but by the time next pay day came along she usually had a tidy sum left over. Within two years they had cleared her father's debts, and in the summer wakes week of 1957 she was able to take her mother for a holiday in Bispham.

But the job was boring. She determined that the flying shuttles would not lull her into the sort of trance which seemed to overcome other women, most of whom appeared to get through the day by switching off their brains, so she bought a book on the principles of textile manufacture and used to watch Abram while he was working on her looms. He helped by bellowing out the procedures he was following when a machine needed attention. But, of course, she would never be allowed to join the select band of loom tuners. That was man's work.

She took advantage of the impenetrable noise to keep up her French and German, declaiming Corneille or Schiller against the competing din. She speculated as to what those who could lip-read made of her ranting. Some called her 'hoity-toity' and many of the younger ones were no doubt jealous of her looks, but this was her form of rebellion against the conditions. They could make of her whatever they liked.

Abram had finished repairing loom number 72. 'You were right, lass. Your pick wheel were buggered.' He tapped her affectionately on the shoulder. 'By the way, come up to the cabin when t' shift's over. I have some carrots for you.'

Every time he picked vegetables from his allotment he brought some in for Jenny to take home. He was a sidesman at the Broadholme Methodist chapel and lived by the precepts of his church (except that he was partial to the odd pint of Thwaites's ale). The first time he gave her some vegetables she sought to thank him but he said, 'Don't talk daft. How do you think me and Sheila could get through that lot?'

He moved off to see if any of his other weavers had a problem.

*

Kenneth also decided against going to university. His knowledge of chemistry enabled him to secure a position at Harrisons, as a management trainee in the dyehouse, so when Jenny also went to work there he used to meet her outside the weaving shed and they would walk home together, just as they had done as children.

On most Saturday nights they went to the Astoria ballroom, over the hill in Rawtenstall. Dancing was a secondary consideration for most of the boys who spent at least the first part of their Saturday nights at the ballroom. Come to that, few of the young women who attended were solely interested in finding an expert partner for the quickstep or the slow foxtrot. No, the attraction of the Astoria was that it provided safe territory where assignations could be made, where, to use the vernacular of the time, the male talent could be spotted and the female stray picked up.

Now that Jenny had become a beauty, she was a prime target. She found that the best way to keep the budding Lotharios at bay was to stick with Kenneth, who was an excellent dancer. They had learned together from a manual written by Victor Sylvester. There were sometimes other young men with whom she would have liked to dance but it became known that she was 'spoken for'.

8

She often practiced how she would sign after she and Kenneth were married.

Jane Thistlethwaite.   *Jenny Thistlethwaite.*   *J. E. Thistlethwaite.*

However she wrote it, she could not make the name acceptable. Then there was the way he spoke. She assured herself that she was not a snob but he might at least try to get the grammar right. They used to argue about it.

'Your parents speak properly, so why don't you?'

'Not at home they don't,' he said. 'They speak normal at home, and I do speak properly when I need to. I speak properly when I'm talking to you, don't I?'

'Usually you do, then why not always?'

'It's not natural. It's not how I were brought up . . .was brought up.'

Of course, it was how she too had been brought up and she was proud of being a Lancastrian. She loved her grand-

25

mother's recitations of the vernacular poetry of Edwin Waugh, some of which Jenny now knew by heart. But, hearing people talking on the wireless, she realised that the English her school friends spoke was not the same as that spoken by educated women.

When she was about thirteen years old she decided to model herself on Kathleen Ferrier. Not the singing of course; that was out of the question. Jenny could sing In tune but she had a weak little soprano voice, and at chapel she used to wait until they were well into the first verse of a hymn before she would join in. It was Kathleen's speaking voice that she emulated; clear, grammatical, yet with a trace of Lancashire still there.

Because of Jenny's aptitude for languages she had cultivated good French and German accents, so she easily adopted Standard English or 'received pronunciation' as she heard it called. She developed it so people would know she wasn't from 'down South' but would have difficulty in tracing precisely where she came from. Her accent was one reason why women at the mill called her 'hoity-toity'. Another was her use of vocabulary.

By chance it was Kathleen Ferrier who had also whetted Jenny's appetite for words. The Clarkes had a record of Kathleen singing *Blow the wind southerly* which was played so often that Jenny could recite the words before she understood them properly. There was one line which particularly baffled her --- *They told me last night there were ships in the offing*. One day she asked her mother, 'What's an offing. Mum?'

'I don't know love, let's look it up.'

They could not find *offing* in their little dictionary so Jenny asked Miss Warburton at St Peter's what the word meant. When it had been explained, she took to using the new word on every possible occasion. "I have a birthday in the offing" or "I gather there is a new Lassie film in the offing".

Gradually she added other words which she heard on the BBC Home Service, some of which she needed to check in Miss Warburton's *Concise Oxford*. In her second year at the Grammar her father bought her a copy of that dictionary and she started to tune in to the new Third Programme, chiefly to listen out for new words.

She told Kenneth he ought to improve his vocabulary.

'I know words you've never even heard of,' he responded.

'Such as?'

'Trinitrotoluene?' he ventured.

'What? That's no use.'

'More use than bloody *offing*. It'll blow up fancy buggers like you.'

9

After graduating from Cambridge, Geoffrey dutifully joined the family firm and began practical training in the mills. When he eventually reached the Lancashire loom shed he was put with Harrisons' most experienced weaver, who was called Elsie Parkinson. Because of the din there was no chance for him to speak to the lovely young woman who worked beam to Elsie and at the end of each day her boy-friend was waiting for her at the door of the weaving shed. Geoffrey had been in the shed just short of two weeks when she disappeared to work on the Northrops.

Geoffrey did meet Jane one Saturday night, at the Astoria ballroom. He knew she turned down invitations to dance and always took the floor with her boyfriend (whom he considered far too wet for someone like her). On that particular night, Geoffrey had a few dances with a girl who worked in the card room at the mill, but he was thinking of abandoning the Astoria and driving up to a pub above Haslingden, when he saw Jenny's boyfriend leave for the gents. Without much hope, he went over to ask her for a dance.

'I'd be delighted,' she said. 'You're Geoffrey Harrison, aren't you? I work at your mill.'

'Yes, I know, and you're Jane Clarke. I used to see you when I was learning to weave.'

'So you noticed me? I did wonder.'

'How could I fail,' he said, and feared he might have gone too far, but she looked pleased. After only one foxtrot the band took its break and the boyfriend had returned.

Geoffrey decided to leave, thinking he may have fallen in love.

*

It was only after Geoffrey had completed his training in Daisy Mill and moved down to the dyehouse alongside the River Coll that he got to know Kenneth Thistlethwaite. Ken was by now the colour chemist, responsible for mixing dyestuffs to the required shade and fastness. One day, while they were having a cup of coffee together in the laboratory, which was Ken's domain, Geoffrey asked him why he had not taken up the place he had been offered at Manchester University.

'It were Dad that made me change me mind. "What do you think you'll want to do when you've finished at Manchester?" he says, and I told him I'd thought of trying for a job in your dyehouse. "You won't need a degree for that", he says, "you might as well be earning money". So that were it, really.'

'But university isn't just about getting a degree,' said Geoffrey.

'I suppose at Cambridge it wasn't, but if I had gone to Manchester I'd have just taken the bus there every day and come home at night. Just like grammar school, only further. And then there was me girlfriend.'

'That's Jane Clarke, isn't it?'

'Yeah, Jenny we call her. I'd have taken up the offer from Manchester if she'd gone with me, but when she got her results we were sure she'd get into Oxford. She did get offered a place at St Hilda's.'

'Why on earth didn't she take it?'

'They had some trouble in the family. She ended up not going to either university and I couldn't see the point of me going neither, so I applied to Norman Howarth for this job.'

'I suppose it all worked out OK for you,' said Geoffrey, 'but I think that one day you'll regret not going to university.'

29

10

Castleberg was an all-male school, so Geoffrey's experience
of the opposite sex was limited. Girls who visited The Little
Lodge during school holidays tended also to be from single-
sex boarding schools, so were seldom relaxed in his company. The few that did appeal to him seemed more interested in his elder brother, Roger. National Service had been
his first entry into the real world but, when he went to town
with the lads, their aim was to find women willing to
provide instant sex, a prospect Geoffrey found intimidating.
There had been occasions when he was tempted to accept
what was on offer but some ingrained prudery, or perhaps
fear, prevented him.

Men greatly outnumbered women undergraduates when he
arrived at Cambridge and the attractive ones were snapped
up within the first few weeks of term by others, quicker off
the mark than the shy Geoffrey. It was not until he started
to go through the mill at Harrison's that he discovered that
it was possible to meet young women on a basis other than
the sort of mating game which his mother favoured.

He started his training on the scutching machines, which
opened and cleaned the cotton lint. Only men were employed there, because humping four hundred pound bales
and pushing trolleys of laps to the carding engines was
heavy work. Geoffrey arrived home each night tired. Curi-
ously, he also felt satisfied, though no mental effort had been
required of him throughout the day. He got on well with the
other men, but to them he remained 'Young Mr Geoffrey'.

It was quite different when he progressed to the card room,
where women were in the majority. They teased him un-

mercifully. For the first time in his life he found that he was able to talk to women as fellow human beings. Despite the constant dust and heat, he enjoyed his month in carding.

The ring spinning room was further proof that one could have pleasant relations with members of the female sex without, as one of them put it to him, "getting right serious." Two of the young women lived in Haslingden and he used to give them lifts home in his MG. Sometimes they would stop at the Coach and Horses for a quick drink.

He reached the preparation section in late spring, a season when the sap rises, even in industrial Lancashire. The department had only four men apart from him and there were at least forty women, most of whom were young, because they needed to be keen-sighted and adept at piecing-up broken threads. He was asked by the forewoman if he would be interested in joining their annual departmental outing to the Mecca of the North, Blackpool.

*

Geoffrey was in the mill car park by nine o'clock on the chosen Saturday, waiting for the 'charas' to arrive. A few women were with husbands or boyfriends, but the rest chatted noisily outside the door of front office. Geoffrey joined the unattached men in a corner of the car park. When the two coaches drew up, the single women boarded straight away, each taking a double seat, leaving a space beside her. Geoffrey got onto the first coach and chose to sit with a woman called Dorothy (he did not know her second name). She squeezed his thigh as soon as he was seated, setting the tone for the rest of the day. But it was not with Dorothy that he spent that Saturday.

A few miles outside Preston, someone pointed out to the driver that it was now opening time and he pulled into the car park of a large pub for the first drink of the day. There were to be many more. He asked Dorothy what she would have but she said, 'Just wait a minute, chuck,' and went over to join the group of women congregated at the far end of the lounge bar. Geoffrey bought himself a half-pint of bitter. He had almost finished it when the huddle broke up and a good-looking woman wearing a short floral pinafore dress came up to join him. She gave him a peck on the cheek.

'Now then, Geoffrey,' she said, 'I know who you are and they call me Maggie.' She wore a wedding ring. Geoffrey offered to buy her a drink.

'There won't be time, thanks. We only stopped here for t' sweep.'

'Sweep?'

'Sweepstake. You know, like they have for t' Grand National. Them as brought husbands or boyfriends don't enter, but the rest of us pick a name from the hat, and I drew you. So, I hope you don't mind but you've got me for t' rest o' t' day.'

He studied Maggie, and decided that fate had been kind to him. They could hear the coach driver sounding his horn. 'Come on, sup up love,' she said, squeezing his hand. 'Let's find a seat near t' back.'

As the last glimmer of daylight was disappearing behind Morecambe Bay, Geoffrey Harrison lost his virginity.

11

Alice often found it difficult to get her husband to pay attention to what she considered important problems, so that particular Saturday evening seemed as good an opportunity as any to put her plan to him. He had returned late from the football match and she could see that he was in a good mood, Burnley having beaten Tottenham Hotspur 3 -1. She had persuaded him to change from his sports jacket to a lounge suit. Ideally she would have liked them to dress for dinner on Saturdays but she knew that was too much to ask, especially when the children were out.

Alice also was happy. Just after six o'clock she had seen Harriet driven away to the Hodder Valley Hunt Ball by a young man in a brand new yellow Triumph TR3 sports car. A very suitable young man, from a family of cotton brokers with an estate outside Cliviger. He was not a prepossessing fellow one had to admit, but ideal for Harriet, who was no beauty. Alice's only misgiving was about the frock, a pale mauve. The woman at Kendals had said how much it suited her daughter, but Alice had had reservations at the time and, as she was helping Harriet to dress that afternoon, she had come to the conclusion that it was a dreadful mistake. Only with difficulty had she hidden her true feelings. But the young man did not seem to notice. However, her main worry was Geoffrey.

They no longer had a permanent cook, though Mrs Foster came in when asked. Tonight she had cooked them a lovely rack of lamb which they had just followed with gooseberry fool. The dining room was one of the few parts of the house that Alice had not altered; she had always approved of it.

It gave the impression of genteel affluence. The walls were half-panelled in light oak, above which she had specified a burgundy flock-wallpaper of Regency design, in keeping with the fireplace, which was modelled in the style of Robert Adam. On the walls hung four pictures which had been chosen by Harold's mother, with advice from the architect. Alice found it difficult to remember the names of the artists, but when showing visitors through the house she had learned to point out that the paintings were by 'English post-impressionists'. She was not quite sure what that meant and fortunately nobody had yet asked her. However, she knew they must be good paintings because their insurance value needed to be increased significantly when Harold had the house contents re-valued in 1950.

Burnley's win was still reflected in the expression on her husband's face. When young Gloria had cleared away the pudding dishes he got up to take a Monte Cristo from the humidor. Alice poured them each a cup of coffee but she waited until he got himself a glass of port and his cigar was well alight before she struck.

'It's nice having a meal on our own, isn't it love?'

'Grand,' he replied. There was no further response.

'I'm worried about Geoffrey.'

'Oh yes?'

'Aren't you?'

'Not particularly. He's doing well at the mill; seems keener than I would have expected when he came down from Cambridge.'

34

'His social life,' she explained. 'You know what I mean.'

'No, I don't see the problem. He seems to get out quite a lot.'

'Exactly, but who with?' She corrected herself, 'with whom?'

'None of our business, I'd say. After all he's twenty-three; I was married at twenty-three, if you recall. And you were just turned nineteen, weren't you? As lovely a nineteen year-old as could be found in the county, and...'

'No, Harold, you aren't going to flannel me out of what I was going to say. Where is our Geoffrey now, for instance?'

'On the winding room trip to Blackpool --- very good for what they call public relations.'

'And where was he last Saturday.'

'Out dancing, I understand.'

'Exactly.'

'You keep saying 'exactly' but I don't see your point. Why don't you stop all this probing around and come out with it.'

'Very well, Mr Harrison, your son . . . '

'Our son', he interrupted.

'All right then, *our* son. Our son is not moving in the right circles. I had hoped he might find someone suitable at Cambridge.'

'You wouldn't want him married to some bluestocking would you?'

'Well, no, I suppose not, but I've introduced him to some of the nicest, most respectable girls in East Lancashire.'

'Say what you mean, love. You mean rich.'

'Yes, Harold, if you must have it, some of the nicest rich young girls in East Lancashire. We are rich aren't we? What's wrong with being rich?'

'Nothing my dear,' he said, seeing that she was becoming upset. 'I was only teasing you.'

'Well, it's not a matter for teasing. It's serious.'

'All right Alice. Seriously, what's your solution to this so-called problem?'

'I think he ought to be sent away from here for a bit. I think you ought to send him out to that new mill you're building in Nigeria.'

Harold could not resist one last tease, 'You think he might find a nice black woman out there, do you?' She was now angry.

'I knew I was wasting my time. You're quite impossible.'

It was rarely that Alice hit on something with which he agreed. Sending Geoffrey to Okante was precisely what Harold already had in mind.

12

Broadholme Wesleyan Methodist Chapel was built by Isaac Harrison to ensure that the people of Colesclough would be able to worship God in the way that he thought proper.

Jenny ceased attending chapel after she started at the grammar school --- not exactly a loss of faith, more that she didn't see the point in working people giving up their hard-earned Sunday morning rest to scrub themselves and show off their best suits and frocks. But Kenneth never gave up, and when they were more or less officially 'walking out', Jenny began going with him. After the morning service he would escort her home to change into casual clothes and would return ten minutes later on his motor bike, wearing a pair of denim trousers, which people nowadays were calling 'jeans'.

The motor-cycle was Ken's pride and joy, a Norton he bought second-hand, but which he kept in perfect condition, polished so as to shine brightly in the infrequent East Lancashire sunshine. They would take off for the Ribble Valley or through the Trough of Bowland, and they had a favourite pub in Mitton where they usually ate a sandwich lunch. Although neither of them touched alcohol, Kenneth was not so prejudiced as to believe that it was a sin to enter licensed premises.

One Sunday in November they walked back to the mill rows as usual after chapel. It was a crisp, sunny day and Jenny was looking forward to their ride, but before she went in to change he said, 'I have a surprise for you, we're not going out on't bike.'

'It's a lovely day. We'll be all right if we wrap up well.'

'Aye, we are going out. He paused, 'I've hired a car!'

'Oh Kenneth, that's lovely. Where are we going?'

'It's a surprise. You can change into that new print frock you bought in Burnley and I'll put me grey suit on. See you in twenty minutes.'

When Kenneth sounded the horn, Agnes came out with Jenny to admire the hire car, a light blue Renault Dauphine. They both waved to their nosy neighbour across the road who was, as usual, peering through the upstairs net curtains. Kenneth opened the car door to usher Jenny into the front seat, then he ostentatiously revved the engine for all to hear, before they sped down Bright Street.

On Blackburn Old Road Jenny told him to slow down; the Anglican church was just emptying and laggards were still trickling back from Broadholme. She wound down the window to wave to people she recognised and, looking through the wing mirror, was pleased to see them turn to stare after the smart little car. They took their usual road out of Colesclough, heading for Whalley. But in Whalley, instead of turning off for Mitton, he carried on along the Clitheroe road. Obviously this was the start of her surprise trip. Jenny felt a surge of affection for Kenneth and reached across to the steering wheel to give his hand a squeeze.

'I love you Jane Clarke,' he responded.

'I love you back,' said Jenny, counting her many blessings.

In Clitheroe he took the wrong road and they had to turn round. 'Dammit, I were looking for t' Slaidburn road and we must have passed it. Keep your eyes peeled to t' right when we go back through.'

Suddenly she was aware what the surprise might be. 'You're not taking me to the Gamecock, are you?'

'I am that,' he said proudly, 'nowt but t' best for my lass.' She forgave him the lapse.

The Gamecock Inn at Waddington was favoured by what Agnes Clarke called 'the better end', the sort of place that people like Geoffrey Harrison frequented. The lounge bar was already quite full when they arrived, but Kenneth said that was OK because he had booked a table. When he went to get the drinks, Jenny took a look around to see if there was anyone she knew. Lo and behold, there *was* Geoffrey Harrison, sitting in an alcove with a well-built young woman whom Jenny knew to be Mabel Butterworth, daughter of Butterworth's Shoes. They were deep in conversation and she tried to interpret their body language to see if this was a close liaison.

Geoffrey was a handsome man. Her best friend Mary had quite a crush on him. His dark hair was already receding; most likely he would go bald early like his father. It was Geoffrey's eyes that women in the mill talked about; deep set, dark olive. 'Bedroom eyes' one of the weavers had called them. Jenny could see what she meant. In an ideal world she might have fancied Geoffrey Harrison, but she was a realist and preferred what was attainable. Her dear Kenneth was attainable. She looked over to the bar where he was waiting to be served, and felt a surge of affection.

When Mabel Butterworth got up for the toilet Jenny assessed her and found little to make her feel jealous. A bit overweight and bottom too large, but she had a good bust and nice ankles. She was glad she had decided not to wear a hat; none of the other women was wearing one and she had had her hair cut shorter that Friday night. Her mother said it looked very fashionable. At school many people had told her she resembled Ava Gardner, which may be true, since even Kenneth had said so.

Jenny felt proud of how smart he looked today. His grey suit was made to measure for his Cousin Donald's wedding and he had worn it only twice that she knew of. His rimless glasses made him look intellectual, which indeed he was, at least as far as science was concerned. If only he had more ambition. Dyehouse manager at Harrisons was likely to be the pinnacle of Kenneth's career.

He returned with the bitter lemon she had ordered. His drink was fizzy and had some ice and a slice of lemon in it.

'I hope that's not what they call gin and tonic,' she said jokingly.

'No gin, but nobody's to know that are they?'

A man who looked as though he must be the proprietor was circulating the room. When he came up to them he shook Jenny's hand and Ken stood up to do likewise. 'Welcome to you both,' said the man. 'I don't recall having you with us before. Are you dining?'

'Yes, we are sir. Could we have a menu?'

'You shouldn't have called him sir,' she said when the man had gone.

Geoffrey had seen them and came over, followed by Mabel. 'Well, look who's here,' he said. 'Nice to meet you again,

Ken. And Miss Clarke. Do either of you know Mabel Butterworth? Mabel, I'd like to introduce Jane Clarke and Kenneth
Thistlethwaite, friends of mine from the mill.'

Jenny did not care for the look of appraisal that Mabel gave
her, but shook hands and remembered not to say 'pleased to
meet you'. Her granny used to tell her that was common.
'No, we haven't met,' Mabel said. Geoffrey must realise that
she and Mabel would never have mixed in the same circles.

'How do you do, Miss Butterworth?'

Kenneth said, 'Pleased to meet you, Mabel.'

'This is obviously a celebration', said Geoffrey, 'so we won't
disturb you. Come along Mabel, I expect they're ready for us
in there.' They moved off towards the dining room.

It was another ten minutes before Jenny and Kenneth were
called. The menu presented no problems. There were one
or two things on the 'a la carte' that she didn't understand
but 'Les plats du jour' were straightforward. Both ordered
prawn cocktail and Kenneth chose filet mignon, well done.
After a long period of indecision Jenny opted for sole
meuniere.

When the wine waiter came over, she expected Kenneth to
send him away. However, without consulting the list, he
ordered a half bottle of Sauternes.

The sommelier raised his eyebrows, 'With the main course,
sir?'

'Yes please,' said Ken. As the man walked away, she
whispered, 'Are you sure you ought to be drinking? You've
not had wine before and you're driving, don't forget.'

'Why not? Look, Geoffrey and Mabel are drinking a full bottle.'

The central heating, along with the blazing log fire, made the room very warm and he looked uncomfortable. She suggested he remove his jacket; other men had.

'It's not the heat. It's just that I were waiting for the right moment.'

'What for? What's the matter?'

'Oh heck,' he said. 'I might as well get it over with. Will you marry me?'
So this was what the special trip was about.

'Yes,' she said. 'Of course I'll marry you. I always intended to.'

He jumped out of his chair and came round the table to kiss her. She stood up, threw her arms around him and kissed him back, careless of the crowd observing them. Someone started to clap. She suddenly remembered where she was and looked round in embarrassment to see Geoffrey leading the applause of the rest of the diners.

The proprietor appeared. 'Do we have cause for a celebration?'

'That we do, sir,' said Kenneth excitedly. 'She's just agreed to marry me.'

They declined his kind offer of a free bottle of champagne but Jenny gratefully accepted the suggestion that they move to a private annexe to continue their meal.

42

The Sauternes tasted a bit sweet, like a drink the man at the herbal bar in Rawtenstall used to serve. As she sipped the wine she did not, as the Reverend Fazackerly promised, glimpse the gates of Hell opening to receive her. On the contrary, it gave her a pleasant feeling, though nothing compared with the joy she felt that she was soon to be a married woman.

*

The following morning Jenny was at work before six and waited in the tacklers' cabin for Abram. He ought to hear the news. Fortunately, he was the first to arrive. She showed him the solitaire diamond ring. No explanation was necessary.

'Congratulations lass. He's a grand lad is Kenneth but a bit on t' timid side. I were despairing he'd ever ask you, but I'm right pleased for you both. Can I tell the others?'

'If you want,' she said, and went down to start her looms.

13

The 1950's was a good decade for the Lancashire textile industry. The end of clothes rationing released a demand that had been pent-up since the wartime shortage of cotton. Windows which had been 'blacked-out' were now draped with brightly coloured curtains in the latest 'contemporary' designs. Women could at last choose a new dress whenever they had the money, no longer dependent on clothing coupons.

Woollen mills on the other side of the Pennines got a more valuable share of the business but the spinning frames of Bolton, Royton and Oldham and the looms of Burnley, Blackburn and Colesclough were now working flat out. Every day one saw the vans of spinning companies carrying bobbins of yarn to be wound onto cones or cheeses, which were carried to another firm for transfer onto warp beams.

The beams went to a size-house, where they were first 'drawn-in' to the prescribed pattern. Then the yarns were coated with a 'slasher's mix', which strengthened the warps for the battering they were to receive in the looms. The formula for each mix varied, according to the family tradition of each company. A blend of starches and gum tragacanth would include a secret ingredient. The formula was passed from father to son and, if it was ever written down, would be kept securely in the family safe.

Now the warps were ready to be transferred to the weaving company, who shipped the cloth to a bleacher, a dyer or a printer, before it eventually reached a finishing works, to be calendered or raised, stentered back to full width, cut into pieces, pressed into hessian bales and dispatched to the waiting merchants of Manchester, often for export to those very countries which had grown the cotton.

But it was not like that at Harrisons. The raw cotton, which had travelled down the Manchester Ship Canal from Liverpool, was collected from Salford docks by the lorries of Harrison Transport Limited and delivered to the central bale store at the highest point of the factory site, half-way up Daisy Hill. Each bale weighed four hundred pounds, whether it came from the United States, Nigeria or Egypt.

Once these bales were lifted by hoist at the top of the site, either into Daisy Mill on the left or Buttercup Mill on the right, nothing emerged from the factories until the grey-cloth was loaded onto a Harrison Transport lorry for the short journey down to the dyeing, printing and finishing works alongside the River Coll, which were the only premises not on the original site chosen by Isaac Harrison in 1862.

But Isaac Harrison's grandson, Harold, knew that this boom could not last. In 1954 he was forced to put Buttercup Mill onto single shifts. The more expensive fabrics were just about holding their own against foreign competition but the 'bread and butter' business was moving away to the Far East, just as Harold had seen the West African trade disappear to India in the thirties.

When he first joined the firm, the whole of number three shed was permanently engaged on making Baft for the Hausa population of Nigeria --- one hundred and forty-four calico looms churned out plain cloth; no need for bleaching or dyeing, just a bit of starch and a heavy calendar. Pure profit that was.

In the old days he used to walk down Whitworth Street in Manchester in the morning, and by the time he arrived for lunch at the Midland Hotel he had sold enough to keep the shed clattering away for another month.

Locked away in a cabinet at the finishing works were the old 'chop-marks' of the firms that Harrisons used to supply. Harold could still recite the names engraved on the metal stamps used to mark the ten-yard bolts. The Greeks, Paterson Zochonis and A. G. Leventis. the Indians, Chanrai and Chelleram, the French Compagnie Francaise. The old British traders, G.B. Ollivant and Gottschalck in Manchester, John

Holt and Edward Bates in Liverpool. Then there was the independent fellow in Kano. Nice chap, sharp as they come. What was his name now? Masoor that's it --- Jacob Masoor.

Greatest of all was the firm which now called itself the United Africa Company. To those steeped in the West African trade it was still known as the Niger Company --- 'Gldan Goldie', the house built by George Goldie who, side by side with Fred Lugard, had made Nigeria the African jewel in the British crown.

Harold still went down to Manchester almost every week, often taking Geoffrey with him. He used to drop in on some of his old pals in the West Africa houses. Occasionally he would come out with an order for dress prints or drill, but his friends of the thirties had now nearly all retired and the younger buyers were not influenced by loyalty to an old supplier. Why should they be? Business is business after all.

But maintaining his contacts finally paid Harold a huge dividend. One day in the late summer of 1956 he walked into the Midland to find three old West African trading pals at the bar, entertaining Harry Tomkinson, a long-retired colleague who had come over from Liverpool for the day. Arthur Barnes of the United Africa Company signalled for him to join them.

'Speak of the devil,' he said. 'What are you having Harold?'

'Orange juice, please.' He had no chauffeur that day.

Arthur smiled, 'Orange juice, indeed! Not like the old days, eh? You're quite right to be careful though, there's too much damned traffic on the roads these days. It's lucky I found you. I phoned you this morning but your secretary said you were on your way here.'

'What can we do for you,' said Harold, hoping for an order.

'We are having a party of Nigerians coming to see us at UAC next week and I said I'd try and arrange a visit to a textile mill on Friday. Would you show them through your place?'

'Glad to,' said Harold. 'Ask them to come in time for lunch? Just tell us how many to expect. What part are they from, by the way? Religion I'm thinking of. I'd like to know what sort of food to tell Mrs Green to prepare.'

'It's a delegation from the Central Region, they've just got self-government. I'm told they may be interested in having a mill built out there. Christians, I assume, though it might be a good idea to steer clear of pork. From my experience they won't object to a glass or two.

*

The heads of agreement for the new mill were signed in May 1957 and, six months later, Norman Haworth, the general manager of the Colesclough factories, went out to Okante to supervise the establishment of the new venture, which Harold trusted would secure the future not only of Geoffrey, but of the grandson he relied on him or Roger to have. He hoped that the production of a male heir would not be left to young Harriet. He wanted the name of Harrison to continue.

14

Nico woke early, as he usually did, and was pleased to find that he had less of a hangover than he deserved. Easing himself off the bed, he stood for a moment to admire the contours of the woman who had spent the night with him. They had never got between the sheets, because London was enjoying an unusually warm spring and the humidity was high. It could only have been four or five hours since they finally abandoned themselves to sleep and she was dozing quietly. Her ash-blonde hair, which at last night's party had been pulled back into a chignon was now draped over the pillow.

Before they went to bed she had asked him to open a window, but he claimed not to have reacclimatized from his recent visit to Africa. The true reason was that he feared she might be a 'screamer'. The mews was narrow and he had never forgotten the occasion when one of his overnight guests created that awful din during her orgasm. The Kuwaiti fellow opposite made a crude comment the following morning. With this woman he need not have feared; she had been responsive, indeed adventurous, but comparatively quiet. She did not wake as he drew the curtains. In the light of day she was not as young as she had appeared last night --- possibly older than him. Thirty? Could even be thirty-five. He tried to recall what she had said her surname was. Nicki was her first name, so much he could remember --- it had been the opening gambit in their conversation at last night's bash at the Rembrandt to celebrate the opening of the *Accra Homestead.*

'Glad you could be here Miss . . .' whatever her name was. 'I'm Nico.'

'Nicki,' she had replied.

'No, Nico. Nico Masoor.'

'Yes I know you're Nico, it's me who's Nicki. Sorry, that's wrong isn't it? It is I who am Nicki --- Nicola, actually. At least we have something in common.' There were traces of a Southern African accent. Looking into her eyes he saw distinct possibilities. 'I hope we shall find much more in common than just our names,' he said. Then a group of Ghanaians had signalled to him.

'Excuse me for a moment Nicki; I'll be back.'

But the party was almost over before he found the opportunity to seek her out again. Most of the guests had drifted away. He saw her standing beside the remains of the nibbles, her hair now somewhat disordered. He went over to resume their conversation, aware that he was rather drunk. So, it appeared, was she.

'Sorry I was away so long. Nicki, isn't it? What do you do, by the way?'

'Deputy Editor of *Africa Business Quarterly*. We are a small publication but influential. I had hoped for an interview.'

'Why don't we continue this conversation over a cup of coffee. I live just over the road.'

15

Saul Masoor sold most of his residential portfolio when his wife died; he had lost the incentive to increase his fortune and the excitement he derived from property trading was no longer there. He got rid of the family home in Chester Square and went to live in Geneva, where he bought a penthouse apartment overlooking Lac Leman, becoming something of a recluse.

Soon after the war, Saul had bought a semi-derelict mews house in Kensington. A few years later, in a moment of weakness, he had taken a mistress and started to have the property renovated for her, but the affair ended long before work was complete. By then, however, he could see the potential for such houses and decided to keep it, though still unfinished.

When he became a widower it occurred to him that this would be a suitable place for his son to live. Although he would have loved to have Nico with him in Switzerland, London was where the boy would learn the property business, so he continued with refurbishment of the mews house while Nicolas was in his last year at public school and the place was ready for occupation by the time he completed his National Service. To look after his son he found Mr Jenks.

*

Percy Jenks regarded himself as one of the few remaining 'gentleman's gentlemen' in London and had acted in that capacity for Nico from the first day he moved into the neat little house, converted from derelict stables.

At the interview Percy had had his doubts; the father was not exactly what he would describe as a gentleman, despite the obvious affluence. But when he met the son he was re-assured. The boy had few visible traces of a middle-Eastern ancestry, thanks no doubt to having an English mother. Although there were, as Jenks told his boyfriend Gus, one or two 'woggish' edges which needed to be smoothed off, he was sure that under his tutelage the good-looking young man could be turned into something indistinguishable from the genuine article.

Now, after eight years, Percy felt satisfied that he had succeeded, although he was concerned about the number of different young ladies paying overnight visits. He thought it about time that his charge took matters of the heart more seriously, despite the fact that, when a permanent young lady appeared on the scene, Percy's services may no longer be required.

He had prepared for such a day. He still lived with his mother in a pleasant apartment near World's End in Chelsea, just a short bus ride from the mews. On fine days he often used to walk to and from work. Percy could not leave Mother, who had a heart condition, but when an apartment on the second floor of the block became vacant, Gustav took it. They had first met in the Catering Corps in 1940 and spent almost the whole of their service in Yorkshire at Catterick Camp.

Although they never went near any battlefront, they were in constant danger, for had the nature of their friendship been revealed there would have been a blot on their service records which would follow them into Civvy Street. But they were still together, or as nearly so as the law permitted. Both of them were saving hard. Percy was very well remu-

nerated by Nico and Gus had graduated from waiter to
maitre d' at one of the leading London hotels. They planned
that when Mrs Jenks died they would retire and move down
to Brighton, where they had several friends. By then, they
hoped, their sort of partnership would be socially and leg-
ally acceptable.

16

Nico took a shower without waking his beautiful visitor. He
had shared his bed many times, seldom feeling any sense of
regret when it was time for his companion to leave, but this
one interested him. She sighed and shifted on the bed, moving onto her back and displaying the dark triangle which
contrasted with her ash blonde hair. He gently placed a
white bath-robe over her and closed the bedroom door
quietly behind him. Then he went into the spare bedroom
to put on swimming trunks, a track suit and tennis shoes.
He put underwear and a large bath towel into his back pack.
As he went down the stairs he was surprised to hear that
Jenks had already arrived; it was only six twenty-five. In the
kitchen his manservant was setting the tray for morning tea,
with two cups.

'Good morning sir. I assume the young lady would like tea.'

'Jenks, are you psychic? How did you know?'

'She left an item of clothing in the sitting room, sir. Should I
give them a quick wash and spin-dry or will she be leaving
shortly?'

'I suggest you just put them into a carrier bag and hand it
over discreetly when she appears. We had rather a late

night, so it may be some time before she comes down. For your sake I hope she puts on the bathrobe I left her, though it's still bloody hot and I can't guarantee that. Now I'm going out for my swim. Do make sure she waits for me and we'll have breakfast together.'

Out of doors it was pleasantly cool for his jog to Hyde Park. Kensington was almost deserted at that time of day. He bid the postman good morning and waved to the milkman, whose float had Exhibition Road to itself. When he reached Kensington Road there was still hardly any traffic. He ran across without having to wait for the lights.

It had been Jacob Masoor who introduced him to the Serpentine. Jack, as he insisted he be called, was Nico's only uncle, his father's twin. Soon after Nico moved into the mews his uncle wrote to invite himself to stay there on his next visit from Nigeria, instead of using Brown's Hotel, which was his usual base. He appeared at seven o'clock on the first morning in the doorway of Nico's bedroom, wearing a sort of dark blue battledress, reminiscent of the one Churchill wore during the war. Over his shoulder he had a large bath towel.

'Up you get, young man. You have some bathing drawers, I hope. At that expensive school you were a swimming champion, weren't you? So come with me. Move yourself.'

'For goodness sake Uncle Jack, it's the middle of December,' Nico had complained. 'Why on earth do you want to go swimming at this time of year? And where? We're in the middle of London, remember. The nearest baths are in Chelsea and they're probably not open yet.'

Since then Nico had become one of the enthusiasts who regularly brave the elements for an energetic start to the metropolitan day by swimming in the Serpentine, heedless of the temperature, breaking the ice if necessary.

17

Originally Nico had difficulty in persuading his father to let him diversify from property development into hotels, but the Masoor Group's *Homestead Inns* had been a big success. He had chosen locations where land was cheap, so despite being told by the experts that a sixty-bed unit was too small to be viable, his concept of compact two-storey hotels had proved a winner. Guests liked his alternative to the anonymous high-rise blocks which are the hallmark of the large international chains. The first two projects, in Lourenco Marques and Mauritius, were financed from the group's own reserves. After that the banks were falling over themselves to lend money.

The success of the first hotels meant that Nico had no difficulty in getting government participation when he moved into a developing country. His strategy was to build where commercial development was taking place rather than in tourist resorts. (The one in Mauritius had been an indulgence, because he liked to holiday there). The recently-opened *Accra Homestead* was the fourth hotel. Another in Dakar was nearing completion.

Okante had been Uncle Jack's idea. He wrote to Nico soon after the geological survey team arrived in Central Region.... *from what I am told it is doubtful if they will find any oil so far from the coast, but several teams are prospecting and the visitors will need somewhere to stay. One of your sixty bed units would be a good risk, because apart from the possibility of oil,*

*there are some commercial ventures on the drawing board --
a Lancashire firm I used to deal with has signed an agreement for a cotton textile factory and there is talk of a new
brewery, possibly also a palm oil mill. Come over to Kano and
I will go down with you to talk to Chief Qgondo, who is an old
friend.*

Nico had himself supervised the commissioning of all the
hotels. Okante seemed as though it would be another pion-
eering job, but sailing to Lagos would allow him to unwind.

When he returned from the Serpentine she had gone. On his
dressing table was a visiting card. Her name was Nicola van
Vleet. There was a message scribbled on the back.

*Sorry can't wait. You were superb, darling. Still no interview!
Phone me.
Love, N*

18

Jenny would have liked a spring wedding, but she was
pleased to see that Kenneth was keen for the event to take
place as soon as possible, though, as he put it, 'Not that quick
as would set folk talking'. It was ironic that he should have
thought of that because so far there had been no danger.
Sometimes, as they embraced, she could feel the evidence of
his excitement and she would have been happy to take
things further, because soon after they became engaged she
had visited her doctor and had a contraceptive device fitted.
But he used to pull away from her with a remark such as
"We'll have to watch it, won't we?" She could not decide
whether her future husband was too considerate or under-
sexed.

One evening she plucked up the courage to say that she would not object if he wanted more than a kiss, but he said, 'There'll be plenty of time for that sort of thing after t' chapel bell's been rung.'

So she began to agree with him, the sooner the better.

Jenny had no doubts about the strength of her own sexuality. When she was about thirteen she started buying *Picturegoer* in order to see what her favourite film actresses were wearing, but she soon became more interested in the men. She used to have arguments with her grammar school friend, Mary, over the relative attractions of leading screen actors. Mary liked muscular men such as Burt Lancaster. Jane was at that time deeply in love with Tyrone Power.

The ice cream kiosk in the Royal cinema in Colesclough sold signed photographs of the stars, of which Jenny built up quite a collection, mostly of Tyrone in various costumes, including her favourite one of him wearing swimming trunks. Then, on the front of *Picturegoer* one week there was a photograph of an actor she had never heard of, but whom she considered to be the most beautiful man she had ever seen. She kept the magazine face down in her bedside cabinet but spent the whole weekend taking surreptitious looks at it. His name was Montgomery Clift.

Mary also bought the magazine. Back at school on the following Monday Jenny asked her friend what she thought of him. 'Lovely looking, of course,' she said. 'But too skinny for me.' Jenny was so angry that she was unable to respond.

When *From Here to Eternity* came to Colesclough, the girls were able to see their two heroes together. Jenny was disappointed that Burt had a far more important part than

56

Montgomery and Mary teased her about Montgomery's body.

'I suppose you'll be fancying that Frank Sinatra next,' she said. 'He was even weedier than your fella.'

So when Jenny read that there was to be a re-showing of *A Place in the Sun* at the Odeon in Blackburn she went on her own. She immediately developed an intense jealousy of Elizabeth Taylor, whom she had previously quite liked. The plot was of no interest to her and she suspected it was not a very good film, but that did not matter; sufficient that she could enjoy her hero without distraction. She left the cinema in a joyous haze.

19

Kenneth knew that what he had in mind was likely to upset his parents, but soon after he and Jenny became engaged an opportunity arose for him to prepare the ground. Jenny was always going on about him having no ambition. He was bloody well going to surprise her. His mother raised the subject of where they were going to live after they were married.

'There's a house for sale in Harrison Street as would suit you two. You'll know the one I mean --- Polly McDonald's? It's really lovely inside; poor Robert spent all his time doing it up before he passed away.'

'I didn't know she were leaving. Where's she moving to?'

'Back up to Scotland. She has no one down here since Bobby died so she's going to live with her sister, she's a widow too. Kilmarnock --- I think that's where she said she were going. I went down to look at the advert in Horrockses' window. With your two jobs you'd get a maximum mortgage and I've no doubt they'll take an offer. One thousand two hundred pounds they're asking.'

'That's a lot of money, Mum. Happen we could rent. Anyway,' he said, drawing a deep breath in preparation for his mother's response, 'We might not be stopping round here.'

'What do you mean, not stopping round here? Surely you wouldn't give up your job at Harrisons? Does your father know about this?'

'It's only a thought, Mum.'

'I suppose Jane put you up to this.'

'No, Mum. I've not mentioned it to her yet.'

'So what's it all about then?'

'I don't want to sound mysterious like, but I can't start explaining right now. Just be a bit patient. Happen nowt'll come of it.'

*

Since the advertisements for spinning overlookers for the Okante project appeared in the *Evening Telegraph* and the *Colesclough Gazette* there had been a lot of talk around the mill, particularly concerning the high salaries that were on offer. For over two years Kenneth had been studying at night school for his City and Guilds certificate in textile dyeing and printing and now, as well as having a good knowledge of dyestuffs, he knew how to operate and maintain all the machines in his department.

One day, while waiting for Jane outside the weaving shed, he encountered Mr Geoffrey. 'Yes, of course,' he was told, 'we will be having bleaching and dyeing out there, but it could be some time before we start advertising for that section. Anyway, it won't be my decision when it comes to choosing staff. If you're interested why not have a word with Norman Haworth? He's coming back from Okante in about three weeks to interview spinning overlookers. You're related to Norman, aren't you?'

'Sort of. My mum's his wife's cousin.'

'Right then. See how the land lies.'

'Happen I might, Geoffrey. But keep this to yourself will you?'

'Mum's the word --- or should I say, Mum's cousin? Best of luck anyway, Ken.'

20

Jane and Kenneth went to see Mr Fazackerly, the minister of Broadholme chapel, and Saturday the fourth of February was agreed upon as their wedding day. Jenny asked the minister if it would be all right for her best friend Mary to be her bridesmaid. Her family was Catholic and Mr Fazackerly was known to be antagonistic to that church, but he said he had no objection to Mary if her priest didn't mind her attending. The two girls had been thrown together from day one at the grammar school because Mary was called Clark (without the 'e'). She now worked in the wages office at Harrisons.

Mary's mother, who was a good seamstress, offered to make both dresses but, because there wasn't a lot of time, Jenny decided to spend part of her Trustee Bank savings on a bridal gown. The two young women chose the first Saturday in December to go down to Manchester to look for one. They caught the early bus and were at Lower Mosley Street by nine-thirty. C and A Modes, which was their first port of call, did not have many bridal dresses, so Mary suggested they go to Kendal Milne.

'You're joking aren't you?' Jenny said. 'C and A's prices nearly gave me a heart attack.'

'I don't mean you should buy one there --- just get some ideas. If you decide on the sort of thing you're looking for we can have a proper look round. There's plenty of other places.'

It was a long walk down to Deansgate and when they reached Kendal's they decided to go for a drink in the coffee shop. One and threepence each seemed a bit steep, but it was lovely coffee. A smart plump woman came to sit at a table under the window. The waitress went over immediately and made a great fuss of her, though it had taken her all her time to come to serve Mary and Jane. Mary whispered, 'You know who that is?'

'Her face looks familiar. I think I've seen her picture in the paper.'

'Mrs Harrison, Harold's wife.'

The woman was smiling in their direction. When her coffee arrived she brought it over to their table, 'You don't mind if I join you, Mary?'

'You're very welcome, Mrs Harrison. Do you know Jane Clarke? She works with me at your factory.'

'I'm a weaver,' said Jenny, not wishing to have her situation misunderstood.

'No, we haven't met, have we dear? Didn't I see your engagement notice in the *Gazette*?'

'That's right. I'm going to marry Kenneth Thistlethwaite.'

'Oh yes, I know Kenneth. I've met him in our dyehouse. You've got a nice lad there, love. You two certainly are early birds.' Then a thought struck Mrs Harrison. 'Would I be right in guessing that you're here to look for the wedding dress?' To Jenny's annoyance Mary admitted that they were.

'Oh, how exciting,' Mrs Harrison enthused. 'Let's finish our coffee and then you must let me take you up to see Marie-Claude. She will find you exactly what you need.'

In the lift up to the fashion floor Jenny wanted to tell Mary that they must escape from this woman, well-intentioned though she obviously was, but she and Mrs Harrison were in conversation. Jenny could not help feeling she was being patronised. However, when they reached the 'bridal suite', as it was called, all such thoughts disappeared from her mind as she looked in awe at the gorgeous gowns on display. One in particular captivated her. In her mind's eye she pictured herself in this dress, walking hand in hand down the aisle with a man who looked more like Montgomery Clift than Kenneth. . . not down the stark aisle of Broadholme chapel but somewhere like Manchester Cathedral, to the waiting confetti and a carillon of church bells. She pulled herself together very quickly after taking a discreet peep at the price tag. There was nothing for it but to face up to Mrs Harrison. 'Excuse me, might I have a word?'

'Certainly dear. Wasn't I right? Aren't they gorgeous?'

Jenny managed to steer Mrs Harrison out of earshot of the vendeuse, who transferred her sales pitch to Mary. After Jenny had explained her circumstances, Alice said, 'Of course I understand, love. You came here just for ideas, didn't you?'

'That's right. I do hope we haven't put you into an embarrassing position.'

'Not a bit of it,' said Alice. 'Marie-Claude won't mind, she's a good friend of mine; actually her real name's Polly. And I'll let you into another secret. When I married Harold I was in the same situation as you. He wanted to buy the wedding dress but I had my pride. So I hired.'

'You mean one can hire a wedding gown?'

'Of course you can, why not? Will you ever wear it again? Haven't you been to dances and seen those wedding dresses remodelled and dyed all sorts of pastel shades? People think they're kidding you. "That's a dished-up wedding gown if ever I saw one" I used to say to my husband.'

'Where can I go to hire one?'

'There's a little place in King Street; I think it's still there. I'll take you. Oh I am glad I met you, Jane . . . I'm having so much fun.'

So, when the time came to issue the wedding invitations, Jenny had no hesitation in including her employer and his wife. She also sent an invitation to Geoffrey.

When she walked down the aisle, only three other people knew that her beautiful white guipure-lace dress and veil had to be back with Cohen's Bridal Emporium by twelve noon the following Monday.

Harold remarked what a good looking young woman Jenny was and Alice had to agree. Quite wasted on an insipid lad like Kenneth Thistlethwaite, she thought. She found herself thinking that if Geoffrey insisted on marrying out of his class he could do a lot worse than a girl like Jane Clarke.

But there were to be important developments before the fourth of February.

21

Since the engagement, Kenneth regularly went to number forty-eight for his evening meal and he and Jane often took a walk afterwards. This evening it was dark by the time they set off, but there was street lighting on their route to the river, across Blackburn Old Road and then down the back lane which led past the dyehouse.

When they reached the river bank the moon was bright enough to light their way, though what should have been a romantic ambience was somewhat marred by the pungent odour emitting from the vicinity of Harrisons' bleach works As far as Jenny was aware, her mother had never revisited the spot where her father had taken his life, and it had taken her some time before she could steel herself to go down to the river, but she was determined she would not be denied what had always been her favourite walk. Now, her father was a remote figure in her memory and the place no longer troubled her.

She and Kenneth held hands as they walked, and from time to time they stopped to kiss. Jenny was normally in bed by nine when she worked early shift but this evening was quite mild, so she agreed to Kenneth's suggestion that they continue across the footbridge and up into Layrocks village for a glass of lemonade at the Lark Inn. It was their favourite, one of those old public houses with a taproom and stone flag floors, little altered since it had been built sometime in the eighteenth century. When they reached the pub, they sat at a wooden bench outside, looking down onto the lights of Colesclough which, in Jenny's present romantic frame of mind, seemed like fairyland.

After Kenneth had told her about making an appointment with Norman Howarth she did not respond for what seemed a long time. She released her hand from his.

'Well, what do you think?' he asked, much troubled. 'It don't necessarily mean he'll give me a job but there's no harm in trying, is there?'

Still she said nothing. 'I hoped you might be pleased,' he continued. 'You keep on telling me I've no ambition."

'Yes, darling,' she said at last. 'I'm very pleased that you should think of it, only --- well, it's a big step isn't it? I'm sorry Kenneth, it's my mother I'm thinking of. I don't see how she could manage without my wage.'

'Don't talk daft. We could afford to send her more than what you're earning now. Do you realise what they're paying? They're offering spinning overlookers one thousand eight hundred pounds a year, and with my qualifications they'd have to pay me that much at least. That's more than the two of us earn put together, plus there's a fully-furnished house, rent free.'

Jenny could see how she had upset him. 'All right dear, I'll consider it. I didn't mean to sound discouraging. By all means see Mr Howarth when he comes, but don't let my mum hear about it until we know a bit more.'

'Thanks Jenny. I had to tell you, because Geoffrey says they'll want to see us both.'

22

Whenever Jenny looked in the mirror she was aware that it was mainly to Tommy Clarke that she owed her good looks, and she had come to regard this with increasing bitterness. Not that her mother was by any means unattractive, but according to one of the weavers who had known him as a young man, Tommy used to be 'a right bobby-dazzler'. He had been a sportsman, something of a local hero --- wicket-keeper and high-scoring middle-order batsman for Colesclough in the Lancashire League, having once been chosen for the county side in a second eleven game against Derbyshire. He had a trial with Accrington Stanley football club, though nothing came of that. Before the war he had worked in a slipper factory, but the second lieutenant's pip he wore on his shoulder when he was demobilised from the Lancashire Fusiliers helped secure him a job as sales representative with a firm of paint manufacturers.

Tommy had always been a ladies' man. As Jenny reached the age of puberty and acquired knowledge of such matters, she realised that her father was a philanderer. He was also a regular gambler, but alcohol had always been the chief problem. His drinking crept up on him gradually, starting with weekend binges and developing into a nightly habit. When he entertained a potential customer at lunch time he was constrained by how much his client wanted to drink but when he ate alone he drank far more than he should. Eventually he was usually the worse for liquor in the afternoons and his order book started to show a sharp decline. Some who had welcomed his visits now refused to see him.

A large part of his income came from sales commission, so the amount of money he brought home declined and Agnes and Jenny became aware that the problem was affecting his work. Eventually he was transferred to the company's headquarters to work in the sales office but proved quite unsuited to the discipline of a desk job.

In 1952 he parted company with the paint firm and joined a local newsagent with a view to a partnership, but by then he was drinking heavily. He began to put on weight and the swagger went out of his step. When the chance of a share in the newsagents business evaporated he took a job in a haulier's yard, supplementing the salary with evening work as a barman, which only aggravated his problem.

Jenny felt only temporary grief when he killed himself. During those first few days of shock she diverted her anger to those callers who hid the true purpose of their visit behind a veneer of solicitude, gradually veering the conversation to the point where they could reveal how much Tommy had borrowed from them. One, whom she respected more than the others, had come straight to the point and within the first few minutes had produced a bunch of properly witnessed records of loans amounting to well over two hundred pounds, taken against the security of 48 Bright Street.

She had gained satisfaction from writing to inform all his creditors that the house was, and always had been, in her mother's name, that solicitor's advice had been taken and that her mother had no legal liability for the debts. However, she concluded by saying, that she, his daughter, had every intention of ensuring they would eventually be paid in full.

Her grief had been modified by disgust that her father had taken the coward's way out, and particularly that he had not even had the courage to reveal to his wife the extent of his debts. His suicide and its aftermath had been the nadir in the family's fortunes, from which she had struggled hard to recover. Now, in the cold light of day, she was tempted to say 'good riddance'.

She had an uncle on her father's side. He and his wife would have to be invited to her wedding, but she had no intention of walking down the aisle with the brother of the man who had come close to ruining them.

*

She could not tell whether Abram was pleased by her request; shocked was more like it. He gazed at her with a blank expression. 'Me? Me give you away? You must have uncles.'

67

'I have one on Dad's side but I'm certainly not having him. It's all right if you don't want to. I don't mind.'

'Not want to?' A broad smile spread over his lined face and he came to embrace her. They were standing in front of the tacklers' cabin window, so the whole of the weaving shed must have seen.

'Oh Jenny, love, there's nowt in the whole wide world as I'd like more. You're all I'd ever have wished for in a daughter if me and Sheila could . . . '

'Shut up, you big soft man,' she said, sharing his emotion. 'You've only got to say yes, there's no cause for crying.'

23

Mr Harrison's secretary showed them into the empty board-room. They sat side by side on rather uncomfortable high-backed chairs, of which there were sixteen around the heavy oak table, though Jenny knew there to be only five directors. It was a long room which faced onto the main car park, but she had never been able to see inside, because the windows were above head height. She could tell that Kenneth was as nervous as she was. In order to cover her excitement she got up to study some of the pictures.

Taking up most of the wall space at one end of the room was a large framed drawing of the two mills, a copy of which she had seen in the entrance hall of the local library. On either side of this were two portraits in oils which she recognised as Isaac Harrison and his son Wesley, but the other walls were hung with modern works, one signed by John Piper.

On a tall marble plinth by the door of the chairman's office stood a bust of Harold Harrison, in the style of Epstein. She asked Kenneth if he thought it might be genuine but he had not heard of Jacob Epstein. There was a fine old cherry wood sideboard on which stood spirits and liqueurs, more than a dozen different sorts. Some of the drinks were in cut-glass decanters with silver labels hung round their necks --- what Reverend Fazackerly would refer to as 'the Devil's armoury.'

They had already waited more than ten minutes. Jenny tried to calm Kenneth, who was beginning to perspire. 'Don't worry, love. It's only your mum's cousin, he's not going to eat you.'

At last the door of Harold Harrison's office opened and in walked Mr Howarth, looking very tanned, followed by Geoffrey Harrison. Both shook hands, first with her then with Kenneth. Mr Howarth seated himself at the head of the table.

'Sorry we kept you waiting,' he said. 'I've been having a few words with Geoffrey here. Mr Harold would normally have seen you but he's in Manchester today, so Geoffrey's sitting in on the interview. Did Mrs Allardyce offer you tea? Or would you like coffee perhaps?'

'Yes she did offer but no thank you,' said Jenny, who knew that in their present state of nerves neither of them could lift a cup without spilling the contents. She had never officially met Norman Haworth before, though she had seen him going through Daisy Mill before he was sent out to supervise the establishment of the Nigerian subsidiary. He was in his mid-fifties and not unlike Kenneth in appearance, despite the fact that there was no blood relationship. Both

69

were not very tall and wore rimless glasses. Norman's hair was a similar sandy shade but more tightly curled than Kenneth's. Jenny glanced at her fiance's immaculately combed loose waves and felt a surge of affection. She prayed that his hopes were not about to be dashed.

As Mr Howarth began to describe the project, she warmed to him and to the possibility of embarking on the adventure of a life overseas. She had strong reservations about going to Nigeria, but he inspired confidence and, by the time he had explained the new life that might await them, she was already won over. But when he got round to the interview proper she became concerned.

'OK,' he concluded. 'Those were the preliminaries. The first thing I must say to you, Kenneth, is that we shall need a person with rather more experience for the dyeing manager's job, but there will eventually be vacancies for shift supervisors.'

'That would do fine for me,' Kenneth replied, more humbly than Jenny would have wished.

'We won't be installing any dyeing or finishing machinery for at least six months, maybe more, but . . . '

'I'm willing to wait,' Kenneth broke in. 'Assuming you can tell me there'll be a job for me.' She wished he would stop being so servile.

Mr Howarth did not answer Kenneth. Instead he said, 'Hold on a bit lad, while I talk to Jane.'

Disappointment was written on Kenneth's face. She knew that he had built up hopes of getting the manager's job. She had come to this interview without any expectation of their life being changed, so she did not feel let down, but she did not wish to wait around to see her future husband belittled.

'No', she said, 'we don't want to waste your time, Mr Howarth, there's no need to go into further details. Thank you for being so straightforward with us. We shall talk it over and perhaps come back later if the firm has something definite to offer.' Jenny stood up and nodded to Kenneth that it was time to leave.

Geoffrey spoke for the first time. 'No, listen please both of you, don't walk out now. Norman has a proposal.'

'I'm sorry,' she said, resuming her seat, 'please carry on, Mr Howarth.'

'Thank you. Yes, Geoffrey's right, it's you I'm after Jane. Last night I had a drink in the Crown with Abram Pickup and we got to talking about you. You see, I need an experienced person to set up a training school for our Nigerian staff. Would you be interested?'

'I hope you realise that Kenneth and I are to be married next month. If you had a job in mind for me I couldn't consider it unless we went out to Nigeria together.'

'Of course, I fully understand. Here's what I suggest . . .'

The proposal was that they should both go out to Okante as soon as possible. Kenneth would act as Norman's assistant, helping with day-to-day supervision of the project. Then, when the dyeing jigs arrived and the bleaching and finishing machinery was being installed, he would be responsible for preparing that department for single-shift working. Kenneth would become a shift supervisor once the Dyeing Manager had arrived and the factory was in full production.

What Mr Howarth had in mind for Jenny she certainly found interesting. A training school was being set up to teach spinners and weavers, and with her experience in both departments she was qualified to take charge.

'And there's something equally important you might help me with,' he went on. 'You see, the local population is predominantly a mixture of Yoruba and Hausa, so we have to keep a fairly even balance in our recruiting. Igbos are more or less barred; I wish they weren't but that's another matter. Most of the Yoruba have a reasonable command of English but few Hausa people have, at least not the sort who would want to become factory workers. Someone with your language skills would be a great asset. Do you think you could learn Hausa?'

'How can I answer that?' I assume you mean quickly. I really don't know, but I would have a darned good try.'

Mr Howarth grinned, 'That's the sort of thing I like to hear. I'll let you have my Hausa manual when we've finished, have a look and see what you think. You don't have to make up your minds here and now, but I would appreciate a decision before I fly back in ten days' time. So now let's talk money: Geoffrey's the chap for that.'

When she heard their terms Jenny was furious. Kenneth was offered twelve hundred pounds a year, well below what the spinning supervisors were to be paid, and she (who Mr Howarth said was to be a key person in the project) would receive nine hundred --- not all that much more than she was taking home now.

Geoffrey wound up by saying, 'So together you would be getting over two thousand pounds a year. That makes it worthwhile, doesn't it?'

'No, it certainly doesn't!' she exclaimed angrily. Kenneth nudged her in the ribs and whispered, 'Hold on, let's talk about it. Don't fly off the handle.'

'No, Kenneth', she said aloud, 'I must have my say. I'm sorry, Mr Geoffrey, but this just isn't good enough. The firm has a reputation for fair wages but I think you're taking advantage of us. Just how many applications do you think you'd get if you put an advert in the *Evening Telegraph* and offered nine hundred pounds a year for a woman to up sticks and set off for a place in Africa she'd never even heard of? Tell me that.'

'But we would never consider a woman going out alone,' said Geoffrey. 'And think of the free housing and how much in total the two of you would be receiving.'

'I'm a person in my own right, thank you very much.'

She realised that she might be ruining their chances but she was now angry and determined to have her say . . . 'and Kenneth isn't some young lad willing to scramble for any pennies you throw down for him. If spinning overlookers, with next to no education, are getting eighteen hundred a year, then why is my future husband, who could have gone to university, only worth twelve hundred?' She rose to her feet. 'Come on Kenneth, we're going.'

'Sit down,' shouted Mr Howarth, and she did. 'For goodness sake take it easy lass and give us a minute. I hear what you're saying and I admire you for it, but we're entitled to reconsider, aren't we? Let me ask Mrs Allardyce to get you that cup of tea, and me and Geoffrey will go and have a chat in Harold's office.'

Norman went out to see the secretary. Geoffrey sat there for a moment, looking highly embarrassed, before he went into his father's room without saying another word. As Norman returned to the boardroom he patted Jenny on the shoulder and said, 'Don't worry, I'll see it's all right.' He followed Geoffrey into Harold's office.

'My word Jenny, I thought you'd buggered us up.' said Kenneth when they were alone. 'I shall have to watch *you*. I didn't know you could get that mad.'

'You still want to go, do you?'

'Aye, it seems like a grand opportunity.'

'Will you leave the money side to me?'

'Looks like I'd better,' he said.

They had finished their cups of tea by the time the two men returned.

'So, when exactly are you two planning to get wed?' Mr Howarth asked, 'Early next month, isn't it?'

'Fourth of February,' Jenny replied.

'That's, how long?'

'Three weeks and two days,' she told him.

'Right then, over to you Geoffrey.'

Geoffrey was contrite. 'I'm sorry if we were a bit insensitive in what we offered you both. I do see your point, Jane, and I can only apologise. Here's the new offer; one thousand eight hundred pounds a year for you, Ken, and for you Jenny, twelve hundred. I'm sorry, but whatever you may think --- and believe me I do understand how you feel --- we couldn't possibly pay a woman the same rate as a man. There'd be all sorts of implications.' Jenny was about to object, but Norman interrupted.

'Wait a bit lass, we haven't finished; there's more. If you can agree to leave right after your wedding, we can offer you a honeymoon. I don't know what you had planned but we'll settle any cancellation fees you have to pay.'

'We were going to Southport,' said Kenneth, 'but we've not booked yet.'

'Right then, what would you say to a first-class passage on the flagship of the Elder Dempster Line from Liverpool to Lagos, calling at the Canary Isles? I've just rung our agent in Liverpool. The M.V. *Aureol* leaves on the seventh and he thinks one of the best cabins might still be available. Beats flying, I'm told.'

'You don't need to decide right now,' said Geoffrey.

Jenny looked quizzically at Kenneth, who nodded. 'Yes,' she said, 'We'll accept. Thank you, and I'm sorry I sounded off.'

Norman beamed. 'It sometimes pays to say what you think, love. I'll be glad to have you both with us. Keep this to yourselves but Geoffrey here may be joining us later. It looks like we may have the beginnings of a Harrison team.'

24

Jane was invited for dinner at Kenneth's place on the Tuesday before their wedding and his parents gave them what she considered a macabre sort of wedding present. Mr Thistlethwaite, who was a representative for the Northern Temperance Assurance Company, had taken out a large life insurance policy in each of their names, for which he was going to pay the annual premiums. He also presented them with the passbook for a joint Burnley Building Society account into which a thousand pounds had been deposited. She later paid in the balance of her Trustee Savings bank account and Ken deposited the proceeds of the sale of his Norton, so they started married life with over three and a half thousand pounds.

*

There was a slight drizzle when Jenny peeped through the curtains at six o'clock on the morning of her wedding day, but the previous night's weather forecast had predicted a bright afternoon for East Lancashire. She returned to bed, though she doubted whether she could get back to sleep. Her mother would be bringing a cup of tea at eight. Her bridesmaid, Mary, would be round at ten and she would travel to the church with Abram, of course. She was nowhere near as excited as she felt she would be.

Broadholme chapel was crammed full. The sun did shine brightly as the couple emerged as man and wife. Abram drove them to the reception at a snail's pace in his white Ford Zephyr, which they were using as the wedding car. Although it was a cold day, those invited to the reception followed the bridal car on foot to the Co-operative assembly rooms, a three or four minute's stroll from Broadholme, with Mr Fazackerly leading the happy group as though this was Whit walking-day.

On the way, Jenny could hear the applause of Saturday shoppers, and there was the occasional cheer from that knew who they were.

Jenny looked round to see who she could recognise. The Harrisons were quite near the front, chatting freely to other guests, many of whom would be employees of their firm. She knew Geoffrey Harrison was not a snob but he did not seem to be happy.

Kenneth's Cousin Robert acted as best man. Although he was only eighteen he looked quite grown up in his hired morning suit. He had just left the grammar school and been accepted to read History at Cambridge. Jenny felt a tinge of jealousy that this boy was having the opportunity she had denied herself, but she had the satisfaction of knowing that her sacrifice had restored the family finances, so that Agnes and Jane Clarke could hold up their heads once more.

It was not an extravagant wedding breakfast. The Co-op supplied a cold buffet and lady members of the chapel congregation had competed to provide beautiful pastries and cake. There was no strong drink available, but tea and coffee were served and there was a variety of soft drinks for the younger guests.

The bride and groom left the reception soon after the speeches were over. Abram, who had finished his speech in tears, drove them to 48 Bright Street. He was taking them to Liverpool. Mr and Mrs Harrison had given them a most generous wedding present, three nights' stay at the Adelphi Hotel before their ship sailed.

'We'll not be more than ten minutes,' said Jenny, as Abram parked outside her house. 'There's a fire in the front room if you'd like to come in.'

He turned the car at the top of the street but did not enter the house. He removed the two white ribbons which he had attached with Sellotape and spent the time polishing his car, though it was already immaculate.

Kenneth had left a pair of grey flannel trousers, a clean shirt and his sports jacket in the spare room and Jenny had a new navy blue two-piece suit and white blouse laid out ready on her bed. She had cleared a space on top of her chest of drawers for the cardboard box which her mother would re-turn to King Street in Manchester by the first bus on Monday. She took off the wedding dress and laid it on her bed, then carefully set it back to its original folds. As she was putting it in the box she rubbed the soft material gently against her cheek, picturing Alice Harrison doing the same thing thirty-odd years ago. Now she wished she had bought the dress; she was loath to surrender it.

She quickly changed into her going-away clothes and re-paired her make-up. Then she walked across to the bedside cabinet, lifted the paper which lined the top drawer, re-moved her collection of film star photographs and slipped them into her handbag. At the bottom of the stairs Kenneth and Abram were preparing to carry the suitcases out to the car. Jenny waited until they were outside before she went into the living room. The fire was still burning. She poked it and watched for a few seconds to make sure the photo-graphs were well alight before she went out to the car. She wouldn't need them now.

Just after four-thirty that afternoon they arrived at the Adelphi Hotel. Ken was rather disappointed when Jenny asked him to sign in for both of them; he thought brides always looked forward to using their married name for the first time. He felt it only right and proper to ask Abram to stay for tea, so he had the suitcases sent up to their room and the three of them went into the lounge. It was obvious they were newly-weds, for Abram still wore the morning suit he had hired and had a white carnation in his buttonhole.

By quarter past five Kenneth was hoping Abram would leave and he could tell that Jenny did too. In her clever way she was trying to steer the conversation in the desired direction. 'I do hope you don't get caught in the football traffic on the way home, Abram. You mustn't let us keep you.'

'Don't worry, love. Liverpool are away today and there won't be so many at Goodison Park. Everton are struggling this season.'

Despite a nervous tightening in his stomach, Kenneth was aching to be alone with his wife. She had surprised him a week or so before the wedding. 'I think you ought to know, Kenneth, I've had a cap fitted.'

'Sorry, you'll have to help me. I don't understand..

'A Dutch cap they call it, a diaphragm. Doctor Pewtress said they're the most reliable way for the woman. I don't want you messing about with those rubber johnnies.' He was surprised to find that she knew about such things.

'Yes,' he agreed, 'I reckon that's a good idea, at least till we see how Nigeria suits us. I don't suppose it's the best place in the world to be having a baby, and you'll have the job, won't you? You seem to know a lot about it', he added.

79

'You mean about contraception? Yes. And I think you should, too.'

She had given him a book called *Now You are Married.* Descriptions of the mechanics of birth control rather put him off, but what worried him most was what was referred to as 'foreplay', which he had never realised was necessary. He developed a fear that this would make him so excited that things would be all over for him before he had even begun to satisfy his wife. So, as Kenneth sat sipping his third cup of tea and trying to get rid of Abram without being rude, he was considering the prospect before him with a mixture of delight and dread.

Eventually Abram took the hint. Well, I'll have to love you and leave you. Don't forget, me and Sheila will want to know how you get on . . . happen you'll send us a postcard from Las Palmas? We've always wanted to go somewhere like that.'

They saw him to his car. There was a tear in his eye as he drove away.

Kenneth's forebodings were unfounded. It all worked out marvellously, because right from the start Jenny took control. Even before they unpacked she said, 'I want a shower. Come in with me and wash my back.'

 Half an hour later they were dozing on the bed. Jenny woke to kiss him yet again and whispered to him, 'Darling, you were wonderful. I hope the noise I made didn't upset you, it's something I just can't seem to help.'

It was eight by the time they came down for dinner. While they were studying the menu the wine waiter brought an ice bucket to the side of their table and produced a bottle of champagne. '*Pol Roger '49* with the compliments of Mr Geoffrey Harrison,' he said, and before they had time to stop him he had popped the cork and poured Kenneth a small measure to taste.

'Isn't that thoughtful of him?' said Ken, and reached over to squeeze his wife's hand. 'Do you know, Jenny, I used to sometimes wonder if you fancied Geoffrey. He fancies you, I can tell that.'

She lifted his hand to kiss it. 'Don't be silly. What would I want with the likes of Geoffrey Harrison when I have the nicest boy in Colesclough? Come on, let's order. I'm hungry, and you need something to keep your strength up. Ask if they have any oysters.'

She could tell that he did not get the joke.

25

When they woke on Sunday morning Kenneth said they ought to go to thank God for their happiness and Jenny said that was a lovely thought, although she would have liked a lie in. After breakfast they enquired at the desk and were told there was a Methodist chapel within easy walking distance of the hotel.

A sidesman welcomed them at the chapel door and showed them to a public pew. He was there again when they left and, at the end of their conversation, he asked if they had ever been to New Brighton.

'No? That's where I was born. You really must see New Brighton while you're here. Take the ferry.'

'I can think of better things to do,' said Ken as they walked back to the Adelphi, but Jenny said she would like to go. She knew what he had in mind and did not want to tell him she was sore. They changed from their Sunday best and took the short walk from the hotel to the ferry terminal. As they stepped onto the boat he said, 'It looks a bit rough. I remember going to Douglas when I were little and being sick all the way there and back.'
'Oh, darling, you should have said so when Mr Haworth offered us the passage on the *Aureol*. I'd never have considered it if I'd known.'

'I didn't want to spoil it for you. I were only young then, happen I've grown out of it. Anyway, this is not so far, and they have pills for sea sickness these days.' But though the crossing took only about a quarter of an hour, he said it made him feel a bit queasy.

'If this upsets you, how are you going to feel when you're on the ship? We'd better ask someone if there's a chemist open where we can get some of those pills.'

It was lunchtime by the time they found the duty chemist. The weather worsened while they ate their fish and chips, the only diners in a large café. Before they were ready to leave, the rain had started and through the misted windows they could discern that the wind was becoming quite strong. There seemed no point in prolonging the visit to New Brighton, especially as they had no umbrella. Kenneth had taken one of the Kwells tablets and he wanted to get back to Liverpool before the effects wore off. Jenny agreed: she had bought some jelly in the chemists, so was now ready to carry on from where they had left off the night before.

*

Monday was spent sightseeing and shopping. They had allocated thirty pounds to buy Kenneth's dinner suit but the
winter sales were still on in Liverpool and he paid only half
that amount, so Jenny was able to buy herself two dresses
with the balance. She pounced on the first one as soon as
she saw it, a fashionably short off-white day dress with navy
blue revers and pockets. The other one, which would be
suitable for formal evenings, was even more of a bargain, a
mid-calf black gown in a new non-creasing material called
Terylene. 'Very Coco Chanel', the sales lady had observed.

When they returned to the hotel there was a message for
them to ring a Mr Penberthy. He introduced himself as Harrisons' shipping and forwarding agent and offered to take
them to the *Aureol* the following day. They could board any
time after two o'clock.

*

They had their bags packed before lunch and by half-past
one they were waiting in the hall, having found that the
whole of their bill had been taken care of by Mr Harrison.
When Mr Penberthy arrived, Jenny had to suppress a giggle,
because he resembled a popular young Liverpool comedian
--- the same accent, protruding teeth. He must have noticed
their reaction.

'I know what you're thinking,' he said. 'Don't worry, my
dears, everybody tells me I'm just like him; in fact, I keep my
hair long because it's good for business and I borrow some
of the jokes. Come along, I think my car may be blocking the
exit.'

Everybody at the port seemed to know Mr Penberthy. He helped them through the customs and passport formalities and was allowed to come on board to guide them to their cabin. As the steward opened the cabin door for them Mr Penberthy said, 'Harrisons have done you proud, haven't they? I've got you one of the very best cabins, there's only the sun deck that's better. Between you and me, when Harold asked me to book you he said you were sort of on your honeymoon so I told him this was all that was left available. He tipped the steward, who said, 'Thanks Pete, Dorothy keeping well?'

When Mr Penberthy left they went to the portholes to see the view over the Wirral estuary. They were on the starboard, which Jenny had heard was not the best side for the outward journey, but it was indeed a fine cabin. The furniture was oak. A dressing table was set between two large square portholes, a desk to one side and a wardrobe unit on the other. The two-seater sofa and a couple of armchairs were covered in pale blue moquette which matched the counterpanes of the twin beds. When Kenneth tried to move the central table he found that it was attached to the floor.

'I suppose that's a precaution for when it gets rough,' he said, with a touch of foreboding.

The bathroom had twin sinks and a separate shower cubicle. There were more towels than they could possibly need.

Jenny was disappointed that the beds were separated by a bedside unit, which had a ship's radio and clock built into it. Kenneth sat on the bed nearer the bathroom. 'I'll have this one if you don't mind,' he said, 'To be near t' toilet.'

He got up and placed a 'do not disturb' sign outside the cabin door. Then he kissed her and said, 'But let's not worry about that yet; I'd like to see how this bed takes the weight of two of us --- unless you can think of owt better to do.'

26

The welcome brochure informed them that dress was informal on that first evening. Kenneth put on his grey suit and Jenny wore a short-sleeved royal blue dress which she had bought at Fothergills in Burnley.

As they entered the dining room they were met by one of the senior stewards who took them to their table, more or less in the middle of the dining saloon. The other four passengers were already seated, an elderly man and a couple who appeared to be in their early forties, with a young daughter. The woman was dressed in a mauve creation which showed too much of her rather scrawny shoulders.

Jane and Kenneth introduced themselves.'

'Hardwicke . . . Paul and Mavis,' the woman said in a posh accent, 'from Norwich but originally from Surrey'. She placed emphasis on 'Surrey' as though there was something slightly shameful about Norwich. 'And this is Alison.'

The daughter, who was about fifteen, gave the impression she wished to disown her parents. She managed a brief smile and then resumed gazing into the middle distance with a bored expression. Poor Kenneth was placed between this daughter and Mrs 'Originally', as they came to know the family. Jenny sat between Mr Originally and the elderly man, whose name was Harry Tomkinson. Some tables at the head of the dining saloon had a vacant seat. Mr Tomkinson explained these would be for senior officers, but that they did not dine with passengers on the first evening.

'That's happen as well,' said Kenneth, causing Jenny to cringe. 'I'd rather they were steering the boat.'

They declined wine with their meal and the tablet that Kenneth had taken at five that afternoon saw him through dinner and into the evening, which they spent walking around the decks and inspecting the night-time activities which the ship had to offer. He took another Kwells before retiring and decided that he ought to try to get to sleep straight away. She said she fully understood.

But the pill did not seem to have any effect. Around one o' clock in the morning the mal-de-mer really took hold of him. At two-thirty she rang for more water. The steward appeared almost straight away. Jenny apologised for troubling him at such an hour.

'That's what we're here for, love,' he said. 'Has he tried a glass of brandy?'

'We don't drink,' said the pitiful voice.

'Purely medicinal, sir. If you're not a drinker a sip or two should do the trick. Believe me, it works.'

'All right,' Jenny said, 'but the bar won't be open now will it?'

'I can find you a half bottle --- keep some in my cabin for just such an emergency. Twenty-five shillings, I'm afraid.' Jenny took out a pound and a ten shilling note from her purse and, though she knew they were being overcharged, told him to keep the change. A small drink of the brandy did indeed do the trick. It was a rough night but he slept through it, and when Jenny awoke at seven the next morning her husband was gently snoring. They had planned that he would join her for an early morning dip in the pool, but she decided not to rouse him.

She loved swimming. Colesclough had no pool but throughout her schooldays she had regularly taken the bus to the public baths at Haslingden, which she preferred to those in Burnley, though Burnley was nearer. She quietly slipped into her swimsuit, put on a bath wrap, took one of the largest towels from the bathroom and eased the cabin door open, then restrained it to shut quietly behind her.

She had not catered for how cold it would be on deck but she steeled herself, knowing that the pool water would have been heated. Since last night the sway of the ship had become a swell, and when she arrived at the pool the water was swilling over the side with each lurch of the vessel. Only one passenger had braved the conditions, a dark-haired young man performing an impressive crawl, quickly completing lengths as though he were competing. She held onto the side of the shower cubicle while deciding whether to go in.

The attendant approached her, 'It's up to you whether you go in Miss, but don't try it unless you're a strong swimmer. It'll be your last chance for a day or two, though. In half an hour I'll be draining the pool; we'll be in the Channel before dark and I gather it's playing up. Then I won't refill until we're through the Bay of Biscay.'

'I'll be fine, thanks,' she said. 'This is what I've been looking forward to.'

She left the robe and towel on a bench by the shower and slipped off her mules. She walked gingerly to the poolside but, just as she was about to dive in, the deck seemed to sink beneath her. She slipped, turning her dive into an inelegant and painful belly-flop. The water first seemed to disappear then to engulf her, so that she was momentarily unable to achieve a stroke. Before she reached the surface she felt an arm encircling her waist to assist her to the side of the pool. Jenny grabbed the handrail and found herself beside the man who had been doing lengths. By now she had fully recovered and could easily have brought herself to this position without the man's help, but she thanked him nevertheless.

'The pleasure is all mine,' he said, 'but I'd advise you not to stay in too long, it really is getting a bit dicey. I've had enough.'

He eased himself from the pool and stood up, shaking himself as a dog would, his long dark hair immediately forming loose curls as the water left it. He was what her mother would call 'a nice height', meaning that he was three or four inches taller than she was. She vowed she would never adopt her mother's habit of regarding every man as a potential partner, but in his case . . . ? Yes, very attractive.

He sat down on one of the slatted wooden benches to dry himself and watched her as she did the breast stroke. Aware of his interest, she changed to the crawl, but it had been some time since she had swum and she soon tired, so after a couple of lengths of the pool she walked up the steps and gingerly set off back to where she had left her towel and robe. This meant that she had to pass where the man was sitting. As she went by she said, 'Thanks once again. Perhaps we shall meet when they refill the pool.'

He moved along the bench and indicated that she should sit beside him, which she had no intention of doing, certainly not without her bathrobe. He stood to shake hands and said, 'Nick Masters.'

As she shook his hand she realised that he would require to know her name. Panic overcame her. She heard herself say, 'I'm Jane . . .' and then there was a hesitation before the ridiculous error --- 'Jane Ferrier. Mrs Ferrier.'

'Then do sit down Mrs Ferrier, and let me ask the pool steward to bring us coffee. It's still early for breakfast.'

'Thank you but I really must go. My husband has been unwell during the night.'

As she walked across to where she had left her things she sensed that he was studying her. Guiltily, she felt pleased. She was quite proud of her little bottom.

When she got back to the cabin Kenneth was sitting on the edge of his bed. He looked much better. 'I'm glad you had your swim,' he said. 'Did you enjoy it? Don't suppose there were many people in while it's like this.'

'No, not many, but it was very . . .' She sought for a word. 'It was very bracing.'

27

Dress for dinner on the second evening was formal. They were now in the English Channel and the sea was even rougher, but Kenneth was finding that a few sips of brandy controlled the problem. As they changed for dinner Jenny reminded him that they ought to take their malaria tablets. He poured himself another brandy with which to swallow his, and asked if she would like to join him. She declined, the smell alone persuaded her that she did not like brandy.

'Anyway, it's nearly finished,' she said, 'and you may need one during the night. But don't get used to it, you know what they say about alcohol.'

'I know what Mr Fazackerly says about alcohol, and now I think it's a load of bollocks.'

'Really Kenneth!' He never used language like that. She realised that her husband was slightly drunk.

When they got to their table, however, she found that both Mr Tomkinson and the Originallies were also tipsy, having been in the bar before they came in to dine. Mr Tomkinson called the wine steward and ordered two bottles of Chablis for the first two courses and some red wine to follow.

Jenny said they would like to pay for the red wine but Mr Tomkinson said, 'Allow an old man his way, Mrs Thistleth-waite. We become like children, you know; we need to be humoured.'

Young Miss Originally was not at the table. 'Is Alison un-well?' Jenny asked.

'I'm afraid she's rather under the weather,' her mother replied, 'Literally under the weather.' She gave a modest chuckle, indicating that they should laugh at her witticism.

The Chablis was served before the first course arrived. When the waiter came to pour some for Mrs Hardwicke she put a hand over her glass and said, rather prissily, 'I think we have had enough, don't you, darling?', but her husband ignored her instruction and accepted what the steward poured. Jenny had not intended to have any wine but decided not to disappoint the old man.

The glasses were oversize, but less than half was poured for each of them because the Channel was proving as rough as the pool steward had predicted: the wine followed the undulations of the ship, not quite spilling. Kenneth solved the problem by draining most of his quickly and Mr Tomkinson reached across to refill it. Mr Originally also had some more, receiving a glare from his wife.

As he drank the wine, Mr Tomkinson blossomed and began to dominate the conversation. 'I am fast approaching eighty and my housekeeper keeps on telling me that I ought to be preparing to meet my maker.'

He had assumed a 'mock-pompous turn of phrase', which Jenny found amusing .

'But that is a step I'm not planning to take for at least another ten years. However, just in case she is right, I've decided to revisit the scenes of a quite outrageously misspent youth. I may even come across some of my children.'

Mrs Originally belatedly gathered the import of this remark and her mouth pursed into something resembling a zip-fastener.

'Did you speak Hausa?' Jenny asked him, in order to change the subject. 'I have begun learning it.' He came out with a sentence, of which she was pleased to recognise a few words.

'That's impressive,' she said. 'How it has stayed with you all this time?'

He gave her another burst of the language, then interpreted; 'That means, what is learned on the pillow remains for life.'

Mrs O's mouth tightened even further. Harry was well aware of the impression he was creating and was enjoying himself. 'I would be delighted to help you, Jane, provided Kenneth can spare you.'

'We can perhaps learn together, darling?' she suggested.

'I'm not that bothered,' said Kenneth.

'So it will be just we two, Jane,' Mr Tomkinson said, sounding pleased. 'Let's meet on the sun deck after breakfast tomorrow morning.'

It became clear why there was no soup on the menu, for the ship was rocking so much that drinking soup would have been nigh impossible. Jenny's melon was not very ripe and she ate only the very centre of it. Kenneth ordered avocado and prawn cocktail.

Mr Hardwicke had made hardly any comment so far, nor did he have much to say for himself on the previous night. Jenny felt she should bring him into the conversation but there was only one topic she could think of. 'Whereabouts in Surrey do you come from, Paul?'

'My wife was born in Sunningdale,' he replied.

'And you?' He hesitated.

Mrs O answered on his behalf. 'You had better admit it, darling,' she said, smiling and raising her chin in a superior manner.

'Well, Croydon actually,' he murmured, as though Croydon was even more shameful than Norwich.

Kenneth did not help by saying, 'I always thought Croydon was part of London.'

'No it is not,' Mrs O replied, 'though nowadays one might be forgiven for thinking so. But certainly it wasn't when we were younger, was it darling? Never quite Sunningdale though,' she added, ending any further conversation on that particular subject.

The Originallies were to disembark at Freetown, where he was an official in the Sierra Leone colonial service. He and Mr Tomkinson had been discussing the colonial service during dinner the previous evening and Jenny had been intrigued by them talking about something which sounded like 'lumpus', that had been distributed by the British government when the Gold Coast became Ghana. It seemed a suitable way of keeping poor Mr O in the conversation.

'By the way,' she said, 'I hope you don't mind my asking, but what exactly is a lumpus, or is it lumpusses?' This caused amusement which she and Kenneth did not share.

Mr Tomkinson explained. 'For people like Paul there are advantages in forecasting which colony is likely to be the next to gain independence, then one can arrange to be transferred there, so that when the British flag goes down one is given a lump sum to terminate the contract. Far be it from me to accuse Mr Hardwicke of such speculation, but the 'lumpers' --- which is Colonial Service jargon for lump sum gratuity --- can add up to a tidy little nest egg.'

'I plead guilty,' said Paul. 'The money I got from the Gold Coast bought us a laundrette in Drayton, and there is another in Catton that I have my eye on. As you say, Harry, the lumpers will be a nice little nest egg for my retirement.'

'So you'll be supporting the Sierra Leone independence movement then?' Kenneth asked teasingly.

Mrs O was clearly annoyed by the facetious remark, 'No, certainly not. You shouldn't say such things, Paul,' she chided. 'I would like you all to know that my husband is a devoted servant of the British Crown. Any benefits that may flow to us from our country abandoning its responsibilities are purely incidental.'

Fortunately Mr Tomkinson changed the subject. 'And you two?' he asked Kenneth. 'You didn't tell us who you'll be working for in Nigeria.' When he heard the name Harrisons he was overjoyed. 'My goodness, isn't that a coincidence. I've known Harold ever since he was a young lad trailing his sample bag round Liverpool.'

'You know Okante, do you?' Kenneth asked him. 'That's where our mill is.'

'Indeed I do; one of my favourite towns. If ever you meet the Regional Premier mention my name. His name is Reuben Ogondo. Reuben started out as one of my clerks.' Mr Tomkinson then went off on a trip down memory lane, back to his first posting in a small bush station near a place called Maiduguri. Jenny listened with half an ear, but took the opportunity to search the dining room to see where Mr Masters was sitting.

94

She found him at a table with one of the officers (the purser, according to the photographs she had seen displayed in the main concourse). Mr Masters was wearing a white dinner jacket. She had wanted Kenneth to buy a white one but he pointed out that there was probably no dry cleaners where they were going and black would be more practical. The other people at the purser's table were an elderly man of about Mr Tomkinson's age, and three women, two of whom were quite attractive --- or so they appeared at that distance. The one on Mr Masters' left was hanging on his every word and Jenny wished that she could have overheard their conversation. She could not suppress a tinge of jealousy, which soon turned to guilt. You're a married woman now, she reminded herself; none of your business what they say to each other.

For the first course Kenneth had chosen pâté again, which she thought may have made him upset last night.

'All right, love?' she whispered to him.

'So far, thanks. The wine's helping.' She would have liked to tell him not to have too much but did not wish to embarrass him.

There was no sign of the fish course arriving and the band had struck up, so she suggested to Kenneth that they dance. The sway of the ship made it difficult to keep rhythm and they found themselves sliding around in their attempt at the quickstep. She found the experience quite amusing --- it was rather like the Noah's Ark on the Pleasure Beach at Blackpool --- but she could tell that Kenneth was troubled by the motion of the ship, so suggested they abandon the effort.

She saw Mr Masters pull back the chair of the woman who had been ogling him and they were coming towards the dance floor. She was relieved to find at closer range that the ogler was not at all pretty; her dark chestnut hair was clearly dyed and she was too heavily made up. She was at least thirty-five and wore a wedding ring.

As Mr Masters passed them he said, 'Good evening Mrs Ferrier'. Her heart sank, but fortunately he did not stop to talk.

'Who's he?' Kenneth enquired on the way back to their table.

'He was at the swimming pool. He must have confused me with somebody else.'

Kenneth managed to eat the fish course but when the roast beef was put before him he did no more than push it around the plate. After his third glass of red wine he stood up and held on to the back of his chair. 'I'm very sorry everyone, but I'm going to have to leave you.'

Jenny also left her seat, took his arm. 'Goodnight. We'll see you again tomorrow evening. No doubt we will be out of the Bay of Biscay by then.'

'No, darling, I want you to stay. I'll be better on my own. Just give me the cabin key and I'll see you later.'

She was not happy about letting him go alone but accepted that there was nothing she could do to help.

This was the first red wine she had ever drunk and she found it very pleasant; St-Emilion, the label said. She accepted a second glass.

After they had finished the main course Harry Tomkinson asked her to dance. He was not a very good dancer but the conditions meant that this made little difference. They managed to slide around more or less in unison.

Mr Masters was now dancing with the other ogler, who was better looking than the chestnut. Her hair was nicely cut, though mousey, and she wore a strapless frock which displayed her large breasts to advantage. Mr Masters seemed to be appreciating this woman more than the other and he whispered something into her ear which caused her to simper.

Harry seemed to read Jenny's mind. 'Yes Jane, I've been watching him too. And you mustn't condemn her: shipboard romances should never be taken seriously. No doubt the husband has been packed off by air and this is her last fling before two years in the steaming jungle or on the arid plain.'

'So you know all about shipboard romances, do you?'

'Of course I do, my dear. Looking at me now you may not believe it, but I was quite a presentable young fellow when I first came out to the West Coast. There were no aeroplanes in my day, of course. We had to go out by sea and it was over a month's voyage in those days. From what I recall of the procedures, that good-looking young fellow will be deciding which of his two dancing partners he will take to bed later this evening... possibly both of them. Neither, I happened to notice, seems unresponsive to his charms.'

'You are a very naughty man, Harry. I realise you are just trying to shock me. Those are both married women.'

He appeared to find this remark amusing. 'Dear innocent Jane, I hope West Africa does not totally disillusion you.

28

Jenny returned from dinner by way of the promenade deck. The atmosphere was balmy, for although the sea was rough, there was only a slight breeze and the temperature seemed remarkably warm for February. She would have liked to have stayed on deck but decided that she ought to see how Kenneth was.

Opening the cabin door quietly, she was pleased to see him sprawled on the bed, gently snoring. He had removed only his shoes and trousers but she decided to let him sleep for an hour or so before waking him to undress.

It was too early to go to bed. She could safely leave him to snooze and take the stroll she had wanted. She took off her evening dress and changed into a pair of slacks and a sleeveless jumper. Then, as the ship lurched, the empty brandy bottle rolled out from under his bed. She looked in the bathroom. There was a bottle of Martell in the holder attached to the wall. He must have ordered this new one from the steward and there was a good measure taken from it. Her sympathy evaporated. She shook him awake.

'What on earth have you been doing?'

He opened his eyes. 'Eh?'

She held the empty bottle in front of his face. '*This*. This I what I mean. Don't you think you'd already had enough?'

'Shut up, woman. Leave me alone, I'm not well.'

'Just how much have you drunk today?'

He got off the bed, holding on to the bedside console.
'What's it matter? This is supposed to be a bloody holiday.'

'Two brandies and four glasses of wine that I saw you have.
And then this!'

'I'll do as I please. I'm not your tame poodle, not like that
pathetic Hardwicke chap, scared to open his mouth. Is that
what you want?'

'Listen, love . . .'

'*Love*! That's a joke, that is. I'm surprised you can remember the word.'

'That's not fair.'

'Since we got on this damned boat it seems you've
forgotten . . .'

'You've no right to say that. You've not been fit to . . . '

'Well, I'm fit now, so stop bloody nagging. Get your knickers
off and do what a wife's supposed to do for her husband.'

'No, Kenneth, listen . . .' He was trying to undo the dress
studs of his shirt, with no success. 'Let me do that for you,'
she said.

He shook her off, 'Leave me alone, I'm not your bloody baby.
Get down on that bed and do what you're told.'

'No!' she shouted. 'I won't. You're drunk.'

She dropped the bottle on the floor, grabbed the key from the dressing table and ran out, allowing the door to slam behind her. Half-way down the corridor she stopped and waited, anticipating that he would follow. Her heart was thumping and she was breathing hard --- angry, but afraid. She let enough time pass for him to dress, but the door of their cabin remained closed. She turned to go back in. At the door she hesitated, hearing him moving about inside.

Fearing what he might do in his present state she carried on up the corridor which led towards the swimming pool. This took her past one of the bars. She wanted a drink; water, lemonade, anything. But when she opened the door of the bar she found it full of people playing cards, still in their evening dress. Her courage deserted her. She hesitated in the doorway, swaying with the movement of the ship and feeling increasingly foolish as people turned to stare at her. Then she summoned a false smile and said, 'Sorry'. The players returned to their game as she closed the door and resumed her walk towards the pool.

She had forgotten to change her shoes. The heels made walking difficult, so she took them off and carried them. By the time she reached the pool she felt so sorry for herself that it seemed the natural thing to cry, something she had not done since she and her mother had sobbed in each other's arms after her dad's body was discovered.

Jenny sat down beside the empty pool on the bench where Mr Masters had sat. She put her shoes down beside her, took her head in her hands and wept.

It seemed no more than a minute later. The voice she recognised said, 'Are you all right Mrs Thistlethwaite? I saw you in the door of the card room. Anything I can do to help?'

Through her tears she could make out his white dinner jacket. The only thing she could think of to say was, 'How did you get to know my name --- my real name?'

'Easily. All I had to do was ask my friend the purser for the name of the most attractive woman on board. Anyway, 'Ferrier' didn't fool me. You hesitated that second too long. Here, have a hankie.' He sat down beside her and pulled a large white handkerchief from his top pocket. She dabbed her eyes, then inspected the handkerchief and was pleased to see that there was no trace of her mascara having run, though she must look an awful fright. She handed it back to him.

'No, keep it, I have plenty.'

'You are very kind.' She gave her nose a most unladylike blow, which made her feel better, though to her surprise she began to cry again, this time not tears of self-pity but of gratitude. He put his arm round her shoulder and, without realising what she was doing, she found herself kissing him. Gently, he returned her kiss, just a light touch of the lips. She found herself wanting more, wanting to lose herself in his embrace, to hide away from her problems in the arms of this man she hardly knew. Gradually his kisses became more intense. Her eyes were closed and she had forgotten where she was, but knew that this is where she wanted to be.

*

It was approaching midnight when she left Nico's cabin. She paused to get her bearings, for she had no idea how she had reached there. The cabin numbers told her that she was on the Sun deck and that she must move down a deck and then traverse almost the full length of the ship to reach her destination. At the end of the corridor she found the stairs and had to cross the hall. The lift doors opened and out stepped a woman whom she recognised as Nico's dinner-table companion, the one with the big bust. She wore a floral peignoir and carried a bottle of wine, which she attempted to hide behind her back. It was clear where she was headed.

'Still rough, isn't it?' Jenny said, bestowing a smile on the embarrassed woman. 'But it's lovely and fresh out on deck. Goodnight.'

'Goodnight,' was the mumbled reply.

As she watched the woman scurry away, Jenny managed to refrain from adding – Good luck to you love, but a glass of wine is all you're likely to share with him tonight.

She opened the door of her own cabin quietly, fearing another confrontation with Kenneth, but found him deep in a drunken sleep from which there was no danger of his waking. He had managed to get out of his clothes, which were strewn on the floor between the beds. It did not seem important that the level in the brandy bottle was lower than when she left, nor did she feel guilt, only euphoria. She ought to have taken a shower but did not want to lose the precious traces of her lover. For the first time in her young life she had discovered the full extent of the power which her beauty gave her. In a perverse way she had begun to resent her good looks, knowing that they were the legacy of her father. As she had grown to despise him, so she had come to despise the face she saw in the mirror. But now she

102

knew that this face had value, that it could give her control over men and that she could cause even a man of the world like Mr Masters to surrender totally to her needs.

It did not occur to her that she had been seduced by a skilled practitioner of the art. Nor did it strike her that within a week of her marriage she was an adulterer.

29

Harold Harrison was having a difficult conversation with his cousin, Pomona Hattersley. They were seated in the drawing room of Daisy Mount, the mansion which their grandfather Isaac had built above his factory site. It still sat amid green fields, albeit the Pennine version of green, the grass apparently stained by years of smoke issuing not only from the Harrison mills but from factories in the valley below, carried upwards on the prevailing east wind.

Daisy Mount was no longer a home, but was used for entertaining visitors, for sales conferences and for musical recitals, which Harold sponsored in his capacity as President of the Coll Valley Arts Club. The upstairs rooms had been modernised to provide a permanent exhibition of the firm's history, along with a lecture hall and a studio where their latest fabrics and designs were displayed, but the downstairs rooms retained the period character of the original house, particularly so the dining room. Harold had become something of an expert on early Victorian furniture and had added to the ambience of the house by purchases of pieces which were in keeping with what had been, by the standards of a successful Victorian mill owner, quite a modest residence.

Pomona was seated on an ottoman which Harold had bought quite recently at a house sale in Bacup.

'People like Plantagenet Sykes are simply vultures,' Harold was telling her. 'You should have shown him the door as soon as you heard his offer. I think I told you he came here with a ludicrous takeover bid last year and I sent him away with a flea in his ear.'

'We must consider the future, Harold. It's my children I'm thinking of. Mr Sykes said that this boom can't last forever and it seemed a generous sum he was offering for the shares.'

'Plantagenet! He must really fancy himself must that chap. Anybody who calls himself Plantagenet has to be a charlatan.'

'I'm sure it wasn't a name he wanted, dear. It's our parents that choose them, as I know only too well. Pomona wouldn't have been my first choice for a Christian name and I'm sure our Leander feels the same way.'

'And has Sykes been to see Leander too? He'll have got a shock if he did. I bought your brother out in 1955, did you know that, Mona?'

'Yes, he told me. We were all very grateful, all our side of the family. He should never have gone into the antiques business. We were shocked when we heard how much he owed.'

'Anyway, I'm having no truck with the likes of this Plantagenet fellow. What he chooses to call Palatine Enterprises is nothing more than a ragbag of tin-pot back-street weaving sheds, despite the grandiose name. Did you know he's a Yorkshireman, by the way?'

'Does that make a difference?' Pomona asked, well aware of her cousin's prejudice.

'Of course it does. What does a fellow like that know about cotton? I happen to know that his dad was a Bradford shoddy merchant until he made a bit of money in the war with army blankets, but then he drank it all away like a lot of 'em do.   A couple of years ago our Mister Plantagenet was nothing more than a jobbing accountant in Leeds.'

'So how does he get the money to go round buying up half of Lancashire?'

'Exactly... that's what I wondered; so after he came flannelling round here with his daft offer I hired a firm of investigators to do a bit of checking up. Seems he married a rich Lebanese woman. That's where the cash must come from.'

'But you have to admit, Harold, it is a tempting offer. What does Geoffrey say? Does he know about it? And Roger? I don't suppose Roger would turn it down out of hand. After all, an army Captain's pay isn't a king's ransom, is it?'

'Even Sykes wouldn't sink so low as to approach my sons behind my back.' Then a doubt crossed his mind. 'Or would he, I wonder? Let's ask Geoffrey. I'll phone his office.'

30

Geoffrey too was having a difficult day. A shipment of cone winding machinery for the new mill in Okante had missed the *s.s. Winneba* and he had to ask the manufacturers to delay their fitters' flights. On top of that, a stage payment invoice for the ring frames had arrived from Platt Brothers, necessitating a difficult phone call to try to persuade Crown Agents to advance the date of the Central Region's next tranche of capital, so the last thing he wanted was a summons to Daisy Mount. The only compensation was that he always enjoyed seeing Pommy.

On his way in through the kitchen he pinched a scone from the tray that Mrs Green had just taken from the oven, receiving a playful slap on the wrist as punishment for the theft. He ran to the drawing room to avoid further retribution and went over to the ottoman to kiss his great-cousin, who started to get up to greet him, so that his kiss landed on one of her several chins.

Harold was pleased to learn that Geoffrey knew nothing of the takeover offer. He outlined Sykes's proposals in as impartial a way as he felt able, though his disapproval was obvious. Geoffrey took some time to respond.

'Well?' asked Cousin Pommy.

'It's nowhere near enough.'

'There you are, Mona,' said Harold.

'Hold on Dad, that's not all I have to say.' Geoffrey went to retrieve the stolen scone, which he had left on the sideboard. He poured himself a cup of coffee and joined Pomona on the ottoman.

'Sykes is a chancer, that's well known. But I must give him a bit of respect for the way he's built up his business, and obviously he has realised how stretched we shall be while we're financing the Nigerian project. Of course, once Okantex is up and running we shall be a high profile company, not just another old-fashioned Lancashire mill.'

'Is that how you think of Harrisons?' his father intervened angrily. 'I'll have you know that . . .'

'No, of course not, Dad. But who's heard of us outside the industry?'

'All my friends know about Harrisons,' Pomona said. 'They've all got our curtains and very pleased they are with them.'

Geoffrey squeezed her hand. 'Yes, of course, Pommy, but I mean people in the City, the sort of people who we would need on our side if Sykes did make a credible takeover bid.'

He could see his father keen to intervene. 'No, listen a minute, Dad. I've just been talking to a woman from Crown Agents. She wanted to know if we would be interested in a project in Northern Rhodesia. Then what about all those new countries that are going to get their independence in the next few years? They'll all want what Ghana and Nigeria are getting, and that will include a textile mill.'

'I'm afraid the lad's right, Mona', said Harold. 'It's daft, I know. There'll be far too many textile mills in these new countries but somebody will have to run them, so it might as well be us.'

'Correct, Dad, and if we want to get further into that side of the business we shall have to increase our capital base, whether we like it or not. It's not the likes of Plantagenet Sykes we shall need to look for, but serious investors such as Joe Hyman. There's a new chap, too. Alliance he's called. Not a bad name for a merger specialist, is it?'

Pomona was obviously puzzled. 'You know I don't understand this sort of thing', she said. 'All I want to know is, are my shares going to be worth more than what this Sykes man is offering? Is that what you're saying will happen, Geoffrey?'

'Almost bound to be, provided we can weather this next year or two. They could be worth a great deal more if we take the right course --- or possibly nothing if we don't.'

It was Harold's turn to look puzzled. 'Now you're not making sense to *me*, son. What is it you're proposing?'

'Go public, Dad. I don't mean just yet. Let's see some profit from Nigeria first, but then we shall be what they call a hot property. We'd have a lot of suitors, but a sale to the public would be the thing.'

The look on Harold's face registered his disapproval. 'You've no sense of history, lad. I'm not going to sit back and let some set of wide-boy speculators get control of everything your great-grandfather created and my dad and I worked so hard building up.'

'You don't necessarily have to. We could offer 'A' shares.'

'Those are all right if you're big enough. Great Universal Stores maybe, not Harrisons.'

'Hold on you two,' said Pomona. 'You lost me five minutes ago. All I really want to know is should I hang on to my shares?'

'Yes, love,' Harold replied. 'We'll make sure it's worth your while, won't we son?'

'Indeed we will, Pommy. And it's my opinion that when we do go public we ought to give our workers the chance to buy shares.'

'Now you're beginning to talk like that Wedgwood Benn fellow,' said Harold, who disapproved of his son's leanings towards the Labour party.

But Geoffrey did not rise to the bait. 'If you'll both excuse me I'd better be getting back. Why don't I put a paper up at the next board meeting? Bye, Cousin Pommy.'

She grabbed his arm. 'No, you shan't escape so easily. Sit down again and talk to me. I'm sure your father will allow you a few more minutes off, won't you Harold?'

As Geoffrey had feared, she wanted to know about his love life, which seemed to be a major talking point within the family.

'Your mother tells me that Mabel Butterworth has disappeared from the scene.'

'Mabel?' he said teasingly. 'Butterworth? Oh yes, I know who you mean. Very nice girl, Mabel.'

'Is he always like this, Harold? At least I get a bit more sense out of my two. Come on Geoffrey. How old are you now?'

'Twenty-five'

'Time you were getting serious then', she said. 'It's ages since there's been a nice wedding."

'No it's not,' said Harold. 'We went to one the other week, didn't we Geoffrey? Prettiest girl in Lancashire.'

'That's right Dad, but I really must go.'

31

Geoffrey used to come across a man called Tom Swan at his favourite pub. They had first met when Tom came to Colescough while the Okante project was on the drawing board. He was export manager for a firm in Blackburn which made air-conditioning systems. Geoffrey assumed he was single or, more probably, divorced. He came to the pub alone and often drove home with a female acquaintance. It therefore came as a surprise when one evening Tom brought a woman to the pub whom he introduced as his wife.

During their conversation she suggested that Geoffrey might like to join her amateur dramatic group. Although he had done some acting at school and at Cambridge, his business commitments prevented him from auditioning for a part with the Colesclough Players. He had had quite a few beers that night, so he found himself volunteering to help build the set for their next production.

Geoffrey did not come across Tabitha again until the dress rehearsal of the play, in which she had the leading female role. He sat at the back and left before the rehearsal was over. The rather silly comedy proved a big success. Geoffrey was helping to strike the set on the last night and had not known that there was always a post-production party. He felt out of place in casual clothes when he entered the green room, to be confronted by the other members in their finery. He considered a hasty retreat.

'Hi there --- it's Geoffrey, isn't it?'. The speaker was behind him but he recognised her by the accent. She had been obscured by the open door as he came in.

'Am I right? When I saw you backstage I thought I ought to know you.'

'Yes, Geoffrey Harrison, and you're Tabitha --- couldn't easily forget a pretty name like that. You're American, aren't you?'

'Correct, a genuine Yankee.'

'I didn't know we were allowed to call you that.'

'Not unless we hail from New England. I'm from Connecticut.'

'Tabitha sounds like a name that came over with the founding fathers.'

'More or less, honey. I'm the fourth generation one: there always has to be a Tabitha in my family.'

She was probably in her early forties but careful make-up made her look not much older than him; a tiny woman, only just over five feet tall. Goes to a lot of trouble not to put on weight, he speculated, for her figure was perfect.

111

'You're very late,' she said. 'Some of us are slightly plastered, me included.'

'I do hope you aren't driving.'

'No, I'm promised a lift. Tom's away in Hong Kong, South Korea, places like that, and my Land Rover's hospitalised. Now that you mention it though, I really ought to be going. Good to have met you again, Geoffrey.'

She gestured across the room to the gay man who had played the lead. He came over to join them.

'You ready sweetie?' she asked him. 'It's my bedtime.'

'Don't be a spoilsport, Tabby. After all, the night is young --- and I'm so beautiful. But if you do insist on leaving maybe Geoffrey could run you back. Haslingden's on your way home isn't it, Geoff?'

'Glad to,' he said, welcoming the excuse for leaving the party.

*

From that first exciting night Geoffrey became Tabitha's pupil. He started to realise how much there was to learn.

She had met Tom Swan at the London School of Economics while her father was working at the United States Embassy in London. When her parents were posted back to Washington she stayed on to complete a master's degree and shared an apartment with Tom, in East Acton.

Having graduated, they applied for jobs that would permit them to continue to live together and each turned down of-

112

fers which would have separated them. It was not until he secured the position in Blackburn and she was offered a post as Reader in Business Studies at the East Lancashire Technical College that they decided to marry. They bought a disused farmhouse up a long lane on Haslingden Grane, which, over a period of four or five years, they converted into a home which would have cost them a fortune had they stayed in the South of England.

Before he met Tabitha Geoffrey's only experience of sex had been that drunken coupling under the pier at Blackpool, an encounter so unmemorable that he struggled to recall the woman's name. Tabitha had no inhibition about telling him exactly what she liked to have done to her and she encouraged him to say what pleased him. She showed him what satisfaction one partner can derive from giving pleasure to the other.

Hers was an 'open marriage', she claimed. Apparently she and Tom did not want children and were allowed to go their separate ways whenever they found someone to whom they were attracted. Geoffrey found this amazing and began to wonder how many other outwardly respectable couples led this sort of life. He now looked on with interest when he saw men or women chatting to other people's spouses, and speculated as to whether this might be the prelude to wild abandon later in the evening.

Nevertheless, despite Tabitha's protestations of a liberated lifestyle, when they went for a drink together she insisted it was never to the pub where he first met her and where he and Tom were well known. Furthermore, she always insisted that they arrive at their chosen venue in separate cars. When he suggested that he might take her out to dinner or to the cinema she declined.

'Let's not set tongues wagging,' she said.

There was no talk of love between Tabitha and Geoffrey and it was understood that he was only to communicate with her when Tom was away. Geoffrey took great pleasure from his evenings with Tabitha.

But he could never forget Jane Clarke.

32

Kenneth woke with two steam hammers pounding directly against his lower temple. In films he had seen, particularly those of W.C. Fields, a hangover had been amusing, but the reality was painful beyond belief. With difficulty he opened his eyes, finding that he could not focus. He peered at the bedside cabinet and identified two clocks. Then he partly closed his eyes until the clocks gradually merged, to show him that the time was almost half-past nine in the morning. His wife was not there and her bed was neatly made. He reached for the water carafe and drained what was left in one gulp, finding it quite insufficient to quench his raging thirst.

He rang for the steward but it was Jenny who opened the door a minute later. Even in his dreadful state he could see how attractive she looked. She wore white shorts, a loose black and white striped sun-top and the rope-soled sandals she had bought in Liverpool. Something at the back of his pounding brain told him that there had been a row the previous evening, a suspicion confirmed by her silence as she busied herself tidying the dressing table. He tried to speak but his first attempt was a mere croak. Before he succeeded in giving voice there was a knock on the door and Jenny let in the steward.

He carried a large jug of water. 'I see I guessed right --- I mean the reason why you rung for me, sir.' The steward filled the empty carafe and, diagnosing the symptoms of the sorry figure sitting on the side of his bed, decided to leave the jug. 'But I bet you slept OK didn't you? I told you brandy would do the trick. Now drink plenty of water, that's the ticket. Take it from one who knows, water clears the system out.'

The victim gave a grunt which the steward interpreted as assent. Kenneth heard Jenny using her 'prissy' tone to the annoyingly cheerful intruder.

'Thank you for bringing the water Alan, but I'd like to say that neither of us will be requiring any more brandy during the voyage.'

She held the door open for him. 'Don't bother to come back. I'll make Kenneth's bed. Lovely morning, isn't it? The sea is much calmer.'

When the man had gone, Kenneth tried again. He found that his voice was pitched much lower than usual but at least he could speak.

'I suppose I need to apologise," he said. 'I let you down, didn't I?' There was no reply. 'To be honest I don't remember much of what happened. Was I drunk at dinner?'

'Not at dinner, not noticeably so.' She chose her words with care. 'I think the best thing is that we should both forget about last night. But we really shall have to make a fresh start, Kenneth. It all seems to be going wrong.'

'I know, and I'll admit it's my fault. You see, I'm finding life a bit strange on this boat. Nowt much to do and lots of time to do it in, if you get my meaning. But now I'm getting my punishment for whatever it was I did last night. The seasickness was awful but this hangover is worse. Far worse. You've no idea what me head's like.' He attempted a smile. 'So am I forgiven?'

She poured him a glass of water. 'Of course I forgive you, darling and I must ask you to . . . '

But she decided that would be going too far. 'Here, drink this.'

*

They were now almost through the Bay of Biscay which they had been warned would be rough, but turned out less difficult than the English Channel had been. Kenneth at last appeared to be 'getting his sea legs'. The sun shone from a clear sky and it was warm enough for them to sit outside.

They settled down to a pleasant routine. After breakfast Jenny would find a quiet corner of the sun deck and study her Hausa manual until Harry Tomkinson arrived to give her the daily lesson. She was pleased to find she had learned enough for them to hold a simple conversation in Hausa.

Kenneth had joined them for the second lesson and they both learned the rather complicated greeting rituals, which Harry made clear were essential preliminaries to even the most casual conversation, but she could tell that Kenneth was not really interested. He did not join them again and she was glad when he was adopted by Alison Originally.

116

Once away from her parents Alison was a pleasant girl and she and her young friends made him a member of their team for deck games.

Jenny continued to make good progress with the language, which she spoke at every opportunity, though not at the dinner table --- that would have been rude to the Originallies and Kenneth. She had learned to recognise which of the Nigerians were from the North and tried out some phrases in the queue for buffet breakfast.

In the afternoons, while she was studying, Kenneth usually went to the card room. His father had taught him bridge and during his grammar school days he had become quite proficient. She could tell that he often had a drink while he was playing but she knew that he would not have too much, needing to keep his wits about him to follow the game. He considered many fellow passengers to be 'posh', so she was pleased when he reported that the other players were friendly.

'That chap Masters was on my table today; him you met at the swimming pool. He certainly knows his onions.'

'About bridge, you mean?'

'Yeah. Looks like the sort of clever bugger who's good at everything he tackles.'

Jenny hoped that her tan hid the rising colour in her cheeks, but decided she must glean what information she could.

'What does he do for a living? Did he say?'

'Summat to do with hotels. He didn't seem keen to talk about it.'

33

There was great activity on the day before they were due to reach Grand Canary, with queues at the purser's office to book tours and change money. The Originallies were going to visit one of their former Gold Coast colleagues who had retired to a villa near Las Palmas. Harry Tomkinson told them not to book a tour, because he was going to call a Spanish friend of his on the ship's radio telephone, to hire a chauffeur-driven car for the day.

Breakfast was taken early on the morning of arrival but Harry said they should let all the tours get away before they disembarked. The itinerary he had planned would mean there would be plenty of time, enough for a leisurely lunch at a restaurant that he knew well, up in the mountains.

'Hope it's still there,' said Ken.

'It is,' said Harry. 'The friend I phoned last night will book us a table.' Jenny kissed the old man on the cheek.

'We are so lucky to have found you. Aren't we Kenneth?'

It was disappointing to find a slight drizzle as they walked down the gangway, having seen the last of the ancient buses draw away from the quay, loaded with passengers who had booked day trips. There was no sign of a hire car, the only vehicle within view was a large yellow sports car parked on the road alongside the customs gate. It had a soft top which looked as though it might be made of chamois leather.

When they disembarked, a group of ladies surrounded them on the quayside, holding up beautiful lace tablecloths, but

Harry advised Jenny not to buy one until she had seen what the shops in the city had to offer. When they emerged from passport control a uniformed man got out of the sports car and opened the passenger doors. Harry greeted the driver in Spanish and the two men embraced.

'This is my old friend Alfredo', he told them, 'owner of the finest vehicle on the island of Gran Canaria. Show your appreciation before we get in.'

Kenneth moved around the old car like a pilgrim at a shrine. 'My word, it's really something is this. I never thought I'd get to ride in a Pegaso. How old is it?'

Alfredo spoke good English. She is old as my youngest son, twenty-three years. Others they must ride in my Mercedes. This old lady is now retired but for the visit of Senor Harry I decided to bring her back to the road.' Kenneth sat in front with Alfredo. Harry knew the island so well that he acted as their guide, only occasionally being corrected by Alfredo.

The visit to Las Palmas city was to be kept until the end of their journey. Alfredo drove south, hugging the coast, alongside what looked like dried up river beds but which Harry said were old lava streams. After about four miles they came to a village, set amid this volcanic rubble. Kenneth turned round to speak to Jenny. 'I wouldn't like to live here, would you? I imagine Hell is a bit like this.'

Jenny hoped Alfredo was not insulted by this description of his native island, but privately she agreed with Kenneth. She had never previously been further from home than the English Lake District and Kenneth's only holiday outside Lancashire was that trip to the Isle of Man, so neither of them had anything with which to compare this strange landscape. It struck her how awful it would be if Okante turned out to be like this.

As they turned inland they left the stark terrain behind and passed by small fields, growing vegetables. Jenny recognised carrots by their spindly foliage, cabbages too, but she had to question Alfredo about one crop, which he told her was melons.

After crossing a stone bridge they entered a little forest of palms and emerged into a valley of orange groves, each plot marked out by a low wall of rocks. An unfamiliar type of sheep grazed among the trees; Harry said they were sheep but to Jenny they looked more like goats. The scent of orange blossom wafted through the open windows of the car, though she could discern none on the trees.

The drizzle had now ceased and the sun was attempting to break through the cloud. Alfredo pulled off the road beside the gate of one of the plots and began to pull down the hood of the Pegaso. Kenneth got out to help him. She now saw that the trees were indeed laden with fragrant blossom, though it had not yet turned white. Harry went through the gate and she saw him break a branch from one of the trees. 'Won't they mind?' she shouted after him.

'Ask Alfredo, it's his field,' Harry shouted back. Alfredo smiled and shook his head. Harry returned bearing a beautiful spray of pale green blossom. He closed the gate behind him, not a real gate but an old brass bed-head which had been placed on hinges.

'This was always my custom, Jenny.' Harry kissed her cheek as he presented the bouquet. 'Alfredo knew exactly where I wanted to stop, didn't you, old friend? I always tried to take my holidays about this time of year. We are a little early for the full effect, but I want you to imagine me as young man and you are my partner in a shipboard romance. Imagine this whole valley permeated by the perfume of orange blossom; would you not succumb to my charm?' He smiled to himself. 'Oh yes, Jenny, orange blossom has served me well.'

When he was in this mood his language became quite lyrical. Charm does not wither with age, Jenny thought. She felt she now knew him well enough to ask the question which had been in her mind since first they met. 'Why did you never marry?' His mood was suddenly serious: she feared she may have offended him. 'That is not a question to be answered here,' he said. 'Wait until our Hausa lesson in the morning.'

The car roof was now safely stowed and Alfredo re-started the engine.

It was just after midday when they reached their lunchtime destination, a small town set in the foothills of a range of mountains which had been in view ever since they emerged from the palm forest. Alfredo parked in the deserted plaza and Jenny looked round for a restaurant. She was disappointed to find Harry leading them to a rather seedy-looking bar. The proprietor greeted them as though they were a great nuisance, but after Alfredo spoke to him in Spanish he mellowed slightly and shook hands with the four of them.

Without asking what they wished to drink he brought a carafe of red wine and a bowl of olives, then went back to bring them tumblers which would have held half a pint. Alfredo asked for lemonade so the carafe would be for the three of them.

Jenny took a sip of the wine. It had a heavy, slightly bitter taste, somehow bearing the flavour of oranges, though this may have been induced by the spray of blossom which she had placed on the table.

'Vino del Monte,' explained Alfredo, sipping his lemonade. 'Bottoms up, isn't that what you say?'

Kenneth took a draught and licked his lips. 'That's great; I could get to like this, Alfredo.'

Just before one o'clock Harry got up, walked to the top of the square and knocked on the door of a villa which Jenny had been admiring since they arrived. There was no sign to identify it as a restaurant. An elderly woman came to the door, hesitated for a moment and then embraced him warmly. He signalled that they should come over. Alfredo took out a banknote which he left on the table along with most of the wine.

It was a meal Jenny would always remember, their first 'foreign' food'. They ate upstairs on the balcony, looking down over the plaza to a distant view of the sea.

There was a bowl of freshly-baked bread on the table but no side plates. She was worried about spilling crumbs on the lovely lace tablecloth, but the men were also leaving a mess. When Senora Gonzales brought a carafe of the same wine, Vino del Monte, she did not seem to mind. This one tasted much more delicate than what they had left at the café. Jenny threw caution to the winds and kept pace with Harry and Kenneth, glass for glass. For some reason there flashed into her mind a picture of Mr Fazackerly in the pulpit at Broadholme, preaching his regular sermon on 'The Demon Drink.'

Kenneth reached out for her hand. 'This is what being abroad is all about, hey love?' It was a happy moment.

The mountain air and the sense of occasion combined to give her an appetite. The Senora brought out the largest soup bowls she had ever seen. A huge tureen then arrived and they helped themselves with a ladle. The chief ingredient was chick peas, with other vegetables, some of which she could not identify. It also contained a variety of meats --- ham, lamb and several different sorts of sausage. It seemed as though everything in the larder had been thrown in, but the result was delicious. The tureen was carried away empty. Only Alfredo had appetite for the pudding. When they had finished their coffee she insisted they each take away a bunch of grapes.

They were back in Las Palmas with plenty of time left to shop before they needed to start their walk back to the ship. Jenny felt a bit tipsy but pleasantly so. It was time for Alfredo to leave them, and Ken took her aside so that the old men could be alone to say their farewells. They could see Alfredo openly weeping as he said goodbye to Harry, for what both must realise would be the last time. After they had watched the Pegaso disappear from view, Harry visibly pulled himself together and said, 'Right then, young people --- it is time now for some serious shopping.'

A tablecloth was top of Jenny's agenda. Choosing one under Harry's guidance involved a tour of the narrow back lanes of the old city. This took the best part of an hour but eventually she emerged with just the right tablecloth, at a price which seemed insultingly low. It was to count among her most treasured possessions, even in the days of her affluence.

Time was now pressing, but Harry said they simply must visit another old friend of his. Again there was a preliminary display of affectionate embraces. The man showed them round his shop, which was full of beautifully-crafted leather goods; hats, gloves and breeches, intricately embossed aprons, pouffes, saddles, slippers. Jenny found a tray of tooled-leather bookmarks and bought two to send as presents to her mother and to Abram; then, as an afterthought, one for Mrs Harrison. Kenneth was wandering around the shop showing little apparent interest, but surprised Jenny by bringing to the counter a beautiful riding crop, made from different shades of leather twisted together and ending in a pretty tassel.'

'That's lovely, Kenneth, but is it something we really need?'

'I thought we might buy a horse when we get out there.' He was full of surprises today.

'What a lovely idea, we can both learn to ride.'

Harry bought nothing but spent the time on a long conversation with his friend, in fluent Spanish. Kenneth said how moving he found this.

'You really are an old softie,' she said, and kissed him. She vowed she would let him make love to her that night, and hated herself for feeling that this was a duty.

34

Soon after breakfast next day, Jane and Harry claimed their usual place on the sun deck, she in her bikini and he in his long khaki shorts and crazy- patterned shirt. She helped him move a reclining chair into the shade and then asked him to put sun cream on her back, which she knew he en-

124

joyed doing. The salt air and gentle sunshine had already given her a golden tan, so she was able to take full sun, despite its increasing power, as they headed for the coast of Africa.

For her Hausa lessons they had now dispensed with the manual, finding conversation was the better way for her to learn. But for the story of his love affair he reverted to English.

'Come closer, my dear,' he said. She moved her lounger, to join him in the shade. 'I am going to tell you a story about a young lad from Liverpool and a beautiful Fulani girl.'

She settled down in great anticipation, delighted to find that he was again in his lyrical mode.

Among her people she was a princess, tall and beautiful. Her father was leader of his clan, nomads who roamed the plains of Bornu. The family owned over six hundred head of cattle and they went wherever their beasts led them, from the edge of the Sahara to the gates of the ancient city of Kano, raising families during their wandering and educating them in the wisdom and traditions of their forebears. Amina was their finest flower.

That was how Harry described her, and who was she to doubt this old man? But the man in the real story was a boy, not long out of public school. He had just over a year's service in the buying office of Liverpool's leading West African merchants before he began the long journey to Nigeria and the loneliness of the most northerly of that great firm's outposts.

One day in the dry season he is supervising the unloading of a newly-arrived consignment which has been delivered by bul-

lock wagons from the railhead.   A red cloud on the horizon warns him of some Fulani approaching, and he runs to tell his assistant to help him pull down the shutters of the store to prevent the invasion of the airborne dust which the herd always carries with it.

When he returns, she is already in the back compound, having dismounted her horse and is using a dagger to tear open the hessian covering of a bale of peacock blue fabric. In his yet-inadequate Hausa he orders her to stop. She turns her head to look at him --- and his heart is lost.

She buys four pieces of the dyed cloth, which the storeman loads onto her horse. Then she smiles shyly at Harry and gives a loud instruction for the herd to move on. His clerk tells him that this is Amina, a virgin, whose bride price has not so far been afforded by any of the young men of Bornu Province, and who is condemned to chastity until a suitor provides her father with at least eighty prime beasts.

Strangely, Harry's face had assumed that of the young man he then was, though the voice was that of an eighty year-old.

At the end of the rains each year the nomads would move South, their cattle were now fat and ready for the markets of Sokoto or Katsina.

'I used to prepare supplies for them to collect on their way westward; salt, candles, blankets, matches, tobacco. I forget what else.'

But when Amina's family arrived the following year she was not with them.

'My clerk spoke with her brothers, who said that when they set off, a rich old man from Birnin Kebbi was considering the

126

bride price. Their mother was keeping her in the rainy season quarters along with the pregnant women, until the demand was met.

I invited the brothers into my bungalow. It was nice to have
company. For dinner we ate the meat of a young sheep and
they shared several bottles of Burton beer with me --- and
far too much whisky, as I remember! I staggered off to bed
and they spread their mats on the floor of the canteen. In
the morning we had a breakfast of porridge, made with the
thin cream of their cattle, followed by eggs and tinned bacon, something which they had never tasted before. They
relished bacon as we would caviar. When they left they
agreed to carry my message, though I feared I may have
been too late.

Before the following rainy season came, I had been promoted and was due for transfer to Maiduguri. I recall that
my last day in the old post was to be the thirty-first of
March, and still the Fulanis hadn't come. I sent a signal to
our Kano office that I was ill with malaria, a deception that
became the truth, because later that week I lay sweating and
delirious in my room above the store. There was no doctor
within eighty miles, but there *was* a mission station at the
railhead. My clerk went there on his bicycle and returned
with more quinine, as well as a bottle of Gordon's gin, which
he had bought from an itinerant trader he met along the
way. I drank most of the gin, took twice the recommended
dose of quinine and prepared for death.

In my delirium I imagined myself back in the infirmary at
Liverpool where, as a child, I had my tonsils removed. A
nurse was applying a cool compress to my head. I opened
my eyes to thank her, and there stood Amina --- the woman
who had occupied my dreams for two years. She was gazing
into my eyes and smiling, more beautiful than I had ever

imagined her to be. She whispered words I didn't understand. It seemed like an hallucination. But then, standing behind her I saw two of her brothers, those handsome nomads I had last seen lying drunk on my canteen floor, now grinning in embarrassment as their sister administered the healing compress which began to draw the fever from me.

The brothers moved on with the herd, but Amina stayed behind and nursed me, for what must have been ten days or so. She shared my bed, hugging me back to health. When the brothers returned, she left with them, still a virgin. As was I.'

His story appeared to be over. Jenny felt huge disappointment.

'Surely that can't be all,' she said. 'Did you never meet her again?'

'Sorry my dear, I would love to give you a happy ending but that was the last I ever saw of her.'

'But you must have wanted to know what happened to her, whether she married that old man?'

'I did find out, but that was not until 1915. When the Great War broke out, what you call the First World War, I joined the West African Frontier Force. It was after we captured Togoland that I met Mecho, the youngest of Amina's brothers. He had abandoned the life of a nomad and received an education at the government school in Kaduna. Mecho was a corporal in another company of my regiment. I'd never come across him before --- he was only a child when his brothers stayed with me --- but he must have known who I was, because one day he came to tell me the awful sequel.'

128

Harry's eyes clouded over and Jenny feared he may not be able to continue.

'Tell me later if it's too painful,' she said.

He took a deep breath and continued, 'The old suitor eventually provided one hundred beasts as the bride price but, less than a year after her marriage, Amina killed herself with her golden dagger. She had become pregnant and would not bear the child of the man she had come to hate.'

'Oh Harry, you poor man --- and poor Amina, of course. That is the saddest story I have ever heard.'

Jenny could see how much these reminiscences had taken out of him. His head was turned away from her and she knew he was about to weep.

'Come on, Harry dear, let's go to the lounge for some coffee. What you've just told me is quite enough for any person to reveal about himself.'

He seemed to pull himself together but did not get up from his chair. 'No, I must carry on, because somewhere in my story there is a moral which may be helpful to you, though I'm damned if I know at the moment what it is.'

He coughed, to clear his throat, and dabbed his eyes with a handkerchief.

'After the war I found myself promoted once more, this time to the company's head office in Lagos.' He gave a slight chuckle, which surprised Jenny. 'By the way, I don't want to give you the impression that I was an angel. I'm sure it would be nice for you to go away thinking I was some sort of medieval knight, forever carrying the memory of his one true love to the grave.'

He stood up and stretched himself, to relieve the stiffness which had come from sitting too long. 'Perhaps we *will* have that coffee, after all. Come along, put your robe on and let's find a quiet corner in the lounge; there won't be many people there this early.'

In Lagos, Harry got himself a housekeeper, who became his mistress. She was a Hausa woman a few years older than him, who was now unmarriageable, having been discarded by her husband for not bearing him a child. He said her apparent infertility was a bonus in those days, when contraception was not a reliable option.

Jenny interrupted him, 'But I thought you said . . . sorry. Carry on.'

'I know what you're thinking,' he continued. 'What I told you the other evening about looking up some of my children was said only to shock that dreadful Mrs Hardwicke. There were no children. I'll tell you about that in a minute.'

In the fifth year of their relationship she told Harry she had met a man who was willing to marry her, a Christian Yoruba. The man agreed that she could continue to clean Harry's house, but of course she must no longer sleep with him.

'That would never have worked', he said, 'because we had become too close for what they call a 'platonic' relationship. Instead, I set her up in a little shop not far from where the army barracks is now. Her husband was a good man. I used to visit them and he and I became friends. They had three children together, two girls and a boy so --- how can I put it? It was not *she* who couldn't have children. Could have been

130

me, could have been pure chance. Who knows? And what does it matter now. By the way, she died before her husband did."

'And you? Did you ever . . .'

'No, there was never anyone else. The odd flirtation, but nothing permanent. Now I have a *genuine* housekeeper in my house on the Wirral, just to do the shopping and keep the place clean and tidy --- I've always done my own cooking, it's a hobby of mine. By the way, I hope you and Kenneth will come over to see me when you are on leave. Hoylake isn't all that far from Colesclough.'

The lounge was filling up and a couple were within earshot, so she suggested they move outside again.

'No, we may as well stay here because that's all there is to tell you.' He hesitated. 'But hold on, we haven't found a moral yet, have we?'

'Does there have to be a moral?'

'I believe every story should have a moral --- so what can I say?'

He was silent for a moment. 'I know what it is. *Follow your heart.* That's a well-worn phrase but it's good advice nonetheless.' He took her hands and looked her straight in the eye, 'Never pretend to yourself that everything is all right when you really know you have made a mistake.'

She suspected this wise old man had found out more than he should.

35

It was going to be a long time before they reached the next port of call. Her lessons with Harry continued and he congratulated her, saying she was nearing fluency. She even persuaded Kenneth to join her in borrowing books from the library. He played bridge most afternoons and was regularly called to join Alison and her friends for deck games. She decided it would be a good idea to have her hair cut short again next time she visited the ship's salon. This would give her time to find a hairdresser when they got to Okante. He also agreed to have his cut, so she booked him an appointment to follow hers.

She was taken aback when he emerged. He saw her face, and said, 'I didn't ask you, because happen you wouldn't agree. It's called a 'crew cut', a lot of them lads I play games with have one. Same as you, I think it may be hard to find a proper barber out there.'

Jenny took a look at the new Kenneth. 'I like it, darling. I think it suits you.'

Although the ship was large enough for Jenny to avoid meeting Mr Masters, she found it odd they had not bumped into each other again and guessed that he might also be avoiding *her*. She sacrificed her morning swim because she felt sure that was the one thing he was unlikely to give up. Once, in the dining room, she unintentionally caught his eye and he smiled, but there was no message in the smile. Kenneth never mentioned him again.

The temperature and humidity rose progressively as they approached the coast of West Africa. Before the Originallies disembarked at Freetown, Ken and Jenny invited them to their cabin for drinks and bid them an almost sincere fond farewell. They exchanged addresses and promised to get in touch when they returned to England, but there was clearly no intention on either side that they should meet again.

Only about a dozen people got off at Monrovia. At Tema, the port of Ghana, there was quite an exodus. Nevertheless, well over half the complement of passengers was still aboard as the *Aureol* set sail for Lagos.   Both Jenny and Kenneth were facing the prospect of arrival with foreboding, though neither admitted it.

They thought they were acclimatised to the heat, but what met them when they reached the dockside at Apapa was beyond their imagining. The atmosphere was fetid and a warm stench rose from the harbour, in which floated debris that may well have lain there for years --- rotten fruit, dead seabirds and other flotsam which it was better not to try to identify.

Surrounding the ship was a heavy layer of mist. From the shelter of the disembarkation deck Jenny could not judge whether it was fog or drizzle, though she noticed that many of those standing on the steaming quay had raised their umbrellas. The activity on the dockside was hectic but without any discernible purpose, save on the part of members of the crew trying to secure mooring lines and pushing back the crowd, so that they could make room to lower the departure ramps. Kenneth remarked that it would be a miracle if they ever saw their luggage again.

After much searching of faces in the dense and noisy throng, Ken pointed out the figure of Norman Haworth standing beneath a multi-coloured umbrella held by a tall African man. Norman had identified them and was waving a white

133

handkerchief. The Nigerian was dressed in a voluminous robe, predominantly green, with a matching headdress. Norman was all in khaki, shirt buttoned down to the wrist and knee-length shorts with long stockings. The pair on deck smiled at the pair on shore and the four of them occasionally waved in a futile manner, until at last the gangplanks were down and disembarkation was allowed.

Jenny could see the second class passengers already rushing off in a mad scramble down the stern gangway. First class passengers were to disembark according to cabin number, which meant that the Thistlethwaites were among the first onto the ramp. Halfway down, Jenny turned to wave goodbye to Harry Tomkinson.

Norman Howarth kissed her on the cheek. 'About bloody time', he said, 'we've been waiting since half-past eight. Give Peter your baggage tickets and let's get away from this stinking place.'

The Nigerian man lowered his umbrella and held out his hand to her.

'How do you do?' he enquired in a perfect English accent. 'I'm Peter Ogondo, here in the capacity of chauffeur.'

His voice was remarkably deep. Illogically, Jenny felt that such a voice ought to belong to some giant of a man but, though he was tall, Peter had a slim figure and the most delicate features she had seen on an African; not that she had seen many. The black men she had previously encountered had been professional cricketers who came to play in the Lancashire League. Then she remembered that those were West Indians; perhaps there was a difference.

Mr Ogondo gave a signal and a small man wearing a blue uniform and battered straw hat emerged from the crowd to take charge of the baggage tickets. A long queue had already formed at the passport control barrier but Peter went to the front and spoke to the officer in charge, then beckoned them forward, causing the rest of those waiting to shout and whistle their disapproval. He took their passports and asked them to wait.

They stood well away from the line of hostile people while Peter went into a glass-fronted office, where they could see him shaking hands with an official who had a lot of gold braid on the epaulettes of his white uniform. He emerged almost immediately and gave them back their passports.

'All done,' he said, 'follow me.'

'What about customs?' Kenneth asked him.

'Also taken care of. Come along.'

His car was a white Rolls Royce. Norman sat in front with Peter, who wiped his large spectacles and then did not bother to put them back on, confirming what Jenny had suspected when she first looked him in the eye... that they were made of plain glass and were worn purely for effect. The air-conditioning started up immediately he switched on the car engine, soon bringing blessed relief from the Turkish bath atmosphere of the dockside. Kenneth and Jenny settled in the back of the car on beaded cool-seats which had been placed over the leather upholstery.

When they set off from the harbour it seemed to Jenny that what she was watching through the tinted windows of the Rolls was one of those travelogues they used to show at the picture house in Colesclough before the main feature.

135

Women sat along the roadside at intervals of only a few feet, with their wares set out on bamboo mats. It was surely not possible for more than a few of them to make a living. With so many sellers, who was left to be a buyer? The houses behind the mud side walk were no more than shacks, some constructed from old packing cases, some of adobe with rusty metal roofs, but nearly all of them were painted in vivid cheerful colours as though their owners wished to make a gesture to deny their poverty.

After about ten minutes, in which they covered no more than three miles, they reached a bridge and the traffic suddenly thinned out. 'Not far to your hotel now', Peter said.

Jenny was excited. They were now truly in the country that was to be their new home and so far it was completely alien. She was sitting directly behind Peter. He had a lovely neck, long and slender, from which the tight dark- brown curls of his hair rose in a perfect inverted arch. It had not previously occurred to her that African men could be beautiful.

They came to a district with apartment blocks. Washing waved from the balconies, there were trees alongside the road, proper pavements. Then the area became more prosperous, smart bungalows with front gardens and cars parked in their drives, children riding bicycles.

After a couple of hundred yards a sign pointed to *Lagos Homestead* and the Rolls turned into a brick-paved lane and down to a courtyard fringed with palms. The central roundabout was packed with brilliant yellow and red flowers which Jenny had never seen before.

'What are those?' she asked Norman. 'They look gorgeous'

'Canna lilies. You'll be able to grow them in your garden. Come on, this is it, out you get.'

A young boy in a red and blue uniform came to open the car doors. He made an obeisance to Peter, who led them into the foyer. Norman went to the reception desk to check them in. Kenneth shook Peter's hand,

'Thanks a lot for the lift. I've never sat in a Rolls before. Can we buy you a drink before you go?'

'Yes please. I shall be waiting until I am sure that your luggage has arrived. A Sprite, if you would be so kind.'

Kenneth said he had never heard of it. 'It is a sort of lemonade,' Peter explained. 'Get one for Norman too, that's what he always drinks.'

Jenny said she would try one.

Peter led them to the veranda. 'I am hoping that one of your fellow passengers will be arriving soon. A chap I knew at school.'

As the waiter was pouring their drinks a white pick-up truck drew up in front of the hotel. On its door was painted a crest of palm leaves and 'Ogondo Construction Ltd'. The man who had taken their baggage tickets got out, dumped their suitcases in the entrance hall, got in again without saying anything and drove off. Three young bellboys came out to pick up the luggage. The senior boy took the keys from Norman and they went off down a corridor with their bags.

'Your heavy loads will be sent by road to Okante,' Peter said. 'They should be on the way tonight, if all goes well. By the way, don't think my driver is rude. He is unable to speak; a problem since birth.'

'By the way,' Norman said, 'I didn't explain that Peter is a director of our company --- and many others,' he added. 'Isn't that right, Peter?'

'Since you mention it, yes. You see, Jane, my father happens to be Premier of the Central Regional Assembly and it also happens that local companies find it convenient to have me on their board. Nepotism is a word we never use in this country, so you will gather that my appointments are entirely due to my business acumen and irresistible charm.'

He gave Jenny a winning smile. She could not imagine why such a person should agree to wait on the dockside and act as their driver.

'We certainly didn't expect this VIP treatment,' she said. 'Now that we know what a busy life you lead we are especially grateful.'

'I will confess why I came. It is because I was told how pretty you are and I just had to come and see for myself. You were quite right, Norman.'

Jenny looked to see how Kenneth had taken this. He seemed pleased.

A Mercedes car drew up and, to her dismay Jenny saw that the passenger was Mr Masters. Peter rushed out to greet him and they stood for a moment, laughing and punching each other on the chest like schoolboys. Then her heart sank as she saw Peter leading Mr Masters by the hand towards their table.

Kenneth went to bring another chair. 'Hi there Nick', he said, 'we had one or two games of bridge together, do you remember? But I don't think you were properly introduced to my wife. This is Jenny.'

'Nico Masoor,' he said, taking her hand.

So she had been deceived, just as she had tried to deceive *him*. His eyes looked deep into hers as she held his hand. The scene came to her as in a flashback; the two of them naked on his bed, she astride him, the undulation of the storm-tossed ship serving to increase the exquisite sensation as her body shuddered with pleasure such as she had never imagined.

She emerged from her reverie to find that someone was speaking and she realised that she had grasped his hand too long.. When she met the discerning brown eyes of Peter Ogondo through his fake spectacles, she guessed he may have discovered her secret.

It was Norman who had spoken. 'Why don't we all meet for dinner tonight? You're staying here are you, Mr Masoor?'

Peter said, 'He had better, since he owns the damn place.'

'I'm not sure what plans have been made for me today,' said Nico. 'Why don't we leave it until we get to Okante. We should be seeing a lot of each other up there.

36

The telephone sounded before Jenny was aware she had gone to sleep. She had lain awake for most of the night tossing and turning, unable to ignore the high-pitched whistle emitting from the trees outside their bedroom, so piercing that it rose above the noise of the air conditioner. She reached out to find the receiver.

A female voice said, 'Good mornin' ma'am, here is your early call.'

She shook Kenneth awake and could tell that he had another hangover. 'Come on sleepyhead, time to get up. You must try and eat some breakfast.'

Peter had not joined them for dinner on the previous evening and, to her relief, Nico did not reappear. So the three of them had dined alone, which enabled Norman to bring them up to date with progress at the factory. It was clear that she was needed urgently to start training spinners and weavers. When the conversation turned to the subject of Nico Masoor she took care to keep quiet.

'I'm amazed how young he is,' Norman said. 'Did you look at the brochure in your room? There are four or five of these *Homesteads* up and down the world and the company's called the Masoor Group, so if this chap Nico owns them . . . '

'He can't actually *own* them,' said Kenneth, 'stands to reason. If he were the boss he wouldn't be comin' to work in a place like Okante, would he?'

Norman persisted. 'Don't forget, Peter's also on the local board of this hotel, so he should know.'

Kenneth was not convinced.

'All right, I grant you he's probably a member of the family, but summat about that chap doesn't ring true. Why did he call himself Masters on't ship if his name's Masoor? A chap I were talking to in the games room said he was knocking off two married women . . . three in a bed sort of caper, they were saying. Looks the type, doesn't he?'

Jenny felt she must intervene, whatever the consequences.

'I can never understand why men want to transfer their fantasies onto some unsuspecting victim --- sorry Norman, I'm not including you --- but what Kenneth says sounds to me like jealousy. Mr Masoor is not only foreign but he's also handsome, therefore he must be a sex maniac? That sort of logic is based purely on jealousy. If I were a million-aire, as he probably is, I would think it a wise precaution to use an assumed name. Now, let's choose a dessert.'

*

Jenny had not realised they were to travel on the same flight as Peter. He was already at the airport when they arrived. Today he was dressed in European clothes, but not anything she would have allowed Kenneth to wear. His lightweight suit was off-white, with thin blue stripes running through it. Jenny considered it made him look rather like an escaped convict, and his shoes were cream and tan; what her father used to call 'co-respondents'. But on Peter the outfit did not look outrageous.

141

Her two companions in the taxi had been quiet, Kenneth almost morose. But Peter was bright and cheerful. She needed cheering, because she was paralysed with fear, at the prospect of going on an aeroplane. Kenneth too was flying for the first time but it seemed that his hangover took priority over any trepidation he may be feeling at the coming ordeal.

'There she is,' said Peter, pointing to the twin-engined aircraft standing near the window of the departure lounge. 'Our carriage awaits. Which, I may say, is a pleasant surprise. In this country one cannot always rely on an aeroplane being there simply because the schedule says it should be. By the way, Jane, may I say what a pleasure it is to see you looking so fresh at this early hour. Would that I could say the same of your companions.'

Jenny refused to believe his flattery. 'Nonsense, I know I must look an absolute fright. I got hardly a wink of sleep for the constant whistle of some creatures in the trees outside.'

'Oh, you mean the cicadas,' Peter said. 'Do not worry, Jane, you will become used to them. In a week or so you will find it impossible to go to sleep without their serenade.' He led the way to a vacant group of chairs. 'So let us make ourselves comfortable. No VIP lounge on domestic flights, I regret to tell you.'

Kenneth's eyes were hardly open. 'Any chance of a drink, Peter? I need a livener.'

'Only minerals,' said Norman. He took their orders and went to the kiosk.

*

As Jenny walked out to the aircraft with Peter, she admitted to being petrified at the coming ordeal.

'Worry not, dear lady,' he consoled, 'this aircraft is a Dakota, the most reliable aircraft in the world. Sit beside me so that you can hold my hand and squeeze it hard whenever you feel a qualm. It will calm you, and it will give me the pleasure of a forbidden liaison with a beautiful married woman.'

Once aboard, her fear immediately increased, for the floor was not flat; they had to walk to their seats up an incline. She asked if she might take the aisle seat. When she sat down she found herself leaning back at an angle and immediately took Peter's advice by gripping his hand, even before the engines had started. He turned to give her a reassuring smile. She noticed a white couple across the aisle look disapprovingly at them. The woman whispered something to the man.

Almost as soon as the last passengers were settled, the engines gave an uneven cough and the plane began to shudder. She squeezed Peter's hand even harder, closed her eyes and silently prayed. It was a few minutes before she heard the noise settle to a drone and realised they must be airborne. She opened her eyes and dared to look at Peter, who was smiling sweetly at her. 'You must think me an awful coward,' she said.

She turned to Kenneth, seated directly behind her, 'All right, love?'

'No problem. Planes rather than ships for me, any day.'

Peter took a small package from his briefcase and handed it to Jenny. It was wrapped in gold and silver paper and had a little red bow on top. She hesitated. 'Go on, open it' he said'.

'I was doing some shopping on the Marina yesterday afternoon and found a little thing which I thought would go well with the costume you were wearing when you disembarked. Take a look. See if you agree.'

She removed the paper to find a padded jewellery box containing a brooch in the form of a silver leaf, set with tiny pink pearls, resembling blossom. In England it would have cost over fifty pounds and she hesitated to guess what he might have paid for it out here in Lagos. She could not possibly accept such a gift from a man she had met only yesterday. She had to risk offending him.

'Peter this is absolutely gorgeous but I couldn't possibly . . . '

'Why not? Did I forget to tell you I am rich --- stinking rich, as a matter of fact. Anyway, I am in love with you, so you must have it.'

'Don't be silly. You have a wife. Norman told me.'

'A tiny problem only. Here in Nigeria we are very good at solving problems.' He changed to a whisper. 'Let us plan how to dispose of Kenneth and then I will marry you.'

'Peter, please stop this nonsense,' she whispered in return.

'No listen, it's easy. What you need to do is bring me a lock of his hair and some clippings from his toenails. I take them to the ju-ju doctor with the appropriate donation and hey presto! Your husband will suddenly disappear.'

'That's not funny. Don't ever again say things like that to me, even as a joke.' She gave the box back to Peter. 'Thank you, but I insist you take it back.'

'All right then. I will give it to my wife instead and tell her that since we parted she has been constantly in my thoughts. And there is one more thing I must tell you.'

'Yes?'

'I am not a very serious person.'

He gave a rich belly-laugh, which made everything all right.

*

The pilot announced that they should fasten their seatbelts for landing. Jenny reached once more for Peter's surprisingly narrow hand and gave it a squeeze to boost her confidence, but found that she did not now have the same feeling of terror as she had experienced on take-off. Indeed she was brave enough to lean across and look out of the window when Peter pointed out the town which was to be her home for the next twenty-one months.

The Dakota made a low pass over Okante then it banked again, giving her a second look. She was agreeably surprised to find much of it quite wooded, though there was a large area of tightly packed streets which Peter said was the 'old town'. He indicated a green-domed building on a high point in the leafy part of town.

'That's the Regional Assembly building. My father works there.'

Terror overwhelmed her again when the engines began a louder roar and the ground grew alarmingly close. She leaned back in her seat, closed her eyes and began another prayer, which was interrupted by a terrifying jolt as the plane hit the runway.

A moment later Peter said, 'You may safely open your eyes, Jane. We're here.'

37

It was reassuring for Kenneth and Jane to be greeted in the arrivals hall by a man with a distinct Lancashire accent. Norman introduced him as Dick Sanderson, the Spinning Manager, who had come in the firm's Zodiac to drive them to their new home. Norman bade them farewell and said he would see them at the mill tomorrow. He was going in the Mercedes which had come to collect Peter. He was to be dropped off at the Government rest house, where he stayed.

From the quite imposing environs of the airport they joined a road of compacted red earth, which Dick said was called laterite. The scattered groups of houses they passed were mostly built with mud blocks and reed roofs. A few were topped with corrugated metal sheets. Between these small settlements there was the occasional neat bungalow, set amid fields of a spindly crop which Jenny did not recognise. Dick told them this was cassava. After another couple of miles, the clay road changed to pot-holed tarmac and they were in the outskirts of the town. Dick slowed down so that he could point out places of interest, but the area they first passed through was not a great improvement on the environs of Apapa docks.

Dick explained that what he called 'the European area' was to the west of the old town. 'That's where the club and the rest house are, and there's a new hotel going up called the *Homestead*. Our firm's building two houses in a new devel-

146

opment behind there for the general manager and his assistant.'

'I didn't know Norman wanted to stay out here', said Kenneth.

'No, I'm not so sure he does. There's a rumour going round that your boss's son is coming to take over. We hoped you might know more than we do.'

Now they had passed the old town and were heading south on a recently constructed bypass, through flat and arid scrubland depressingly similar to what they had seen on the outskirts of Las Palmas. Eventually they joined what Dick said was the main road out of town and Jenny registered with disappointment how far from Okante their home must be.

They came to a wide river, flowing lazily between high banks. The water was dark brown, similar to how the River Coll had looked before the effluent laws caused it to be cleaned up. Dick slowed the car to snail's pace before negotiating the bridge. It was a rusty metal construction, only just wide enough to allow two-way traffic, the carriageway was made narrower by pedestrians on both sides. Half-way across they encountered a mammy-wagon with a load of timber overflowing its sides. The people who were perched on top smiled and waved their thanks as the Zodiac moved over to hug the side of the bridge, but the pedestrians shouted complaints at having their passage restricted. Someone banged the car in protest.

About a hundred yards after they left the bridge, Dick turned onto a laterite road and they entered a forest of bamboo, but soon emerged into a road of bungalows with well-tended gardens, each behind a neatly trimmed hedge.

147

'These are nice houses,' Jenny remarked. 'Is this where we're going to live?

'Further along,' Dick replied. 'Ours is a new estate, not so well established.'

Jenny calculated that they were probably five miles from what Dick had called 'the European quarter'. The road began to deteriorate and the car had to negotiate pools of standing water. After about a quarter of a mile the surface improved again and they were in an area where building plots had been marked out. A pavement had been laid at one side of the road but there were no houses built there yet.

'That's us down there,' said Dick, pointing to their right. Jenny picked out a group of bungalows with green roofs. At the junction to their road was a sign which read:

ANOTHER OGONDO DEVELOPMENT. CLIENT-- OKANTEX LTD.

Jenny was becoming increasingly depressed. They passed more houses still under construction and then turned into a close with a single palm tree in the centre of the turning circle. Dick drew up the Zodiac beside a stand of bamboo.

'This is your bungalow,' he said. 'We live next door but you won't see us --- our garden boy's got a hedge established.'

In front of their house was a patch of ground marked out by a single wire on metal posts. A few weeds had established a foothold in the bare earth. Dick turned the Zodiac into the barren plot and stopped in front of three steps, which led up to a veranda. A Nigerian man ran out of the house to open the car door and a tall young boy appeared from behind the

148

house to carry their cases inside. Jenny smiled at him, hiding the overwhelming sense of disappointment she felt.

Once through the door, however, her spirits rose. The large open-plan room was light and airy and the furniture modern --- a settee and four easy chairs with side tables, a glass-topped coffee table and a bookcase. She was pleased to see that an electric roof fan had been provided. The walls were a neutral off-white but she could change that. At the far end of the room, in an alcove, was the dining area.

There was no carpet, which did not displease Jenny as she would prefer to choose her own. The floor was made from the same multi-coloured material as the front veranda, a type of broken mosaic. She asked Dick what it was and he said it was called terrazzo. A glass sliding door to her left led onto another veranda. The man who had met them at the car slid the door open and walked out. Jenny and Kenneth followed him.

'Here you find the side stoep,' he said. 'It is a most convenient place. This is where you will sit in the evenings to observe the setting of the sun.'

Dick joined them. 'You won't have heard of a 'stoep'. It can mean your veranda or your front porch. By the way, I got Musa for you on approval,. If you don't like him you can get rid of him. That's right, isn't it Musa?'

The man looked offended. 'But madam and master will not wish to sack me away because I am a very good steward and expert cook. I know how to make English chips and fish.'

Kenneth reached out to shake hands with Musa, who wiped his hand on his trousers before doing so, looking slightly embarrassed. Jenny thought that shaking hands was probably not the right thing to do, so she just smiled, and saw relief on Musa's face that she had not followed her husband's example. She led the way back into the living room. The boy who had taken their suitcases now appeared silently through a door which must lead to the bedrooms. He went into what Jenny could see was the kitchen but Musa called him back. He was a lovely looking fellow, about sixteen years old.

'Here is Adebayo, madam --- he is your small boy.'

'Do I need a small boy?' she asked.

'Every European person needs a small boy, madam. He will perform all those tasks which are not convenient for me to do.'

'Such as?' Kenneth asked him. Musa thought for a moment.

'Like chopping wood for fire, sir.'

'Do we need firewood, there's no fireplace?' Jenny asked him.

'I need firewood,' he said, as one would explain to a child.

So that appeared to be settled.

Dick said, 'I'll show you quickly round the house and then we'll go and have a cup of tea. Rosie's looking forward to meeting you. Musa, go to my house and tell George to put the kettle on.'

'Tea is available here, master.'

'My house I said.'

His tone was abrupt. Musa reluctantly went through to the kitchen and Adebayo silently slipped after him. Jenny did not like having her servant spoken to in that manner, but thought it premature to object.

38

Although Ken Thistlethwaite was now in a foreign country, he felt more at home than he had done on the ship, despite the fact that most of the passengers had been British. They had not been 'his sort' but, here in Nigeria, in the confines of his workplace and in the little community housed in the Okantex compound, he was among his own people. Twenty of the expatriate staff had already settled in Okante, most of them from Lancashire.

The spinning and preparation sections were on single-shift production, building up stocks of warp and weft. Fitters from Northrops in Blackburn were setting up and tuning the looms, which could begin production once Jenny had trained enough weavers. None of the bleaching or dyeing equipment was yet on the water, which meant that it would be January before Kenneth could start work on his speciality. In the meantime he became Norman's 'errand boy', as he told Jenny.

Each morning at seven o'clock he and Jenny were picked up by one of the factory mini-buses. She would go straight over to her school and he went to the general manager's office to wait until Norman Haworth emerged from the mill to give him his daily orders. Norman was always on site earlier than anyone else, usually an hour before the rest of the staff arrived. On one occasion Kenneth went into the mill to seek him out, failed to find him, and was given a telling-off for not being there when Norman returned to his office. So now he just sat and waited.

It was made patently clear that he was there simply because they needed his wife. The tasks he was given could easily have been performed by one of the Nigerian staff --- searching the local shops for a particular gauge of nut and bolt, collecting mail from the Post Office, drawing cash from the bank. He got the impression that he was being given things to do simply to fill his day, and Norman never complained if he was late back from his errands in town, so he began calling in at the club around ten o'clock.

This was breakfast time for employees of the Public Works Department, chaps with whom Ken got on very well, though 'breakfast' for many of them was their first beer of the day. He had developed a taste for the local Star beer, so he often joined his PWD friends for what they called their 'eye-opener'. He began to look forward to his morning chats, and he invited some of his new friends round to the house. Jenny agreed it was a good idea to get to know people other than what she called 'inhabitants of the ghetto', which was how she viewed the Okantex housing compound.

With two salaries coming in, they were now well off. Jenny arranged with Barclays Bank DCO to have two-thirds of her salary transferred to the account she had opened for her mother at Martin's Bank in Colesclough, but they were still left them with a healthy surplus at the end of the month.

Although the Sandersons were very good about giving them lifts, they really needed a car of their own. Many expatriates were leaving before Independence, taking their 'lumpers' rather than staying to be 'Ordered around by some

152

Black', as one of Ken's pals put it. This man wanted to sell his Ford Consul, which had done only three-thousand miles. They were able to buy it for two hundred and twenty pounds, for which Kenneth took an advance on his salary. He started to give Jenny driving lessons, but they had a row every time he took her out, so he got one of the firm's drivers to teach her. She was progressing well.

Kenneth grew tired of Jenny nagging him to do something about making a garden, so one day he borrowed a rope, a sledge hammer and a measuring tape from the mechanics' shop at the mill. He always finished work before she was free from her duties in the school, so he drove straight home after work instead of going for drinks at the club, as he usually did. He went round to borrow a spade from the Sandersons' garden boy.

When Jenny arrived home in the company minibus, he had begun to measure out flower beds. She gave him a 'thank you' kiss before going in to ask Musa to make their afternoon tea. Kenneth used the measuring tape to find a spot directly ahead of the front steps, sufficient to allow a turning circle for cars, then he called for Jenny to ask how large she wanted the central bed to be. She paced out what she thought should be the size and he used the sledgehammer to drive in a metal post, which the builders had left in the garage. To this he attached the rope, ready for describing a circle of the right diameter.

A man who was walking past with a cardboard box on his head looked to see what Kenneth was doing, before turning into their plot. The box contained grapefruit, which he offered for sale.

'Can't you see I'm busy, 'said Ken. 'Go round to t' kitchen and see Musa.'

153

'Master does not have a garden boy?'

'What do I need a garden boy for? I haven't got a bloody garden yet.'

'I will be your garden boy,' the man said.

He appeared to be about fifty years old and he was small, with a lined pinched face and puny body. Even lifting the box of grapefruit seemed difficult for him. Nevertheless, Ken was already sweating from the effort of driving in the post, so he asked the man, 'What do you know about gardens?'

'Everything, master.'

'All right, name me three different types of plant.' The man creased his already furrowed brow, before replying, 'lemon, lime and grab fruit.'

Kenneth laughed. 'All right you old bugger, you can have the job. How much do you want?'

'Salary master?'

'Aye, salary, wages, whatever you call it out here.'

'At the present time, master, no salary is required. For one week I will work without recompense. Only when you see that I am a highly capable gardener will we negotiate salary.'

'Done,' said Kenneth, but don't call me 'master'. My name's Ken.'

'Thank you, Kenmaster. I am Emmanuel. Now you will buy some grabfruit?'

Jenny and Musa had been listening to this exchange from the front stoep.

He said, 'That man is not a convenient person to be our garden boy.'

'What is inconvenient about him?'

'You may not know this, madam, but that man is an Igbo.'

'Is that bad?'

'Not bad,' he grudgingly admitted, 'but he is not a convenient person to be our garden boy. Adebayo would not agree for that person.'

'And you? Would you agree?'

'I too would not agree, madam.'

'Then you had better go and tell my husband he has made a mistake.'

Musa looked shocked, 'But I am your servant, madam. It is not convenient that I should tell Mister Ken that he has made an error.'

'But I am his wife, Musa,' she echoed. 'Don't you see that if I go and tell my husband that he has made a mistake he will lose face? Do you allow your wives to tell you that you have made a mistake?'

'No, madam.'

'Then what are we to do?'

'It is a problem, madam.'

So Emmanuel became their garden boy. Eventually Musa and Adebayo accepted him, and she used to hear them laughing and joking together outside the kitchen door. Emmanuel made a garden which was the envy of the other wives on the Okantex compound. She and 'Kenmaster' took pride in the good relations between their household staff and Jenny considered they had a microcosm of how the independent Nigeria would develop, the three main tribes working together in harmony --- Musa the Hausa (in overall control), Emmanuel the Igbo (with his domain in the garden) and the Yoruba Adebayo, (arbitrator, go-between and, when it became necessary, the pourer of oil on troubled waters.)

*

A couple of months later Musa suggested it would be more 'convenient' if the three of them had uniforms. Jenny agreed. A tailor came round on his bicycle the next day with wads of fabric samples attached. Musa chose a uniform of white drill, with a long tunic and narrow trousers. He already owned a green sash and matching cap, which his former employers gave him. Jenny thought this outfit was a bit 'old colonial' but Musa said that was how a senior servant should be dressed and that it was very convenient.

She let him have two sets of the uniform but she allowed Adebayo only one, because his was more expensive than Musa's. He chose a light grey safari suit in the new non-crease material Terylene, which she guessed was intended to impress the girls. Adebayo continued coming to work in

156

singlet and shorts but she made it clear that he must wear the suit if they gave a dinner party. Emmanuel opted for two sets of khaki shirt and shorts, the sort of thing he already wore.

Jenny was so pleased with the tailor's workmanship that she asked him if he could make her a dress, but Musa advised her that it would not be convenient for a man's tailor to undertake such work and that Adebayo had an elder sister who was 'most skilful' at dressmaking.

Although she knew that Musa recommended the sister in order to receive a 'dash', Gladys Adebayo did indeed prove to be a find. From rough sketches and pictures which Jenny cut from magazines, Gladys made her some beautiful dresses for a fraction of the cost she would have paid in the stores. It was grudgingly admitted by most of the female club members that she was the belle of the ball.

*

From the outset, Jenny knew that she was not going to get on with her next-door neighbour. Dick and Rosie Sanderson had been recruited from Southern Rhodesia where they had worked at a spinning mill for several years. Both had been born in Rochdale and he had kept his Lancashire accent. Rosie's vowels, however, had been modified into a passable imitation of educated Afrikaaner-English and she had developed what Jenny's mother would have called 'ideas above her station'.

The Sandersons had brought up quite a lot of furniture with them from their Rhodesian home and had discarded most of the company issue, which gave Rose's house a character distinct from those of the other Okantex staff, most of whom had shipped out few of their own possessions. The newlywed Thistlethwaites, who had very little to send, were at a particular disadvantage in the prestige stakes.

Jenny had got the measure of Rose while she and Kenneth were having tea with the Sandersons on that first day. Rose said, 'I understand Kenneth is related to Norman Haworth. Won't it be nice for them to be working together?'

A little later she commented, 'Of course, I suppose you know that Lafiya Close is meant to be for the management staff, but since you know Norman so well I don't expect he will make you move when the Dyeing Manager arrives. That would be unfair wouldn't it – once you get settled in, I mean?'

It later transpired that Mrs Sanderson had wanted Jenny's job as Training Officer. She was about forty years of age and still good-looking. Her dyed blonde hair set off a deep tan and she was remarkably trim for a woman of her age. Her svelte figure was probably due to her having brought an exercise machine with her from Rhodesia. Rose invited Jenny to use it whenever she wanted. She took satisfaction in saying, 'Thanks, Rosie dear, but I don't have a weight problem.'

Despite their implicit dislike of each other, the two women kept up the pretence of friendship and their husbands believed them to be chums. Only later did Jenny discover another reason why Rosie might be so antipathetic. Dick had warned Jenny that local staff usually invented a nickname for expatriates. Kenneth proudly reported that hers was *Mama Beauty*.

39

Hepzibah was greatly looking forward to seeing Nico, not having met her nephew since they attended his baptism in Golders Green. Jacob met him every time he visited London but Hepzibah always stayed in Kano to look after the business.

Early in the twentieth century Jacob's parents left Lebanon to make a new life for themselves in Nigeria, taking with them their infant twin boys, Jacob and Saul. The Masoors were from the Lebanese Christian minority. Jacob's father chose not to settle in the south of Nigeria, which was mostly Christian, but went to the far North of the colony where Islam predominated. The family were reconciled to being outsiders, so it came as no surprise that when Saul decided to move to Britain he chose to live in Golders Green, the heart of Jewish London. But no matter where a Masoor might settle, however isolated he might appear to be, he remained united to an extended family by unbreakable bonds.

Jacob was waiting for his nephew's arrival outside the large upstairs room which he used as his office, seated in his favourite cane rocker on the veranda. He put down his two-day-old copy of the *Financial Times* and took a silver hunter from the top pocket of his linen jacket. The old watch had been his father's; he kept his Rolex Oyster in the office safe and only used it when he was away from Kano, knowing that customers might regard it as ostentatious of him to be flashing such a symbol of wealth while haggling over ten shillings on the price of a bale of cloth. It was twenty-past four, still more than an hour before the afternoon flight from Okante was due to land at Kano airport.

He and Hepzibah still lived over the store, but all their children had now left home. The eldest boy looked after the
soap factory in another part of Kano, their second son managed the transport and freight businesses in Lagos, the other
was the manager of Nico's hotel in Conakry and his daughters, Ruth and Janna, were in England.   Ruth was studying
economics at Leeds University, a choice favoured by her
parents, because it meant she could lodge with Janna, who
had gone to Leeds to train as a nurse and was now married
to an Englishman.

If you had known the Masoor twins you could be forgiven
for thinking Saul the richer. After all, he was a property ty-
coon with a chain of hotels, a penthouse in Geneva and a
motor yacht on Lake Leman. He drove a Bentley and had all
the other appurtenances of a leading international businessman, while his younger brother (by fifteen minutes) lived
above a shop in a town not far from the edge of the Sahara.
But you would have been wrong.

A passenger flying into Kano airport in the 1950's would not
have been able to identify which of the huge pyramids of
groundnut bags belonged to Masoor and Sons, but each season there were at least six. Expatriates in West Africa would
pass by the display of Roosam toilet soap in the pharmacy to
look for a more famous brand name, but almost five hundred cases of Roosam left the Masoors' factory each week
and millions of Nigerians regularly washed their clothes
with Onak soap.

Had you travelled by road past the small town of Zaria you
might notice that several of the wagons leaving the depot of
the British Cotton Growers Association belonged to Masoor
Transport Ltd. They carried bales of cotton which had been
bought by Masoor Traders (Northern) for export by J. M.
Freight and Forwarding Ltd. Those same lorries would re-

turn from Apapa docks, packed with dried saltfish to be sold in Kano, Kaduna or Sokoto to housewives who would fry it in Jayem cooking oil. The match used to light the stove was likely to be one from a packet of Masoor's 'Gecko' brand.

Nigeria had been kind to the Masoors. Jacob's father was one of the first individuals to set up in competition with the European trading groups in Kano, and Jacob had successfully expanded the business. He could usually undercut 'Gidan Goldie' or the Frenchmen by a penny or two, because he was not paying foreign managers, who closed their canteens at four-thirty and who insisted on having big cars and air-conditioned bedrooms.

Masoor's Store in Liverpool Road was open until seven in the evening and it was either Jacob or Hepzibah who served you. A retailer could always obtain credit at Masoors if he wanted a couple of bales of textiles before the groundnut payment came through, or he could barter if necessary.

Though Kano had been kind to Jacob, the London stock market had been even kinder. He began to accumulate spare capital while the investors of New York and Europe were still cooling their burnt fingers after the great crash of 1929. It occurred to Jacob that this might be a good time to buy a few shares. So, with a letter of recommendation from the Bank of British West Africa, he chose himself a London stockbroker from a list given to him by the bank manager. The firm he selected had offices in Cheapside. 'Cheap' was a word guaranteed to attract a Masoor.

The broker regularly sent him advice, but only in the early days did he follow it. Once Imperial Airways began a daily service to Kano, he was able to receive the *Financial Times* by air, though always a day or two late, which made it frustrating to find that a stock which he would have bought had often 'run away' by the time he could act. The brokers suggested that he give them what they called 'discretion to deal', but to Jacob that meant losing control of his money. So he worked out his 'system'.

On Fridays, the Moslem holy day when the shop was closed, he would take a week's copies of *Financial Times* and laboriously record those shares which had fallen below their annual low point. From among these he would select ten (never more, never less) and would send a telegram to his brokers, which would arrive by the time they opened for business on the following Monday.

He invested the same amount in each chosen share; at first fifty pounds, eventually a thousand. The broker was given a selling price for each. Jacob invested in several companies which rapidly plunged into bankruptcy, others reached heights far above the price at which he sold, but at the end of each year a healthy surplus had accumulated in his bank account in Jersey.

Over a period of time the brokers so valued his business that, in 1952, they sent out a senior manager to try to persuade Jacob to abandon his system and build up what they called a 'steady portfolio'. But that was not his way. He was a trader, brought up to believe that it was turnover that produced profits. Shares were there to be traded, not held in stock. After all, he was Lebanese and the Lebanese love a gamble.

But now Nigeria was about to change. There was already regional self-government and in October 1960 there was to be full Independence. Jacob admired the Premier of the Northern Region, the Sardauna of Sokoto, a scion of the Emirate, and Central Region was in the safe hands of Reuben Ogondo. Though undoubtedly a populist, Reuben was also a practical businessman, schooled in one of the great British trading companies. Further south, however, were Chief Owolowo and Dr Azikwe, whom Jacob regarded as firebrands. How a unified nation would accommodate such disparate characters troubled him.

He and Hepzibah had spent all their adult lives in West Africa and they still hoped to end their days in Kano, but if things went really wrong he needed a bolthole. Most of all he wanted to see his children and his seven grandchildren safely away from what, in his darker moods, he considered could become a blood bath. Today, though, his thoughts were on an altogether more cheerful subject, a family dinner with his nephew.

*

The house had been built by his father in 1913. It was then the finest private dwelling in Kano and was still a credit to Abraham Masoor, who designed it himself.   In the yard were godowns sufficient to hold a season's supply of goods, ensuring that Masoor & Sons did not need to trade with any of its European competitors. The whole of the spacious ground floor comprised the shop. Now that his son had his own branch close to the soap factory there were not the same demands on the ground floor space, so Hepzibah was able to have one of the stockrooms converted into a laundry and larder. In the larder were three large freezers full of meat and vegetables, which meant that she could defy the seasons and be independent of the big stores, such as Kingsway and Leventis. Despite their great wealth she and Jacob resented what they considered to be excessive mark-ups.

The veranda, on which Jacob now sat, ran round all four sides of the house, so that the living quarters were an island surrounded by a walkway, shaded by jalousies and open to whatever air might be available in the heat of Kano, for the outer windows were covered with mosquito wire instead of glass. Even in the hot season, when strong men wilted, Gidan Masoor was an oasis cooled by even the slightest breeze.

He got up and went back inside to use the telephone. His son Saul answered straight away and agreed to go to the airport to pick up Nico. From the second drawer of his filing cabinet Jacob took out a folder which he placed on the large oak table behind his desk. Then he went downstairs to tell his wife that they would close the shop as a mark of respect to their nephew.

40

Nico put a hand over his dessert dish. 'I'm sorry. I couldn't eat another morsel, Auntie. This mango tart was delicious, but don't forget you gave me two helpings of guinea fowl.'

There were eight round the table... Nico, Hepzibah, Jacob and Nico's Cousin Saul, with his wife Tania and their three children. There was little resemblance between Nico and any of the others: his English mother had bequeathed him her fair skin and he was a good deal taller than the rest.

His cousin's ten-year old daughter had done nothing but stare at him since he arrived. She spoke to him for the first time. 'How many brothers and sisters do you have Uncle Nico?'

'I'm sorry, Hannah, I don't have any.'

'Why not?' This was a perfectly reasonable question for a little Maronite girl to ask; a family of less than three children would seem to her unusual. Nico wondered how much she had been taught about the birds and the bees.

He was relieved to hear Tania say, 'You see, darling, after Nico's mummy gave him birth she became ill, so she could not make any more babies.'

Hannah looked at her uncle with the most piteous expression. 'Oh dear, I am very sorry for you. When I grow up I will have a baby and I will give it to you.'

'That's very kind of you, Hannah,' he replied, 'but when you do have one I think you will probably want to keep it.'

'No,' she insisted. 'I will give it to you, because I like you very much and you speak a very nice sort of English. My other English uncle does not speak like you do.'

'Which uncle is that?'

'I can't remember. He has a funny name.'

Her mother explained. 'She means Janna's husband, Plantagenet. He speaks like they do in the North of England. Hannah liked him too though, didn't you dear?'

'Yes,' she said, 'but this one is more pretty.'

Saul, Tania and the children went home soon after eight.

*

When there was a family party, Jacob and Hepzibah dispensed with their servants, so that private conversations

165

would not be overheard. Jacob always helped his wife with the washing-up, but before he did so tonight he led Nico to his study. From the file on his desk he took copies of the last four annual reports of Isaac Harrison Limited and left his nephew to study them. He was confident that the young man would notice what had been obvious to him as soon as he glanced at the Harrison accounts. When he returned from his washing-up duties he was not disappointed.

'Yes Uncle, I think I have found what you may be interested in. The land they own is shown as an asset but can't have been re-valued for years. But if you are then going on to say that it will have appreciated in value I must point out that the site has no development potential without planning permission. Part of it is commercial land, the rest open country. You would have to establish a precedent for residential use.'

Jacob smiled. He took a magnifying glass from a desk drawer, gave it to his nephew and led him to the table. He opened the folder he had brought out earlier, removed several aerial photographs and arranged them carefully into a rectangle.

'Residential use did you say? Take a look. The third photograph from the left, bottom row. See? Four streets already are there.'

Nico picked up the glass for a closer inspection. 'That's interesting, but would they fit in with a modern housing development?'

'Not ideally, I agree. Sykes thinks we may be able to have them condemned. If not, I would put some terraced blocks at the lower end of the development, so they would not be totally out of place. And look there,' Jacob used a pencil as a pointer, 'that is a fine Victorian mansion, with two servants'

166

cottages behind.   Also Plantagenet tells me there are water mains leading from the mills to the four streets, street lighting along each boundary, a feeder road to the main thoroughfare. It appears that the founder of the business intended to build houses right across the hillside. So, young man, any chance of getting planning permission, do you think?'

'Quite a good chance, I'd say. The British government is desperate to build more houses. But you still have the mills on – what is it called?'

'Daisy Hill,' his uncle prompted, 'a pretty name isn't it.'

'Indeed, but not many people want to live next door to a factory. According to the accounts the business isn't very profitable, but the mills are still viable. Then this new venture in Okante should be a money spinner for them. How much did Mr Sykes offer them for the business?'

'One and a quarter million pounds, but I expect to have to go to nearer three.'

'That's a lot of money to pay for a declining business. Rather than make a full takeover bid why don't we get our foot in the door with an offer for around half the share capital? After all, the Harrisons ought to see the value of developing the hillside, just as we do. I take it that developing the site is your main interest. And if we can get half the profit it's better than an outright refusal.'

Jacob was pleased to hear his nephew already saying 'we'. He hesitated, thinking over Nico's suggestion.

'Maybe you're right. They turned down Plantagenet's offer out of hand. Do you smoke cigars?' He took a drum of Havanas from the bottom drawer of his desk. They each lit one. Then he went once more to the filing cabinet and withdrew from the bottom drawer a cardboard box marked,

Private and Confidential. Higher Colesclough Village Development.

41

Jacob Masoor had strong reservations when Janna told them she was going to marry a Yorkshireman. Had you called him bigoted he would have been indignant, but his English business acquaintances were mostly from Lancashire and he had unwittingly absorbed some of the prejudice that runs deep within many inhabitants of the two counties. Although he understood little about the game of cricket he always paid attention to the BBC World Service sports bulletins when the 'Roses' match was being played and was pleased if Lancashire won.

His daughter brought her fiance to Kano for approval. Neither Jacob nor Hepzibah had been impressed, but they accepted that the couple were genuinely in love and Jacob was pleased to find that Mr Sykes had proposed to the young nurse before he knew of her family's wealth; in fact, Janna herself was not fully aware of how rich she would be one day.

Jacob did recognise in the oddly-named accountant something of his own qualities, an assiduity and aptitude for business, which had led the young man to search out undervalued companies and appreciate the worth of their hidden assets. What swayed him in favour of Plantagenet Sykes was that his elder daughter would be independent of the family's support.

Plantagenet had identified Isaac Harrison Limited as being what he described to his father-in-law as 'a potential break-up situation', though the prize proved beyond the reach of his fledgling business. But, after the Okante project had been announced, it was obvious to both Jacob and his son-in-law that there would be a temporary period when their target would be vulnerable. What particularly appealed to Jacob was not only the possibility of controlling the company's Nigerian mill, indeed expanding it, but of developing the Lancashire site.

By early 1959 the concept had become even more appealing. Jacob read his *Financial Times* carefully. Britain was embarking on a major road building programme. At the opening ceremony for a new bypass around Preston in December 1958 the Prime Minister announced 'the opening of a new era in motor travel'. In March the following year the government declared that it would spend £140 million per annum to build up a modern road network to transform communications throughout the kingdom. The new roads were to be called 'motorways'.

*

The ceiling fan rotated slowly, riffling the papers laid out on Jacob's old desk. As he outlined his proposal he could see a gleam of interest in his nephew's eye.

Colesclough was just over twenty miles from Manchester, handy commuting distance once the feeder roads to the motorway were established. Jacob had visited the town many years ago and remembered it as quite a pleasant place, at the western end of what was then a prosperous valley. The hillside which the company owned would accommodate six

169

hundred houses, possibly more. Jacob would provide a cinema and one of those general stores they were calling supermarkets. His son Paul could run that. This would be a new village, of which Jacob Masoor, the twin born of poor Maronite parents in a small apartment in the heart of Beirut, would be the Squire.

'So you see, Nico, that's why I wanted your opinion. I want your property company to undertake the development.'

'We would have to consult Pappa.'

'I rang Saul in Switzerland before you came up to Kano. My dear brother says he has no objection provided you approve.' He laughed. 'You know why, boy? Because it is *my* money we are using. But to you I would give a share.'

'Fine, thanks --- but what about the mills? They don't just disappear, do they?'

'Well, yes, as a matter of fact they do --- eventually. The boom in Lancashire textiles is already ending. Let me explain. We start building on that part of Daisy Hill looking out over the Rossendale valley.' He used a pencil to indicate. 'Here, beyond the four streets. That's well away from the mills, so there should be no problem selling the first batch of properties. By the time that phase is completed I am sure even firms like Harrisons will be struggling to find orders, and I am convinced that the family would be more than grateful to accept the second stage.

'Which is?'

'Pull down the factories. That gives us the land for around another three hundred and fifty houses. I remember visiting Colesclough many years ago when I used to do business

with Harrisons. The mills were built with fine stone blocks.
No longer is such excellent stone quarried, and it would be
ideal for building some more expensive properties at the top
end of the village . . . see, there. That slope of the hill looks
out over the valley of the River Ribble.'

Nico's enthusiasm was growing. 'And what's this complex
down by the river?'

'That's their dyeing and finishing works. It would make an
excellent soap factory. I have plans for an international
brand.'

'And the machinery? When we empty the mills what do we
do with the machinery? Who wants second-hand textile machines these days?'

'Who wants it? We do. Don't forget that by then we would
also own a share of the Okante business. The machinery in
the mill they call Buttercup is out of date and will only bring
its value as scrap, but Daisy Mill could provide the machinery for a second mill in Okante. Money for --- what is
that English phrase?'

'Old rope, I think you mean,' said Nico.   He picked up the
glass again for a more detailed inspection of the photographs. 'What about the big house? Surely you wouldn't
pull that down.'

Uncle Jack drew deeply on his cigar. 'No, of course not, that
is where your auntie and I will live.'

42

Adebayo had borrowed two pounds from his sister, which he paid to Musa so that he could be there when the new people came. He had expected to be turned away, as he had been on previous occasions by couples who decided that they did not need a small boy, but the beautiful lady had smiled at him and taken him on.

There were two rooms in the servants' quarters behind each house of the Lafiya Close compound, but Musa kept his wives in the village. He let Adebayo have the other room, which was next to the washing place. Every morning he washed himself all over with Roosam soap so that he would smell nice. His sister said that Mama Beauty told her she thought he was a good-looking boy. When she bought him that safari suit he was convinced that she liked him.

Adebayo grew to hate his master. Musa and he used to discuss how often Mama Beauty and Kenmaster quarrelled, and they were listening in the kitchen that time when he hit her. They even considered what to do if he sacked her away and agreed that, if that should happen, they would not stay on to serve Kenmaster.

Adebayo's room was at the end of the block, so no one could see him when he crept out during the night to listen outside the bedroom when Kenmaster and Mama Beauty came home from the club. The watchnight was always fast asleep as soon as they had locked their front door. Sometimes there was no noise after they went to bed and Musa would go back to his room and not worry, but two or three times each week, and especially on Saturday, he would hear her moaning as if Kenmaster was hurting her and then sometimes she would give a scream. It made him very angry that Kenmaster should hurt Mama Beauty. If he had a woman like her he would give everything he had to make her happy, not hurt her.

When he found a whip in their wardrobe he decided to pay a visit to the ju-ju man.

*

It was particularly hot during that harmattan season and everyone was praying the rains would soon come. A barely perceptible breeze did nothing to cool an atmosphere bereft of any hint of moisture. This Saturday afternoon Jenny was cutting flowers in the garden, wearing a large straw hat to protect her from the sun. Her husband had found a shady spot on the garage runway and was polishing the Consul.

'Can you hear me, Kenneth?'

'Yeah, what do you want?'

'Do you realise you haven't had a haircut since we were on the ship?'

He did not reply.

It was becoming fashionable for men to wear their hair long and his was not untidy. The crew cut hair had regained its usual wave. However, it was nearing shoulder length. She persevered. 'I can trim it for you if you'd like, but why don't you let that man who comes round on the bicycle do it? You sent him away last time but he cuts Richard's next door and his looks very smart. I can get one of the servants to send for him.'

173

'All right,' Ken muttered, 'get him to come on Monday afternoon.'

When Jenny was dropped off by the minibus the barber was waiting, sitting patiently on the wall of the stoep. He declined the offer of a cup of tea and asked would she please let him have the use of a chair. Adebayo brought one of the dining chairs out. The barber was setting up the tools of his trade on the wall of the stoep when Kenneth arrived in the Consul. It was going to cost three shillings.

Jenny had never had the opportunity to watch a man having his hair cut. The barber seemed to take an unconscionable length of time, and the process was carried out in silence, Kenneth sitting rigid, staring straight ahead. When she had hers trimmed there was always a conversation and the hair was cut off in reasonable amounts but this man snipped away at Kenneth almost hair by hair, as though afraid to commit himself, continually stepping back to admire his work. Kenneth did not appear to object, so she assumed that this was the way it was always done.

After about twenty minutes she asked if Kenneth would like his cup of tea brought out but he explained that the procedure would soon be finished. She continued to watch through the front window. When at last it was all over the barber held an ancient mirror up to the back of Kenneth's head and he spoke for the first time.

'OK, thanks', Kenneth said. He got up and gave the man his money. As the barber pedalled away, Jenny felt privileged to have witnessed this male ritual.

Adebayo too had been watching. He came out the back way from the kitchen with a dust pan and brush and carefully gathered up every hair from the veranda. He already had the toe clippings. Now he must start to save the money that the ju-ju man required. It might mean having to sell his radio.

43

The *Okante Homestead* was to be opened in time for Independence Day. By then only the bars and restaurants would be open, residential rooms were not yet ready. Kenneth and Jane found that they and Norman Haworth were the only members of the Okantex staff to be invited to the opening party, a fact which did not go down well with Rose Sanderson. Jenny attempted to mollify her neighbour by stressing that their inclusion stemmed solely from having travelled out by sea with Mr Masoor.

She had not caught sight of him since he arrived in Okante and she spent a long time rehearsing how she would greet him when they did meet again. Some of her friends had seen him out riding and he sometimes played tennis, but he never came into the club afterwards. Despite the low profile he kept, he was much talked about and women envied her when she said she had met him.

Gladys Adebayo made her a rather daring dress to wear to the hotel party, which was to be held in the afternoon. The design was copied from *Vogue.* It had a low neckline and the back plunged half-way to the waist. She discovered there was no way she could wear a bra with it. Several fittings were required and she would need a good deal of nerve on the day.   The material was some mauve chiffon which she found in one of the Indian shops and was the last piece in the bolt, so she was confident that no one else would have a similar outfit.

She persuaded Kenneth to let the tailor who made the servants' uniforms have a go at making him a new suit. Kingsway Stores had some new material called Trevira and she chose a length of light cream fabric. When they tried on their new clothes they looked the smartest couple she could imagine.

They had arranged to pick up Norman and go together to the hotel party but, when Ken drove into Club Road, the traffic policemen would not let him turn into the rest house. The hotel car park was already full, so they were ushered into a parking space at the far end of the racecourse. Jenny waited outside the front gate of the hotel, under a flamboyant tree, while Kenneth walked quickly back to the rest house to bring Norman.

By the time she saw the two men rushing to join her, she could hear that the speeches had already begun and the three of them hurried down the hotel drive. Waiters were still lining the route, holding trays of drinks. Kenneth grabbed a glass of whisky and Jenny and Norman took lemonade. All the shaded areas were occupied, so they sat in hot sunshine.

A raised platform had been set up near the hotel entrance, across which a wide red ribbon had been stretched. The Regional Governor, Sir Fergus Abercrombie, was coming to the end of his speech. Chief Ogondo was seated next to the Governor's empty chair and beside him was a lady who must be Peter's mother. Both the Chief and his wife were quite plump. Jenny wondered if Peter would end up fat, though she thought probably not, because he was a good deal taller than his father.

176

Nico was seated beside Lady Abercrombie, whom Jenny recognised from the photograph displayed in the club. The rest of the dignitaries she did not know. There was only one other white person, a small man of middle-Eastern appearance sitting at the end of the second row.

There was applause as the Governor sat down after a short speech, but then he got up again and began the same thing in Yoruba and when that was finished he repeated it in Hausa. When he finally ended, the clapping was a gesture of relief. Nico stood up and introduced the Premier. For him there was a genuine ovation.

The Chief spoke in English, a very amusing speech. Then, instead of the translated repeats that everyone feared, he said, 'If anyone here did not understand that, let me say to them, go back to school and pay more attention this time. It is too damn hot for you people to be sitting in the sun, so I now invite Lady Abercrombie and my dear wife to cut that ribbon over there.'

Nico got up and held open a red box, from which each lady took out a pair of golden scissors. They walked together to the hotel entrance and each cut one end of the tape. As it fell to the ground a band struck up from somewhere in the garden, playing the British national anthem rather badly. Some of the Europeans started to sing the words but soon gave up in embarrassment.

When the band stopped, the Chief stood up and held his arms aloft to call for silence. 'Right everybody,' he said. 'Now it's time to dance. If you want to see the hotel right now you can go in, but I suggest you look at it in little groups. Me, I'm going to dance first.' The band struck up again, this time more tunefully, with a 'High Life' number.

177

The Premier took the hand of the Governor's wife and, already dancing to the rhythm, he led her off into the garden.

Ken said, 'Thank God that's over. I thought we'd be sitting in this bloody sun all afternoon. He's a great chap is that Chief Ogondo, don't you think? Come on, I could do with another drink.'

They followed the crowd through to the garden. The Nigeria Police band was seated beneath an awning, in front of two open marquees set side-by-side on the lawn. Wooden floors had been laid in each marquee and the central area was kept clear for dancing.

One of the marquees was already full, but they found three chairs in the other one and sat down to watch. Jenny and Norman took another glass of lemonade from one of the waiters but Kenneth had to go to the bar for his whisky. Jenny sat down with care, to ensure that she did not disturb her décolletage. She noticed a constantly changing line of partners dancing with a beautiful Yoruba girl, whom she recognised from advertisements in the newspapers. She asked Norman if he knew who she was.

'That's Peter's sister,' he replied, 'isn't she lovely?'

'Bloody cracker', said Kenneth, who had returned with his drink.

Norman said he would take a quick look round the hotel and then he had to get back to the mill, but he told them they should take the rest of the day off. They saw Peter go to speak to his sister, who then left her partner and walked towards the hotel. Peter looked round the crowd, waved to them and came over to where they were sitting.

'Hello you two, nice to see you again', he said. 'Jane, would you grant me the favour of a dance? You don't mind do you Kenneth, if I borrow your lovely wife for a moment or two?'

'That's OK with me Peter,' she heard her husband reply, 'but she doesn't come cheap'. He held out his open palm. She would have slapped him had there not been so many people around. Fortunately Peter pretended to find the remark amusing.

Jenny had become quite a proficient dancer of High Life and Peter was a natural, as she had expected, but after a few minutes he suggested that they go into the hotel. She said they ought to pick up Kenneth.

'He looks happy where he is,' Peter replied, indicating the bar, where Kenneth was in conversation with a lady member of the club committee. 'I want you to meet my sister, Jumoke. She's in Nico's office with his uncle.'

As Jenny entered the room she was disappointed to find that Nico was not there. Peter's sister looked her up and down, before exchanging a glance with the small man, whom she assumed to be Nico's uncle. The man nodded to Peter. She felt like a prize cow in a show ring. Miss Ogondo wore a plain white sheath dress and no jewellery, except a gold wristwatch and two dress rings; with a figure like hers there was no need for adornment.

Jenny decided that her own outfit was a mistake for such an occasion. 'How do you do, Miss Ogondo?' she said.

It was the last time Jenny used her surname.

The Yoruba girl stepped forward and hugged her. 'Call me Jumy, please,' she said. 'From now on it will be Jenny and Jumy, if that is all right with you,' and she giggled, in a softer-pitched version of her brother's belly laugh. Jenny was cross with Peter for hijacking her without warning, but she felt an immediate rapport with Jumy.

Nico's uncle came to shake her hand. His eyes were like Nico's; there was no other similarity.

'Hello, I am Jacob Masoor. My nephew has told me a lot about you and I can only agree with what he has said. Please don't think me rude but I must be on my way back to Kano. We shall be meeting again.' As he left, he nodded again in Peter's direction, making Jenny feel that she was the only one in the room who was not privy to some secret.

Peter took her by the hand. 'Come on, let's pick up Kenneth and have a look around the hotel.' Jumy came part of the way with them but diverted to the dance floor, saying, 'Bye-bye, Jenny, see you soon.'

Before they reached the bar they encountered a group of dignitaries from the Northern Region who wanted to speak to Peter, so she excused herself. Kenneth was sitting by himself at the bar. He had another glass of whisky and soda but was not yet drunk.

'Have you had a look round?' she asked.

'No, I got talking. Have you?'

'I got talking, too. Come on, let's go and have a look.'

They saw Nico outside the front entrance, saying farewell to Chief and Mrs Ogondo and other members of the official party. They stood aside and smiled, in response to the Premier's friendly wave, as he and his wife walked towards the Government cars lined up along the drive. She wanted to slip through another door but Kenneth said he would like to speak to Nico.

'Thank God that's over,' he said. 'How do you think it went?'

'I could have done with a bit less from the Governor,' said Kenneth.

'Me too,' Nico agreed.

'Come along in for a drink and tell me how you've both been getting on.'

When they reached his office she was pleased to find it was now empty. She declined another drink but Nico poured two neat whiskies for himself and Kenneth. She would have to drive home, even though she hadn't yet passed her test. Having her husband there relieved her of the problem of what to say to Nico, but she could not suppress a feeling of disappointment that she was unable to deliver the speech she had been rehearsing.

'I do apologise for not having been in touch,' Nico said. 'Life is still pretty hectic, as you can imagine, but we must meet up when things quieten down. Why don't you join me for Christmas lunch here, so we can catch up?'

She was preparing to make their excuses, but Kenneth immediately responded, 'No, sorry, we're having a do at our place. Why not join us?'

Oh no, she thought, Nico would be totally out of his element. With immense relief she heard Nico say, 'I can't I'm afraid.

I've invited Chief and Mrs Ogondo and quite a big party. How about Boxing Day? Are you free?'

'That will be lovely, said Jenny with genuine enthusiasm. 'Now, may we see the hotel.'

Kenneth gulped his whisky down as Nico led them to the door. Kenneth went out first. Nico held her back and whispered in her ear, 'Phone me.'

44

It was a Sunday afternoon ten days after the hotel party, and there had been another argument. As usual it started with a small disagreement and ended with them shouting abuse at each other. Kenneth had been to the club before lunch and had heard that one of the Italians who worked for Ogondo Construction wanted to sell his motor bike.

'At least come with me and have a look,' he said.

'There's no point in me looking. We can't afford it.'

'It's a bargain. He only wants two hundred and...'

'I don't care how much of a bargain it is, we still have the car loan to pay off.'

'It'll be less than what I got for me Norton.'

'I thought we were supposed to be out here to save money.'

'You'd have nowt in t' bank if it weren't for my family,' he yelled.

'That's not fair. It's *our* money not just yours. That was our wedding present.'

'Right then I'll go on me own,' He went to the sideboard and grabbed the car keys, 'and I'll send home for the bloody money if I want.'

She stood in front of the door to block his way.

'No, Kenneth, you mustn't drive. You've had too much to drink.' He pushed her aside. The Consul threw up a cloud of dust as it sped out of the Close.

To take her mind off this latest quarrel she picked up one of her old French books and sat on the sofa with her legs tucked under her. Proust usually took her mind off her troubles --- but not today. She stared at the book, unable to concentrate, depressed by this latest example of their grow-ing estrangement.

There were so many quarrels these days. His drinking was the problem, that was clear, but she knew that it stemmed from his not having enough work to do and she accepted her share of the blame. She found her job fulfilling and spent time most evenings working on lessons for the training school, which only exacerbated his lack of motivation. Ken-neth resented Norman Haworth's praise for what she was doing and was hurt by criticism of his own efforts.

The marriage was fast becoming a purely physical arrange-ment. Sex still drew them together but even that had be-come a routine. At first it had been fine, often exciting. Soon after they arrived, Kenneth had found a book called *Secrets of the Kama Sutra* in one of the less salubrious shops in the old town. They experimented with new positions, some of which were downright impossible, others so comic that they found themselves collapsing with laughter, before they had even begun the attempt. Yet, despite these experiments, she suspected that for him there remained something lacking in their lovemaking.

One night she asked outright if there was anything else that he wanted, but all he would say was, 'I'll let you know.'

Saturday evening at the club was the highlight of her week. Kenneth was happy at the bar with his cronies but she always had plenty of dancing partners. The most attractive bachelors were to be found among the British army officers. They used to monopolise her and the evening would be a crescendo of arousal, heightened by knowing what was to come, for it was understood that when they returned from the club on Saturday nights she and Kenneth would make love 'her way'.

It was not that she wanted to dominate him, more that she needed to have one occasion during the week when she could ensure herself the maximum pleasure. By the time they were home and in bed she had no need of foreplay, though she would deliberately control and prolong the lovemaking, closing her eyes to relish the sensation, stretching out the point at which she would achieve her climax.

Gradually she would enter her fantasy. Back on the ship, bringing herself and the man she loved to the pinnacle of excitement, delaying his response and choosing the moment when their pent-up tension was ready for release --- the moment when she could surrender herself totally to Nico.

When the excitement of the act was over she invariably experienced a profound sense of shame. Shame that the demands of her body had caused her to compromise her true feelings, overriding her increasing estrangement from Kenneth, whom she no longer loved and doubted if she had ever truly loved.

Their differences were heightened now they were removed from their native surroundings, for he seemed to draw nothing from this new environment. He was happy to be set apart from the 'real' Africa, whereas she felt it a constraint to be segregated on this estate of houses, which closely resembled an English suburb.

He chose his friends from among those who, like him, wanted to create a cocoon against contact with this foreign place. Okante Club was a substitute for their pub, their conversation related to what was happening in Britain, they exchanged English newspapers sent out by airmail and kept up to date with the progress of their home football teams. Kenneth hardly ever glanced at the Nigerian paper, which was delivered every day. But at the root of it all was his drinking. Having seen her father on the same slippery slope, she was sure that this was at the heart of their problems.

He had boarded the ship at Liverpool a virtual abstainer but within six months he was well on the way to being an alcoholic. What more could she do to help Kenneth? Norman must have noticed the change in him. Jenny decided that in the morning she would seek the help of Norman Haworth.

A car turned into the drive. She recognised Peter Ogondo's white Mercedes and fled to the bedroom, because she wore only a tee shirt and shorts and had no shoes on. She hoped that when he saw the garage empty he would think they

185

were both out. Then she heard two male voices, and re-membered she had left the front door ajar.

Peter called from the sitting room. 'Hello! Ken?... Jane? Are you there? She could hear him talking to the other man, then ... 'Sorry to disturb you,' he persisted. 'It's me, Peter

She decided she must answer. She opened the bedroom door and shouted, 'Hold on, I'll be out in a minute.' She took off her shorts, changed into a white skirt, slipped on a pair of flip-flops and was already in the sitting room before she realised she was not wearing a bra. She managed a smile, but it quickly faded when she saw that the other man was Nico.

Peter kissed her on the cheek but Nico stayed beside the door. He smiled but did not speak. Both men wore tennis clothes.

'I hope you weren't sleeping,' said Peter. 'Send us away if it's not convenient, but we saw the front door was open so we ...'

'I'm here alone, Kenneth is out,' she interrupted, and real-ised this sounded rude. 'I mean, I can't say exactly when he will be back.'

'It's really you we hoped to see. Would you like to have a look at the new television studios? We decided it was too hot for tennis so I'm showing Nico round and you were more-or-less on our way.'

'I'm not properly dressed.'

'Course you are, look at us. To be honest Jane, we have a suggestion to put to you and it would be better to do it down there.'

Intrigued to hear what they had to say, and faced with the alternative of an afternoon of depressing introspection, she said, 'OK. I'll leave a note for Kenneth.'

*

It had not been officially announced that television was coming to Central Region. Peter's father's last election campaign had made much of the dangers of exposing young people to the malign influence of European and American popular entertainment. The TV station, which had just been completed half a mile beyond the Okantex factory, was still anonymous. It would eventually be justified by it's news service and broadcasts to schools, subsidised by a grant from USAID. Of course, once enough sets were purchased by the bourgeoisie of Okante and the other towns within radius of the transmitter, programmes such as *I Love Lucy* and *The Flintstones* would quickly follow. For the moment, however, the sign outside the studios read simply:-

ANOTHER OGONDO DEVELOPMENT   Client: Ministry of Communications.

Local gossip had it down as a secret service headquarters.

This being Sunday, the place was deserted. Peter had a key to the main gate and they parked in a bay marked *M.D.*

A watchman opened the glass front door and bowed them through. Jenny was impressed by the opulence of the entrance hall. There was a glass dome over the spacious foyer, the floor had large blue and white rubber tiles, there was a

187

long reception desk with blue Formica top and buttoned moquette base. Matching bench seats lined two walls and light oak tables and chairs were set out in the centre of the foyer.

Peter preceded them to unlock another glass door, which led into a passage with nameplates on the office doors. The first read,

> *J. K. BARAU   Managing Directo*r

'Don't tell me you are not the man in charge here, Peter?' Jenny asked with a hint of irony.

'Not of the TV station. That might seem like nepotism might it not?' He gave one of his chuckles.

> On a panel above the double doors at the end of the corridor, was inscribed,

> CREATIVITY (NIGERIA) LTD.

Nico pulled his friend aside for a brief whispered conversation before Peter opened the doors and called Jenny forward. He smiled and said, 'Come into my parlour, little fly.'

This reception area was small and totally empty. They went through yet another glass door. Peter's office was the third along the final corridor. It was not yet fully furnished, there was just a desk, a refrigerator, empty bookcases and four cheap cane chairs, such as were for sale in Okante market. On the wall were several mounted coloured photographs and a gilt-framed mirror.

'This is my little empire, Jane. At least it will be when I have moved my company up from Lagos. Now, I hope you don't mind if I leave you two alone for a while. Nico will explain.'

Peter was on the point of leaving when Jenny started to panic. 'You said I could see the studios. May I have a look round now? I can't stay long because Kenneth will be . . . '

'Soon,' said Peter in a tone designed to calm her. 'Listen to what Nico has to say. I'll be back.'

The door closed, leaving her alone with the man who monopolised her fantasies. They stood at opposite ends of the room, he behind the desk, she beside the door considering whether to open it again and follow Peter, but rooted to the spot. She could not help gazing into his eyes. Unwittingly she moved towards him.

'I asked you to get in touch', he said.

'We're not on the phone.' She realised how feeble this sounded.

He appeared lost for words.

'You have something to say to me?' she prompted.

'Yes, that's why I asked Peter to let me have a few moments alone with you.'

But he could say no more, because she was already in his arms. Their lips closed hungrily together, her need for him as obvious as his for her. Her unprotected breasts pressed against him, giving her eager body the same message she received during those precious moments on the ship. Then he abruptly pulled away.

'I'm sorry', he said. 'That shouldn't have happened, I apologise.'

He hesitated, as though calling to mind a prepared speech. 'I want you to understand that . . . I mean . . . Oh God, I've practised it so often and now it won't come.'

She tried to help him. 'I think I know what you're going to say. I do understand, believe me.'

'No, let me say it.' At that moment he seemed like a callow schoolboy. Her heart, which was already won, warmed to his vulnerability. He cleared his throat.

'Since we . . . um . . . since the ship, and . . . Oh God, Jane, I've not been able to get you out of my mind. You see, I think I love you. I've never been in love before so I've no way of telling. No, that's wrong again. I really do love you, I'm sure of it, but it's hopeless isn't it? Just let me say that if ever you are free, that I shall be . . . but that I'd never . . .'

'Stop Nico. No more.'

'Hear me out, please. The reason I asked Peter to go is that I want to explain something. You see, I shall be having a friend to stay --- well, not exactly a friend, just someone I met in London.'

'Look Nico,' she began, 'it really is no concern of mine who comes to stay with you.' But she wanted to know more. 'I suppose the reason you are telling me is because this friend is a woman. Am I right? If so, I'm pleased for you.'

'Yes. She's a journalist doing a feature on Nigerian independence and she wrote to ask where there was to stay in

Okante --- it will be a good base for her, being so central, and she can get around . . . '

'OK. Thanks for telling me but please go now and find Peter. There must be a reason why he asked me here and I'm sure this is not it.'

After he left the room she felt weak. His kiss seemed to have drained all the strength from her body, so that her legs would no longer support her. She sat on one of the cane chairs to wait for them, still aglow with the thrill of his arms around her. Several minutes passed and they did not return. She got up to look into a mirror above the bookcase and saw flushed cheeks, her hair awry. She ran her fingers through it, wishing she had a comb, wishing she had taken more time to prepare herself.

The coloured photographs on the wall looked like stills from movies; an attractive young black woman walking along a beach with the sea spray splashing her legs, holding a bottle of soft drink close to her lips. There was another with the same woman holding hands with a good-looking Yoruba man in front of the counter of a bank. Then she realised the woman was Jumy.

Then the men were back. Peter gestured towards the fridge. 'Jane my dear, would you see if there are some drinks left in there?'

It was empty. For a few seconds she allowed cool air to play over her heated face.

'No, nothing in here.'

'Sorry,' he said. 'My sister and her agent must have finished them. I gather that Nico failed to explain why we asked you here.'

'We decided you would do it better,' she said.

'OK. Let me tell you about my company. I call it *Creativity*. We make advertising films for cinemas in several West African countries and we're expanding into television. The other two directors are also from Central Region, which is why we are moving the business up here from Lagos and we aim to be in production before the new TV station starts broadcasting. Right, there's the background. Now it's your turn, Nico.'

'OK, here's what I was supposed to tell you. You met my uncle, I gather.'

'Yes, a charming man,' she said, though in fact she thought him rather creepy.

'Well, he has a soap factory in Kano . . .'

'Among other things,' Peter interrupted.

'Just leave this bit to me will you, Conker.'

'Conker?' Jenny asked. Peter seemed embarrassed.

'That's what they called me at boarding school. My friend has never quite outgrown his childhood nor his nickname. So carry on then --- Knickers.'

'Knickers!' She was amazed to find two successful business-men still using school nicknames. 'That's hilarious.'

'All right, go on,' said Nico. 'Laugh, if you must.'

'Sorry.'

'OK then. Uncle Jack started the factory by making washing soap. Your servant probably uses it.'

'Onak?'

'That's the one --- *Kano* spelt backwards. Then he added a toilet soap called *Roosam*. I leave you to work that one out for yourself.'

'Got it', she said after a moment's thought.

'Well, *Roosam* is popular in the local market but it doesn't have the cachet of other soaps like *Lux* or *Palmolive*. So he's launching another brand that he hopes will challenge them and he wants to back up the launch with a new advertising campaign. Over to you, Peter.'

'You met my sister Jumoke, didn't you? She appears in a lot of our commercials, like those you see on the wall. Even I will admit that Jumy is beautiful. Good looks run in our family.'

'Yes, she's gorgeous', Jenny agreed. 'I'm not going to say anything about you.'

'Well, Mr Masoor has employed a French chemist to come up with a completely new soap. It's very good, by the way --- I got several of my lady friends to try it before I took on the contract. It's designed for the West African market, but everyone is meant to think it's an established international brand like *Palmolive*. That's why he wants a white model to appear alongside Jumy.'

He looked at her as though she was expected to respond. The truth dawned.

'Me? You mean you want *me* to be the white woman in your adverts?'

'Who better?' said Peter. 'You have lovely skin and those cheekbones will photograph like a dream. You and Jumy will get on like ... what is that phrase, Nico?'

'Like a house on fire,' his friend replied.

And they did.

45

By the time she had been shown through the television studios it was after six o'clock and already dark. She sat next to Peter in the front seat, considering how she would explain her absence when she got home. She was worried how Kenneth might behave in front of the two men, and asked to be dropped off at the end of Lafiya Close. Peter refused, saying it would be dangerous for her to walk even that short distance in the dark. As they approached the bungalow she noticed that the lights were on and the garage door had been closed. Kenneth would see the Mercedes arrive and she dreaded facing him alone, so she decided to ask Peter and Nico to come in, praying that Kenneth would be in a fit state to receive them.

But he was not there. Her note was where she had left it'. Musa must have come to shut up the garage and turn on the bungalow lights for security reasons. She asked the men to have a drink but they said they ought to go.

'No, wait please.' She hurried into the bedroom, opened her underwear drawer and found the handkerchief. She had laundered and ironed it herself, away from the prying eyes of the servants, for Musa would have been quite capable of interpreting the initials. She came back and handed it to Nico.

'This is yours. You kindly lent it to me on the ship.'

'But I wanted you to keep it.'

'No, please take it.'

'Do as Jane says Nico,' said Peter. 'Remember Othello? Our School Certificate set book?'

'I don't get you.'

'I'll explain in the car.'

Peter shook her hand. 'Bye Jane. Do say yes. I promise you it will be a lot of fun. You have my number --- give me a ring when you've talked it over with Ken. I want to do a shoot as soon as our equipment comes up from Lagos.'

'We don't have a phone. There's a long waiting list.'

'I'll have one installed for you next week', Peter said. 'Give our regards to Kenneth when he gets back. Come on Nico, don't stand around like a lovesick loon.'

Standing by the garage in the darkness, Adebayo watched them drive away.

*

It was after seven-thirty before she heard their Consul turning into the drive. When she met her husband at the door
his breath told her that he had been drinking heavily, but he
appeared to have had the right amount. If he had too much
or too little he would be tetchy, but now he was more or less
stable. In fact he was apologetic.

'Sorry I've been so long, love. I took that Italian chap to t'
Club. Thought it right and proper --- that motor bike were a
real bargain. Know what? It's a Norton just like I had at
home. It'll want doing up, but we settled on a hundred and
seventy-five quid.'

'You bought it then?'

'Had to. Couldn't miss a bargain like that. He's bringing it
round on Tuesday. It'll be worth twice what I paid, once I've
done it up.'

'But I know you. You won't sell it, will you? I don't really
mind, though, so long as I can use the Consul when I pass my
test.'

'It's a deal,' he said.

'I left you a couple of sandwiches in the fridge. You ought to
eat something.'

'Thanks love. I don't deserve you.'

'No, you don't', she replied.

He went into the kitchen and she heard him opening another bottle of Star beer. She decided that this was not the time to tell him about Peter's offer. Before she did that she ought to speak to Norman Haworth.

*

'Well, I never,' said Norman next morning. 'Wouldn't that be something, eh? Our Jenny a movie star.'

'Hardly that. But you don't mind, then? Peter says we could do the filming at weekends, so it wouldn't interfere with my job.'

'To tell you the truth I've been wanting to talk to you about this. When we discussed the job at Colesclough I was so keen to get you out here for the training school that I didn't think it through properly. You see, in a month or two you'll have given me all the people I need to get us onto two shifts.'

'And then what? Yes, it had occurred to me too, Norman. There won't really be enough for me to do, will there?'

'Not till we start a third shift. I didn't want to upset you, but if Peter can give you something to do it would solve my problem. You still get paid, of course, but I wouldn't like you to be sitting at home with nothing to do. Congratulations Jenny. I'm sure you'll do well.'

'I wouldn't really call it a job and I don't suppose I'm much of an actress.'

'Who'll care about that? It's advertising, not Hollywood, and you're the bonniest lass I've seen in a long while. Don't tell Bessie I said that, she's coming out for Christmas?'

'Is she? That's wonderful. I hope you can both come for lunch at our house.'

After he agreed she said, 'Now, may I talk to you about Kenneth?'

46

Kenneth almost exploded when she told him about the advertising job.

'Who the hell do you think you are – some kind of high class tart? Do you think I want to go to t' pictures and see my wife poncing about on t' screen with some African woman? No. Definitely bloody not!'

But, when she reported what Norman told her about the security of her job, she could tell he was thinking things over.

'It's not your fault if Norman's got nowt for you to do,' he said. 'He'll have to keep paying you because your contract says twenty-one months, like mine does.'

'Yes, he says I still get my salary.'

'That doesn't mean you have to go making an exhibition of yourself, though.' But his tone indicated that he was becoming less hostile to the idea. 'I'll have to think about it.'

Later that night, as they were preparing to go to bed, he said, 'That thing of Peter's. You want to do it, do you?'

'Very much.'

'What'll they be paying you?'

She realised she had not discussed money with Peter. She picked a figure from the air'

'Two pounds an hour.'

'All right then.'

*

When Jenny got home from work on the following Wednesday she found Musa waiting on the stoep, in a state of great excitement. He ushered her towards the new addition to their household, which had been placed in the alcove behind the dining area.

'See madam, the number is Okante 238. That is a very low number. New numbers which are being issued are now beginning with two thousand. It is my opinion that this is a ministry number.'

'Do you know how to use the telephone?' she asked him. He looked pained.

'Of course I do, madam. My former employers also had a telephone machine installed in their house. When it rings I answer and I inform you who it is that is calling you, and then you take hold of the telephone and make a reply. That is the convenient way.'

'Yes, that is the correct procedure. Perhaps you'd be so kind as to teach Adebayo how to use it, so that he can take over answering duties if you aren't available?'

199

'No, madam, it would not be convenient for a smallboy to undertake such a duty. Now please sit down and I will bring your tea.'

The telephone did not ring at all until Thursday evening. Kenneth was still at the club and Jenny was alone in the house.

'You didn't phone,' said Peter. 'I rang this afternoon to check it was working but there was no one in. Anyway, what I wanted to tell you is that all our equipment arrived from Lagos yesterday. I've got my staff working overtime getting it set up and we want to do a trial shoot of the soap ad at the airport on Saturday. Is that OK with you? You are willing to help me, aren't you?'

Now this was becoming a reality she was having second thoughts. 'I'm not sure. Maybe I'm not suitable, I don't have any acting experience.'

'Of course you're suitable; it's not *Gone with the Wind* we are making. Can you get yourself to the TV studios on Saturday morning by nine o' clock? We'll have you and Jumy dressed and made-up there before we all drive up to the airport. Bring the nice dress you had on at the hotel opening, but not those shoes. What shoe size are you.'

'Five.'

'That's excellent, the same as Jumy. I'll tell her to bring a selection for you to choose from. My friend Alo has written us a script but you don't need to learn anything. You'll love Alo, by the way, he's good with words like you are. Bring Kenneth along, by the way.'

'I don't think he will be interested.' The remarks about her facility with words served to dispel her anger at Peter's implied criticism of her shoes. 'Have you got a name for the soap?'

'It was Mr Masoor who suggested it. Nico told his uncle the name that the workers in Okantex have given you. Would you mind if we called it *Mama Beauty*?'

'If you like,' she said, highly flattered.

47

Jenny did not get much sleep on the night before the filming. She went to bed early, but woke soon after midnight when she heard the motor-bike come down the Close and Kenneth rolled in from the club, or wherever it was that he went these days. She never asked. When he came to the bedroom she pretended to be asleep, though she was wide awake and remained so for most of the night. When Musa brought in their morning tea she felt completely drained; she could not imagine how awful she must look.

Musa pulled back her mosquito net, as he did every morning, and was beginning to pour the tea when she stopped him and whispered, 'Master won't want any tea yet and I'm getting up right away, so take mine to the bathroom please. I'm in rather a hurry.'

'Of course madam, it is the day of the filming, isn't it?' She had no idea how the servants had found out.

The image in the bathroom mirror reassured her and she thanked God for her good complexion. There would be time for a quick bath. When she emerged for breakfast she was rather annoyed to find that Musa has given Adebayo the morning off so that he could go up to the airport to watch.

'How did you know?'

'The cousin of Adebayo is a servant at the bungalow of the young Miss Ogondo, madam. Miss Jumoke is a most friendly type of person and she tells Miss Adebayo many things. Plenty people will be at the airport to see you --- that is for certain.'

Half-way to the television studio Jenny stopped the Consul by the side of the road and took a look into the driving mirror to confirm that the sleepless night had had no harmful effect on her appearance. She was not a vain person, but to bolster her confidence she said to herself --- Not bad, Jane Clarke, not bad at all.

On arrival she was ushered into a parking bay between a *Creativity* van and a white Wolseley saloon. She locked the doors of the Consul and took several deep breaths before walking through the swing doors. The place was greatly changed since her last visit. Although this was Saturday there was a good deal of activity in the entrance hall and a pretty young Fulani woman was on duty at the reception counter. Jenny was casually dressed, in her Slimma slacks with a pale blue long-sleeved blouse. She carried her dress over her arm. Stockings and make-up were in her holdall. As she approached the desk she could sense that she was being appraised, and was embarrassed when the girl said, 'Hello. You must be Mama Beauty'.

She picked up the phone. 'I will tell them that you are here, madam.'

Jenny went to sit on one of the banquettes but before she reached there the door from the corridor was flung open and Jumy came and grabbed her, planting a kiss on her cheek and tugging her by the hand along the corridor. She was wearing a voluminous white overall.

'I know how nervous you must be feeling,' she said, 'but don't worry, I have brought some whisky. Come along and let me make you up.'

She was already heavily made up. To Jenny's inexperienced eye she looked rather tarty. They went into an unmarked room. It had a long dressing table with bright strip-lighting above the mirrors. Jumy placed her in a chair like those at the hairdressers, put a tumbler on the dressing table and half filled it with Johnnie Walker whisky.

'Good gracious! I couldn't possibly drink that, certainly not so early in the morning,' Jenny said, never having tasted whisky.

'Take just a little sip. It is what you need to make your colly-wobbles go away.'

Jenny had a taste, which did, in fact, make her feel better.

'Take off your blouse and trousers,' Jumy ordered. Jenny felt embarrassed to be standing in her underwear but Jumy wrapped her in a white overall, then she took a long swig from her glass.

'Right, here goes,' she said. 'Sit down and let's get rid of that suntan.'

'Hold on a minute, Jumy. I've brought my own make-up.'

'Leave it to me my friend. You need more than a dab of Yardley today.'

Jumy swung the chair round and gently rubbed in a variety of Leichner sticks, chatting as she worked. 'Has Peter mentioned money?'

'Well, no. Not exactly, he just said what fun it would be.'

'Typical! Just like my brother. He exploits people, do you know that? You must speak to Ranjit before we do another shoot. Ranjit's my agent and he'll make sure they pay you properly.'

Jumy continued making her up. After the application of lipstick and eye liner, Jenny looked in the mirror and was appalled by what she saw, but before she could say anything Jumy took her by the hand.

'So now come quickly and get dressed --- and don't forget your glass.' Jumy grabbed the whisky bottle and led Jenny to a room further down the corridor.

There was no furniture apart from a clothes rack, a glass-topped table and some cane chairs, like those she had seen in Peter's office. Jumy took Jenny's dress and hung it on the rack. The other outfit hanging there was a traditional robe of red satin with gold lurex embroidery. A matching headscarf was spread over the rail. In the centre of the floor lay a pile of shoes which reminded Jenny of a chapel jumble sale, except that these were the most gorgeous shoes she had ever seen.

'Take your pick,' Jumy said. She chose a pair of mid-heeled kid leather courts almost exactly the shade of her dress.

'Surely you didn't buy these in Nigeria, Jumy?'

'Course not, silly. There is a shop in Dakar which is having all the latest Paris styles. Nothing like as expensive as Lagos. You can stock up with shoes when we go there. Ranjit has plans for us to make some personal appearances, and with you speaking French so well we . . . '

'Personal appearances? Jenny was shocked.

'Yes, provided Mr Masoor approves the first advertisement. Peter says everyone is going to love you and me together and he is going to make the commercials into a story with different episodes. He says they do that in the United States. They call them 'soap operas' --- but we don't have to sing,' she added. She held out her hand and said, 'OK, pardner?' in an approximation of an American accent.

Jenny let Jumy shake her hand, but she was staggered by what she had just heard. The implications were too much for her to think about at that moment, amid her trepidation at the coming ordeal, but she appeared already to be involved in this business far deeper than she had anticipated. As they both changed into their outfits she glanced at Jumy in her smart underwear and could not avoid a tinge of envy at the black girl's figure; envy mixed with admiration. Jumy had the prettiest bottom she had ever seen. Having met both the parents, she was amazed how they could have produced two such lovely creatures as Jumy and Peter. She had never been able to understand how a woman could fall for another woman. But with Jumy? She quickly cleared her mind of such disturbing thoughts and started to put on her stockings.

205

Before they left the dressing room she took another fortifying sip of whisky, but her restored confidence was shattered immediately they entered Peter's office, because when he saw her he burst out laughing.

He apologised at once. 'Sorry Jane. Please forgive my laughter but it's such a surprise to see how Jumy has changed you back into a white woman. You may have liked your tan but, believe me, this is just how we need you to look. We Africans expect Europeans to look pale.'

There were four people she did not know; a tall European woman, two Yoruba men and a Sikh, whom she assumed to be Ranjit. The woman was seated on the edge of Peter's desk with her long legs crossed, clearly making herself the centre of attention. Her hair was dyed ash-blonde and gathered into an untidy chignon. In her left hand she held a cigarette holder containing an unlit black cigarette. Her heavy brown-suede boots were quite out of keeping with her beige trouser suit. She appeared to be in her early thirties, though she could be older. Not pretty, but attractive in a snooty kind of way. The men clearly did not view the woman with Jenny's critical eye.

The Nigerians could have been twins. They were the same age and height and wore white baseball caps, blue denim trousers, white shoes and identical yellow T- shirts printed with the word 'Creativity'. The Indian man was short and plump. He wore a pink turban with his grey safari suit. Peter introduced Jenny to the men first, as was the custom in Nigeria.

'OK Jane. Let me introduce Alo, our creative director --- his full name is far too difficult for you to remember.'

Alo came to shake hands and immediately Jenny could tell that he was what her mother used to call 'a pansy'. The other Nigerian came up to her, grinning and displaying perfect teeth.

'And this is Cosmos Adegoke. He looks after production. I do the marketing.'

'Whenever he finds the time,' said Cosmos pointedly.

The white woman had adopted a smirk, clearly miffed at not being introduced first. She took a gold lighter from her purse, lit the black cigarette and blew a puff of pungent smoke.

'Finally, this is Nicola'.

Peter moved one arm in a sweep towards the woman sitting on the desk. It might have been taken as an ironic gesture, were it not for the fact that his face betrayed him a devoted admirer.

'Nicola is a leading international journalist and she is helping us with the launch. Now, let me get this right ... Nicola von Flate (it sounded like). Is that correct, Nicki?'

'That's perfect, Peter darling.' She did not move from the desk but held out a hand, which Jenny had to come forward to shake.

The score was love-fifteen.

Jenny was too excited to be truly angry, but determined to even the score in the near future. She and Jumy took the two remaining seats. Peter's new metal-framed chairs were obviously expensive, but not as comfortable as the cheap cane ones they had replaced. The von Flate woman did not move when Peter sat down behind his desk.

'Do please take a chair, Nicki,' he said, somewhat abruptly.

'What about me?' asked the little Sikh man.

'Oh, sorry. That's Ranjit', said Peter. 'Jumy will explain about Ranjit. Now everybody, listen carefully to what Alo has to say.'

The run-through took no more than twenty minutes. Jenny was disappointed that she had only one line to say, but at the same time she was relieved that there did not appear to be much she could do wrong. Peter had organised the use of a Dakota at Okante airport. Cosmos would photograph the eleven-twenty flight arriving from Kaduna and then they would use the other plane for their advertising film.

All Jenny had to do was to emerge from the aeroplane, wave to an imaginary crowd, be presented with a bouquet of flowers and then be greeted and kissed by Jumy. She merely had to mouth the words 'Hello Jumy darling, in English; then in Hausa, Yoruba and French. What Alo referred to as the 'voice-overs' were to be dubbed later at the studio.

'Who is going to present the flowers?' Jenny enquired.

'We'll find some decent-looking fellow at the airport, don't worry,' replied Cosmos.

Jenny was sure Adebayo would be wearing his nice uniform. 'I think I know someone suitable who will be there,' she said.

'Good', Peter said, 'any more questions?'   There were none.
'Right, let's hit the road. Ladies with me in the Mercedes,
boys in the van, OK?'

'Not OK', said his sister, 'I want Jenny and Ranjit to come
with me in the Wuzily, so Ranjit can talk to her.'

The 'Wuzily' proved to be the white car parked alongside
the Consul. On the way, Ranjit explained that Jumy had been
engaged to do an advertising film to promote the car and
had such difficulty in pronouncing the name 'Wolseley' that
the agents had decided that 'Wuzily' is how the car should
be marketed in Nigeria. Peter had bought her the demon-
stration car as her twenty-first birthday present.

Having seen how much whisky her friend had consumed,
Jenny entered the car with some trepidation, but Jumy
threaded her way expertly through the busy Saturday morning traffic. Ranjit sat in the back seat with Jenny and led her
through the details of a contract he proposed that she
should sign with Creativity.

Later that day she was able to tell Kenneth that for this one
film alone she was to earn the equivalent of her monthly
salary with Harrisons (Nigeria) Limited.   But she did not
mention to him the possibility that she might be buying
shoes in Senegal.

48

Around eleven o'clock the following Monday morning a
messenger came to the training school to tell Jenny that she
was wanted by the general manager. As she approached the

office block, just a short walk away, she saw Kenneth on the veranda outside Norman's office, talking to Nico.

'Hello love,' Kenneth said. 'I've just been showing Mr Masoor and his friend round the mill. She's having a talk with Norman now but he wants you to go in to join them and tell her about our training scheme.'

Nico hesitated slightly before kissing her cheek. 'Kenneth has given us the grand tour of the factory. Most interesting, thanks a lot Ken. Are you coming in with us?'

'No, I'd best get back to the dyehouse. It won't be long now until me first machines come. Oh, and thanks once again for the invite to the hotel do Nico. It was great.'

As Jenny opened the door, Kenneth said, 'Bye love,'and kissed her. That was unusual these days and she wondered whether the gesture was for Nico's benefit.

Norman beckoned Jenny to sit beside him. Nico took a chair in the far corner of the office. As she had expected, the visitor was Miss van what's-her-name.

'I'd like to introduce Nicola van Vleet.' (Norman pronounced the name as it was spelt on the business card which he handed to Jenny). 'She's a journalist friend of Nico's and wants to know about industrial development in Central Region.'

'Oh, but Jane and I already know each other, don't we darling?' said Nicki in her gushing manner. 'I've just been telling Nico how superb you were on Saturday. It really is very good of you to lend her to us for the filming, Norman, and Kenneth has been so kind in showing us through your factory. I've learnt a lot from him in such a short time.'

What gullible creatures men are, thought Jenny as she read the expression on Norman's face. Just a few minutes with Nicola had been enough to charm the pants off him. Then she remembered those occasions when she herself had turned on such charm and grudgingly admired the older woman's technique.

Norman said, 'Fine. So let Jane explain to you a bit about our training scheme and then we'll walk over and take a look at her school.'

Jenny directed her little lecture to Nicola. but glanced at Nico from time to time, to find him almost beaming approval at the way she coped with Nicola's deliberately difficult questions. Eventually Norman said, 'Well, I think that's enough technical stuff. Let's take a stroll.'

On the way across to the training school Nicola linked arms with Jenny, who resisted the temptation to shake her off. This morning the woman appeared to have gone to more trouble with her appearance and looked quite presentable. She wore a two-piece suit in a shade somewhere between green and khaki. The skirt was shorter than was recommended for European women to wear in Nigeria, but her legs were her best feature. Instead of the inelegant safari boots she now wore a pair of taupe canvas loafers which made her height less obvious. Nicola was slightly taller than Nico, a good four inches above Jenny. She looked down with the pretence of affection, though both were now aware that they were adversaries.

'Shall you be here long?' Jenny asked.

'Probably about two months, though I won't be spending all that time in Okante. I've taken a sort of sabbatical to do a free-lance feature on Nigeria's preparations for independence.'

Jenny did not know what a sabbatical was but was darned if she was going to ask. 'And where are you staying while you are here?' she enquired, already knowing the answer.

'I'm using the Okante Homestead as my base. It's a delightful place, isn't it? As you probably know, the residential part isn't open yet but darling Nico has kindly found me a room in his private quarters.' The two men were walking only a couple of paces ahead of them and must be hearing the conversation. In a voice loud enough for Nico to hear, Jenny said, 'That sounds very convenient --- for both of you, no doubt.'

The visitors had gone, and she was alone again with her students. She set them a written test which would last until lunchtime and sat at her desk pretending to make notes, but actually reflecting on the hurt which this episode had caused her.

What right have I to be jealous? I'm a married woman and he is a free, unattached young man. Is he not entitled to have his own friends? And what if they are sleeping together? But that last thought was too painful for her to bear.

She loved Nico, more than she had ever loved Kenneth, and he had said he loved her. But, when this friend from his past turns up, he capitulates. The bitch's motives were crystal clear to Jenny. Because she loved him she would be willing to abandon him to someone who would be good for him --- but not this one. Something had to be done about the van Vleet woman.

49

A representative of the advertising agency was coming up from Lagos the following Thursday and Peter arranged for some interior scenes to be shot at Jumy's bungalow that same evening. Since the house was in the private compound of Chief Ogondo, Jenny looked forward to seeing where and in what style her new friend lived. She was not yet used to driving in the dark, so Jumy agreed to collect her in the Wuzily

Kenneth was still at the club when the white car drew up. The servants had somehow got to know that this celebrity was coming and a small crowd had assembled in Lafiya Close to witness her arrival. Musa, Adebayo and Emmanuel were lined up below the front stoep, dressed in their best clothes. Musa's wives and Gladys Adebayo stood by the garage and Musa came down to introduce everybody to the Premier's daughter.

Jumy appeared rather overwhelmed by this formal reception but spent a few minutes talking to the women, before going back to young Adebayo to congratulate him on his part in handing over the bouquet on the previous Saturday. Later, as they drove over the bridge, Jumy said, 'That boy has a very nice body. We must use him again.'

They were admitted to the Premier's compound by two soldiers who appeared to be bored out of their minds, or possibly drunk. One raised the barrier while the other gave a perfunctory salute. Presumably they had to do this many times a day. Jumy's bungalow was larger than Jenny expected. It was built of big cement blocks finished in pale-yellow distemper, which was starting to flake. The frames of the narrow windows and their security bars were painted a matching daffodil shade --- not a colour scheme Jenny would have chosen. There was no veranda to break the stark frontage, which had artificial crenellations on top. This facade reminded Jenny of the desert fort in the *Beau Geste* movie she had seen as a child.

Jumy stopped the Wuzily by the front door and said, 'Go along in while I put the car in the garage.' The front door was open. Jenny walked through a passageway into a court-yard with a central lawn. When she stepped onto the grass a gardener appeared and turned off a sprinkler. Jenny went to sit down but the garden chairs were wet. The gardener hurried to wipe one for her. Jumy appeared, carrying the studio make-up case, which she placed on the table.

'We will have a cold drink before we start, or would you prefer coffee?'

'Coffee would be lovely, please.'

'Let's go indoors then.'

Dusk was gathering and it would soon be dark. She called the gardener to bring in the make-up case.

'What an interesting house,' said Jenny, hoping she did not display her disappointment.

'It's OK, I suppose. Mummy and Daddy used to live here be-fore their new place was built.'

'Does Peter live in this compound?'

'No, thanks to God. He has a house in the European quarter.'

214

'Might I have a look round before we start?' Jumy seemed unwilling,

'OK, but it's a bit untidy.'

She didn't show her one of the bedrooms. When they were back in the drawing room at the end of the tour, Jenny managed to find a complimentary remark, but she decided that her own little bungalow was far cosier than this. A maid brought in their coffee but Jumy looked at her watch.

'Better we start now,' she said, and led the way to one of the single bedrooms. The servant followed them and left the tray on a dressing table. When the door closed, Jumy said, 'Were you told that we have to take our tops off?'

'Not to show everything, surely?'

'No. I'm in my bra and you are wrapped in a towel, because you have just had a shower with *Mama Beauty* soap.'

Jenny took off her skirt, blouse and bra and Jumy enveloped her in the towel, leaving it rather too low on her cleavage. She managed to hitch it up a fraction without her partner noticing. This time the make-up was not excessive, more a heavier version of what one would use for a normal evening function. Jenny congratulated her friend on her skill.

'Martin taught me,' she said. 'He used to be an actor.'

Jenny wanted to ask who Martin was, but she continued. 'OK, let's begin. I will have to make up your arms and back and you need the front and the top of your bust done. You can do that bit yourself --- unless you would enjoy me doing it.' She giggled. 'But I don't think you are that sort of woman, are you?'

When returned to the drawing room Jenny was glad she had
a dressing gown over the towel, for there was a young
European man waiting for them. Jumy gave one of her little
squeals and ran to kiss him. On the lips, Jenny noticed.

'Martin, this is my new friend Jenny. I'm not very good at
saying her second name, so we call her Mama Beauty. Isn't
she lovely?'
'Er . . . yes. Very,' said the young man, embarrassed. He
shook hands with Jenny.

'How do you do? I'm Martin Donovan. I work for the distributors and I'm doing the English voice-over for your film.'
He was not very tall but had those brooding good looks
which brought back memories of her beloved Montgomery
Clift. It seemed to be the day for compliments from Jumy.

'Tell me the truth Jenny. Don't you think that Martin has the
sexiest voice you have ever heard?'

'Stop being silly, darling', he said. 'We have less than half an
hour before Alo gets here and I need to run you through
your lines. Let's go into the big bedroom.'

Jenny now understood why she had not been shown this
room during her tour of the house. It was set up with lighting and sound equipment, as was the adjoining bathroom.
Pink was the predominant colour but the whole of one wall
comprised white wardrobe units, with a built-in dressing
table. The walls were painted off-white with a slight tinge of
pink, the king-size double bed had a pink and white striped
cover and the Regency-style chairs and settle were up-
holstered in matching fabric. This was so much more taste-
ful than the rest of the house that Jenny wondered if the

room had been specially furnished for the filming, but decided it would be impolite to ask.

The English dialogue consisted of only three or four sentences, which they both memorised in a few minutes. For the translations Martin had brought cue cards. They were to speak first in English, then Hausa and finally French. Jenny and Jumy discussed a couple of alterations to the French text, which Martin accepted. Jumy's French accent was delightful and she said the same of Jenny's Hausa. 'Anyone can tell you are English, but it is like a French person speaking English --- sexy.' By the time they had run through the script twice in each language, the maid knocked on the door to say that Mr Alobayundike had arrived.

The air-conditioning had to be switched off and, although the filming did not take long, the bedroom became extremely hot. Jenny was grateful to be wearing only a towel. As the equipment was being removed, the maid brought cold drinks and some sandwiches for the two actresses.

'Leave those,' Jumy ordered. 'We'll get rid of our makeup first.' It was the first time she had taken a shower with another woman.

When they had dressed and returned to Jumy's bedroom for their drinks and sandwiches, the lighting equipment had already gone. Martin was
 unpacking. He hung his clothes in a section of her wardrobe unit.

50

Peter telephoned on Friday evening, to say that the first
episode of the commercial was ready and would be shown
at the TV studios the following afternoon. Kenneth took the
call and Jenny was pleased to hear him agreeing to go along
with her. She asked Peter how the film looked.

'I haven't seen it yet, but Cosmos says you and Jumy look
marvellous. I knew you would. I'll pick you both up after
lunch tomorrow. About two o'clock, OK?'

'I'm so glad you're coming, darling', Jenny said after Peter
had rung off.

'Suppose I've got to show some interest,' was his rather
grudging response.

*

Peter came early. When they reached the studios he took
them to his office to wait for the others. After about five
minutes Cosmos and Alo popped their heads round the
door, to say hello, and immediately went to the projection
studio. Then Martin Donovan arrived. He had come by taxi,
explaining that Jumy was not ready and would drive herself
in the Wuzily. The telephone rang while Martin was still
speaking. Jenny was becoming increasingly excited and
wished she had Jumy with her.

Peter replaced the receiver. 'That was Nico. Mr Masoor got
in from Kano last night but they are waiting for Nicki to get
ready. Apparently, like Jumy, she has a reputation for being
late.'

The last thing Jenny would have wished for was the van Vleet woman being at the showing, but presumably she needed to be involved, as their press adviser. Martin said he would show Kenneth round the studios.

'Make sure you're back in five minutes,' Peter told them.

'Alone at last,' he said when the men had gone, and gave one of his laughs. 'But, seriously Jenny, I wanted to talk to you, because we have to choose a name for you.'

'What do you mean? I thought I was to be Mama Beauty --- not that I like the name much.'

'No, I mean we have to decide what you shall be called in real life, a stage name as it were. Thistlethwaite isn't very suitable, I hope you agree. What was your maiden name?'

'Clarke.'

'Well?' he pondered. 'Not really, unless you feel strongly about it. Think of another English name you might use.'

After only a moment's hesitation Jenny said, 'How about 'Masters'.'

So Jane Thistlethwaite (nee Clarke) alias Mama Beauty, became Jane Masters.

The little film lasted only a few minutes but Jenny was impressed by how professional it looked, and amazed to see herself at the centre of it. This was an entirely different person from the woman she saw every day in her mirror; far more glamorous, she thought. She sat on one of the middle rows of the small viewing studio, between Kenneth and

219

Jumy. In the half-light she glanced to see Kenneth's reaction and caught him looking at her, quizzically.

When the lights went up Martin said, 'We need to lose fifteen seconds.'

'No problem,' replied Alo. 'Well, Mr Masoor?' he enquired.

'Just what we need,' said a voice from the back. 'Can you have the rest of the adverts finished in time for Independence?'

It was a tremendous relief.

51

We all have priorities in our lives. For Alice Harrison, her children naturally came top, taking precedence over her charitable work, the garden, *The Little Lodge* and her husband. Harold ought to come higher up the order, but she was always available when he wanted her --- not so frequently as when they were younger, but that too was entirely natural. Having Geoffrey sent out to Nigeria would take away some of the pressure. It was taking longer to get him out there than she would have wished, but Harold assured her that he would be on his way as soon as he could be spared from the Colesclough mills.

Knowing something of the appetites of men, she believed that Geoffrey would return from Africa in need of feminine company and it was her plan to have a suitable young woman available to present to him while he was still 'hungry', so to speak. She was sorry that he had broken off with Mabel Butterworth, whom she considered a highly suitable girl for someone like Geoffrey, but at the Women's Institute conference she had met a solicitor's wife from Bolton who had three daughters of the right sort of age. The middle girl played golf for the county. She hoped that one of them would still be available by the time Geoffrey got back.

Until the recent disturbing news, Harriet had been Alice's chief source of worry. Piers Waddington, the young man who had taken her to the hunt ball, still appeared interested, and Harriet used to go over regularly to his place at Cliviger, but when she was there she apparently spent most of her time out riding with his sister, a girl named Clarice. As Alice remarked to Harold, nothing could come out of that.

Her elder son Roger had previously never caused Alice to lose a single night's sleep. Rather as the mother of a nun can rest easy once her daughter has taken the veil, Alice had readily surrendered her son to the Royal Artillery. It occurred to her that Roger would one day wish to marry. It was therefore something of a shock when Harold came back from his lodge meeting with the news.

'I've been talking to Fred Butterworth,' he said. 'Did you know Mabel has been out to see our Roger?'

'What? To Germany? What would she want with Roger.'

'I can only guess,' said Harold, smiling.

'Don't be vulgar, dear. I had her in mind for Geoffrey, you know.'

'Well, that's all over, according to what Fred tells me. It seems Mabel has changed her plan of attack.'

221

'But she can't just have turned up out of the blue; Roger must have invited her.' Alice's mind was working hard. 'I wonder if that's why he's coming here for his leave this time.'

Roger usually tried to take leave in August or September, for the shooting. He would stay with friends in Yorkshire and visit The Little Lodge for a couple of nights at the beginning and end of the holiday, but this time he was coming in October and would be staying with them for ten days. Alice had a sense of foreboding. Mabel was a very nice young woman, ideally suited to be married to a mill owner, but something different would be required of an army wife, or so she assumed. She began to worry on Roger's behalf. He had always been easily led.

Roger owned a boat, which he kept on Steinhuder Meer, only a short drive from the barracks. His German girlfriend used to join him there most weekends. The British Army of the Rhine still discouraged 'fraternisation', as it was called, particularly for officers, but Hilde was a keen sailor and it was not considered untoward that she should come to crew for Roger. They both enjoyed having sex on the boat but there was never any talk of love, certainly not of marriage. Hilde had no wish to marry an Englishman and she knew that there would be a nice clean break when Roger was eventually transferred from Germany. He, for his part, had no plans to look for a wife until he was promoted. Having inherited his mother's pragmatic approach to such matters, he realised that the choice of partners available to a Major was wider than for a Captain.

It had been a surprise when he received the first letter from Mabel, whom he had considered to be his brother's girlfriend, but it was couched in the language of a pen-friend. He remembered her as a girl who had always been around

222

at parties, probably five or six years younger than him, but an early developer (which, in the euphemisms of polite Lancashire society, meant she had a big bust). Nice legs too, if he recalled correctly; and when she sent him a photograph he was impressed by the way she had blossomed. In return, he sent one which Hilde had taken of him on the yacht, at the tiller in his bathing trunks.

He began to enjoy writing to her as much as he enjoyed her amusing, gossipy letters. As their correspondence flourished, the tone became more affectionate and, once it was clear that her affair with Geoffrey was at an end, Roger felt able to put on paper some of the things he would not feel it proper to say to Hilde; not without inferring a more intimate relationship. Mabel replied in kind.

He had a seventy-two hour pass due to him for extra field duties, so he wrote to ask whether Mabel might be interested in a short sailing holiday on Steinhuder. She immediately booked herself on a plane to Hanover.

Roger had a very important question to put to Mabel during his leave, but the prime purpose of his visit to Lancashire was to see his father about the offer he had received from Plantagenet Sykes. A couple of hundred thousand pounds was not to be sniffed at.

52

The extraordinary meeting of the directors of Isaac Harrison Limited was not held in the boardroom but in the conference room at Daisy Mount, where there was no danger of interruption. Harold had set the meeting for ten-thirty, hoping they could be finished by lunchtime. Alice had organised a buffet at The Little Lodge.

There were five round the table, all family apart from the company secretary, Mostyn Stainforth. Mostyn was a solicitor, the great-grandson of Isaac Harrison's lawyer who had drawn up the original company articles and helped finance the building of Daisy Mill. Every director was there, except Geoffrey's sister, Harriet. He could not recall Roger having attended a board meeting before, not since he himself had been made a director at the age of twenty-one. It was also rare for Pomona Hattersley, Harold's cousin, to attend. Today, she was here to represent the interests of her side of the family.

His elder brother was the first to respond to their father's introduction of the thorny subject, which was the sole item on the agenda.

'I'm sure none of us would wish to deny that you do a splendid job, Dad --- and you too, Geoff . . .'

'Hear, hear,' said Pomona.

'. . . but dividends are one thing and capital is another. I'll be first to admit that I don't keep my finger on the pulse of the industry, but I do read in the papers that competition from places like Portugal and India is hitting us, now that we are forced to pay these ridiculous wages. Sykes says he has been having machinery reconditioned from some of the mills he's bought up, and he's exported it to South Korea . . .'

At the mention of the name 'Sykes' his father burst in, 'Don't believe anything that . . .' He struggled to find a suitable word for the detested individual and then remembered what Geoffrey had called him. 'Anything that bloody chancer says. Apologies for the language, Mona, but that man brings out the worst in me.

Listen Roger, I've been doing a bit more research on Mr so-called Plantagenet and he turns out to be nothing more than a front man for some Lebanese fellow.'

'In that case,' said Roger, 'why don't we get in touch directly with the main chap. The organ-grinder, I believe the phrase is. Have him round.'

'The reason is that the 'chap' lives in Nigeria. We used to do business with him before the war and, to tell you the truth, I'm a bit surprised that he's gone round to the back door for what he wants, because as I remember him he was as straightforward as they come.'

'Do you mind if I say something?' said Pomona.

As Harold listened with half an ear to what his cousin had to say, he did some quick mental arithmetic and decided that, even if Mona and Roger went for Sykes's offer, there was no contest. Then he included Mostyn's twenty percent and he was still safe.   In some ways he regretted having given the three children their shares. His accountant had suggested that each should be given part of the equity when they came of age, as a precaution against estate duty. He held proxy for Harriet --- but just suppose both his sons voted in favour of the takeover?

He could count on Geoffrey, surely? But just suppose? OK, count Geoffrey out and that left him on his own, voting his twenty percent, plus Harriet's six percent and the twenty percent he had bought from Pomona's brother Leander. Forty-six percent. Not enough. Belatedly, he turned his full

225

attention to what Mrs Hattersley was saying. 'Can you just repeat that, Mona?'

'I thought I'd made myself clear,' said his cousin. 'Since Geoffrey is due to go out to Nigeria soon, could he not tackle this . . . what's he called, Harold?'

'Masoor.'

'. . . this Mr Masoor, and see if he might be interested in buying just a few shares. Then you and Geoffrey could go on running the mills, as you do so well. I can't see what he would gain from putting in new management.'

Geoffrey had taken no part in the discussion so far. He took the formal course of asking the Chairman if he might speak. 'Go ahead, Geoffrey, please,' said Harold.

'I agree with what Pommy says. We ought to let Mostyn and Roger know that the three of us discussed this when Pommy was first approached by Sykes, and that I believe we ought to investigate the possibility of going public, rather than considering this private offer. Perhaps Mostyn will give us his views on that.

*

An hour or so later Harold and Geoffrey strolled on the damp lawn of The Little Lodge, each with a plate of smoked salmon sandwiches in his hand.

Harold said, 'Well, son, I reckon that's about the best that could come out of it. I make no secret of the fact that I would have been happier for things to carry on as they are, but I can understand Roger wanting to have some brass of his own when he gets married. He won't need it though.

226

She's an only child is Mabel, and I reckon Fred's better off than I am. I expect you know that your mother thought she would have done for you.'

'Yes, Dad, I did know that. I'm sure half Lancashire knew that. But, as Mostyn said, we shall have to time the offer carefully, because the blokes in the City don't like anything less than a full flotation, and we'll have a Labour government by then.'

'Never', his father insisted. 'They'll go for Mac again, you mark my words. This Gaitskell talks well, I'll grant you, but everyone knows he has out-and-out reds lurking behind him. Anyway, politics apart, if Jacob Masoor wants our shares let him damn well buy them on the stock market. To be honest Geoffrey, I couldn't bear to have that Sykes chap on our board. But Jacob Masoor --- as I remember him he's a different kettle of fish.'

'Why don't I go out and see him, as Pommy suggested? It would be good to have a month or so in Okante, to see what I might be in for. I know you're not sure if you want me to move there permanently, but Norman might appreciate a bit of help. He said in our last phone call that Ken Thistleth-waite is turning out to be a bit of a dead loss. Hitting the bottle, he said.'

'You'd have to move fast, if you do go. Roger wants a quick decision one way or the other. Let's make it soon after Christmas.'

'It might be fun to spend Christmas in Nigeria,' said Geoffrey, hoping to avoid another family celebration.

'I wouldn't dare suggest that to your mother. No, make it the second week in January. Come on, let's get some of that Chablis before Mona drinks it all.'

53

As Independence Day approached, there was a swelling tide of expectation; joy among Nigerians and disquiet among many expatriates, particularly those who worked for the Government. One of Kenneth's PWD friends said, after too many beers at the club bar, "They'll have me out of my house and in the street before the end of October, just see if they don't. I'm fuckin' off while I've got still got the old wedding tackle intact."

By early September, Sir Fergus and Lady Abercrombie were giving farewell dinners and preparing to move out of Government House into what was to become the residence of the British Deputy High Commissioner.

Jenny had no doubt that the handover would be peaceful and that Chief Ogondo would remain a benevolent leader of the region. She was pleased to be witnessing such an historic event. Workers at the mill were to be given two days' holiday, plus a special bonus, and the whole of the expatriate population of Okante was invited to the flag-lowering ceremony on the lawn of Government House on the evening of September 30th.

*

The rest of the soap commercials were filmed in Jumy's bungalow. Jenny was cast in the role of a beauty consultant and

Jumy was her actress friend. After the second episode they began to devise their own dialogue, which Alo adapted to fit the brief he had been given by the distributors. To Jenny, it all seemed like an enjoyable game and each time she saw the finished result, she was amazed that it appeared so professional. She even began to suspect that she might be what she had seen referred to in *Picturegoer* as a 'natural'. On most evenings, when the filming was over, an informal party began. Peter turned up on several occasions but never brought his wife.

Kenneth no longer showed any interest in what she was doing. She was invariably home before he returned from the club, or wherever it was that he spent his evenings these days. They still had sex every Saturday night and most Sundays, but only occasionally during the week, because he was rarely capable.

Love had ceased to be a factor in the exercise. For her it was now little more than a routine. She resented the fact that her body still demanded this satisfaction. As to how he felt, she had no inkling. It was a long time since she had sex with him when he was completely sober.

*

Because the servants were given leave on the eve of Independence, Jenny and Rose Sanderson prepared a cold buffet in Rosie's bungalow for the residents of Lafiya Close, before everyone set off for Government House. Kenneth spent the afternoon of the holiday at the club and was not home until just before they were due to go next door for the meal, though he returned relatively sober. Jenny decided it was likely to be quite cool at the outdoor reception, so she wore her grey two-piece. Kenneth wore his wedding suit, which had become rather tight for him.

229

Rumours of impending doom had grown in intensity as the day for handover grew nearer. The atmosphere was far from festive when they all gathered at the Sandersons' house.

'Could this be the Last Supper?' said Tim Rostron, who fancied himself as a wit.

'At least we're all on contract,' Dick Sanderson pointed out. 'We'll get paid compensation if owt goes wrong. We're not settlers here like we were in Southern Rhodesia. If the blacks make trouble down there they'll be buggered. That's one reason why me and Rosie got out.'

'Don't talk like that, Richard,' said Jenny, determined to lighten the atmosphere. 'We have nothing at all to worry about. Tonight is a celebration. The Nigerians are pleased to have us here and we should be proud that Britain is handing over such a unified country. Come on, tuck in everybody. We'll drive up to the party in convoy if you are all so worried.'

She meant that to be a joke but nobody appeared to appreciate it.

It was an exciting moment as they were ushered onto the lawn of Government House, having taken their fill of the Governor's hospitality. As midnight approached, all the lights were extinguished, except for a single spotlight which picked out the Union flag fluttering in the slight breeze.

Conversation gradually died down and, when the spotlight was turned off, all was quiet. They stood, whispering, in the dark for what seemed a long time. Then train whistles started to sound from the marshalling yards of Okante station

on the Northern outskirts of the town, fire-crackers exploded from down below in the Sabongari, but the crowd on
the lawn remained silent, both Nigerians and expatriates.
Now the spotlight shone again, this time trained upon the
green, white and green flag of the new Nigeria, which
fluttered atop the flagpole where the British standard had
flown. Jenny checked her watch. It was the first of October.
A new nation was born.

For a split second it appeared as though no one knew how
to react, but a sporadic cheer by the Nigerians soon grew
into a yell of triumph, then the police band struck up the
new national anthem. Most of the crowd began to sing the
well-rehearsed verse. Some in Yoruba, others in Hausa.
Jenny, alone of her group, joined them in English:

> *Nigeria, we hail thee, our own dear native land.*
> *Though tribe and tongue may differ, in brotherhood we*
> *stand...*

There were tears in her eyes, but joy in her heart; joy that
her friends were at last in control of their own destiny. She
hoped Nigeria would become a shining example to the rest
of Africa --- of unity, prosperity and peace.

54

Musa was looking forward to preparing Christmas dinner.
He knew how to cook everything that Europeans ate on
their special day and the steward from next door had been
enlisted to help. Musa ensured that it was made clear that
the Sandersons' servant was second-in-command on this occasion.

Kenmaster told him they did not want any decorations because 'It won't feel like Christmas out here.' When Musa
asked Mama Beauty what that meant, she said it would be
too hot for Christmas, but he explained that it was always
hot at Christmas. So they gave him money to buy some paper chains and streamers at the market and Kenmaster
brought home a plastic tree from Kingsway Stores, which
Musa and Adebayo decorated with fancy balls. Gladys Adebayo made a pink dress for a tiny doll for Mama Beauty to
place at the top of the tree.

A few days before Christmas, Emmanuel had found a large
cobra at the bottom of the garden and cut off its head with a
panga. It was moving from right to left when he killed it,
which he told them was not a good omen, but Musa assured
Adebayo that such superstition was Igbo nonsense and that
everything would go well. It was up to the three of them to
make sure that Mama Beauty's Christmas party was a big
success.

What Jenny would have liked most as a Christmas present
was a horse, but since that day in Las Palmas, when Kenneth
bought the riding crop, he had made no mention of them
having one. Their relationship was on a knife edge. After
the row about the motor-bike she did not want to risk another one, by reminding him of what he said when he
bought the whip. There was not a great choice of Christmas
presents available in the local stores. They decided to buy a
Black Box record player as a joint present. For the 'surprise'
element, each would buy the other a record.

They slept in late on Christmas morning. Kenneth had
brought the Christmas parcels into the bedroom the night
before, so that they could be opened without the servants
looking on. Since Jenny knew what her present was there
would be no surprise, apart from seeing what record Ken-

neth had chosen for her, and she had given him hints.. A few of the neighbours had left them packages and the servants had clubbed together for a gift, inexpertly wrapped and obviously a bottle.

She was delighted by Kenneth's choice of record, Mozart's 'Jupiter' symphony, not one of her 'hints' --- and he appeared pleased with his Glenn Miller LP. From the neighbours they received a set of ashtrays, some candied fruits, chocolates and an alarm clock; a useful present, since this was one of the few items not supplied by the company. The servants had bought a bottle of Liebfraumilch. The record player lay on the floor by the door. There had not seemed much point in wrapping that.

When they had opened all the packages and she was starting to tidy up the paper, carefully saving that which might be used again next year, Kenneth said, 'Hey up, I've not finished yet.' He reached under the bed and pulled out another parcel, wrapped in expensive paper.

'Oh darling, you shouldn't have done this,' she said. 'I'm cross with you. I've only bought you the one thing. I thought we agreed only the records --- apart from our joint present.'

'Wait till you open it. You'll see it's more like a present for me – I should say *they* are. Not the sort of things you'd want me to put under t' Christmas tree.'

She regarded herself as fairly broad-minded, but when she opened the parcel she was shocked that he could imagine her wearing such an outfit, a red bodice of the type she had seen advertised in some of the cheap magazines, and matching knickers with no crotch. He had also bought her a black suspender belt and black net stockings.

'Where on earth did you find this sort of rubbish in a place like Okante?'

'You can get a lot of things if you know where to look. Well? Will you? Wear them, I mean.'

'Really, darling! What would I do with an outfit like this?'

'Want me to show you?' He went to the wardrobe, placed the whip alongside the costume and said, 'Now you know. That's what I'd like. That's why I bought that whip.'

She was appalled. 'No, Kenneth, never! Is that what you've wanted me to do to you? No way would I ever do such a thing. That's sick, darling.'

He raised his voice. 'There you go again with your bloody *darling*.'

She sensed the beginnings of another conflict, on this day of all days. Before she could say anything emollient he began his attack, almost as if her response was what he had hoped for.

'You didn't seem to mind flashing your tits in them films of Peter's, did you? And yes, if you must know, that is what I've wanted all along, ever since Liverpool, ever since we got married. But if you're too much of a bloody prude to . . .'

'And what about the horse? Do you mean to tell me you never . . .'

'Of course not. What would I want with a fucking horse?'

He put on his dressing gown. 'All right then,' he said. 'For-get it --- *darling*!' On his way out he added, 'Happy Christ-mas, I don't bloody think!'

By eleven o'clock that morning he was well on the way to being drunk and they had exchanged hardly another word. Jenny suggested a walk around the housing estate, hoping that may sober him up, but he said it was too hot and he was enjoying himself. Musa had everything under control in the kitchen. She was superfluous, unloved and desperately un-happy.

'Look, Kenneth,' she said, 'whatever you feel about what I said this morning, I want you to think about yourself, self-respect, about the job.'

'What do you mean – the job?'

'Our guests will be arriving in an hour's time, including our boss and his wife. What are Norman and Bessie Haworth going to think if they see you in this state before we even start?'

'It's supposed to be Christmas. Who cares?'

'Then there's the Sandersons. Just imagine what Rose Sanderson will make of this; it will be all over the compound that my husband was incapable by lunchtime.'

'That's it, isn't it? *My* husband. My common husband who can't even talk proper. You don't have to tell me you're ashamed of me, that's been obvious for ages. I saw the look on your face when Masoor said he couldn't come --- bloody relief. Thank God, you were thinking. Thank God I won't have to expose my posh friend to my uncouth husband and his common accent.'

235

'No, you've got it all wrong Kenneth, it's not like that at all. You act as though I think I'm something special, which I know I'm not. I just want us to . . . '

She was determined not to cry, but his accusations had made her doubt her motives. His face now showed some satisfaction; that he had wounded her.

'Go on then,' he taunted. 'Turn on the waterworks again.'

She willed herself not to cry. 'It's just . . . just that I want us to make something of this opportunity. It's a wonderful chance we've been given, and we mustn't spoil it. I've already had to ask Norman to give us time to put things right. He knows you've been going through a difficult . . .'

'Norman? You've been talking to Norman Haworth about me?'

'Only to tell him that you really are trying to control the drinking. You must, Kenneth, really you must. Otherwise . . .'

'Right! That's it.' He took his motor-bike keys from the side-board. 'That's the limit --- the absolute bloody limit! I'm off. Enjoy your fancy dinner party with your fancy fuckin' friends.' He stormed out.

Emmanuel opened the garage doors for him but Kenneth ignored his greeting of 'Merry Christmas' and she heard the Norton roar off out of the Close. She ran to the bedroom and allowed the tears to flow.

Ten minutes later there was a knock on the bedroom door. 'Cup of tea for you, madam. May I come in?'

'Come in, Musa.'

There was no need for subterfuge, for the servants would have heard every word, as they had during so many of the other quarrels. She dabbed her eyes with a tissue.

'Bless you,' she said. 'A cup of tea is just what I need.' She sat on the side of her bed while Musa poured, and he put in half a spoonful of sugar with just a trace of milk, as he knew she liked it.

'Kenmaster has gone to hospital, madam. That is what has happened. Sick for tummy and he cannot eat the Christmas luncheon. That is so, madam, isn't it?'

'Thank you Musa. Yes, that is what we will tell everybody. I will be out in a short while.'

55

Norman and Bessie Haworth were first to arrive. Jenny had met Bessie while Norman was showing her round the mill earlier that week, so she did not have the added problem of meeting a stranger. Tim Rostron, the weaving manager, came next. He was a regular visitor, a bachelor she found it easy to get on with. Finally the Sandersons, who may well have heard the row. Nevertheless, Jenny could think of no alternative but to use Musa's explanation for Kenneth not being there.

'He insisted we carry on as normal. I said I would go round to the hospital see him later, to find out if they will be admitting him. It's bound to be a while before he is seen, on a day like today.'

Norman took charge of the drinks. Once everyone was settled on the side stoep he took Jenny aside. Her explanation of Kenneth's absence had obviously not fooled him, nor probably did any of the others believe it. Their pretended concern for her husband's health had been unconvincing.

'You're coping well, lass,' Norman said, 'but wouldn't it be better if we all went home?'

'No Norman. A lot of hard work has gone into this party and Musa has been looking forward to it.'

'I can pop over to the club to fetch Kenneth. That's where he'll be, I reckon. I'll drag him out, if necessary.'

'That's very kind of you but I would prefer it if we carried on. I suppose I had better get used to this sort of behaviour.'

The lunch was a success, despite the fact that each of them had one eye on the front door, expecting Kenneth to appear. Bessie Haworth proved to be the catalyst, the sort of woman to enliven any party. She was younger than Norman but must have turned fifty, because they had two married sons and a grandchild. She had a fund of amusing stories. Jenny was amazed to find herself laughing, despite the pain deep inside her.

When the meal had been cleared away, she asked the servants to come back and gave them their presents. Norman went to his car and brought in Musa's bicycle, which he had been keeping for her. There was a watch for Adebayo and for Emmanuel five pounds, so that he could buy himself two pigs.

After that she told the servants they could leave, and she tuned in to the BBC World Service on the short-wave radio. They listened to the Queen's Speech.   Apart from the heat it was like being at home. Just before six o'clock the Sander-sons excused themselves to prepare for the party at the club and Tim Rostron left with them.

'Right Norman,' said Bessie, 'now you and I will go to the club to find Kenneth.'

'We can all go,' Jenny said. 'That would be best. I know how to handle him.'

'No,' said Norman, 'I'll go on my own. If he isn't at the club I think I know where he may be and, if I'm right, you two shouldn't be with me.'

*

The Christmas party at the club was just getting into swing and quite a few of the mill staff were already there. They said that Kenneth had been asked to leave an hour ago be-cause he was still in his shorts. Two of Kenneth's drinking pals were in the golf bar. He was 'well away', one of them said, but he planned to move on to the Goodluck Inn in the Sabongari.

As Norman walked across the club car park there was a crack of thunder, so he called at the rest house to collect his plastic mac and an umbrella. The rain was pouring down when he emerged.

He had no trouble finding the Goodluck Inn but Kenneth was not there. The place was almost empty; a few Nigerians were at the bar and a drunken European man sat at a table by the window embracing a young whore, who looked extremely bored and eyed Norman as a potential replacement. Two women came over to show him to a table and he ordered a Heineken. The woman who brought it sat down with him, assuming he was a client for her services. He asked her if Ken Thistlethwaite had been in.

'Yes. Kenny's just gone. Little bit pissed.'

'Do you know if he was going home?'

'No. He say him no agree with his wife today. Big quarrel they had. Goin' to see Patience, he said.'

'Patience?' He recalled some of his men talking about Patience. 'Can you tell me where she lives? I need to find Kenny.'

'Look mister, I don't want no trouble for Patience. She's a good clean girl and she always looks after Kenny nice when he comes here. Better you leave them be.'

Ten shillings bought him the address. He left half his beer and before he reached the door he could see that the woman was drinking it.

It was now dark. The rain was sheeting down and, as he ran to the car, he could feel it penetrating the collar of his plastic mac. Lightning shot across the sky and the street lights went out for a few seconds, then flickered back to life, faintly illuminating the deserted road, along which flowed a tide of rainwater.

He did not know exactly where to find the address he had been given but he headed for the part of town notorious for its warren of honky-tonks and brothels. The windscreen wipers could not cope with the downpour, so he stopped the car a little way off the road, waiting for the rain to ease. Three rain-sodden women emerged from their doorways to proposition him. He asked one of them where he could find Patience.

'You'll like me better, Johnny. Special rate for Christmas. One pound and you do what you like. Any way you want me, Johnny.'

He gave her a pound note but did not leave the car. 'Do you know Kenny?'

'The motor bike boy? Yes, I know him.' She looked suspicious so he gave her another pound.

'Have you seen him tonight?'

'Yeah. He just now came look for Patience.'

'Where can I find them?'

'She is Christian, so not workin' tonight. Gone home to her village I think.

That's what I tell Kenny. Patience is the only girl he likes to fuck, so him gone.'

'Home?'

'Dunno.'

Norman left the old town and joined the bypass, heading back towards Lafiya Close, but long before he reached the bridge he met a line of stationary traffic. Already soaked to the skin, he dispensed with the umbrella and got out to question the driver of the lorry in front of him.

'Ten minutes and never I move, sir. Some people say the bridge been struck by lightning. The police have been there since before I got here.'

Norman edged the Zodiac off the road, feeling the left-hand wheels sink into the sodden shale. He turned out the lights, locked the doors and set off towards the bridge. The impatient hooting of motor horns did not drown out the noise of the thunder. As he began to thread his way through the crowd he met protests, but when they saw he was a white man it was assumed that he had some authority and they let him pass. Nearer the front of the line of stationary vehicles the din of complaint had ceased, drivers no longer sounded their horns and passengers had drawn themselves under tarpaulins, resigned to the inevitable wait. From below the bridge he could hear the roar of the river, now grown to full spate with the evening's downpour.

The police had organised a single file of access for those who chose to continue the journey on foot and Norman joined the line heading south, prepared for a long walk back to Lafiya Close. Although heavy rain continued to fall he had dispensed with his umbrella and had reached that stage where there was no point in trying to keep the water from trickling down inside his clothing. The heat of his body made it feel as though he was wrapped in a wet warm towel.

When he drew close to the bridge there was a blockage, as people stopped to see what had happened. He stood on tip-toe to peer over the heads of the crowd and saw the Inspector from Okante South police station in charge of operations. The bridge had been cleared of traffic at the southern end, except for a lorry with a crumpled front bumper and radiator grille. Two policemen were using crowbars in an attempt to extricate the wreckage of a motor cycle from the railings of the bridge. An ambulance was parked in front of the police van.

The Inspector had obviously been off duty when he was called out. A long police mackintosh covered his peacock blue robe, the hem of which was sodden, and he had a pair of embroidered slippers on his feet. He recognised Norman's white face among the crowd and beckoned him through.

'I'm sorry, Mr Haworth. He's one of yours. It's the one they called Kenny.'

Norman noted the past tense. 'May I look?'

'He is a mess, I'm afraid.'

The Inspector signalled Norman to follow him to the ambulance. They passed a police Land Rover. The back doors were open and Norman could see an Igbo man sitting inside, dressed in a soiled white suit with a black cowboy hat, handcuffed and weeping. He looked no older than Kenneth.

Norman identified Ken more from his clothing than from what remained of the body. 'He was a relative of mine, will my identification do? I wouldn't want his wife to see him like this Inspector.'

'Yes, I agree it is better that she does not see him in this condition.' The Inspector replaced the black plastic sheet over the body and closed the doors of the ambulance.

243

'I ought to be the one to break the news,' said Norman. 'Any chance of a lift? My car's blocked on the other side.'

'We will go together. Shall we take a policewoman?'

'No, that won't be necessary. My wife is with her.'

'Right. Give me your car key, I will have it taken care of. By the way, I have had a blood sample taken. I expect the coroner will require a post mortem.'

As the police car passed the crowd which had gathered at the southern end of the bridge, Adebayo hid behind a tall Hausa man, though there was little likelihood of his being recognised by the manager. He was appalled by what he had brought about and that it had happened so soon. He still owed the ju-ju doctor four pounds.

56

Geoffrey noticed that the train was nearing Settle. He was on the way home from Scotland., and quickly left the dining - car for his seat in the first-class carriage, hoping to catch a glimpse of the green dome of his old school chapel.

It had been a long way just to interview one person, but the outcome of his trip to Hawick had been worthwhile. Iain Stewart was the ideal man for the dyeing manager's job. Geoffrey was surprised that someone of his experience was willing to accept a job in Africa, but Iain explained that the cashmere industry was going through hard times. His wife was a sister in the local hospital and a condition of their acceptance was that there would be a job for her out there. Geoffrey and his father had a standing arrangement to telephone Norman Haworth every Sunday at nine in the evening, Nigerian time. He hoped Norman would be available that Sunday, so soon after Christmas, for not only did he need to find out whether Mrs Stewart might get a post at Okante hospital, he had to ask Norman to tell the Thistlethwaites they would have to move out of their bungalow into one of the new semis.

He was expecting to be picked up by the company chauffeur at Preston station, so it was a great surprise to find his father waiting for him. They were well on the way to Blackburn before Harold got round to telling him the awful news.

'Thank God Bessie Haworth was there,' said Geoffrey. 'Did Norman say how Jenny is taking it?'

'Remarkably well, it seems. Shocked of course, hardly says a word, but no tears. They weren't getting on apparently, but there's bound to be a delayed reaction.'

Geoffrey pictured Jenny on that day not long ago, beautiful and happy, as she walked down the aisle on the arm of Abram Pickup. Despite the jealousy he had felt then he could never have wished for this to happen.

'We'll have to bring her home, Dad.'

'I've left Norman to decide that when he's talked to her.'

'What about Kenneth? The body I mean.'

'He's being buried out there. That's what the parents say they want. I've booked them to fly from Ringway tonight. They catch the Sabena plane in Brussels.'

'I can talk to Jenny when I get to Okante and find out what she wants to do.'

'Just a minute, lad, there's one more thing. You're not going to Nigeria to see Masoor. He's coming to us. I told him I wouldn't have Sykes on the premises but he's bringing his nephew.'

57

Jenny was not called upon to give evidence at the inquest. Norman was of the opinion that the coroner wanted to spare her the ordeal of recalling the events of that terrible day but, as Bessie later reported to Agnes Clarke, her silence left an element of uncertainty in people's minds, not least in the minds of Kenneth's parents.

After Norman and the police inspector came with the terrible news, Bessie made up a bed in the spare room of the bungalow and had Norman bring her things from the Rest House. She decided immediately that she must cut short her holiday and travel home with Jenny, but a date could not be fixed until after the inquest. Fortunately, they were able to bury Kenneth immediately after the autopsy, but the coroner was away in Jos until after New Year and, despite pressure from the Deputy High Commission, nothing could be done to have the case heard before the second of January.

Norman found tea chests and Bessie packed away the young couple's possessions, though she got no thanks for it. Not a single tear had the girl shed, not that Bessie had seen anyway. No sign of grief, even at the inquest. Bessie was convinced it was that servant of theirs who was responsible for the problems at the hearing. The coroner chose Musa as the first witness, after the police evidence had been given. Even Jenny appeared surprised at that and, as things turned out, it would have been far better if she *had* been called.

Musa began by sticking to his silly story that Kenneth had been taken ill on Christmas morning and had set off for the hospital, but when the coroner started to question him he soon let slip that there had been a quarrel. Then, after the lorry driver and his passengers gave evidence about the motor bike heading straight for them, it seemed there might be a suicide verdict. Things got even worse when they called that awful Sanderson woman from next door and all the gossip came out. It was a relief when the coroner stopped her and brought in a verdict of accidental death, but the damage had already been done.

After the verdict, Kenneth's parents did not speak to their daughter-in-law. They stayed at the Government rest house and Norman tried to patch things up, but they seemed convinced that Jenny had driven her husband to drink. They left without calling at the bungalow and took the Sabena flight from Kano on the fourth of January.

Jane and Bessie were driven to Kano the following day and shared a room overnight at the Central Hotel before their early morning flight to Amsterdam. Jenny said scarcely a word during the journey. Bessie did not press her into conversation. Better let nature take its course, she thought.

At Schipol they had less than half an hour to wait for the BEA connection to Manchester. Her elder son, Keith, met them at Ringway. On the way to Colesclough Jenny talked to him about the journey as though she were returning from holiday, but the brittle chatter was a facade; she still had that immobile face and her eyes were those of a sleep-walker.

As they drew near to Bright Street the curtain of silence came down again.

Mrs Clarke opened the door to them, already in tears. Her daughter just said, 'Hello Mum. Mrs Haworth can explain why I'm back better than I can. I'd like to go and lie down now', and went upstairs.

58

Mrs Clarke had taken a job in the Co-op drapery depart-ment, so she left each morning before her daughter was up. Seeing Jenny looking so drawn, and sallow beneath the tan, Agnes insisted she go out for fresh air and exercise. Jenny obeyed because that seemed the easier course.

She spent the early part of each day wandering aimlessly around the house, doing the occasional bit of cleaning. Just before twelve she would make sandwiches and a flask of tea, put on her old grammar school raincoat with its weather-proof hood, wrap a scarf round her neck and, with sand-wiches in her shoulder bag, she would take the path up Daisy Hill. Often it was raining when she set off but she did not care about getting wet. At the summit there was an Ord-nance Survey benchmark from which one could see the whole town of Colesclough and, further up the valley, the outskirts of Blackburn. On a clear day, if you looked the other way, past the breast of the hill, you could follow the River Coll to the point where it met the Ribble. Low cloud and drizzle had shrouded the moors since she came home,

248

but that did not matter to Jenny, for she could look either way and in her mind she could recall the view as it used to be on those warm spring days of her childhood.

The miserable weather was in keeping with her mood. In the daytime she was able to make her mind a blank. It was during the long nights, as she lay in her old bed drifting in and out of sleep, that she relived the events; memories and dreams confused. Her mind could not distinguish the nightmare from the reality, for both were equally terrible.

On Thursday of the third week the weather improved slightly. Instead of going up the hill she walked down Bright Street for the first time since her return home, then along Blackburn Old Road, past the entrance to the factories and across the main road to take the path which led down to the river. When she reached the dyehouse she tried to open the wicket gate in the boundary fence, but it was locked. At the main gate she almost went in, but then remembered that Kenneth would not be there. She carried on along the river bank towards the footbridge. One or two people greeted her but she did not reply. She had no appetite, so from the middle of the bridge she fed her sandwiches to the ducks, but some swans flew quickly downstream to chase them away and steal the bread she had thrown in.

Mist still lay over the river, but when she looked up she saw that the sun was beginning to break through, A shaft of sunlight illuminated the pub where she and Kenneth used to sit drinking their lemonade. She continued across the bridge and took the lane which would lead her to Layrocks village.

There were only two people in the pub, a young couple in hiking gear seated at one of the scrubbed wooden tables, eating what smelt like steak and kidney. She managed to say, 'Good morning'. There was no one behind the bar so

249

she rang a little brass bell on the counter. The landlady emerged from the living quarters wearing a pinafore over her floral dress.

'Ee, hello love,' she said. 'It's a good few months since we saw you here. Joan, isn't it?'

'Jane.'

'Sorry. Didn't I see in t' paper as you'd got wed, Jane?'

'Yes.'

'You're looking very brown.'

'We've been away.'

'You and Kenneth, that's what they call your lad, isn't it?'

'That's right, they did. But he's dead.'

At long last she had been able to say the word. Now the tears came, quietly at first, then uncontrollably. She supported herself on the bar by her elbows, with head lowered, sobbing.

'Oh, my poor love,' the landlady said. 'You'd best come through.' She lifted the flap of the bar, took Jenny by the hand and led her into the kitchen. The landlord was sitting by the fireplace reading his newspaper. Seeing Jenny's distress, he got up. 'Sit her down here, Mollie. You give her a cup of tea. I'll go and look after t' pub.'

It was easy now, the nightmare had been broken and she could talk freely, though what she was saying between the sobs could hardly have been intelligible, the words tum-

250

bling out in a jumbled cathartic stream, triggered by the simple admission. He's dead. The tea was far too sweet, but she drank it gratefully. Gradually her sobs subsided. She recovered her self-control and began to feel embarrassment at having unburdened herself to this woman, who was little more than a stranger, whereas for weeks she had been unable to talk even to her own mother. For the first time in many days she was hungry.

'You've been very kind to listen to me', she said. 'I'm better now. I'll go back into the taproom. Do you think I could possibly have some of that steak and kidney those two were eating --- and a glass of red wine, please.'

'No, you stay where you are, love. There's some pie left in th' oven but we've no wine, we get no demand for it up here, you see. I could let you have some sherry. Or a glass of port, happen.'

'Another cup of tea would be lovely, but just half a spoonful of sugar this time, please.' Then she realised how rude she had been. 'I'm sorry, I don't even know your name.'

'Heyworth. Mrs Heyworth. They call me Mollie.'

The clock on the mantelpiece said five-past three by the time she had finished the meal. 'I must be getting back down the lane before it gets dark, Mollie. You've no idea how grateful I am. Is that clock right?'

'We keep it five minutes fast, makes us sure to open up in time.'

'Still, I ought to go.'

'You live in t' mill rows, don't you?'

251

'Yes, Bright Street.'

'I wouldn't advise walking back along by t' river, love. It'll be dark soon and there were a woman attacked down there last November. Best catch t' bus. There's one goes at a quarter-past. Layrocks is where it finishes and it'll probably be waiting now on t' other side o' t' road.'

As Jenny was putting on her coat and scarf, the landlady kissed her on the cheek. 'Come and see us again, Jane. And don't trouble yourself; nobody's going to hear a word of what you said from my lips.'

'Goodbye then, Mrs Heyworth.'

'Mollie, please.'

'Goodbye Mollie . . . and thanks.'

As she was preparing to leave from the back door the landlady called her back.

'I know it's none of my business, but could I give you a bit of advice?'

'Good advice is exactly what I need at the moment.'

'What you told me about that place where said you were, Nigeria. You want to get back there, love. There's nowt for a girl like you round here.'

59

She got off the bus outside the Co-op and went in to see her mother. As soon as Mrs Clarke saw her daughter she knew that some change had taken place, but she was engaged with a customer. She measured out the six yards of curtain netting and cut it carefully, so as to keep a straight edge for hemming.

'Don't bother wrapping it Agnes,' the woman said. 'Just fold it up and I'll slip it in me bag. We don't want to keep this young lady waiting.' Then she recognised Jenny. 'Oh, it's your daughter, isn't it? How are you love? We were that sorry to hear your sad news. It must be very difficult for you.'

'Thank you Mrs Maloney. Yes you're right, it has been difficult, but from now on everything is going to start getting better.'

Jenny told Agnes not to buy anything for their supper; she would make their evening meal. At Macfisheries she bought two salmon steaks. Next door was Crabtree's greengrocery, where she had little hope of finding asparagus, but they had some. She bought a bottle of Chablis at the off-licence. Only now did she realise how rude she had been to those who called to give their sympathy. She had to begin mending fences. The person who deserved the biggest apology was her mother.

Abram Pickup had been the first to come. He and his wife Sheila called on their way back from chapel on the Sunday morning, but they stayed no more than five minutes. As he was leaving he said to Agnes, 'I'm sorry, we shouldn't have come. It's too soon, isn't it?'

Her bridesmaid, Mary Clark, came on Monday evening. She and her fiancé brought a huge bouquet with them. Jenny spoke hardly a word to them. Neighbours and women from the mill called, faces to whom she could no longer put names and to whom she had nothing to say. The house was still full of flowers, expensive at that time of year.

The shopping in her bags weighed heavy as she walked home and she stopped from time to time to put them down. There were a lot more cars parked in Bright Street than she had previously noticed. Some of the Pakistanis must be quite well off these days. Since her return she had been going around with her mind closed to what her eyes were seeing. It occurred to her that she would need her mother's help in remembering who had been to see her, or written letters of sympathy. She would call on them, or write to apologise for her rudeness.

Most important on the list of people she must see were a couple who had neither called nor sent condolences --- Mr and Mrs Thistlethwaite.

When she had almost reached home, she saw a car make a three-point turn at the top of the street and then pull up outside their house. A woman got out to ring their doorbell. Recognising who it was, Jenny was tempted to slip down the passage which led into Peel Street, but she remembered her new resolution and decided that she would face her visitor. She quickened her pace when she saw the woman abandon ringing and start to return to her car.

'Hello, Mrs Harrison,' she shouted. 'Here I am.'

Alice came down the hill to meet her. She kissed Jenny's cheek and took one of the shopping bags. 'I hope you don't mind my calling unannounced like this, but I saw these freesias in Crabtree's window and I decided I must take some up to Jane.' Entering the flower-filled front room, Alice remarked, 'Oh dear, coals to Newcastle I see. These make my little posy look a bit inadequate.'

'No, believe me, freesias are my favourites. It's very good of you to think of me.'

'I intended coming as soon as you got back but Geoffrey said you would need some time on your own.'

'That was very thoughtful of him. He was right, I did. But now, since this afternoon . . . I can't explain, but I really am genuinely pleased to see you.   It's rather cold in here, come through to the sitting room. Have you time for a cup of tea?'

There was no need to talk to Mrs Harrison, one had merely to listen. The conversation soon became a monologue, centred on Alice's family problems. Jenny failed to grasp why the forthcoming marriage of her elder son to one of the district's most eligible young women should be a problem, but she accepted that the intricacies of life among the moneyed classes were beyond her comprehension. It was comforting to have her introspection disturbed by this kind, rather stupid, woman. Only when the tea things were cleared away and she and Alice were in the kitchen drying the cups and saucers, was the real purpose of the visit re-vealed.

'I've got to admit, Jane dear, that I came with an ulterior motive. I want your help.'

Jenny owed the Harrison family a lot.

'Anything I can do, I will,' she replied with sincerity 'What is it?'

'I want you to come for luncheon at our house next Tuesday week. Shall you be able?'

Having lunch at The Little Lodge would certainly not be an unpleasant task. It had been one of her ambitions to see inside what was reputed to be one of the show-places of East Lancashire.

'Of course, I'd be delighted. Thank you very much. I don't have transport, though, is there a bus that takes me near to where you live?'

'Silly girl, I wouldn't dream of you coming on the bus. I'll have you picked up. Would eleven o'clock be too early? I want to be sure you're there when they arrive.'

'I'm sorry, Mrs Harrison...'

'Alice.'

'I'm sorry, Alice. Who shall I be meeting?'

'Oh dear, I am hopeless aren't I? Harold's always telling me my brain can't keep up with my tongue. No, I should have explained that the reason I want you to be there is that we are having some people from Nigeria and Geoffrey suggested you would be able to help me --- I'm useless with foreigners. It's an important meeting to do with the mill, so I thought having you there would mean they wouldn't keep on talking business when they come back to me for luncheon. I suppose they'll eat normal food? What do you think? I'll have to remember to ask Harold about that; he's very good about what different people will eat and won't eat. Perhaps you could . . . '

Once Alice was in full flow it w as necessary to interrupt. 'You didn't say who these people are.'

'Oh, I didn't, did I? It's a foreign man and his nephew. I should be able to be able to remember the name, it's something medical.'

Alice visibly racked her brain.

'They're called . . . just a minute. Yes, I've got it. The name is Masseur or something like that.'

60

Mrs Harrison had left by the time Agnes Clarke got back from work. Jenny decided not to mention that she had had a visitor, until she could think of the best way to explain the Masoors, more particularly Nico. But she did tell her mother how much she regretted her behaviour since she returned home.

'You really don't have to apologise, least of all to me. I'm sure everybody understood how upset you were, but I think you ought to go across to see Jack and Dot Thistlethwaite. I really don't know why they should bear a grudge, but I can understand how shocked they were. Bessie Haworth told me all about the inquest.'

So, soon after nine the next morning Jenny went the short distance to Cobden Street and knocked on the door of number 22. She was surprised to find Kenneth's father opening the door, because she had hoped he might be on his rounds. He stood for a few seconds, expressionless, before he took her into his arms and hugged her.

'Come in love, I'm right pleased to see you.' Then he shouted up the stairs, 'Come down, darling . . . it's Jenny.'

He took her into the front room. 'Sit yourself down. I'll put the kettle on. We've been that worried after the way we parted in Nigeria but we didn't know what to do for t' best. It's us as should have come to you.'

'I'm glad you didn't,' she said. 'I might have given you the wrong impression.'

The room was a mirror image of that at number 48 but more elegantly furnished. Jack Thistlethwaite was still a collector for his insurance company, but he now acted as area supervisor, responsible for five or six other representatives, who called on households throughout the Coll valley to collect the sixpence or shilling a week which working people traditionally paid towards their burial insurance. Many accused the Thistlethwaites of being penny-pinching, for they still lived in the home they had occupied since marriage, whereas it was known they could have afforded to move to somewhere more prestigious like the new 'executive' development, Gorsedale Close.

The interior of the house betrayed their affluence. They used their front room on a daily basis. A log-effect electric fire glowed in the hearth, purely decorative, because the Thistlethwaites had central heating. There was an Indian carpet on the parquet floor, they had a four-piece suite and matching jacquard curtains from Harrisons' 'Queen Anne' range. Not only did the curtains reach to the floor, a clear sign of affluence, but there was a pelmet which Jenny knew from her mother had been specially made by the Co-op furnishing department.

Jenny had been unsure of what welcome she might receive from her mother-in-law but as soon Dorothy Thistlethwaite entered the room she knew that all would be well. At once the women were hugging each other, shedding tears.

Eventually Dorothy said, 'Now then, this won't do will it? There's nothing can bring him back, as Father keeps reminding me. I was wanting to come and see you, love. Believe it or not it were in my mind to go across this afternoon, because how we left each other out there wasn't how it should be, was it?'

'No, but I do understand,' Jenny said. 'I don't suppose Kenneth told you how things were between us. I used to make sure he wrote to you, but of course I never read his letters.'

'We thought it were all OK with you and him. He seemed to like the life there, but Cousin Bessie came round last week and told us a bit more about what had gone on. It made us feel we happen ought to apologise.'

Jenny had not brought a handkerchief. Mr Thistlethwaite fetched a box of tissues for her. 'We've got through a fair number of these in the past few weeks, I can tell you, Jane,' he said. 'I reckon you must have an' all.'

Jenny dabbed her eyes and blew her nose, then went to sit beside Jack on the settee. 'I really did love Kenneth, she said. 'you must believe that. We were working very hard to put our problems behind us. Maybe it was because it was Christmas, but . . .'

259

Jack interrupted her. 'That's enough of that: you mustn't go over it all again. We both realise now that you did all you could. Don't we, Mother? Look Jane, I've got to start on me round, but before I do there's something important I have to tell you. I didn't get the death certificate through from Nigeria until last Friday. Did they send you one?'

'I haven't got one yet. Who sent yours?'

'Never mind that now. Suffice it to say that I took it round to our District Office in Bolton yesterday. You remember our wedding present? We never dreamt in our worst nightmares it could come so soon, but I had you both put down for twenty-thousand. They'll be sending you a cheque.'

'Twenty thousand?' She was aghast. 'Twenty thousand pounds! I couldn't possibly accept that.'

'It has to go to you love', Dorothy said. 'There's nowt sentimental about insurance. It's yours is that money.'

'No, you must have it.'

Mrs Thistlethwaite was adamant. 'We had him insured for more than that, love. Just think if it had been you instead of him, wouldn't you have wanted Kenneth to have it? Nowt will bring him back, but this could help you towards the sort of life you both might have had if... I'm sorry.'

She had broken down in tears again and Jenny went to comfort her. Kenneth's father pulled a watch from his waistcoat pocket, then went out to the hall and returned in his overcoat, carrying a briefcase and Homburg hat.

'Excuse me, Jenny. I've got to go, I'm late already. But don't forget you are part of our family now. If you want advice about what to do with the money, my firm has a department that helps.' He put his hat on. 'I'll see you around half past five, Dorothy. Now you two must go on and have a good cry if you like. It'll make you feel better.'

They heard the front door close behind him.

*

That afternoon Jenny took the bus to Burnley. In her new financial situation she had no hesitation in going straight to Fothergill's, the town's most exclusive ladies outfitters. She explained that she was invited to lunch at The Little Lodge.

'How nice,' the saleslady remarked. 'We used to get Mrs Harrison in here, but from what I'm told it's all Kendal Milne's and Samuels for her nowadays.   However, I do re-member the sort of thing she used to like when she was younger.'

She went to the stockroom and returned with a mid-grey woollen dress with a light pinstripe running through it. The dress fitted perfectly and the hemline was fashionably short, but the matching jacket was slightly too large for Jenny. Luckily the assistant found a smaller one.   This was not at all the sort of thing Jenny would have picked but, looking in the mirror, she decided it was a good choice.

When she showed her mother the outfit that night she said, 'Yes love, that's exactly right. Just the image you want, the attractive young widow.'

'Oh, Mum,' she replied. 'Don't talk like that. You make it sound as though I'm fishing for another man.'

Nevertheless, she decided to see if Dr Pewtress would let her have some of those new oral contraceptive pills.

61

If Percy Jenks and his friend Gustav were not working on Sundays they often took the coach from Victoria to Heathrow airport. Neither of them had ever been on an aeroplane, but they enjoyed the ambience and used to fantasize as to which exotic destination they might be travelling. They also loved what they called 'talent spotting'. Gus had a particular liking for young men in airline uniforms, so they would stand and watch crews coming through the arrival gates and speculate as to which of the pretty boys might be 'possibles'. They had both fallen for one particular fellow, a Swissair steward who was often on the midday flight from Geneva, though they had never got closer than smiling at him.

This Sunday, however, Jenks had come to the airport to collect Nico and his uncle, having driven there in his employer's Bentley. The flight he was to meet was already an hour and twenty minutes late. Earlier he had been down to stand beside the arrival gate when the Geneva plane came in and was thrilled when the lovely Swiss boy returned his smile. That had been the highlight of the day, but the prospect was gloomy, for when the uncle had last stayed at the mews cottage they 'had words', as Percy expressed it to Gus. He was not used to being treated like a servant and was glad that this time the Lebanese man was staying for only three days before travelling north.

At last he saw the Kano flight signalled on the arrivals board and refilled his cup from the expensive pot of tea he had bought. There was just time to finish it before he must go down once more to stand by the gate.

Eventually they appeared, and Percy was surprised to see the woman called Nicki with them. He quite liked her. She had been very generous to him when he gave her Nico's Nigerian address and it occurred to him that the fact that she had travelled with his employer might mean that she was 'the one.' This suspicion was strengthened when the uncle was dropped off at Brown's Hotel.

When they reached the mews, Percy was asked to carry the remaining luggage upstairs. Nico said, 'Miss van Vleet will be staying with us for a couple of nights, Jenks.'

'Shall I make up the spare bed, sir?'

'No, don't bother', was the reply.

Percy contemplated redundancy.

62

Harrie Harrison was predisposed to dislike Jane Clarke or whatever she called herself now. For years Geoffrey had sung her praises, and after she married that chap from the dyehouse he had mooned about the house for weeks like a sick colt. Now, Harrie's parents were going on and on about 'the poor young widow'. 'Quite sick-making,' she told her friend Clarice. So she protested when her mother said she must pick the woman up for the lunch party, because the chauffeur was collecting Cousin Pommy from Lytham. Alice had to drag her daughter from the stables at ten-to-eleven, still wearing dirty slacks and an old hacking jacket.

Harrie had been given one of the new Mini cars as a twenty-third birthday present. She drove to Colesclough in a time which her brother could not have beaten in the MG, and at the top of Bright Street the little car allowed her to do a single turn on full lock. She jumped out and rang the door of number 48.

Harrie took a gulp when she saw Jane.

'You must be Harriet,' the vision said. 'It's very kind of you to collect me.'

The zip of her dress was half-way down, revealing a vest. Harrie studied the delicate shoulders, the golden tan, the slender arms with just the slightest trace of soft down, bleached blonde by the sun.

'But I'm terribly sorry,' Jenny went on, 'I've got myself into a bit of a mess, can you possibly help me? I'm glad your mother didn't send a man. I don't normally wear a vest, but after Nigeria this feels like the Arctic. I'm terribly ashamed at the state of it and I've got it caught in my zip.'

'Come here, let me try,' said Harrie with some enthusiasm. The zip was irretrievably snagged in frayed wool from the vest, which was almost threadbare in places. 'I think I'll need to cut some away, do you have a pair of scissors?'

Jenny brought some from the kitchen. Harrie trimmed away part of the vest, freed the zip and pulled it down to Jenny's waist.

'I'm not going to risk that happening again,' said Jenny. 'I'll take it off.' She removed the dress, pulled the vest over her head and revealed a perfect little bust in a lace bra. Harriet stood enchanted, but the excitement was over all too soon. Jenny put the dress back on and asked Harriet to zip her up. She added a matching jacket which had been over a chair. The outfit was smart but severe, rather masculine; very much to Harriet's taste.

'That's better,' said Jenny, glancing in the mirror above the fireplace and running a comb through her short dark hair. 'Thanks a lot. Let's go.'

Harriet drove more slowly on the way home, in order to prolong the pleasure of sitting near to Jenny. Once, as she was changing gear, her hand accidentally brushed against a nylon-stockinged thigh and a frisson surged through her body. At first she could not think of anything to say. Awkward at the best of times, she was dumbstruck whenever confronted by anyone who sexually aroused her. Her affair with Clarice Waddington had taken ages to get off the ground. Clarice was three years her senior and a qualified solicitor. She worked in Blackburn but still lived with her parents, which limited their opportunities. Not until they attended the Horse of the Year Show did they spend the whole night together. It transpired that they were too much alike in their sexual preferences to be ideally suited as partners, and both agreed to allow other relationships. A couple of years ago Clarice had taken up with a barmaid from Clitheroe, but the affair ended when the girl became engaged to a coal merchant. Clarice took the rebuff badly, despite insisting that it had never been more than a fling.

Jenny remained silent and Harrie realised she would have to find something to say. 'We were terribly sorry to hear what happened... to your husband, I mean.'

'Thank you Harriet. Everyone has been very kind. Your mother brought some lovely freesias.'

'Yes, Mum's good at that sort of thing. By the way, call me Harrie would you? Except when Mum's listening.'

'Is that like Belafonte?'

'No, just drop the T'

Jenny could not at first relate this tall, lumpy young woman to any of the other members of the Harrison family that she had met, but then she recalled the portraits in Colesclough museum and immediately identified Harriet as a throwback, the same square jaw and broad shoulders, strong capable hands --- just like her great-grandfather Isaac.

'My brother says you're awfully clever,' Harrie said at last.

'How would he know that?' she responded, and then realised that she appeared to be agreeing. 'I mean, no of course I'm not.'

'Oxford? You were accepted, he told me.'

'Yes, that is true.' She did not wish to follow this through, so she asked, 'And you, Harrie, what do you do?'

'Work you mean? Well, nothing I get paid for. I help out at a vet's near our village. Just with the horses.'

'That must be fun. I've never ridden but I've always wanted to try.'

Silence again.

266

They were through Padiham and only a few minutes from Sabden before Harrie plucked up courage to make the suggestion, and it came out in a girlish gush.

'By the way, I don't know whether you would have the time. I mean, if you really would like... you see I have these three horses and I could pick you up from home. That is, if you would like to come for a ride sometime, you could come over to Sabden and...'

'Oh, would you? That would be lovely, Harrie. Would you be willing to teach me?'

'I would really enjoy that,' said Harrie, with more sincerity than Jenny could possibly have discerned.

63

As soon as they entered the drive of The Little Lodge two dogs ran out and chased the Mini all the way to the garage. Harrie parked alongside a Rover. Never having been used to animals of any kind, Jenny was afraid that the dogs might jump up and dirty her new outfit, but Harrie stilled them with a fierce word of command before she left the car. They sat obediently side by side, panting. Harrie patted both dogs as a reward for their obedience.

'Let me make the introductions. Do you know about dogs?'

'Almost nothing.'

'Well this one is Argo, he's a red setter, and the little scruff is Nemo. His ancestors must have been very sociable, because he's part labrador, with a trace of spaniel and possibly some terrier. Nemo was to become Jenny's favourite.

When they reached the drawing room Mrs Harrison was not there. A tall plump lady was arranging flowers. Harrie ran across to kiss her. The resemblance was remarkable, closer than between Harrie and her mother.

'Jane, I'd like you to meet my great-cousin, Pomona Hattersley, whom we call Pommy but everyone else is supposed to call Mona.' Jenny thought how elegant it was to refer to someone as a great-cousin.

Mrs Hattersley bent to kiss her on both cheeks. 'Thank you so much for coming, Jane. We appreciate that this is a difficult time for you to be socialising, but Alice and I are dreading meeting this Mr Masoor. He is said to be very rich. You've met him, I gather.'

'Yes, and he is really very nice. I'm sure you will all like him.'

'Excuse us, Pommy,' said Harrie. 'We'll go and find Mum and then I'll have to change.'

Alice was in the kitchen with a lady whom she introduced as Mrs Foster. She kissed Jenny on both cheeks, as Pomona had done. Jenny registered this as the polite way to greet women friends in future. Alice appeared to be flustered and the atmosphere between her and the cook was obviously strained.

'Thank goodness you've arrived, Jane. I'm expecting the men back from the mill directly. Harriet set off so late that I was afraid you wouldn't be here for another half-hour at least. And you, young lady,' she said to her daughter, 'get yourself washed and changed straight away. Would you mind going up with her, Jane? To make sure she puts on something suitable. By the way, that's a lovely outfit you are wearing. Where did you get it?'

'Fothergills in Burnley.'

'Really? Still there, are they? All right girls, off you go. Be sure to be down   again by one o'clock.'

Harriet's bedroom was at the back of the house, overlooking the garage, stables and tennis courts. It was almost twice the size of the living room of number 48 and surprisingly tidy, considering Harriet's obvious lack of organisation. No doubt there was a maid to clear up after her. There was little about the room which spoke of Harriet's personality. The brass bedstead and the rest of the furniture were early Victorian, the bedspread and matching curtains were heavy damask and there was a large oil painting featuring two scantily-dressed women.

Harrie indicated a chesterfield beneath the window. 'Sit down there and talk to me while I wash.' She stepped out of her working clothes and partly opened the door to a bathroom, so that she could continue to talk while she washed. 'What's the chap's nephew like? I gather you and he were quite friendly.'

Jenny's tidy nature led her instinctively to pick up the clothes which Harriet had left in a heap on the floor and she folded them into a neat pile, which she placed on a mahogany chest at the foot of the bed. 'Not exactly friendly. We were on the same ship going out. Who told you we were friendly?'

269

'Geoffrey. He told me you fancied him . . . the nephew I mean.'

'That's nonsense. How would Geoffrey know, anyway? He seems to believe he knows a lot about me.'

'He phones Norman Haworth every week.'

Jenny wondered what other gossip Norman passed on during these calls. 'I saw very little of Nico in Okante.' Why was she being so defensive? If she were not careful she may confirm Geoffrey's suspicions.

'Is that his name? Nico?'

'Nicolas, he calls himself Nico for short. Very handsome. You'll like him.'

'I'm not all that keen on men.'

Harriet stepped out from the bathroom, naked. She dropped her wet towel on the floor, opened a drawer in one of the tallboys, took out some underwear but did not begin to dress. It seemed as though this rather ungainly girl was inviting inspection of her body. Jenny got up and stared at the erotic painting rather than witness the exhibition. When she turned around she was pleased to see that Harriet was now standing in front of her huge walnut wardrobe, encased in sensible knickers and a bra. Her figure would have been improved by a corset. She threw open the wardrobe doors.

'All right then, tell me what I should put on?' There were lots of lovely clothes but Jenny decided that a plum-coloured trouser suit was the right thing for the occasion.

Harriet laughed at the choice. 'It's amazing you should pick that. You see, it's my old favourite. Mum and Pommy will have seen it hundreds of times before. But that won't matter, they never notice me.'

'Sit down and let me have a go at your hair,' Jenny said. It was what could unkindly be called mousey, though it had some natural curl. It could also have done with a wash, but there was no time for that. Jenny pulled it back and used hairpins and two combs to keep it up. She turned Harrie round to admire the effect in the mirror.

'Thanks,' she said, 'you're brilliant. Now come and choose me some shoes.'

'No, wait a minute,' said Jenny. 'Let's give you some make-up.' The whole of the dressing table was covered with bottles and jars.

'Good heavens, Harrie,' she exclaimed. 'Just imagine you having all this. I never saw such a collection.'

'Mum keeps buying stuff for me but I never bother with it. When you look like I do there's not a lot of point in slapping paint on.'

Jenny did not believe the bit about her not liking men; probably it was a compensation for the fact that her appearance put them off. She determined that, should they become friends, she would take Harrie in hand. With proper handling, and bearing in mind that she was rich, Jenny felt she could make Harriet Harrison into a highly marketable commodity.

271

64

The Lagonda arrived just after twelve-thirty. Alice went out to the front steps to welcome her guests and saw Mostyn Stainforth get out quickly from the back seat to open the front passenger door for Mr Masoor. Geoffrey had gone in his MG and would presumably be following with the nephew. The fact that they were early could mean that the meeting had broken down in disagreement. Alice looked for the expression on her husband's face to see how things had gone. Far from looking depressed, Harold had an un-characteristic grin.

'Alice dear,' he said, 'I would like you to meet Jacob.'

She had expected some sort of Arab sheikh but this fellow looked almost European; small, but handsome in a foreign sort of way. After she had shaken his hand he gave her a little parcel wrapped in expensive gift paper.

'A small token for you, Mrs Harrison,' he said.

Alice was unsure of the etiquette; should she open it now or later? Curiosity won the day. As she tore off the paper she noted that the box was from Asprey's. It contained quite the most gorgeous ruby and diamond bracelet she had ever seen. How could she possibly accept such a gift from a per-son she had never met before? Hoping for guidance, she turned to catch her husband's eye. Obviously he read her mind, for he merely raised his eyebrows as if to say, how should I know?

Jacob misinterpreted her indecision. 'I am sorry. No doubt you already have such a thing. I can easily take it back and have it changed for whatever it is that you prefer.'

'Oh no! It's wonderful, Jacob. Here...' Alice drew him to her and gave him a kiss on the cheek. 'Thank you ever so much. I hope you don't mind me kissing you, but you're in Lancashire now. We don't have London manners up here. Come on in.'

There was still no sign of Geoffrey and the nephew.

*

Harrie and Jenny were ready by one o'clock, as promised. On the way down they heard male voices among the buzz of conversation. Harrie froze, looked at her watch and listened. 'Oh, God; it looks like I'm in trouble. The chaps have arrived.'

'Don't worry,' said Jenny. 'We're not late.'

Immediately they entered the drawing room, Jacob Masoor came across to Jenny and kissed her hand.

'Mama Beauty, it is lovely to see you, we have missed you so much. You look enchanting, my dear.'

These remarks silenced all conversation and Jenny was aware that everyone was looking in her direction.

'Why do you call her that?' someone asked. It was Pomona.

'I do apologise, said Jacob. 'I did not mean to embarrass you, Jane.'

273

Harrie stood by Jenny's side, shuffling. 'And I am also impolite to you, young lady,' he went on. 'You are Miss Harriet, no doubt. I am Jacob Masoor.'

After he had kissed Harriet's hand she stared at the back of it, as though searching for evidence of the exchange. He turned to answer Pomona's question. 'The name I have just used is that of a new soap which one of my companies is manufacturing. Jane has been helping us by taking part in some publicity films.'

'How exciting,' Alice said. 'I expect to hear all about that later.' She took Jenny's arm. 'I wonder if you know the Stainforths, Jane?'

Jenny vaguely recognised the short, thin lady standing beside Pomona. The pair of them together looked, as Jenny's mother would have put it, 'like a penny-farthing'. The small woman was introduced as Margaret Stainforth. She was in her late fifties with close-cropped grey hair. She wore a floral suit which would have been more appropriate in late summer. Her husband came over to introduce himself. Jenny knew him to be the leading solicitor in Colesclough, senior partner in Hall and Stainforth.

'I'm glad we have met, Mrs Thistlethwaite,' he said. 'I'm company secretary of Harrisons and I need to have a little talk with you sometime. We can leave it a week or so if you wish, in view of – um – I mean due to . . . your bereavement.'

'Is it about Kenneth?'

'Well, yes it is. I can't really explain here and now. Shall we make an appointment?' The following Wednesday afternoon at three was agreed upon.

274

Jenny searched the room. 'I do hope Nico is not unwell,' she asked Jacob. 'I was told he would be coming today.'

'He and the young Mr Harrison will be here shortly. Nico said he would like to take a walk on the lovely hillside near the mills. No doubt you know it well.'

'That's where I live.'

65

Mostyn Stainforth held power of attorney for Roger, who had returned to Germany. Pomona did not attended the meeting, because Harold assured her that it was unlikely that any decision would be reached that day. In case her vote was needed she had given Geoffrey proxy, trusting him to act in the best interests of her side of the family. She too had seen the look of satisfaction on Harold's face and was intrigued to know what had gone on. She cornered him by the drinks table.

'Well?'

'Later,' he said. 'In the library when they've gone.'

Conversation was beginning to flag. Harrie tapped Jenny's arm and whispered,

'Let's nip out to the stables, I'll show you my horses,' but the opportunity for escape vanished when Mrs Stainforth came up to Jenny.

'How is your mother, dear? I knew Agnes when we both worked at Harrisons, before I married Mostyn.'

Alice intended to have a sharp word with her younger son when he eventually appeared. The party was becoming a disaster. Nobody wanted more sherry and the Lebanese man drank only mineral water. Clearly they were all hungry. She had told Mrs Foster to have the first course ready by a quarter to two. It was only avocado and prawns, so wouldn't spoil, but unless they started soon, the lamb would be either overcooked or cold. She was on the point of going to the kitchen to check progress when she heard the front door close. The room immediately became quiet.

'Stick your coat in there, Nico. We're late, so prepare to grovel. They'll be in the morning room.'

Everyone turned towards the door as the two young men entered. Jenny studied the faces of the women to see their reaction to Nico. She could sense three middle-aged hearts a-flutter, and even Harrie showed interest. He had had his hair cut to a reasonable length. He and Geoffrey were about the same height and both wore similar navy-blue blazers.

Jacob set off round the room introducing his nephew. As they came towards where she was standing her heart began to pound, but before they reached her she heard Alice say, 'Right everyone shall we go in? Harold, lead the way please.'

Jacob Masoor sat on Alice's right at the far end of the table and Jenny was placed opposite him, next to Geoffrey. She had been invited as an intermediary, but her services proved unnecessary, as it was clear that Mrs Harrison and Jacob hit it off from the start. He appeared to be fascinated by Alice's monologue concerning the history of the Harrison family. She had reached the point where her elder son had taken up his military career.

'I recognised your nephew's tie,' she said. 'I wonder if Roger and he may have met while Nicolas was serving in the Royal Artillery. It's nice, don't you think, that men can so easily identify themselves?' No comment was needed from Jacob, for she immediately went on to the subject of Roger's engagement.

Harrie had spent the whole meal so far simply staring in Jenny's direction but saying nothing. When Jenny smiled at her she looked away. Harrie was seated next to Jacob and was obviously relieved by her mother's monopolising of their guest. Geoffrey had been hardly any more communicative than his sister and spent more time talking to Mrs Stainforth. He seemed to be treading on eggshells, in case he upset Jenny by reviving memories of the last time they had met --- at the wedding.

In reality there were few recollections of her life with Kenneth that now disturbed her. It was as if she had played the lead in a tragedy that had concluded. The curtain had come down and the actors had left the theatre. Then she looked to where Nico sat, talking animatedly to Pomona, who was giving him rapt attention. No, she was wrong. Not all the actors had departed.

Hoping to relieve Geoffrey's anxiety, she said, 'By the way, I was never able to thank you for the champagne. Remember? You arranged for a bottle to be sent to us at the Adelphi in Liverpool on our first night there?'

'Oh yes. I hope you both, er . . . ' he began, but did not seem to know how to finish. Instead he asked, 'Did Mostyn tell you he wanted to see you?'

'Yes, I have an appointment for three o'clock on Wednesday.'

'I'll try to be there too. There are one or two things we need to discuss.'

'Are they not things we could talk about now?'

'Well, if you really don't mind. Are you sure it's all right?'

'Go ahead.'

Apparently he and Norman Howarth had been discussing her in their last telephone conversation. Musa had called on Norman to ask what he and the other servants should do. They needed to have some money but did not want to start looking for other jobs if madam was coming back. Norman had agreed to continue to pay their wages until Jenny let him know whether it was in order for them to try to find other work.

'Maybe the new dyeing manager will want them,' she said. 'I would be sorry to lose them but I think they should go to someone else. And could you arrange for them to have an extra month's salary and deduct it from what's due to me.'

'All right, I'll arrange that with Norman.'

'Do you know what's happening to my training school? I should hate that to fizzle out.'

'That woman from Rhodesia is looking after it; I can't remember her name.'

'Mrs Sanderson.'

It had not taken Rosie long to get her foot through the door.

'Is there anything else we need to talk about?'

'Well, yes,' he said. 'The contract --- about your salary principally.'

'I assumed that would all be over.'

'No. Mostyn and I had a word about it before today's meeting. This first month will be considered compassionate leave and after that there will be terminal leave, based on how long you served.'

He hesitated, 'Perhaps we should talk some other time?'

'Please go on. This isn't upsetting me, really it isn't. It's better to get it all settled. The firm has been very considerate in letting me come home like this but I should feel happier not to be even more deeply committed. I'd be grateful if you could arrange for my salary to be stopped at once.'

'Are you sure? You're still entitled . . .'

'Please,' she insisted.

'All right, if that's what you want. I can understand how you feel. I'll tell Norman in our next telephone call.'

'And?'

'There's the question of your belongings. I'm sorry, but we're going to have to use the bungalow for the new dyeing manager. I understand you had all your stuff packed up before you left so we can easily arrange to send it on.'

'Thanks, Geoffrey. May I have a little time to think?'

That was the end of the conversation because Jacob had turned to her.

'Now, Jane my dear, forgive me. I have been so enthralled by what Alice has been telling me, that I have completely ignored you. Tell me, when will you be returning to us?'

66

It was almost four o'clock. The Masoors were being driven back to their hotel in Burnley and the chauffeur was going to drop Jenny off at Colesclough on the way. Margaret Stainforth was helping Alice and the maid with the clearing-up. The rest were in Harold's study, which was called the library, though there were few books there: he was not a great reader nor had his father been. Harold was just concluding his summing-up.

'So that's just about all we have to tell you, Mona. I agreed to let them have a reply within the month, although Masoor originally wanted the answer before he flies back next week.'

'I think we'd be daft not to accept.' said Geoffrey. 'It's a far better deal than either Dad or I ever expected.'

'Do you mind if we go through it again?' Pomona asked. 'Mr Stainforth, you
explain it. You put things more clearly, being a lawyer. I'll write some notes, so I can tell the boys.'

'If you wish,' he agreed, 'but I'd rather you didn't put anything in writing. Let me visit your sons, Mrs Hattersley, so that I can explain in person. What was proposed today must remain absolutely confidential until we give Mr Masoor our answer, and if there are pieces of paper around . . .'

'All right,' Pomona broke in, her tone somewhat acerbic. 'I understand, but surely you will be telling Margaret? And you, Harold --- you'll want Alice to know, won't you?'

'No love, not at this stage. Alice isn't good at keeping secrets, bless her. For the moment Mostyn and I will tell our wives as much as we think they need to know. Carry on then Mostyn, but make it quick. I think we all could do with a cup of tea, or maybe something stronger.'

Mr Stainforth checked the shorthand notes he had made at the meeting:

J.M. Holdings (Nigeria) Ltd to acquire 48% of I H L @ £350 per share = £1.68 million.
2. Masoor Société Anonyme to have option to purchase title to Daisy Hill for £250,000 (contingent upon planning consent). Note --- check archives re original building permission granted to Isaac.
3. JM to join board. (P. Sykes as alternate)
4. Decision by 21 March 60. (Harold to telephone Roger)
5. Palatine Amalgamated to merge with IHL effective 1 August 60. Geoff to be consultant for rationalisation study.

'All right,' he said. 'Here goes . . .'

*

When he had finished Pomona said, 'Well, that all seems very generous. But what puzzles me is why the Masoors are interested in us, if they aren't taking control. I don't mean to be rude, Harold, but there must be other investments that would give them a better return?'

'It's our land they want, Mona. Grandpa got planning permission to build houses right across Daisy Hill and Mostyn thinks we might have a chance of getting it renewed. So if they do develop it we'll get a sizeable cut.'

'I see. This deal seems to get better and better. But --- I promise this is my last question. Can you tell me what this Palatine Amalgamated is all about, and what are you supposed to do with it, Geoffrey?'

'Go back to your school days, Pommy,' he said. 'I'm sure at Casterton you were taught that Lancashire is the 'County Palatine'. That's where Plantagenet Sykes got the name for his company.'

'Yes, I do know what Palatine means, Geoffrey, but what are you supposed to do with Mr Sykes's business?'

Harold intervened. 'It's Masoor's business really. Sykes started it but now he's only a front man. You know, what sticks in my craw is that we have to have him as Jacob's alternate. But we'd best make him as welcome as we can, I suppose. Sorry, son. Carry on.'

'OK,' Geoffrey said, 'Palatine has so far acquired seventeen spinning and weaving mills up and down the county. I suspect that a lot of them must be rubbish but, if the duds were weeded out, I've no doubt the rest could be made profitable, especially with the back-up our firm could give them. But Dad insists that before we take it on we send somebody round to have a look at them, and Masoor asked me if I would take the job.'

'But you are off to Nigeria, aren't you?'

'Not yet awhile he isn't,' Harold replied. 'This inspection is more important. In fact, I can't manage these changes alone, so he may not be going out to Africa at all. I intend to try and persuade Norman Haworth to carry on in Okante. We might put him on the Board as a sweetener.'

'Well, you certainly seem to have had a good meeting,' Pomona said. 'You can count on my vote. And I imagine Roger will turn a cartwheel when he hears about it.'

67

Jenny sat beside Mr Foster, the chauffeur. She had hoped to be put in the back of the car with, Nico but he and his uncle wanted to talk. She was intrigued to know what it was all about, because during the luncheon party there had been an atmosphere of suppressed excitement. Possibly some deal had been struck over the Okante mill. Had it been sold to the Masoors? Whatever had happened, she had no means of eavesdropping, since they were talking their own language. Arabic it sounded like.

Mr Foster was the husband of the lady who had cooked the lunch. Jenny occasionally used to see him at the mill but he wasn't very popular with the workers. Gives himself airs and graces, they used to say. She planned to ask him to drop her at the bottom of Bright Street because she didn't want the Masoors coming into the house. When they were approaching the junction of Bright Street with Blackburn Old Road, she said, 'Thank you, Mr Foster. It will be fine if you drop me here.'

'Certainly not,' she heard Jacob say. 'We must deliver the young lady to her door and, if my watch is correct, it is time for afternoon tea. Maybe Mrs Clarke would be so kind as to make some for us. I would very much like to meet her.'

'She will still be at work, I'm afraid,' said Jenny, hoping this may deter them from coming in. There was no fire laid in the front room, which was where important visitors were entertained. It was rarely used and was always spick and span. Her father had completely redecorated it while he still had his job with the paint firm. The fireplace was marble, the carpet was a Wilton and the furniture was in good condition. All in all she was proud of their front room, but she couldn't very well ask her guests to sit in the cold; she would have to take them to the back living room. Then it suddenly struck her that her old school vest was lying over the back of the sofa and she started to panic. With enormous relief she heard the driver say, 'I'm sorry, Mr Masoor, but I promised to get straight back when I've taken you to Burnley so that I can drive Mrs Hattersley home to Lytham.'

'In which case,' Jacob said, 'we must make an appointment to see you before we leave, Jane. I wonder if you could join us for lunch. We are staying at the Kierby Hotel in Burnley but young Geoffrey tells me there is a pleasant restaurant at a place called Waddington in the Ribble valley. Do you know it?'

'The Gamecock, you mean.'

'You know it?'

'Yes, it's a very nice place. I would love to come.'

'We shall see you tomorrow then. Nicolas will arrange to hire a motor car and we will pick you up --- at what time, my dear?'

'It may pay to get there early,' she said. 'Would quarter-to-twelve be all right for you?'

'So it shall be,' said Jacob. 'Nico, open the door for Jane.'

It was then that he kissed her. As she turned to wave them goodbye she noticed the net curtains twitching in the bedroom of number 45. She didn't care.

68

Harriet and Geoffrey were very close. Despite the bickering which had been their habit since early childhood, they would always go to great lengths to defend each other, not only from outside attack but from within the family. There was not quite three years between them, and more than five between Geoffrey and Roger, which made their elder brother a respected but somewhat remote figure, whom they regarded as likely to take their parents' side whenever sides needed to be taken. Geoffrey was the only member of the family who knew of Harriet's proclivities, though he suspected that their father realised she was 'not the marrying kind', as he might have put it. Geoffrey quite liked Clarice and, since he knew that she made his sister happy, he had never done anything to discourage the affair. Harrie, for her part, was always more than willing to intervene in what she

285

considered to be Geoffrey's best interest. She prided herself on having been the prime mover in breaking his attachment to the scheming Mabel Butterworth. The coup de grace had been her suggestion to Mabel that her elder brother was terribly lonely out there in Germany and would greatly appreciate having a pen pal.

Harriet and Geoffrey had become used to sharing their secrets, so it upset her when she became aware that her brother had struck up a relationship which he had not told her about. Her spies confirmed that Geoffrey had stopped visiting the Astoria ballroom in Rawtenstall some time ago, but still claimed to spend his Saturday evenings there. One night he telephoned to say that his car had broken down and that he was being put up by his friend Richard; a story which Harrie did not in the least believe. When he returned home she demanded the true details, but Geoffrey stuck to his story. She assumed he was having an affair with a married woman.

They were in Geoffrey's bedroom after the meeting in the library.

'You're wasting your time Harrie. I knew you'd fall for her but I'm certain she's not your sort.'

'You don't understand the least thing about the way I feel,' his sister replied. 'Anyway, *you've* no room to talk. All those years you've been dreaming of getting close to her and then when you do, all you can talk about is business. I heard you. Really, Geoffrey, you're quite pathetic, I despair of you sometimes.'

'You don't expect me to declare undying love at the dining table, do you?

With all that lot present? Besides, she needs to be treated very gently after what she's been through. It's you I'm thinking of, Het. Don't get yourself hurt. Stick with Clarice.'

'This has got nothing to do with Clarice and me. Yes, of course I'm well aware that Jenny's straight, but that doesn't prevent me falling in love with her. Love doesn't need to be reciprocated.   All I could ever wish for is that I might just stay close to her, look after her --- and talking of sticking to what we've got, I could give you the same advice. Stick to your mystery woman, whoever she is. You stand no more chance with Jenny than I do, because whatever she might say it's obvious she's besotted with Nico. Didn't you see the way she looked at him?'

'He is a nice chap though, isn't he?' said Geoffrey, ever gen- erous. 'I'm sure we're going to get along famously.'

69

The bedroom curtains of the house opposite twitched again, as the black Humber Hawk drew up outside number 48 and the same young man got out and rang the doorbell.

Jenny was ready and stepped out immediately, in case they said they wanted to come in. Not that she was ashamed of the house. Her mother always kept it spotless and Jenny had maintained the standard now that she had taken over the cleaning. She intended to ask them in for tea when they brought her back, but this time she would have her mother for support and there would be a fire lit in the front room. This was half-day closing at the Co-op.

Jacob Masoor was in the back seat of the car and Nico opened the other back door so that Jenny should sit next to his uncle. Before they set off, Jacob presented her with a white gardenia which he pinned to the lapel of her jacket. Both men wore expensive sports jackets, so her tweed suit had been the right choice. She did not have a suitable top coat to wear, but it was warm inside the car. However, snow began to fall as they left Colesclough.

'Do you know the way?' she asked Nico.

'He has been studying the map,' said his uncle, 'but when we get to... where was it, Nicolas?'

'Clitheroe. The turning towards Waddington seems to be in the town centre, so could you let me know when we are approaching it?'

'Yes, it is hard to find. I remember.'

'Now Jane,' said Jacob. 'I have asked you to sit with me because I have some things to tell you, which I did not wish to say in public.'

He told her that the *Mama Beauty* advertisements were now being shown in Nigerian cinemas and the agents were delighted with the response. They wanted to mount a follow-up press campaign and later they hoped to make some shorter black and white films for showing on television in Lagos, Senegal and the Ivory Coast. Jumy had been photographed for some press shots but the agents wanted pictures of 'Mama Beauty' herself. Ideally, he said, they would have liked to have the two women together again.

'Of course,' Jacob went on, 'Peter Ogondo and I both realise it is too soon to think of asking you to come back, although

288

we do hope that eventually you will. He suggested that you might agree to go to a photographer in London who could make a portfolio for the press campaign. These photographs could be used alongside those of Jumoke and possibly they could --- oh dear, what is that word, Nico? Put alongside?'

'Juxtaposed.'

'That's it. They could have someone photographed alongside you in London and juxtapose photographs of Jumy with those of that person, to make it appear that you are together.'

'I'll do anything I can to help.'

'That is wonderful, my dear. Thank you. The London office of our advertising agency will arrange it. I will ask Miss van Vleet to contact them as soon as we get back.' Hearing that name, Jenny wished she had never agreed, but it was too late.

By the time they reached the inn the snow had ceased to fall and the sun was out again. They were given a table in a window alcove. The summit of Waddington Fell wore a white cap and there was a light powdering of snow on the fields below; a romantic backdrop, in keeping with her mood. She had grown to like Jacob Masoor but she could not avoid wishing she was alone with Nico.   She was determined not to ask after Nicki van Vleet. Today Nico was hers and she would savour the moment. Let the bitch go hang.

They all followed the proprietor's recommendation of Truite Colbert for the main course, even though she had chosen smoked salmon as a starter. The men began with Pendle duck pate. Jacob drank only mineral water so she and Nico shared a bottle of Sancerre, though she ensured that he took most of it. Half-way through the meal he sought her hand under the table and gave it a squeeze. She asked him to bring her up to date with news of Okante. He said he would do so as far as he could, but that Jumy wanted her address, so that she could write to her. (Jumy was the one she could rely on for the really important gossip).

The Okante hotel was now taking residents and there was to be a big official opening in October to celebrate the first anniversary of Independence.

Jacob said, 'I shall be in Kano among my family, but I will raise my glass to Mama Beauty and regret that we do not have her back with us to join the celebrations.' She did not believe a word of what he said but it was charming of him to say it.

Then, much to her surprise, the conversation turned to the subject of Daisy Hill. Nico said how much he had enjoyed his walk there with Geoffrey before lunch on the previous day and Jacob more or less invited himself to tea when they took her home, saying that he was looking forward to seeing the houses in Bright Street. 'I do hope we shall have the pleasure of meeting your mother,' he said. 'I am sure she must be very proud of you.'

This had never occurred to Jenny. She found herself saying, 'Yes, I suppose she is,' then realised she must sound to be conceited.

After lunch, as they walked across to where the car was parked, Jacob said, 'I will drive back. You young people can sit in the back and pretend that I am your chauffeur.'

They sat close together and she took hold of his hand. Suddenly reminded of their last real conversation, at the TV studio, she felt intuitively that she was about to be given bad news. Jacob had tactfully switched on the car radio so they could talk freely, but Nico still spoke in a whisper.

'I wish I didn't have to be telling you this, but I'll soon be announcing my engagement. I would hate it if you were left to find out from the newspapers.'

Her mouth was dry and her heart was pounding, but she managed to mouth the word "Congratulations." She was even able to say, 'Pass on my best wishes to Nicola. It is her, I assume.'

'Yes,' he said in a flat tone. 'It's Nicki. Oh Jane, I've made the most damn-fool mistake.'

'You are telling me she's pregnant?'

'Yes, and she wants to keep it."

Of course she wants to keep it, you stupid man. How else can she get hold of your money? That is what she wanted to say

'And do you love her?'

'No, but I think we can make it work. Obviously she's delighted to be having the baby.'

At her age, Jenny wanted to add, but managed to refrain.

Instead she said, 'You have a lot in common don't you? I meany you like to travel and . . .' She could think of nothing

else which might unite them, apart from a shared enthusiasm for sexual intercourse.

He helped her by interrupting, 'So am I, of course, pleased
about the baby, I mean.' Jenny still had hold of his hand and
tried tactfully to release it, but he would not let go. 'It's you I
love, though,' he said.

Though she tried to avoid it, she was beginning to cry. Fortunately, this time she had a handkerchief. They spent the
rest of the journey in silence, her head against his shoulder,
his arm around her. By the time they reached Colesclough
she had regained her composure.

Seldom had Jenny seen her mother so elated. Jacob was at
his most effervescent, compensating for Nico's rather dour
performance.

When they had gone Agnes said, 'The uncle is absolutely
charming, isn't he? Not a bit of side on him. But that Nico!
Is there something wrong with him today or is he always
like that? Good looking though. A few years back I could
have fancied that one.'

70

Bright Street was unexpectedly quiet when she got up on
Saturday. The clatter of the milk float usually woke her, but
when she went to the window she saw it was still struggling
to get up the street. A coating of snow lay on Daisy Hill and
she saw that children had already rediscovered the thrill of
sledging, just as she and Kenneth had done each year. They
were in for a traditional Lancashire winter.

On Sunday morning she went to chapel for the first time since she came home. Mr Fazackerley embarrassed Jenny by making a reference to her in his sermon, which was always an impromptu oration, thought by some of the faithful to be a direct message from the Almighty. At the end of the service she was greeted as though she had never been away. People queued to say kind things to her. Kenneth had been a regular member of the congregation and they were genuine in their faltering expressions of condolence. Abram and Sheila Pickup walked with her to the bottom of her street. They thanked her for her letter.

'There were no need to write like that, though', said Sheila. 'We took no offence, did we, Abram?'

He said how upset he was by the latest slump, the extent of which Jenny had not fully appreciated. As usual, Harrisons was bucking the trend, though Daisy Mill was back on single shifts. 'As you know, Jenny,' he said, 'we've seen some ups and some downs in the cotton trade, but I reckon this could be our last slide down t' Big Dipper.'   He mentioned the names of several people she had worked with, who had lost their jobs.   'You'd know hardly anybody in t' shed today,' he said. 'All me weavers are chaps now --- Pakistanis. They're good workers, I'll say that for them, but what I want to know is, what'll happen to 'em if we have to close down? They won't want to go back home, will they?'

As she walked up Bright Street she kept to the slushy road. The council had treated the four streets with salt grit. Householders were trying to clear the pavement. She noticed how many were of Asian origin.   Everyone bid her good morning.

293

The snow continued to fall throughout Monday and Tuesday.

*

On Wednesday morning, Jenny found her long leather boots and walked through what was now deep snow to the top of Daisy Hill to look down on the valley. It was a scene from Lowry --- matchstick people battling against the wind along the four streets below her, smoke blowing across from Harrisons' boiler house chimney, but down in the town she could see that the roofs of several mills and slipper works were still covered in a white blanket, evidence that they were no longer in business. Looking down on this panorama, once so familiar but now alien to her, she remembered the words of that kind landlady. 'There's nowt for a girl like you round here.'

After her lunch of soup and toast she went upstairs to change for the meeting with Mr Stainforth. She had intended to dress up, but from the bedroom window she could see more snow falling and being formed into drifts by the increasing wind. Instead of the tweed suit she had planned to wear, she put on a blue turtle-neck jersey and grey corduroys, and carried her Fair Isle sweater downstairs with her so that she could slip it on before she left the house. Her boots were by the fire, not yet quite dry, but she pulled them on. She left a note for her mother, donned the sweater and her father's old blue duffel coat, which still hung on the stand in the vestibule. She set off for the High Street feeling nervous, as she used to do when on a visit to the dentist.

71

The entrance to Messrs Hall and Stainforth's office *did* resemble that of her dentist's surgery. It was along a corridor which it shared with the Burnley Building Society and Horrocks' estate agency. She had passed by the entrance countless times. The stairs to the first floor were not carpeted, but had rubber edging to protect the risers. One did not get an impression of the prosperous business she knew this to be. At the top of the stairs was a half-glass door with the firm's name in gold lettering and the message, *Please enter.*

Mr Stainforth was standing in the small reception area, in conversation with a man whom he introduced as his partner Alec Ainsworth. (She knew there was no longer a Mr Hall).

'You're a few minutes early, Jane, but that's a good thing, because I have another client at half-past.' He held open the door of his office, 'Come through.'

The receptionist followed them with a tea tray, which she left on a table in front of the ancient leather settee.

He poured two cups of tea. 'Let's sit on the sofa. Help yourself to milk and sugar.'

Jenny noticed that he had a file with Kenneth's name on it. She plumped down far too deeply and was glad she was not wearing a skirt.

'I gather from your late husband's father that there was no will.'

'We didn't think,' she replied.

'No. Few young people do, unfortunately. However, Mr Thistlethwaite has instructed us in the matter and I'm sure we can sort things out with no problem, but I told him you must also agree – as the next of kin. I'm not touting for the business but it would be most convenient if we were also acting for you.'

'Please, if you would.'

'That's fine then. Did you bring a copy of your late hus-band's contract with Harrisons?'

'No, you didn't mention that and I suppose it must be packed up in Okante. Before I left I didn't think about that sort of thing.'

'Of course you wouldn't. Sorry. Never mind, I have the firm's copy. We'll share.'

She recognised the document he took from Kenneth's file. He spent a moment looking for the clause he wanted.

'There we are --- clause eight. As you may remember, it starts off with bits about injury at work, then . . . ah, this is the part we want. Let me read it to you,

In the event of the death of the Employee while in the service of the Company it shall pay to the estate of the Employee an amount in pounds sterling equivalent to ten times the annual salary mentioned at clause 3(a) of this Agreement or such greater sum as may then be the basic annual salary of the Employee... I'm sorry that's in what you may call 'legalese', but do you follow how it affects your situation?' He paused.

'Yes. I must have read that before we signed but I'd forgotten all about it.'

'So, did Kenneth have any salary increase since he started at Okantex?'

'No, we'd been there less than a year.'

'Then let's look at 3 (a). Don't let your tea get cold, by the way. OK, there we are, one thousand eight hundred pounds was the salary, so that makes it a round eighteen thousand. I shall need the death certificate. Do you have it?'

'No, but I understand his father has.'

'Shall I get in touch with Mr Thistlethwaite then, or will you?'

'I'd rather you did,' she replied and added involuntarily, 'Oh dear, I find this so embarrassing.'

Mostyn feared she was about to cry. 'Do forgive me, Jane. It was insensitive of me to be so direct. Would you like a tissue?'

'No, thank you. When I said embarrassing, that's not what I meant exactly. I'm not at all sure whether . . . you see, I'm already getting twenty thousand from an insurance policy that Kenneth's parents took out for us, and there's more than six hundred in our bank account in Nigeria, and about nine hundred in the Trustee and then there's our building society --- it's all too much for me to handle, Mr Stainforth.'

'My word,' said Mostyn. 'That makes you quite a rich young lady, doesn't it?'

297

'Oh, and I forgot about a payment I should be getting for some advertising work I did in Nigeria. That could be a lot more --- I'm not sure how much. It seems such a responsibility; what to do with it, I mean.'

He stood and took her by both hands to help her out of the sofa. 'Come on over to the desk, my dear.' He picked up the telephone.

'Wendy, will you ask Alec if he can look after my three-thirty. It's right up his street, a contested divorce. And could we possibly have some fresh tea? Some chocolate biscuits too, if we still have any.'

72

After her talk with Mr Stainforth Jenny passed the Horrocks estate agency. She had a look in their window, hesitated, then decided to go in. The person she assumed to be the manager was talking on the telephone. He smiled and gestured to her to go over to the desk of his woman colleague, whom Jenny recognised as someone who had been at her school.

'Hello,' the girl said, 'Jenny, isn't it?' She offered a chair. 'Remember me?'

It suddenly dawned on her that this it was one of those who had originally made Jenny's life such a misery at her infant school. They became reconciled when both moved on to St Peter's but lost touch after that, because this girl failed her eleven-plus. As a child she had been unusually tall and wore spectacles. Now she obviously had contact lenses and, though still above average height, she had a good figure. Her hair, which had been nondescript, was piled into a blonde beehive. The overall result was that she looked quite attractive. She wore a wedding ring.

The young woman's face took on that expression of pity which Jenny had come to dread. 'We was all very sorry to hear about . . .'

Jenny cut her off, 'Thanks.' She could not remember her name. 'I came in to ask about the new properties. Those called Gorsedale Close.'

'You've had a look in the window, then? They're lovely aren't they? Let me give you the literature.' She went to a rotating display stand, took out some brochures and handed three to Jenny.

'Right, let's look at the semis first. I'm supposed to call them *Linked Executive Homes* but you and me understand each other, don't we? They're really nice I can tell you. Me and my husband took the show house. A bit pricey, which you have to expect that these days, but because I work here we got a discount.'

'How much?' Jenny asked.

'I don't see that's any of your . . .'

'No, I don't mean what discount did you get. I mean how much do the houses cost?'

'Oh sorry. Hold on, I'm supposed to tell you about them first.' She adopted the tone of a schoolgirl reciting poetry. *Three beds, downstairs loo, galley kitchen, oil central heating, double glazing throughout, own choice of colours for the bathroom suite.*' She paused and consulted a notebook.

'Trouble is I think them might all be spoken for.' She shouted to the manager who was still on the telephone, 'Gorsedale Close? Linked executive?'

He spoke into the receiver, 'Hold on just one sec, would you,' then he covered the mouthpiece. 'Sorry, all gone.'

'I could put your name down in case there's anybody gives back-word,' said the saleswoman, whose name, Jenny now remembered, had been Heather Robinson.

'So how much were they?' she asked.

'Two thousand eight-fifty.'

'Carry on. What about these?' She picked up the brochure entitled *Detached Luxury in a Rural Setting*.

'Oh, them's really super.' Heather had abandoned her 'posh' voice. 'Still only three bedrooms but the main bedroom has enn sweet facilities. Farm'ouse style fully-fitted kitchen, L-shaped lounge diner --- it's nearly all glass is the lounge diner. Big patio doors and further up the hill than me and my hubby's. You can see right over to Rawtenstall from t' patio. But, wait for it --- three thousand nine hundred and fifty pounds.'

'And is there one of those available?'

'There's six almost finished and they're all reserved, but there's eight more goin' up. I'll take you tomorrow provid-ing the snow's not too bad. I couldn't bring me car in this morning, the Close were blocked.'

'What about these,' Jenny enquired. She picked up the brochure headed,   *Ranch-style living. Move into 60's luxury!*

Now you're *really* talking. Absolutely bloody marvellous, pardon my French. I'm supposed to call them 'Ranch-Style Residences' but in the language you and me understand they're big luxury bungalows. There's none finished, yet but I can't begin to tell you how smashin' they're going to be. You know Tommy Capel, him as has the garages?'

'I know *of* him.'

'Well, he's put his name on one, has Tommy, so that just shows you doesn't it?
Three reception, four bedrooms, two of them double enn sweets with sunken luxury avocado bath and gold-plated taps. Just imagine? Gold-plated taps! And the other two bedrooms are called 'singles' but they're big enough for doubles. At any rate one of 'em's bigger than me mum and dad's living room at home. Then behind t' kitchen they have what they call a 'utility room' with direct entry to heated double-garage --- I could go on forever. But I hardly dare tell you how much.'

'Go on, surprise me,' said Jenny.

'Are you ready? Five thousand seven hundred and fifty pounds. Domestic appliances not included, and five hundred quid non-refundable deposit.'

'Put us down for one of those, would you, Heather.'

'Us?', Heather echoed, apparently jumping to a wrong conclusion.

'My mother and me.'

301

'Oh, sorry. I thought perhaps . . .'

'Five hundred pounds, did you say?' said Jenny, opening her cheque book.

73

The cheque from the Northern Temperance arrived in the first post the following Friday, before Mrs Clarke had left for work. Agnes had been told there was to be an insurance payment but not the amount. 'Gracious me!', she said. 'That's certainly a tidy sum; you'll have to get some advice on what to do with it.'

'I did Mum. Mr Stainforth and I discussed it, and I might as well tell you, there's more to come from Kenneth's contract with Harrisons.'

'No wonder you were upset. If only your Granny was alive. She'd have known what to do; she was always good with money. I haven't time to talk it all over now but we'll have a word when I get home tonight.' Agnes was putting on her coat and scarf.

'Meantime, give me your building society book and I'll pay it in right away, so it can be earning interest. Don't forget to sign your name on the back of the cheque.'

Jenny had decided to follow Mostyn Stainforth's advice. The £18,000 from Harrisons was to be put into an investment trust, from which she could draw the income if she needed it, but for the moment the dividends would be re-invested in more shares. Half the £20,000 from the insurance would be put into the building society and the rest kept on deposit at Barclays, until she decided how much of it she wanted to spend. Five hundred pounds had already been spent as deposit on the 'Ranch-style residence'.

That evening, after the supper dishes had been washed up, Jenny and Agnes sat down together at the sitting-room table. Jenny took out the financial summary that Mostyn had made for her and they went through it carefully. Then she mentioned that she had put their names down for one of the Gorsedale Close houses. She had not expected her mother's reaction.

'What on earth would someone like me want with a ranch? I was born in Bright Street and Bright Street is where I'll end my days.'

'But Mum, you don't seem to realise. In four or five years this will be like a suburb of Karachi.'

'Shame on you, girl! I never thought I'd hear a daughter of mine talking such rubbish. They're very nice people are the Pakistanis. I'll take you down to Mr and Mrs Quereshi at number seven. A pleasanter young couple you couldn't wish to find, and the way she keeps the house is a credit to her, especially when you think how many people she has living there. Plus the rent's in the bank on the dot at the beginning of every month.'

'I didn't mean to say they weren't nice people, Mum. I'm sure they are, but just think about what it will be like when you're the only white person round here. What will you have in common with the neighbours? Number 45's been sold to some, I hear.'

303

'Good riddance,' said Agnes, 'she's an old Nosey Parker. We'll be better off without her sort.'

'All right then, think about me. I'm not sure I want to stay in Bright Street. Do at least come with me and take a look at the new estate.'

Agnes was beginning to get angry. 'Don't talk so daft, girl. You're going on as though this was the end of the world for you. You're a young woman, for goodness sake, twenty-three. You've your whole life ahead of you.' Then she added, 'Anyway, have your own fancy house if you want. I'm not so sure as I want you hanging round me.'

'Mum. Don't say such things. It's your happiness I'm thinking of.'

'I'm sorry, love. I didn't mean it like that, but you're a normal healthy young woman and you need a man. We all do. Why do you think God gave us these bodies and these urges? Don't think I didn't hear you in your bedroom of a night time.'

Jenny felt herself blushing. 'Oh dear, you make me feel so ashamed.'

'Rubbish. It's natural; part of growing up. All girls do it one time or another. All I'm trying to tell you is that you mustn't start thinking that side of life's over.'

*

Jenny was alone in the house when the postman came with the express delivery, which turned out to be merely a handwritten note.

Jane darling,

304

My heart went out to you when I heard of dear Kenneth's tragic accident, but what can one say? LIfe must go on, I suppose. Nico gave me the <u>super</u> news that you agree to have piccies taken. Can you make it end of next week? Up on Thursday, to be done on Friday? Would have phoned, but N says you don't have one. Have provisionally booked you 4 nights at Rembrandt Hotel (in Thurloe Place) Confirm soonest to my secretary on above number advising arrival details.

Understand N told you our wonderful news. I'm in <u>7th heaven</u> darling! ! !   Wedding will be in Salisbury (<u>our</u> Salisbury I mean, not Wilts). You will get invitation and <u>must</u> come.   I'll be in Africa to see my parents about wedding arrangements but not to worry, because you'll be met at Euston by Nico's man.

> *Fondest love,   Nicki*

P.S. Chap meeting you is called Jenks. Wears grey bowler and will wave a card with your name on it.

74

Jenny had never been to London before. As the train neared Euston Station in the foggy dusk, she could not suppress a feeling of intense disappointment. The run-down terraced houses with back gardens full of rubbish and rickety sheds, were not what she had expected of her capital city. It was the rush hour. Even before she left the train, she could see that all the traffic was in one direction, a mass of people escaping the city. When she had surrendered her ticket she hugged her small suitcase to her body, to prevent the charging horde from banging into it.

The concourse of Euston was larger and grander than either of the main Manchester stations, but she recognised Mr Jenks immediately, a plump man of medium height. He wore the promised grey bowler hat, and a grey overcoat with an Astrakhan collar. A piece of white cardboard was attached to the top of his rolled umbrella. It bore the name MASTERS.

'Hello, Mr Jenks. I'm Jane.'

He had a posh voice. 'Welcome to the metropolis Miss Masters. Here let me take that.' She gratefully surrendered her suitcase. 'It is hard to find taxis at this hour, so I regret that we shall be travelling by public transport.'

'Could we go on the underground, please,' said Jenny. 'I've always wanted to.'

'Certainly madam.' No one had called her 'madam' since Nigeria. 'There will be ample room on the trains going our way. As you may have noticed, the Gadarene swine are all heading away from town, and we happy few shall soon have London all to ourselves.'

She was slightly claustrophobic and had anticipated that descending into the bowels of the earth might be a frightening experience, but having Mr Jenks beside her gave her confidence, just as Peter Ogondo had done on the aeroplane. People on the other escalators appeared blasé about what she found an exciting experience and no one seemed even to notice the advertisements along the escalators, some of which Jenny considered to be very rude --- women with their private parts evident through skimpy knickers. Even the men seemed to ignore them.

As Mr Jenks had forecast, their carriage was almost empty. They were to change at Leicester Square and she was looking forward to seeing the heart of London's entertainment district, but Mr Jenks explained that they would be remaining below ground. He was not unfriendly, but spoke only when spoken to. She asked him whether she would see Mr Masoor when they reached the hotel.

'He is away today in a place which I understand is called Hemel Hempstead,' he said, 'but he asked me to tell you that he will be back tomorrow afternoon and will call on you at the Rembrandt around tea time.'

They walked the short distance from the tube station to the hotel, where a letter awaited her. Mr Jenks handed her suitcase to one of the bellboys and gave him a tip. 'Now, if that will be all, madam?'

'Yes, thank you, Mr Jenks. I'm most grateful. I could never have got here on my own.'

'Just Jenks, please madam. I will wish you good evening, then. We shall be meeting again, no doubt.'

The letter was from the office of an advertising agency. A cab would collect her at nine the following morning to take her to the photographer, whose studio was in Soho. She was to charge all expenses at the hotel and make a note of any extras, which she should give to Mr Masoor before she left. When she got to her room, there was a box on the bed containing a gorgeous pale-blue afternoon dress. It fitted perfectly.

She did not have an enjoyable evening. In the bar before dinner she had a glass of dry sherry, but no one seemed to want to talk to her, not even the barman. The restaurant was empty when she went in and she had almost finished her meal before an elderly couple came in. They merely nodded as they went past. After taking coffee in the deserted lounge, she went to her room and switched on the television set. It was only eight-fifteen. She had never seen television before, but was not impressed. When the nine o'clock news and the weather forecast had finished she switched off and wondered if she dare take a walk outside, but from the window she could see that it was raining quite hard.

She felt very lonely. Only the prospect of seeing Nico tomorrow made the visit seem worthwhile.

75

A taxi arrived as promised, at five minutes to nine the following morning.

'You know where we're going, do you?' she asked the driver. 'Beak Street, the Tiptop Studio.'

'Yes darlin', Sid's a mate of mine.' He eyed her up and down as he held the door open for her. 'You what they call an exotic dancer, are you?'

'I am making an advertising commercial.'

'Please yourself ducky,' he said, as though he did not believe her.

The fare was already paid, but when he deposited her in Beak Street she gave him a generous tip, which caused him to say in an apologetic manner, 'No offence, darlin'?'

As she entered the building it struck her that this studio could have been the choice of her adversary, Nicola van Vleet. After the cab driver's remark she could imagine Nicki's plan to demean her, but she was determined not to fall for the bait and give up. The basement was a strip club, closed at that time of day. Tiptop Studio was at the top floor up a dingy staircase. One of the doors on the first floor had a card bearing the name *Madamoiselle Lucille*, another read *Private Model (No clients without appointment)*.

When she rang the bell of Tiptop Studio she heard a male voice shout, 'Half a mo.' She waited more than two minutes before the door was opened by a small man with lank blondish hair which must have been dyed, for he was in his late fifties.

'Sorry to keep you, I was developing.' He looked her up and down and remarked, 'Yes, I see what they meant; very tasty.' Jenny's face must have registered her annoyance.

'Don't mind *me*,' he said, 'only thinking aloud. It's just that I get a fair lot of old scrubbers through 'ere --- not often I see the genuine article.'

Having come up such a seedy staircase, she was surprised to find the studio to be a pleasant open-plan room. It had a parquet floor and some beige rugs. The furniture appeared to be Ercol G-Plan. On the tables in the waiting area were fashion magazines and copies of *Country Life*. The man, who did not introduce himself but must be Sid, opened a drawer in the reception desk and studied a letter. He inspected her more closely.

'Mind if we wash your 'air? That's what the instructions say.'

309

'I suppose so, if they think it necessary,' she said, further offended.

'April,' he shouted. A young black woman appeared through bead curtains in the rear wall of the studio.

'April, dearest, would you give this lovely young lady a quick rinse? Keep it wet but plump it up a bit.'

'You tanned like that all over?' the photographer asked Jenny.

'Where it shows,' she replied. Both he and April found that amusing.

'Come through please,' said the girl.

The dressing room was cleaner than she had feared. 'You want I wash it or you do it you'self?' April said in a strong West Indian accent. She had a good figure but a spotty face.

'Would you, please? I don't want to splash my dress.'

'It's very smart. That what they gave you to put on?'

'Yes, it is lovely, isn't it? They sent it round to my hotel. I can keep it.'

'OK, lean back.' April started to shampoo her hair. 'You don't want to mind what Sidney say, by the way. He's sweet really. Him don't mean no harm.'

'No doubt he knows his business. Are you his model?'

'Used to be, but now he's teachin' me photography. Very good photographer he is, too --- an' him quite safe."

'Safe?'

'I mean no messin' about wit' people like you an' me, because him queer. Sometime back he used to work for *Picture Post* an' suchlike' but now he's just doin' glamour. That client what sent you, they know he's good, so they don't mind that he take them other type pictures.'

'Did you do glamour?' Jenny asked her.

'No, me face ain't that good so I just use to do tit an' bum. But I never done plumbin'. Nothin' like that type o' thing.'

'Plumbing?'

'Yeah, you know. Like between the legs.'

'Oh, I see.'

Sidney popped his head through the bead curtains. 'Sorry to disturb you my sweeties but I've just finished reading up the gen what they sent me. Says you're supposed to 'ave just come out of the shower, Miss Masters, so you've got to wear a white bath towel. Get her one April, there's some big ones in the prop cupboard.'

Jenny thought it time to draw the line, 'I'm sorry, Sidney, but I don't think I'm prepared to do that sort of shot.'

He held out the letter for her to read. Look, there --- "just above the bust", it says. Don't worry, I promise I'll keep it decent. I'll not give them no tit, just a bit of cleavage.' She noticed that the instructions came from the genuine agency, but she still suspected the hand of her adversary.

'All right then.'

'We'll do them shots first, if you don't mind, then you can dry your 'air for the dressy bit.'

She returned to the studio wearing the towel. 'How do you want me?'

'Don't tempt me, duckie,' he replied with a camp giggle, then apologised once he saw the expression on her face. But when he started the photography he became serious; she could tell she was in the hands of a professional. It was hot under the lights and her short hair quickly dried, so she had to go back and wet it again.

'I enjoy this,' he said when she returned, 'Reminds me of my legit days. You're a very pretty woman, did nobody tell you that?' She warmed to Sidney.

'Head up, just a bit, please --- that's it. Lovely! Now look away from the light, left profile please. Now look at me --- no, not like that. Don't pout.'

'I didn't know I was pouting.'

'It's them lips,' he said. 'Suppose you can't help it. You know, Miss Masters, a girl like you could earn a fortune round here in Soho. Don't mean tommin' neither.'

Jenny guessed what 'tomming' might mean. 'Does glamour photography pay well?' she asked.

'Yes, good money. Someone like you could earn twenty sovs a session, easy.'

'And how much do they pay for plumbing shots?'

'Oh, dearie me!' he exclaimed with a high-pitched shriek. 'What has our naughty April been telling you?'

'Don't be cross with her. I'm just curious. Not that I'd ever consider...'

'No darlin', don't even think about it. But just supposing. If a girl like you was willing to do open-legs stuff it would be minimum fifty. Fifty quid an hour... might be more if you sold yourself proper. And you could double that if you was took with a bloke.'

'My word,' said Jenny, 'it beats what they used to pay me in the weaving shed.'

After another few poses Sidney said, 'Right, that's enough of that. You can get dressed now.'

As she was leaving he said, 'Just a mo, I don't suppose you'd be willing to drop the towel for one or two shots? Just to please Uncle Sidney?'

'You suppose right,' she replied, and went back to put her dress on.

The instructions from the agency required that Jenny should appear to be talking to another woman (who would, no doubt, become Jumy in the final print). Sidney called April in for these shots. Then he carried on with Jenny alone for five more minutes, speaking only to give instructions. Before the poses were completed, a good looking blonde girl arrived to be photographed. She seemed to be a regular visitor because she went straight through to talk to April; one of his 'glamour' models, Jenny assumed.

When the photography was finished she asked, 'What happens now?'

'Now I develop, edit and touch up where it's necessary, then it all goes to the agency. By the way, make sure they send you duplicate copies --- you can make a nice little portfolio from what I just took.'

'Thanks for the advice, Sidney. I didn't mean to be rude but I couldn't contemplate the sort of thing you suggested.'

'Quite right too, luvvie. That face of yours has value, a higher value than the likes of me can afford. Bye now. I'll phone for a cab.'

'No' she said, 'I'd like to walk down to Piccadilly Circus.'

'All right, but don't talk to no one; there's some naughty people round here, even at this time of day.' He held the door open for her and shook hands.

'Bye darlin', and don't forget, if you ever want to earn some real money.' He handed her his card.

As he closed the door she heard Sidney say, 'OK Doris, ready now. Let's be seeing that lovely bum of yours.'

76

This was London as she had imagined it to be. Even the sleaze of Soho was more the reality than that grey approach to Euston had been. In Swan and Edgar she bought a head-scarf for her mother. Then she walked up Regent Street to Oxford Circus. Her feet were telling her she had walked enough: she wanted to save some energy for Harrods, determined to buy something for herself in this store, to which she never thought she could aspire.

She caught the tube to Knightsbridge and took lunch in the hotel. Despite the expense account, she was brought up not to buy a meal when there was one already paid for.

It was only just after three when she got back from Harrods but she found Nico waiting for her in the hotel lobby. He kissed her on the cheek.

'I'm awfully sorry,' she said.' I do hope you haven't been waiting long, I didn't think you would be here so early. Mr Jenks said teatime.'

'I got back from Hertfordshire an hour ago, had a quick bite and came straight round. They said you'd gone shopping but I decided to wait. By the way, you look absolutely gorgeous.' He was excited; he didn't normally talk so freely. 'Is that the new dress Nicki chose for you?'

'Did she? It was delivered to the hotel with a note from the shop saying I was to keep it but I didn't realise it was her choice.' Much as she liked it, she now doubted if she would want to wear it again.

'Look,' he said, 'why don't you pop upstairs with your parcels and then we'll walk over the road to my place and have tea there. It'll be cosier than here. Then this evening I'm going to make a meal for you. Do you like...'

'Hold on. Let's sit down and think about this.'

'All right,' he said, 'but I don't want to waste any time that we can spend together.'

She went across to one of the settees and he joined her, unwillingly it seemed.

'Listen Nico, it's lovely to see you again, but is this wise? I'm not sure I should be spending *any* time alone with you. I hope I don't have to remind you that you're engaged to be married.'

'Of course not, and that's exactly why the time we spend together is so precious to me. She's gone to Africa to arrange the wedding, but she's expected back tomorrow afternoon and I have to fly to Newcastle in the morning. We only have tonight.'

'You don't seem to understand. I ought *never* to be alone with you.'

He looked downcast, but then he smiled. 'I'll tell you the phrase that springs to mind, Jenny. "The condemned man ate a hearty breakfast." Please don't deny me that.'

'All right then,' she said. 'Wait here. Give me twenty minutes, I want to wash the filth of Soho off me.'

*

'What a lovely little house,' she said as he held the front door open for her.

The ground floor was 'open-plan'. To give the impression of greater space the settee and chairs seemed to be smaller than average. After he had shown her the neat galley kitchen he said, 'Come and see the rest, and ran ahead of her up the stairs. There were two bedrooms and a small bathroom. The main bedroom covered the whole frontage of the house and was large enough for a house twice the size of this one. She searched for evidence on the dressing table, and was pleased to find no make-up, no powder or perfume; not a sign of a feminine presence in the room. She was immensely relieved, unreasonably so, since she was well aware that Nicki must at least be a regular visitor. On top of the chest of drawers was a stuffed toy, a pink panther.

'He's lovely, Nico. Fancy you having something like this.'

'It's not mine,' he said. Jenny quickly replaced the animal.

Nico had noticed her reaction. 'OK, we'd better get this straight. Nicki thinks this place is a bit poky, so she has kept her old flat in Dolphin Square. Also she's a bit of a stickler for, what does she call it? Propriety --- that's the word she uses. However, she does stay over from time to time. But that doesn't necessarily mean that I love her, does it?'

'It's no business of mine what you do or how you feel. Let me see the other bedroom then we'll have that tea you promised me.'

In the spare room he kissed her. Afternoon tea was forgotten.

*

By the time they heard the key in the front door Nico had completely undressed, she had removed her blouse and skirt and was beginning to unhook her bra. Each instinctively recoiled, then Nico said, 'Don't worry, that will only be Jenks. He won't bother us.'

But the intrusion had disturbed her and quenched her excitement. 'I'm sorry Nico, I can't go on. Not with him in the house.' She saw disappointment written on his face and the evidence of his arousal was all too obvious.

'Can I . . . I mean . . . is there something else I can do for you?'

'No not that, it's you I want?' He drew her to him. 'At least may I have another kiss?'

It was then that they heard a heavy tread up the stairs. Someone moved about in the main bedroom for a minute or so before their door burst open.

'Bastards,' Nicki yelled. Instinctively, Jenny jumped into the bed and pulled up the duvet.

'Get out of there you little cow.' Jenny was struck dumb.

'It's not . . .' Nico began.

'Shut up,' she said, returning the offensive to Jenny.

'Talk about the Merry Widow! I've never seen such a bloody hypocrite. You're nothing but a scheming whore.'

She took her large handbag by its metal chain and took a stride across the room. Nico placed himself between the two of the assuming Jenny would be the target. He stood with arms outstretched and his still-erect organ pointing bravely at the aggressor. Nicki took a swing at Jenny, who covered her head with the duvet. When the bag caught Nico's arm, the chain broke and it flew open, causing most of the contents to disgorge around the room. Something heavy must have fallen on Nico's foot because he yelled in pain and sat on the side of the bed to nurse his toes.

The loss of her personal belongings appeared to have taken some of the edge off Nicki's wrath and she went on hands and knees to retrieve what she could find. Nico handed back the quarter-bottle of vodka which had hit his toes. By this time the sign of his ardour had subsided and he began to help Nicki gather up her belongings, which Jenny felt sure the woman must be embarrassed to see displayed. Apart from the obvious things such as purse, enamelled powder-compact, cigarette lighter and Balkan Sobranie cigarettes, there was not only the vodka but some packets of male con-traceptives.

Nicki stuffed the retrieved items back into her bag. 'Where's my lipstick?' she demanded. 'Look under the bed.'

Both women stared involuntarily at Nico's bare buttocks as he lifted the valence to search underneath.

'Here you are,' he said, handing back the lipstick, 'that's about it, I think.' Unembarrassed by his nakedness, he stood to confront her   'Now listen, Nicki . . .'

'Don't try to think of some bloody excuse,' she said, almost laughing. Your cock said it all. You're a dead loss Nicolas, do you know that? Thank God I found out in time.'

'You can't just walk out, darling.' Nico's pleading tone sickened Jenny. 'What about our baby?'

'There never was any bloody baby, you fool.'

Jenny spoke at last. 'You mean to say you're not . . . ?'

'No, of course I'm not. I was amazed when he fell for the oldest trick in the book, and if you think he's going to be faithful to you you're even more stupid than you look. You're welcome to the randy sod.'

She turned to Nico as she left. 'You can fuck the arse off her for all I care.'

At the door she delivered her parting shot, 'If you think you'll get your ring back you're one off, matey. You'll be hearing from my lawyer. Tell Jenks to bring me my stuff.'

While she was trouncing downstairs they heard the front door open and Jenks say, 'Oh hello, madam, what a pleasant surprise. It's tomorrow I thought . . .'

'Out of my way, you smarmy poof.'

Five minutes later they were dressed and ready to face Jenks.

'Am I to assume that this is the last we shall be seeing of Miss van Vleet, sir?' he enquired,' as he poured their tea.

'Not you I'm afraid, Jenks. She wants you to take her belongings over to Dolphin Square.'

'That will be a pleasure,' he said. Since the engagement, he too had seen the rougher side of Nicki's character and was glad to be rid of her. Was this pretty one to be the replacement, he wondered.

'And you, Miss Masters? Shall I be bringing your belongings over from the Rembrandt?'

'No, thank you Jenks. Tomorrow is my last day in London and Mr Masoor and I will not be seeing each other again.'

Nico stared in amazement. After his manservant returned to the kitchen, he said, 'Just what did that mean?'

'I'm sorry, Nico, but one of the awful things she said struck home. It's far too soon for me to be considering any attachment. I was carried away by the novelty of all this.'

He looked crestfallen. 'Why? Surely you aren't afraid of silly gossip. With Nicki gone there's no need now to pretend, and I'm not going to let you just walk out of my life for the sake of what she would call 'propriety'. To be perfectly brutal about it . . .' He hesitated. 'No, sorry..'

'What? Go on,' she said. 'What was it you were going to say?'

'All right then. I'm willing to risk upsetting you if I can make you change your mind. You and Kenneth were totally wrong for each other, everybody knew.'

'That's not true. It's just that we . . .'

'And he was unfaithful to you with the lowest sort of women in Okante. Peter was amazed that you hadn't found out. Don't you realise you could have caught the most awful diseases.'

She interrupted him. 'That's enough, I won't hear any more. I'm going back to the hotel.'

'No Jenny. Forgive me, I shouldn't have said all that, but I'd do or say anything that might make you change your mind. I can't bear to lose you.'

When she did not reply, he said, 'OK, I'll do what you say. I'll wait until you tell me the time is right, but don't leave now. Just let me spend the rest of today with you. If you leave me like this we may both regret it for the rest of our lives.'

Fortunately, at that moment the door from the kitchen opened. 'I'm sorry to disturb you, but I failed to offer cake. There are some maids of honour or we have a rather yummy Simnel cake that I bought yesterday in Fortnums.'

The banal intrusion served to lighten the charged atmosphere.

'Not quite the time yet for Simnel cake, is it?' said Nico. 'Do you like it, Jenny?'

'A small slice of simnel cake would be lovely. Thank you Jenks.'

*

She decided not to let Nico make their meal that evening; her resolve might weaken if she stayed alone in the house with him. Instead, they walked along the mews for a snack at his local. As they neared the pub she suggested, 'Would it not be better to go somewhere else? Won't they be surprised to see you with me rather than Nicki?'

'No they won't be surprised,' he replied. Then he quickly added, 'I mean they know I have a wide circle of business friends, many of whom happen to be women, of course.'

But it was too late. Some of what Nicki had said that afternoon had hit the target. I'm just another of his conquests, she thought. It was not yet seven o' clock. There were just a few men in the pub, obviously sneaking a quick one on the way home from the office.

'This is my friend Jenny Masters,' Nico told the landlord. 'We've been working together on my Nigerian project.'

The publican smiled in a way which disturbed Jenny. 'What will you have, Miss Masters? Nico's lady friends always have the first drink on me. It's a house rule.'

It was then she was sure she had made the correct decision.

77

When she returned to her room in the Rembrandt that night, she cried. The van Vleet woman's filthy tirade had achieved more than she could possibly have hoped. Though the evening at the pub had done something to return her to normality, Jenny felt soiled by the afternoon's encounter. She was no better than those women she had seen hanging around Soho hoping for early trade.

Yet she had to admire Nico's technique. When he said he loved her she had been more than prepared to believe him, since that was exactly what she wanted to hear. But the landlord had almost a leer when he said, "Nico's lady friends always have the first drink on me."

Amid her shame and disillusion there lay frustration: she had been so tantalisingly close to the realisation of all she desired. She was physically exhausted, but her mind would not rest. She telephoned room service and asked for a mug of Horlicks, a remedy which usually helped. When her head finally touched the pillow she sank into a dreamless sleep.

Next morning she woke early, refreshed, and ready for her last day in London; a day she could call her own. She knew she had escaped from what could have been another misalliance, but in her heart she still loved him. In the hotel foyer, as she made her way to the dining room for breakfast, she saw a man opening up the desk assigned to a travel agency.

'Do you offer tours of London?' she enquired.

'Of course we do, Miss. We have one starting at half-past nine. Can you be outside Harrods by nine-fifteen?'

As she stepped out of the hotel she saw that it was a lovely day, mild, with an early hint of spring in the air. She easily identified the group waiting for the tour, all of whom appeared to be American. Before the coach arrived, one of the women came up to her and asked, 'Don't think me rude dear, but did anyone ever tell you you're the living image of Ava Gardner?'

She called to her husband who was studying a window display, 'Hey, Morris, who does this young lady remind you of?'

'I know who you mean,' he said. 'That movie star --- could be her younger sister. Can't remember the name.'

'Ava Gardner, that's who.'

'Sure, that's the one. Look folks,' Morris said to the assembled party, 'we got a movie star with us.'

From then on she was the centre of attention for the Americans, being the only English person among the party. They were shown almost everything in London that she had always wanted to see --- Hyde Park, Buckingham Palace, St Paul's, Westminster Abbey, the Tower of London, the Houses of Parliament.

Then the coach dropped them off at Westminster Bridge, where they transferred to a river boat for a trip down to Greenwich. They had lunch on board. Everyone wanted to take her photograph. She ended the day with a sheaf of addresses and business cards, and was made to promise that she would not fail to visit them all, if ever she went to the United States.

This day alone in London had given her new confidence, which must have showed because, when she went down for a drink before dinner, she found that people in the bar wanted to talk to her.

But in her dream that night she was once again Mrs Nicolas Masoor.

78

A letter awaited her on her return home, informing her of progress on the Gorsedale Close development and requiring a second payment of fifteen hundred pounds. Only now did she admit to herself that her decision to buy one of the most expensive properties on the estate may have been influenced by a desire to impress her former schoolmate. She went down to town the following morning and spoke to the owner of Horrock's estate agency

'If you really are having second thoughts, Mrs Thistleth-waite, I might be able to make an exception and let you have your deposit back. You see, we've had huge interest in the ranch-style residences. The developers have decided to fill up the site, that means another batch of eight ranch-styles, and they're putting them up to seven nine-fifty.'

'I beg your pardon?'

'Seven thousand, nine hundred and fifty pounds. You see, Jane . . . I may call you Jane?'

'Jenny, please.'

'Well Jenny, I can tell you in confidence that there's a lot of interest coming from folk looking for property within reasonable commuting distance of Manchester. Seven-thousand odd quid may seem a lot to someone used to Colesclough prices, but for people who have been looking on the south side of Manchester --- Wilmslow, Prestbury, places like that, our prices must seem an absolute snip.'

She made allowances for the fact that she was talking to an estate agent. Still, she was already sitting on a profit of, how much? Good heavens, two thousand two hundred pounds already. For doing nothing! An idea came to her.

'What if I decided to rent out this house?'

The manager looked wary. 'Well, I'm not so sure your building society would agree to that. Most mortgagors don't like . . .'

'There won't be a mortgagor,' Jenny told him.

He looked surprised, 'I see. You can manage the cash, can you? That, Jenny, is what they call a different fish kettle.'

'Would there be people interested, do you think?'

'Certainly. We have to disappoint someone almost every week, the sort who turn their nose up at places like the mill rows, where there's plenty of houses to rent . . . oh, sorry, love, I'd forgotten that's where you live, but I hope you'll agree that a senior executive on temporary transfer from London or Edinburgh would want something a bit, shall we say, more prestigious than Bright Street.'

Mr Horrocks opened his desk drawer and presented her with a brochure. 'Right Jenny, there you are; the solution to your problem. Have a read of that and I'm sure you'll agree that the Horrocks Property Management Service is exactly what you need. As soon as you've coughed up the readies we're in business. The bad news is that we charge twelve and a half percent, but the good news is that I can get you a hundred and fifty pounds a month, happen a bit more if we have any Yanks interested. In the meantime, let's go up to the site and talk about colour schemes.'

As they set off she said, 'Before I forget, may I have just ordinary taps, please? I'm not a 'golden girl', if you know what I mean.'

*

Now that she would be spending time between Bright Street and the new house she decided to buy a car. Fortunately, her Nigerian licence was still current and she was able to be it for a UK one. She new exactly what car she wanted, and the local agents were Capels.

When she went to their showroom she happened to mention to the receptionist that Mr Capel would soon be a neighbour. He came out of his office to show her round.

'Thanks Mr Capel,' she said. 'I definitely want a Mini but I gather you have a choice of versions,' He took her to the Mini section and she found there was a choice of four versions, Austin, Morris, Riley and Wolseley. She had no hesitation.

'I'll take a Wuzily, please'.
That's pronounced Woolsley, by the way,' he corrected her.

'No, Mr Capel, mine isn't. She's a Wuzily --- I'll have a white one, please.'

79

Jenny now spent much of her time at The Little Lodge with Harriet. She was made welcome by Alice Harrison, who obviously considered her to be a good influence on her daughter. From the start she showed an aptitude for riding. Harrie usually took her to Cliviger to take lessons on Clarice's pony, which was more suitable for a learner than were any of the Harrisons' horses. Although Clarice must have been aware of Harrie's infatuation, she accepted Jenny as a new friend without any outward sign of jealousy. For Harrie, of course, life was now bliss.

Geoffrey was seldom at home during Jenny's visits. He was spending most of his time visiting factories within the Palatine Amalgamated group and usually stayed overnight in the various locations. As Harrie suspected, he did not always spend the night alone. However, whenever Geoffrey and Jane did meet, they seemed to get on well together, a relationship which Harrie did her best to foster, for she too had a fantasy. The three of them would one day set up home together and she and her brother would share the person they both loved.

*

The summer passed happily for Jenny. She was flattered when Harrie began to let her use Tempest, the dressage mare, and when they went over to Cliviger she was now able to jump the course built behind the stable block. Clarice congratulated Jenny on her progress and said she was now quite capable of taking part in the hunt. She usually wore a sweater and corduroys, which she kept in Harrie's room at The Little Lodge. On colder days, she borrowed an old leather jacket which no longer fitted Harrie.

80

'You ought to get a riding habit,' her friend said one morning. 'Specially if you are going to come with us to the hunt.'

'Sorry Harrie, I don't think I could do that. I told you I think it's cruel, and I hope to persuade you and Clarice to give it up.'

329

'Rubbish. We've never been at a meet where there was a kill, it's the fun of the chase we go for. Give it a try and you'll see.'

Jenny admired the outfits that her two friends sometimes wore and she could well afford one, even if it were only for riding around Sabden and Cliviger. So she yielded to Harrie's pressure.

'All right,' she said. 'I'll try one on, if you can tell me where they sell them.'

'That's super,' said Harrie. ' I suggest a blue coat rather than hunting pink. And some tight white riding breeches --- jodhpurs too. You'd look delectable in jodhpurs.'

'I suppose I have to go to Manchester for them?'

'No, there's a place in Clitheroe. Why don't I drive you there today? We'll have lunch at the Swan and Royal.'

The shop was an old-fashioned draper's and outfitters, with a side room devoted to riding gear. Jenny had to admit to herself that she did look rather fetching in jodhpurs. Then she tried some white breeches and riding boots. The assistant disagreed with Harriet's choice of blue for the jacket.

'With modom's colouring,' he said, 'black would be my suggestion. May I try you in our latest arrival? And a black billycock, perhaps?' He brought a coat and hat which fitted perfectly. Jenny was terrified at what all this was going to cost but had already decided to go the whole hog. She looked in the mirror to find she looked every inch the country gentlewoman.

'God, you do look stunning,' said Harrie. 'Just a minute, I'll get you a little present to top it all off.' She went through to a showcase at the back of the shop.

'Here,' she said, returning with a riding crop, 'with my love.'

'*No!,*' Jenny screamed. 'Take it away!'

Still wearing the riding clothes she ran out into the busy street, dodging shoppers who turned to stare after her. She kept on running until she reached a little park, went in and sat down on a bench, panting and breathless, starting to per-spire. There was a sea of red before her.

Some children stopped their ball game and gathered round her, gawping.

'Are you all right, Miss?' asked a little boy.

'Go away, damn you,' she shouted. The little girls screamed and they all ran off towards the swings. Jenny sat with her head in her hands and sobbed.

After a couple of minutes she felt strong arms embrace her and heard the breathless voice of her friend. 'My poor sweet darling, what's the matter? There now, just put your head on my shoulder. Cry as much as you want, Harrie's here with you. Whatever the matter is, let it all come out.'

The boy came back when he saw Harriet arrive.

'She said damn you. That's rude, that is.'

His gang stood close behind him in solidarity.

'You'll have to forgive her,' Harrie told him. 'She's very upset.'

'Why is she dressed like that?' a girl asked. 'Is she going to kill a fox?'

'No, not today, dear. My friend has just had a shock. I'm sure she didn't mean what she said.'

'That's all right, Miss,' said the boy. 'Would you like us to go away?'

'Please love,' said Harrie.

'Half -a-crown, then?'

She gave the boy a coin from her purse and he began to marshal his gang back to the play area. The girls appeared reluctant to leave, but they followed when they heard the boys discussing how they planned to spend the money.

Jenny released herself from Harriet's embrace. The steamy tropical morning had become a summer's day in England. She was surprised to find herself dressed in riding clothes. Then recognition dawned.

'What did I do?'

'We're in Clitheroe, dearest. Don't you remember? You were buying these clothes? Come on, take my arm and we'll walk back to the shop. Whatever it was that upset you, I don't want to know. Ever.'

81

Geoffrey was enjoying his assignment. He was to present his report on the Palatine Amalgamated Textiles Limited group at a Harrison board meeting on the twentieth of October. Before he began the survey he arranged a meeting with Sykes and found him not to be the ogre his father led him to expect. In fact, they got on quite well. He was an intelligent man of about forty, balding and running to fat, with quite a broad Yorkshire accent. He professed himself relieved to be able to pass the responsibility for his group into more experienced hands, though Geoffrey doubted his sincerity.

Sykes said Jacob Masoor had warned him of Harold Harrison's antipathy and advised him to keep well away, but he would have to be at the October board meeting, so whenever Geoffrey gave his father an interim report he took the opportunity to improve Plantagenet's image.

He spent at least a week at each of the factories and, though none of them was more than a couple of hour's drive from Sabden, he found it more convenient to stay in a hotel in the town he was visiting, rather than return home each night.

This made him realise how much his life was restricted by living at The Little Lodge. His friends used to tease him that, at the ripe old age of twenty-five, he had not broken away from the parental home. Now that Norman Howarth had agreed to stay on at the Okante mill, Geoffrey believed that his future would remain in Lancashire, so he decided to look round for a place of his own, preferably not far from the Rossendale Valley, where Tabitha Swan lived.

Her husband Tom was the export manager of his firm, so he spent more time away from Britain than he did at home, which meant Tabitha could often join Geoffrey in one of his hotels after she had finished work at the college. They decided she should play the role of his personal assistant and chose a name, 'Mrs Templeton'. They hoped that hotel managements would suspect nothing other than a business relationship between young Mr Harrison and his older 'employee'. Although they always booked separate rooms they found that the size of a hotel bed did little to restrict their lovemaking. The pretence added spice to these late night encounters, but Geoffrey always resented having to sneak back to his own bed, before the room service staff began delivering early breakfasts.

Some of the small factories in Plantagenet Sykes's empire surprised him. Most of the firms which Sykes had taken over were family businesses and they usually had antique machinery, but most had a skilled workforce and loyal customers. Geoffrey set off on the project expecting to be a butcher, which was how he was usually greeted by the managers of the mills when he first arrived. Closure was the inevitable solution in many cases, but in some he saw justification for more capital expenditure. Managers who had long since abandoned hope of ever having new machinery started to regard Geoffrey as a potential saviour.

He always came home for the weekend, and his journey back to Sabden was brightened by the possibility that he might find Jenny there. As he crossed Rochdale moor on that particular Friday afternoon in late July he was singing to himself in tune with the car radio, unaware of what awaited him at The Little Lodge.

He was greeted by his sister, dressed to kill, with the news that Jenny would be arriving at half-past six and that she was making a meal for the three of them.

'Mum and Dad have gone to Sharrow Bay for the weekend. So this could be your big chance, brother dear --- a balmy evening, the three of us alone. Go on upstairs and smarten yourself up. You need a shave, by the way.'

While he dried himself after the shower he started to open his post. Bank statement... remarkably healthy for a change... it pays to live off expenses... more bumf from a wine club he had once thought of joining, straight into the waste paper basket... surprise letter from Roger, who didn't often write. It seemed to be about the arrangements for his wedding in November. He would study that later. Geoffrey was having most of the best man's duties thrust upon him, though the actual job had gone to one of Roger's fellow officers.

Then he came to the letter with a Rossendale postmark endorsed PRIVATE AND CONFIDENTIAL. He tore it open.

*

Under normal circumstances he would have taken Harriet into his confidence straight away, but when he had dressed and got half-way downstairs, he could see through the landing window that Jane's Mini was parked beside the front steps.

When he went down, she and Harrie were seated in the conservatory.

'For goodness sake wipe that awful frown off your face,' his sister said, 'and give Jenny a kiss, at least try to *look* as though you are pleased to see her.' Harrie had been at the gin bottle he could tell.

Geoffrey gave the woman he loved a polite kiss on the cheek. She was wearing a short-sleeved dress of plain shantung, with a low neckline which he found disturbing. The skirt was fashionably short. He had never seen so much of her lovely legs. He literally did not know where to look.

'I'm sorry, Jane,' he said, 'business problems. I really am delighted to see you, though.' She gave him a pretty smile which cheered him immensely.

Harrie was pleased by this opening exchange. She knew her brother well enough to realise that his apparent detachment was a facade. Like her, he must be bowled over by the way Jenny looked tonight.

'Forget about your boring business,' she said. 'We have the house to ourselves. Besides, I have an announcement to make.'

Jenny and Geoffrey looked at her expectantly.

'But I'm going to drag out the suspense until after we've had dinner. Come with me to the kitchen, Jenny. You can help me with the hors d'oeuvres. Let's leave this old sourpuss to his gloomy thoughts.'

As they were leaving he heard Harrie say, 'On second thoughts I'll tell you my news but we'll make him wait.'

Geoffrey went to the drawing room and mixed himself a dry Martini. Why on earth had Tabitha not warned him? It was only last Tuesday that they had spent the night together. Come to think of it, she *had* seemed tense. He knew that

Tom would be back from Ireland. Now that the cat was out of the bag, so to speak, there was nothing to prevent him from telephoning her directly, instead of leaving the usual coded message at the college. He decided to ring her after Jane had gone home and Harriet was in bed. But he must remember to stay sober.

He sipped the martini as he caught up with local news from the *Colesclough Gazette* which the family took every week. He had begun to think of buying himself his own place and there was a full page advertisement for the second phase of the Gorsedale Close development. He got a shock when he saw the prices they were charging. Now he realised why Jacob Masoor was so keen on buying Daisy Hill.

After about fifteen minutes the women joined him in the drawing room.

'By the way Jane, I love your dress,' he said.

'Good heavens above,' exclaimed Harrie. 'That must be a first, my brother noticing a woman's frock.'

'Shut up Het. Pour us a drink. I'll have a G and T this time, what will you have Jane?'

She would have liked him to call her Jenny, but Harrie said he considered that the more ladylike version of her name better suited her, which she found flattering.

'I suppose I'd better have lemonade or something. I shouldn't have anything alcoholic because I'm not used to driving in the dark.'

'Oh, come on,' said Harrie, 'don't spoil the evening. Tell you what, why not phone your mum and say you'll be staying the night? Roger's old room is made up and I can put the electric blanket on. I'll let you have whatever you need --- nightie, toothbrush, anything. Go and use the phone in the hall.'

'Do you know, I think I will,' she said. 'Thanks, I won't be a minute.'

While Jenny was away and Geoffrey went down to the cellar, Harrie poured herself another stiff gin and tonic. Things were going according to plan.

Geoffrey looked through the private stock he had been laying down. His father's taste in wine was restricted to hock and Beaujolais. He decided on two bottles of sparkling Epernay.

They ate in the kitchen. The meal Harrie had prepared was not ambitious, though compared with her mother's cuisine it was bordering on the adventurous – avocado and anchovy salad, followed by Spanish omelettes served with fried rice, mushrooms and aubergines. They raided the larder for one of Mrs Foster's apple pies and some fresh cream.

It was not until they had cleared their dessert plates that Harriet was prepared to give Geoffrey her news.

'I'm leaving home.'

'Why on earth? No, I can understand why --- but how? How will you be able to afford?' Their father gave her a more than generous monthly allowance but he knew she had very little capital.

'And where do you plan to go?'

'Downham. We're going to make an offer for an old smithy on the road out to Chatburn. It would need some doing up, but Clarice knows a good man in Colne who did their stable block.'

'So it would be you and Clarice, then?'

'Of course. I've just asked Jenny if she would join us but she says two's company and her own house will soon be ready, anyway.'

'I'm awfully pleased for you, Het,' said Geoffrey, 'but have you told Mum and Dad?'

'No, it's not definite yet. I wondered if you would help me tell them.'

'You do realise that Mum will never agree? She's determined to get you married and she's quite capable of persuading Dad to cast you from the door without a penny to your name.'

'I don't care if they do. Clarice has a good salary so she should be able to get a mortgage, and her Grandpa left her ten thousand. There's a couple of acres of land that go with the smithy. We could start breeding.'

Geoffrey could never resist teasing his sister. 'You realise, Het, that's a biological impossibility?'

'Don't be disgusting. I mean horses, you fathead. And I could make some money by doing livery and giving riding lessons.'

Geoffrey could see that Jenny was embarrassed by this family conversation. 'I'm sorry, Jane, but we must get this settled before our parents get back.'

'Of course she doesn't mind, do you darling? We tell each other everything. Oh, I forgot to mention --- I'm thinking of selling some of my Harrisons shares.'

'To whom?'

'I don't know. I suppose Dad is the only one, unless you can afford?'

'Mum would never let him buy them. Not unless you somehow talk her into agreeing to your bunking off. I wish I could help, but I'm saving up for a house myself.'

'I can sell them to anyone I want. As soon as we're sure about the smithy I intend to see Mostyn Stainforth about selling some. Mr Masoor would gladly have them, I'm sure.'

Geoffrey had raised his voice. 'On no account must you do that. It's quite out of the question. Don't you realise that you would give them control?'

Jenny got up and started to stack the plates. 'I'll do the washing up,' she said.

'No, we'll all do it,' said Harrie, 'so Geoffrey and I can carry on sorting things out.'

'I have a little sorting out of my own to do next week,' he said; but he did not explain.

*

It was after midnight before he was able to phone Tabitha but he hoped she would still be up; she always was a night owl. To his dismay, Tom answered.

'Geoffrey old chap, how are you?' He sounded slightly drunk but not unfriendly, certainly not like a wronged husband.

'To tell you the truth I have had better days. I got your lawyer's letter.'

'Oh, I see. Sorry about that, hope you don't mind.'

'Of course I bloody mind,' he yelled. The man must be stupid. May I speak to Tabitha?'

'Yes, hold on. She's a bit pissed though, we both are.' He heard Tom shout 'It's Geoffrey.' Then, still audible, 'Shall I tell him you've gone to bed?'

A moment later a small voice said, 'Hi. It's not a real good time to talk just now, Geoffrey.' Her speech was slurred. 'Maybe we can meet?'

'Can he hear?' Geoffrey asked her.

'No, he's gone back to the parlour.'

'You've given me quite a surprise,' Geoffrey said with a hint of irony.

'I did try to tell you, honest I did, but I chickened out. It never occurred to me he'd go right ahead and have that letter sent. Are you mad at me?'

'Yes, I am. After all, you're not some school kid are you?' He realised how hurtful that must sound, so he tempered the remark. 'I mean we're both adults. You could have warned me he wanted a divorce.'

'Look honey, I think I have a cold coming on. I don't think I can articulate all that well at the moment. Where are you next week?'

'Chorley.'

'Same hotel?

'Yes.'

'OK, I'll join you Tuesday around half after six. Can you book a double room this time?'

'Might as well. Love you.'

'No you don't,' she said. 'Goodnight.'

82

Jenny had not enjoyed an evening so much for a long time. Roger's room was even larger than Harriet's and more modern, 1950's rather than 1890's. It was not a masculine room, probably decorated to Alice's taste rather than Roger's. Jenny sat on the double bed and bounced up and down to test the mattress. Then she put her hand between the sheets, to find the bed so warm that she switched off the electric blanket. Harriet had thoughtfully left her a nightie and a new toothbrush and tube of paste. She took a leisurely bath and cleaned her teeth.

The nightdress was pink satin with mutton-chop short sleeves and a low, lace-trimmed neckline, a most surprising garment for her friend to have bought. When she put it on and looked at herself in the mirror she laughed out loud, for it was at least two sizes too large for her and reached the ground. She knelt to say her prayers, as she did every night. Tonight she certainly had a lot to thank God for. As a girl she would never have dreamed that one day she would have such friends as Harriet and Geoffrey Harrison.

After such an exhilarating evening she was not at all tired, so she sat in bed looking through some old copies of *Lancashire Life* and *Horse and Hound*. But she could not concentrate.

She wondered what 'sorting out' Geoffrey had to do next week. She was worried by the sudden change in his attitude when he came downstairs and didn't believe him when he talked of a 'business' problem. When she heard a knock on the door she half hoped it might be him. She put down the magazine and pulled the sheets over her.

'Come in.'

It was Harriet, wearing a blue woollen dressing gown and a pair of striped flannelette pyjamas such as Grandpa Entwistle used to wear.

'I came to see if you were all right.' She had sobered somewhat.

'Perfect thanks. I'm as snug as the proverbial bug.'

Harrie sat on the side of the bed. 'Is the nightie OK?'

Jenny got out of bed to show her and Harrie giggled, 'Sorry, I should have realised, I'm quite a bit bigger than you, aren't I? Don't imagine that's my choice by the way, it was a Christmas present from Geoffrey, an example of his warped sense of humour. He knew I'd never wear it. I'm the pyjama type, as you see.'

'I can't pretend it suits me either,' said Jenny, 'but thanks.'

'Goodnight then. Sleep tight' Harrie came to kiss her good-night. Jenny had not expected a kiss like that.

'Sorry,' said Harrie, 'I didn't mean it to turn out that way. Put it down to the booze. I'd better go.'

'No, wait a minute. Don't be upset. It's just that you and I are not made the same way. Stay and talk. I'm worried about your brother and I'm not a bit tired, are you?'

'No, but get back into bed, it's cold in here.' Harrie started to tuck in the bedclothes. 'Can I come in while we talk?' she pleaded. 'I promise I won't do anything.'

Each kept to her own side of the bed throughout the night. Jenny was glad not to be alone in this strange room. Harriet slipped off to her own bedroom soon after dawn broke.

When Jenny woke it was not yet eight o'clock but there was activity downstairs. She opened the bedroom door and heard Harriet and Geoffrey talking in the kitchen. She put on the dressing gown that Harrie had left behind, tidied her hair and went downstairs, lured by the smell of frying bacon. They had finished breakfast. Geoffrey still had his dressing gown on but Harrie was fully dressed.

'My word, you two are early risers,' she said. 'I hadn't expected any sign of life until after ten, certainly not from you, Harrie.'

'I've told you about the delights of owning horses, haven't I? I've already fed them but they need mucking out.'

'I'll do that when I have got dressed,' said Geoffrey. 'You two girls can sit and have a nice chat.'

Harrie refused his assistance. 'Leave it to me. I'll phone young Kathy to come and help. The dogs need taking out, though; that's what you two can do. Take them for a good long walk and then we'll meet here at eleven and stroll down for lunch at the pub.'

'I really can't,' Jenny said. 'Not in last night's dress.'

'Don't you remember --- after that time we got caught in the rain? You have a pair of socks and some cords in one of my cupboards. I can lend you a sweater.'

'Of course I have --- but what about shoes?'

'We'll borrow a pair of Mum's flatties. We can clean them up before she gets back. She'll never know.'

That was a close-run thing, Harrie said to herself. But I managed to get them to go out together. Now let's see.

*

When Jenny had washed and dressed, she came downstairs to find Geoffrey waiting for her, wearing the tweeds and brogues of a country gentleman. He seemed ill at ease, now

345

that he was alone with her, but here was her chance to get his opinion.

'Before we go for our walk, Geoffrey, may I mention something that occurred to me last evening. Did you know I bought a house in the Gorsedale Close development in Colesclough?'

'Yes, Harrie told me. I was surprised, they seem overpriced.'

'My idea was to take Mum with me to live there, but she won't leave Bright Street. However, I'm convinced it will be a good long term investment. It's one of the top range houses and it's almost ready for me to move in. Now that Mum has taken a lodger, Number 48 seems a bit crowded.'

'Won't you be lonely on your own?'

Exactly the response she wanted. 'OK, what do you think of this? Mr Masoor wants me to go back to Nigeria to finish off the advertising work I was doing for him. I'm more or less thinking aloud but I believe I have an idea that may help Harrie.'

'Go on.'

'Well, next week I shall be getting the house ready for me to move in. If I did go back to Nigeria, even for a short while, I would want to let it.'

'I see,' Geoffrey said. 'Now I can guess where this is going -- - you think you might let it to Het and Clarice. If so, I must disillusion you. She would still have to persuade my Mum.'

'I've thought of a possible strategy for that. Why don't I ask your mother to help me with the decor and then I could put

346

my 'problem' to her. I think I know Mrs Harrison well enough to suggest to her what a good thing it would be for Harriet to get some experience of independent living, by house-sitting for me. I certainly wouldn't mention Clarice, but she could quietly slip in later if that suits her.'

'What a cunning little schemer you are,' he said admiringly. 'Let's put it to Het after we've had our walk.'

83

There was no question of which dog each should take, for as soon as Geoffrey mentioned the word 'walk', Argo made a lunge for him and Nemo started nuzzling Jenny. The animals were kept on their leads through the village and along Sabden Brook. Several people greeted Geoffrey, who knew most of them by their first names. When he introduced Jenny as 'Harriet's pal' she received some knowing stares. Not me, she wanted to say, you've got me wrong mister. I'm a man-eater.

Surprisingly, Geoffrey said hardly a word until they left the stream to take the path to Churn Clough. Then he asked, 'How was London?'

'Quite exciting. It was my first visit.'

'Yes, I remember how excited I was when I first went. Mum and Dad took us to see the Festival of Britain. Did you see Nico while you were there?'

She must take care. 'Briefly, we had a drink together.'

'I read about his engagement in the *Telegraph*. She's foreign, isn't she?'

'Well, not really. From Southern Rhodesia --- I don't call them foreigners. But I gather they've broken it off.'

She could see him digesting this information. 'I gather you were to have some advertising photos done for him and his uncle. How did it go?'

She gave him an edited version of her visit to the Tiptop Studio in Soho, which he found amusing, and she carried on with an account of her sight-seeing tour.

'Those Americans really made my day. I'd never met any before. They seem to take life much less seriously than we British. I've decided I like Americans, do you?'

'I've only ever come across one,' he said, 'Tabitha her name is. We met when I was helping at the Colesclough Players.'

Then he paused and looked her in the eyes. Jane's quick brain may have anticipated what he was about to say.

'You and Het probably noticed me saying I had a problem to solve. Between ourselves, Jane, she and I have become rather close. Last night I discovered that Tabby and her husband are divorcing and I was wondering if I should ask her to marry me. I'd really appreciate a woman's advice, and Hetty's hardly qualified in that department, is she? Before you begin, I suggest we walk on a little bit further.' He pointed his finger. 'Can you see that gap in the hedge? There is a lovely view of Pendle Hill from there. It's a long time since I have been this way, but I think there are a couple of benches. It would be nice to sit down while we talk.'

He ensured the bench was not wet before he asked her to sit beside him. Each dog found a place in front of its chosen human.

'Do you think I ought to offer to marry her? Is that what she'll expect?'

'Really Geoffrey! How can I possibly answer a question like that? I've never even met the lady. Do you love her?'

'Not yet, but I believe a lot of people get married first and later find they love one another. By the way, she's quite a bit older than me. Did I say?'

'No, but that shouldn't matter.'

'She's great fun,' he said, as if trying to convince himself. If only she *could* help. It was true that she knew nothing about this American woman but she suspected that Geoffrey might be on the brink of making a huge mistake.

'I got hardly any sleep last night,' he said. 'I think perhaps I *will* ask her. I'll be seeing her on Tuesday.'

'Look,' she said, 'it's no business of mine and you can tell me to shut up if you like, but I do have some experience that might help.' She hesitated, not for fear of upsetting Geoffrey but because she was about to reveal something about herself that she had told no one else.

'Carry on,' he said, expectantly.

'Don't. Don't marry her I mean. Not unless you're absolutely certain that each of you loves the other. There's got to be love --- on both sides. Even someone you think you know well, can turn out to be an altogether different person.'

'You and Kenneth? Is that what you're talking about?'

'Yes,' she admitted.

Geoffrey feared she was about to cry. He hated himself for being so insensitive, raising bitter memories simply to help him correct his stupid mistake. She looked so vulnerable, having just lost the man he knew she loved. He wanted to put his arms around her and tell her that it was she whom *he* had always loved. To kiss her and drive away those tears. At any other time his love for her could have been declared. But not now. He stood up and took her hands, to help raise her.

'I can't thank you enough, Jane. How insensitive I have been – do please forgive me. Come on let's get back. Het will think we have eloped.'

84

Geoffrey was waiting in the bar of the Queen's Hotel in Chorley, the only remaining customer. Last orders for dinner were taken at eight-thirty.

'Just yourself tonight is it, Mr Harrison?' the barman enquired.

'No, I'm still expecting Mrs Templeton. She's been delayed in Manchester I guess.' His courage had deserted him when it came to booking a double room, and it had since occurred to him that single rooms might prove a better idea. This was going to be a difficult encounter and spending the whole night together may not turn out to be what either of them wanted. He walked back to the lobby to phone her home number, just as she arrived.

'Sorry, I'm late, Geoffrey,' she said in her 'senior executive' voice. 'I had to call in at the factory.' The subterfuge was no longer necessary, but it had become a habit. The porter took Tabitha's overnight bag.

'Don't bother with that, I'll take it,' Geoffrey said. Mrs Templeton's in room seventeen, isn't she?'

'Correct sir. Thanks.'

Once inside her bedroom they did not immediately embrace. She looked at him warily, anticipating his reproof.

'I'm sorry for being so late,' she said. 'I set off and then lost my nerve. I've been in the Duke of Wellington for nearly an hour, getting myself ready to face you.' She looked even tinier tonight.

He bent to kiss her. 'Don't worry Tabby, we'll work it out. Come on, we'd better get down to dinner. I'm hungry and I need a full stomach for what we have to talk about.'

Two hours later they were in her bed. Neither wanted sex but it was easier to talk like this.

'So? Who is Tom's woman?'

'His secretary. I knew he was screwing her --- he often lays his secretaries, but he says he *loves* this one.'

'If I talk to him, do you think he would agree to be caught with some tart? I'd be willing to pay. Would he do that, do you think?'

'That's what I suggested but he says he isn't prepared to sully his new relationship. Sully! Would you believe he could ever use a word like that? At the back of it all is that I think he's jealous of you and me.'

'What happened to the 'open marriage'?'

'To tell you the honest truth, Geoffrey, I'm not too sure that my dear husband ever saw it that way. Open for him, sure. But for me? I doubt.'

Geoffrey got up to pour two more whiskies from the bottle he had smuggled in.

'I'm gonna miss that lovely ass of yours, she said as he walked towards the dressing table.

'No you're not.'

'I sure am.'

'No, he said, because you are going to be my wife.'

Tabitha sprang out of bed to hug him.

'Hold on, don't make me spill,' he said, and put the glasses on the dressing table. He held her at arm's length. 'And you don't get your hug until you've said yes.'

'Geoffrey Harrison, what a big sweet clown you are. Of course I won't marry you – not unless you are willing to come back to Connecticut with me.'

'Why not stay here and we'll get married? We could make it work.'

'It's the most ridiculous thing I have ever heard.'

'Why?'

'Because you don't love me, that's why. And I don't love you. The sex has been marvellous, but that's all of it. Come on, admit.'

A huge wave of relief flooded over Geoffrey. 'Are you sure?'

'Yep --- but thanks a million for asking.' She drew back the sheet and jumped back into the bed.

'OK, that's enough talking. Come show me how much I've taught you. Regard this as your final examination.'

85

Jumy's letter arrived in the first week of August. It was no surprise to find it written in French, since Jumy's secondary education had been in a French school in Senegal. Although she spoke English fluently she once told Jenny she was more comfortable writing in French. It proved fortunate that she did so on this occasion.

'Is that from your pal out there?' her mother asked. Jenny had told her a great deal about Jumy (and a little about Peter) so it would have been churlish not to let her know what was in the letter, but when she glanced through the contents she quickly decided to stall.

'Oh dear, I'm not sure I can read it to you straight away. It's in French and I'm a bit rusty.'

Her mother did not seem convinced. 'I'm surprised at you; Mr Hopkinson said you were fluent. You can't have lost it already.'

'A lot is what they call patois.'

'Is patois not French?'

'It's like a dialect or slang. I'll get out my French books and type it out; we'll go through it when you get back from work.'

The letter did indeed contain large chunks of patois, and from time to time Jumy lapsed into English. She had also picked up a lot of French West African slang, some of which was still obscure, even after Jenny had searched her Larousse. But the burden of the letter was perfectly clear, Jumy was in love. The unfortunate Martin had been banished and now there was only one man in the whole world. His name was Malachi and God had never before placed upon this planet a human being of such perfection.

They met at an official function. He was a graduate of Edinburgh University who had worked for a firm of London publishers, before coming back to Nigeria with the intention of setting up his own publishing house. There was another bonus, for this paragon was totally acceptable to her father and mother. Being from Rivers Province, he was politically neutral, which was important to Chief Ogondo, who had ambitions at national level. The cruel twist to the idyll was that she would have to cease modelling and to live in Lagos when they were married.

She enclosed cuttings of advertisements from the local press, including some of the photographs for which Jenny had posed in London, which were so skilfully edited that no one could have suspected that she and Jumy were not together in the same room.

Mr Masoor wanted Jenny to return for a final set of pictures. He planned a whole range of cosmetic products under the *Mama Beauty* label and Jenny's face was to appear on each package.

Peter will pay your air fare by first class. I would love to see you but I am sorry you will not meet my darling Malachi. He needs to stay in Lagos.

Remember, we are 'pardners'. Do not disappoint me. (And be sure to grow your hair longer because of the shampoo advertisements). You must come back soon. You are Mama Beauty, not me.

When the time came to report the contents to Agnes there was one paragraph which Jenny completely edited out, though she had typed a translation of the whole letter.

Peter has received a letter from Nico. You will be pleased to hear that he has dumped that awful South African woman and Peter agrees with me that Nico loves you greatly, so now you must become his wife. Did you know he is very rich? If I were you I would seize hold of him before the woman tries to grab him back. Please, please come when you receive your ticket. There is so much more to tell you.

86

At the outset, Alice had doubts about the suitability of the match between Roger and Mabel, but now she considered the forthcoming wedding to be the pinnacle of what she had achieved for her family. She had convinced herself that she alone had engineered it. Her change of heart may have been occasioned by the fact that the bride's father was now a Deputy Lord Lieutenant of Lancashire. Consequently, not only was *Lancashire Life* covering the ceremony but *The Tatler and Bystander* had promised to send its photographer to the reception, which was to be held in a huge marquee in the substantial grounds of the Butterworths' residence, Upper Clough Hall.

Jenny did not receive an invitation to the wedding of Captain Roger Isaac Harrison R.A. to Miss Penelope Mabel Butterworth. She never expected one nor did she particularly want to attend, but Harrie took it as a slight to herself as well as to Jenny.

'Mabel knows how close you've become to our family and this is her way of saying she doesn't approve of you.'

'That's rubbish and you know it,' Jenny said. 'Why should they invite me? I've met Mabel just once and that was only for a minute or so, and I have never even seen your elder brother.'

'Oh him! He won't mind either way. I got Mum to put you on the list for our side but obviously that woman had you crossed off.'

'Honestly Harrie, I don't mind.'

'Snobs, that what those Butterworths are. Just because you happen to live in the mill rows in Colesclough you're persona non grata. They invited Clarice, even though she doesn't know either Roger or Fat-bum, but she comes from a rich family so she's OK. Quite sickening.'

'Much more importantly, Harrie, what progress have you made in escaping from The Little Lodge?'

'None, I've funked mentioning it. I think Geoffrey was right. Mum's probably never even heard the word lesbian, but as soon as anyone explains it to her she'll cast me out for ever. Not that I'll mind that so much, but I do need somewhere to live until we've got the old smithy done up.'

'I may be able to help you there,' Jenny said.

87

When Geoffrey decided to confront his father it turned out to be less of an ordeal than he had feared. 'About time,' Harold said, 'I've known for over a week. I suppose you were plucking up courage.'

'I had a decision to make before I saw you.'

'Decision? Don't tell me you were thinking of wedding the woman?'

'It was a possibility, Dad.'
Harold's face clouded. 'There's not a baby involved, is there?'

'No.'

'Thank God for that. I told Mostyn I'd pay her off if there was, but he says she didn't want you.'

A brutal way of putting it, but Geoffrey had to admit it was true. 'You don't have to worry now, Dad. She's on her way back to America.'

'Of course we've got to worry', his father said. 'There's still this divorce hearing to worry about. Seems this Swan fellow won't do the decent thing. Wants to rub her nose in it; yours too, I imagine. Mostyn says it's set for November twentieth.'

'I believe so.'

'Well, let's have a look.' Harold consulted a desk diary. 'You'll be giving us your report at the next board meeting. That's, hold on . . . . October seventh. Then there's Roger's wedding, you mustn't miss that.'

Geoffrey was puzzled. 'Why would I miss it?'

'I'm sending you out of the way, to Nigeria, that's why. We'll work it out later, but right now we'd better go and tell your mother.' Harold knew the tactics which could soften the blow. 'Best let her think you might be marrying this woman.'

If Geoffrey had been surprised at his father's response, he was positively flabbergasted by his mother's. The timing was fortunate, because her euphoria over Roger's forthcoming marriage had put her into a mood where she could receive bad news with equanimity. In fact, what Alice had just heard from Geoffrey brought back happy memories of Harold's brief courtship; during that lovely summer of nineteen twenty-eight. It had been a particularly warm season, which now lived in her memory as a haze of joy and excitement, permeated by her love for the young man who opened her mind to such wonderful prospects, just as he had opened her young body. Harold had not always taken precautions during their meetings on Daisy Hill, but she had been lucky. Roger was born a respectable fourteen months after the wedding.

Her comparatively mild reaction to her younger son's dis-grace was occasioned not only by the forthcoming nuptials, but by the way Geoffrey described the woman with whom he had the liaison.

'What was it you said her father did?'

'He was a diplomat, Mum, but he's retired now. A very senior diplomat,' Geoffrey added.

'Really?' Alice was taking the bait. 'And she's a graduate, you say'

'Yes Mum. She has two degrees, a BSc in economics and a business degree. It's called an MBA.'

'Has she now? But she's gone back home I understand.'

'Yes, she lives in a place called Bridgeport. It's in Connecti-cut.'

'You've been a very silly boy; you know that do you?'

Crikey, is that it? He had expected far worse.

Alice echoed her husband's words. 'Thank God there isn't a baby involved.'

Geoffrey knew how his mother's mind worked. He could sense her thought processes, following on from the word 'baby.' He was right. Alice was, indeed, considering that some good may be extracted from this divorce.

'Perhaps . . .' She paused. Geoffrey could have prompted her. 'Perhaps you might like to go over and visit --- I'm sorry, what did you say she is called?'

'Tabitha Mum.'

'A nice name, that.'

'Yes, there's a Tabitha in each generation of her family. They came over on the Mayflower,' Geoffrey lied, hoping he was not over-egging the pudding.

'What I was going to suggest,' Alice continued, 'is that you might like to pop over to America when you get back from this visit to Nigeria. I can't remember when you last took a holiday and it would be nice for you to see how she's settling down.'

No one had mentioned that Tabitha was sixteen years older than her son and that a grandchild from the liaison would have been most unlikely.

88

Jenny soon got her opportunity. Only ten days after her overnight stay at The Little Lodge she was back there to get some practice over the jumps on Harrie's new horse, Midnight, a strong but docile gelding. A sudden shower ended the lesson and by the time they had returned their horses to the stable they were both wet through. After her last visit she had driven home in the sweater and cords she kept in Harrie's wardrobe, so she was glad she had brought some more clothes today. She had parked by the stables and took her small suitcase from the Wuzily. When they came in they found Alice in the kitchen.

'Oh, hello, Jenny darling, I didn't see your car. I hope you have some dry clothes to change into.'

'Yes, I have them in this suitcase. When we've changed, can you spare me a minute. I am going to ask a favour?'

'How exciting,' said Alice. 'I'll make us some tea and then you can tell me what it is I can do for you.'

Mrs Harrison reacted just as Jenny had planned. They were to meet at the Gorsedale Close house at ten o'clock the following Thursday.

*

'This is gorgeous,' Alice enthused as she entered the house which Jenny had decided would be called *Okante*. 'What a very sensible young woman you are, my dear. I do wish I could instil some of this enterprise into Harriet.'

This remark prepared the ground perfectly but Jenny decided it was too soon for the attack. She did not need to say anything, for Alice at once started going from room to room. 'All right, decor first; none of these downstairs colours will do, I hope you agree. Let's go upstairs.'

They went first into the biggest double bedroom. Fortunately, this colour received approval. 'What a lovely big room. With so much light coming through in the early morning I think this beige is quite acceptable, though I don't generally approve of beige.'

Jenny had sought Alice's advice purely as a diversionary tactic but, as they went on to discuss furniture, carpets and curtains, it became clear that Mrs Harrison had a taste very much in tune with Jenny's. In fact, when eventually the house was fully furnished, Alice could rightly have claimed most of the credit.

The 'consultation' visit lasted almost two hours, including a coffee break, during which Jenny put forward her proposal. She began by explaining that she would be revisiting Nigeria and hoped to have the redecoration done while she was away.

Alice went off on one of her diversions, about what a lovely man Jacob Masoor was and how surprised she was that his handsome nephew was still single. Jenny could see that Alice had an agenda of her own and was preparing to steer her into the arms of Nico, so it was with some difficulty that she regained territory.

'Yes, I'm sure he will soon be snapped up by some beautiful debutante; but do you think it would be a good idea for me to get some sort of house-sitter in while the workmen are here? It struck me that it might be unwise to let them have a key. As you have seen, the kitchen is ready and I've fitted out one of the small bedrooms. Of course, it would have to be somebody I know and trust, but at the moment I can't think of anybody who could spare the time.'

'I suppose you could pay someone. I understand there are firms that do that sort of thing. I'd be happy to pop in from time to time, except that with Geoffrey's wedding coming up, I doubt . . . '

Jenny needed to stop this. If she did manage to get Harrie into the house, she wanted Alice kept well away, so she interrupted, 'Oh no, Alice, I couldn't possibly trouble you. I've been taking notes of what you suggested and I'll be able to make a clear schedule for the workmen, so all the person would have to do would be open up in the mornings and make tea for them, that sort of thing.'

She managed to create a pause by going to refill the milk jug, and then she said, 'Do you know, something has just occurred to me. Do you think that Harriet might be able to help me? It's what you said when you first came in that brought it to mind. Do you remember? About her lacking enterprise?'

'Well I'm not exactly sure that . . .'

'Please, Alice, may I be frank with you? Since we first met I have been terribly impressed by the wonderful way you help your children.' Alice sat back with a rapt expression, waiting for more of the same. 'The fact that both Geoffrey and Harriet are still living at home is clear evidence of how devoted to you they are.'

Could she yet risk a 'but'? She decided she could. 'But, in Harriet's case, I wonder if you might agree that she could have become *too* dependent. If she came to house-sit for me you would find out whether she can manage on her own? Dip a toe into the water, so to speak.'

This was the tipping point. Ominously, Alice remained silent, but not for long.

'What a clever girl you are, Jane. That's exactly what we should do, but let *me* put the suggestion to her --- she may take some persuading. Now let's carry on. It's getting on for lunch time and I want to take you to that new restaurant that's opened in Bank Street.'

*

She was hoping to have the house substantially ready before she left for Nigeria. When she took her mother to see the house Agnes said, 'It's nice.' High praise, coming from her! She was anxious to get her mother involved. Later that week she broached the subject.

'Would you help me Mum. I've been looking in the carpet shops and furniture stores in town, but there's not much choice. Would you be willing to take a day off and have a look round Manchester with me?'

'Didn't you go in the Co-op?'

'I had a look in the window, but I fancy something a bit better than Co-op furniture.'

'Go and get a catalogue and you'll have a surprise. You don't have to buy their own furniture; they sell branded stuff as well. They'll paint the house for you, lay your carpets and assemble your beds. And I can happen get a discount for you, being an employee. In any case, if we buy in my name I'll earn a lot of divi.'

She was right. They provided everything, and her Mum got a discount for pre-payment. Jenny also bought Co-op sheets and bedding. Before she flew to Kano the painters were hard at work. They started upstairs, so Harrie would have a carpeted bedroom, albeit still smelling of paint.

89

The divorce proceedings took place at Burnley. Because it was an uncontested case Geoffrey was told that neither of the respondents was required to be present in court. His trip to Nigeria was therefore abandoned. He did not attend the hearing and Tabitha was already home in Connecticut. Harold Harrison sat in the gallery to see justice done. Tom Swan nodded to him as he came in.

When the sworn statements were read out in court, they proved far too bland to be of much interest to the hard-boiled reporters who attended the hearing. What they wanted were the 'juicy bits' which would have been revealed had there been cross-examination. Only the depositions by the manager and chambermaid of the Scarisbrick Hotel added any colour to the proceedings, which were concluded within half an hour.

After it was over, Mr Swan was seen to embrace a good-looking young woman outside the court, so the photographer from the *Haslingden Observer* got the picture he wanted. When publication day came round there was a paragraph in the Haslingden paper and slightly more in the

Rossendale Free Press, but few readers of either paper would know who the Swans were, and those who had heard of them would not be surprised at the sort of things that Southern folk got up to. The co-respondent was named as Mr Wesley G. Harrison.

The editor of the *Colesclough Gazette*, who by chance happened to be a member of the same Masonic lodge as Mostyn Stainforth and Harold Harrison, saw no need to mention the case in that week's issue. He did not consider it relevant that the co-respondent was the son of a local businessman, since the family were not, technically, residents of Colesclough. When he discussed the matter with his news editor there was no dissent.

Both agreed that they should give over the whole of their legal section to the main story of the week, the resignation of the Reverend Thomas Fazackerly as minister of Broadholme Methodist chapel, after being found guilty of driving while under the influence of alcohol. The case appeared to have aroused very little interest.

However, for one reader of the *Gazette* this report was a revelation. They imagined the co-respondent creeping cautiously down the cold corridors of these commercial hotels, knowing what excitement awaited him, and reluctantly leaving the warm single bed before any other guest was likely to emerge.

Jenny's opinion of Mr Wesley G. Harrison totally changed. Why had she been so blind?

*

Since the arrival of Jumy's letter, Jenny had spent long hours in bed, considering whether she could ever return to NI-

366

geria. *There's nowt for a girl like you round here*, that kind
landlady had said. But when she finally got to sleep she had
a nightmare ---usually the same one. Musa brought her a
cup of tea in bed, then some woman picked her up and she
was driven over a bridge, where she saw Kenneth's body in
the middle of the road, lying in a pool of blood. Nobody paid
attention to her screaming and begging them to stop and
pick him up.

Never again could she cross that bridge.

She had not yet told Geoffrey what should be done about the
remainder of her belongings in Okante, and he had not
pressed her for a decision. Now she could give him an answer.

She had two Nigeria lives. In one she taught textiles in a
training school. In the other, she and a beautiful friend
dressed up and pretended they were using lovely soap.
When she replied to Peter's invitation she told him that she
would love to see him and Jumy in Kano but could not go
down to his headquarters in Okante. Knowing how sensit-
ive he was, she knew that no explanation was needed.

90

As Jumy promised, the ticket was for a first-class flight from
Manchester to Heathrow by BEA, then to Kano with Nigerian Airways. Although it was open-dated, Peter's letter
made it clear that he wanted her to arrive in Kano as soon as
possible. It had been intended that she would stay with the
Masoors, but Jacob was not well. This was a great relief to
her, though she hoped he was not seriously ill.

The plane from Ringway to London had no First Class section, but at Heathrow things changed. She found a trolley for her two cases and took the short walk to 'International Departures'. She needed to wait only a few minutes at the First Class check-in desk, behind a Yoruba couple. Then she was directed to passport control. The lady Customs officer did not wish to inspect her luggage and pointed out the courtesy lounge. She felt like a seasoned air traveller, though she scarcely recalled that flight back home from Nigeria.

This was one of the new VC 10 aircraft. First-class passengers had priority boarding and she was surprised how few there were. Once on board, she found she had a block of seats to herself. The stewardess demonstrated how her seat could be brought down almost horizontal, which boded well for a good night's sleep.

In preparation for this working holiday she had visited Manchester and spent a day buying a new wardrobe of tropical clothes, this time unconstrained by the cost. For the flight she wore a lightweight grey Terylene trouser suit which she had picked up in Kendals. She was glad to have dressed up, because none of the other first-class passengers were in casual clothes.

The soap in the toilets was *Mama Beauty* and she was embarrassed to find that the wrappers on the spare tablets bore her picture. This could explain why she had noticed one of the cabin crew giving her more than a casual glance.

After a gorgeous dinner and two glasses of champagne, she was ready to sleep as soon as the cabin lights were dimmed at ten o'clock.

It was a nine-hour flight and she woke at six in the morning, having had an undisturbed night's rest. The other passengers appeared to be still sleeping. As soon as she switched on her reading light a stewardess appeared to ask if she would like a drink. When the girl came back with her orange juice she whispered,

'Are you who I think you are, Madam --- Mama Beauty?'

'Yes, but do please keep it to yourself. By the way, what is the local time when we land?'

'There is only one hour difference, Miss. Set your watch forward, we should be landing in about an hour and a half.'

Plenty of time for a good wash and a spot of make-up.

After breakfast the duty-free trolley soon appeared. The brochure showed that they had Jumy's favourite, *Ma Griffe*, so she bought two bottles, hoping Mrs Masoor may also like it. To her amazement, she saw *Mama Beauty* perfume for sale. She bought ties for Mr Masoor and Peter. Almost as soon as the sales trolley returned to base, the 'Fasten seat belts' warning was given and they were on a rapid descent to landing. There was only the gentlest bump before she was back in Nigeria.

Walking down from the plane, she could see huge pyramids covered with tarpaulins. The man in front explained these were sacks of groundnuts, waiting for delivery. The air was suffused with the pleasant smell of the nuts. Though it was only early morning the heat was intense, and she removed her jacket on the way to a waiting bus. It took less than a minute to deliver them to the Arrivals entrance.

From then on there was a contrast to her swift progress through the Heathrow formalities. She stood in the baggage hall for what seemed an eternity, before the first luggage appeared. Almost all the bags had gone before her two new Samsonite cases came round. This made her one of the last passengers in the queue for passport inspection. The officer was a pretty young Hausa woman, so she thought that addressing her in her own language may speed things up. There were only four entries in her passport, but the girl inspected every page. When she reached the back of the document she did a 'double take' before her dour demeanour changed to a grin and she said, 'Mama Beauty! Welcome back to Nigeria.'

The overweight male Customs Officer, unfortunately, did not respond in the same way. He carefully checked both cases. The man spent far too much time looking through the portfolio of pictures taken at Tiptop Studio in Soho, which she brought with her for Peter to photo copy. Had this not been Nigeria, she would have remonstrated. All this meant she was the last to leave for the arrivals hall and it was a huge relief to see Peter waiting for her; dressed in the same dodgy suit he had worn for their flight to Okante. It took her a few moments to recognise the man standing beside him. A blue turban solved her problem. What was Ranjit doing here?

91

Peter confirmed she would not now be staying with the Masoors, and it was a relief when he told her that she and Ranjit were booked into the Central Hotel. He was driving a Mercedes lent by the District Governor, with whom he was staying. He said he would be happier with them at the hotel but protocol decreed that he could not refuse the invitation. She could remember nothing about Kano as they drove, though she knew that she and Bessie Howarth had been here. Then he gave her the bad news.

'I'm afraid you won't be seeing Jumy --- not unless you can stay for more than three weeks. Even then, since you won't be going to Okante, it wouldn't be worth her while coming up here just to say hello.'

'I hope she's all right,' she said.

'Oh yes, Jumy's fine. Sends her love and will write to you, but this weekend she has to go down to Malachi's parents. It seems there is to be a big celebration. His mother's relatives from Upper Volta are coming down to meet Jumy and there is going to be a gathering of the clans.'

Though there had been a significant deterioration in Jacob's health it was hoped they would meet him for a brief discussion the following day. Ranjit sat quietly in the back seat. She had shaken hands with him at the airport but so far his presence had not been explained.

She recognised nothing as they drive through Kano, though she knew she and Bessie Howarth had been here. But when they reached the hotel she *did* find it vaguely familiar. Peter had her cases sent to the room and asked if she would like to go up, but she was keen to find out why Ranjit was there. She said she would like to know what programme had been arranged for her and would love to have some coffee.

After a brief visit to the toilet she found that the two men had moved to a larger table, where Ranjit was setting out papers, in front of the chair on which she was to sit.

'Let me explain why I am here,' he said. 'You may remember that, before you started helping Peter with his publicity films, you and I arranged a contract which he and Mr Masoor signed. My accountant has been recording how much is due to you and an interim statement has been prepared. That's the top item on the paper in front of you. Have a look at that before we carry on.'

The coffee arrived while she was inspecting the account.

'As I remember it, you take just one lump of sugar,' said Peter, as he poured her coffee. 'Help yourself to milk'.

Suddenly she was transported back to that meeting with Mostyn Stainforth in Colesclough when she discovered she was now a rich young woman. When she saw the figure at the foot of this statement she was amazed to find that, so far, she had earned more than twenty-eight thousand UK pounds.

'OK,' said Ranjit, 'may I continue'.

She needed time to recover from the shock. 'Yes please.'

'Well, Jenny, there is a problem. I don't suppose you are familiar with the Bank of Nigeria's new currency controls, so I will ask Peter to explain.'

A group of businessmen had taken a nearby table and were within earshot, so Peter went to the reception desk to speak to the duty manager, who ushered them into an adjoining conference room. He signalled to a waiter to transfer their coffee cups and Ranjit put the documents back in his brief case.

Peter explained that no way had been found to transfer Jenny's earnings out of Nigeria. A solicitor was consulted, and he and Ranjit's accountants had met with Jacob Masoor shortly before his heart attack, to try to find a solution. Jacob was keen for Jenny to carry on as 'Mama Beauty' and had come up with a most generous solution. He had set up the cosmetics business as a separate company, registered in Jersey. Jacob had offered to convert Jenny's earnings into shares in the new company, provided she could accept the proposed valuation.

'Think it over, Miss Masters,' said Ranjit. 'You may wish to take other advice, but the offer which my people negotiated is one thousand pounds per share. That would give you twenty-eight shares, with a bit left over. You could use that money for expenses you incur within Nigeria.'

Peter said. 'I hope this may persuade you to come back to see us, Jenny. Remember, it appears the only way you can avoid having a big lump of money stuck out here. The Mama Beauty business should soon begin paying dividends. Mr Masoor has offered me some shares at the valuation Ranjit just told you. I've jumped at the chance of joining in. Now I'm afraid I have to leave you. I'll phone you here tonight to fix a time for me to pick you up in the morning to see Jacob. It's just the two of us. He said he has private things to tell us which he doesn't want Ranjit to hear. Anything else before I go?'

'Yes, hold on, I have some photos you may like to have copied.'

She ran upstairs to bring her 'portfolio'. He said he would post them to her when the job was done, but she said she would prefer to take them back with her. Local post offices often 'accidentally' mislaid valuable items.

She did not know Ranjit well but she was glad to have him with her.

He asked her to sit down again. 'Before I flew to Kano I called on Mr Haworth at Okantex. He sends you his love and asked me to tell you he fully understands why you didn't feel able to come down. Anyway, the reason I went to see him was to check that you still had an account open at Barclays DCO. He gave me the number. I don't suppose you brought out one of their cheque books, did you?'

'No, I must have left it in Okante. I brought travellers cheques, they are in the safe.'

'Take those home with you. After lunch we will call on their Kano branch.
Show them your passport and I then I will pay in the money that is stuck here. They will give you a cheque book we can start using today.'

He warned her there was little chance of her remaining anonymous and asked if she would prefer to have meals sent up to her room. Seeing her image on the *Mama Beauty* toiletries in the bathroom made her realise that her identity could hardly be kept secret, so she reluctantly accepted the downside to this new career. She had no wish to be imprisoned in the Central Hotel and wanted to see more of Kano.

When they went down to lunch, Ranjit chose a corner table and suggested she take a chair with her back to the room. Nevertheless, before they had finished the first course, a young girl shyly approached with a menu for her to sign. She smiled at the pretty teenager.

As she signed, she asked herself, 'Who the hell do you think you are, Jenny Clarke?' The answer came from an unlikely source --- Sidney, at Tiptop Studio.

That face of yours has value; a higher value than the likes of me can afford.

Ranjit spent the morning giving her a tour of the huge sprawling city. There was still the pleasant smell of ground-nuts everywhere. Her first purchase was the essential cam-ouflage, dark glasses, which she would have needed anyway, as protection against the already strong sun. 'Please put that purse away,' he said. 'I pay for everything, remember?' She also bought and some beautiful silk scarves.

When they got back to the hotel Peter had arrived. After kissing her cheek he merely said, 'Well?'

She realised that she had not yet given either of them a def-inite answer about accepting the share offer, though Ranjit's insistence on not letting her pay for anything was a tacit as-sumption.

'Well,' she said. 'The answer has to be yes. Like it or not, I am still Mama Beauty.'

92

As soon as she saw this gem of a house in the heart of com-mercial Kano, Jenny understood Jacob Masoor's attachment

to the city. They entered through the shop. Peter introduced
her to Mrs Masoor, who appeared surprised and delighted
to be receiving a present. There were several customers in
the shop and only one assistant, so she apologised for not
coming upstairs with them. She took Peter aside and Jenny
could hear her asking him not to keep her husband long.

He was sitting up in bed with his head resting on many pil-
lows. The pyjama top was now too big for him and his skin
had a pallid cast. Nevertheless, the bright eyes were those of
the active businessman she remembered. She went over to
give him the tie she bought on the plane. In a week voice he
said, 'My dear Jane, how kind of you. May I kiss your cheek?'
As she bent down she felt his scrawny shoulders and was
glad she had not delayed this visit.

'So now, Peter,' he said, 'tell me --- am I in the presence of
Mama Beauty?'

Jenny decided to reply. 'Yes, Mr Masoor, I am delighted to
accept your generous offer. I have some decisions to make
when I get home but I intend to play as close a part as I can.'

'That is good news, Jane, but now let me tell you *my* immediate plans. I asked that only the two of you should come this
morning because what I have to say affects all my other
businesses. Peter, if you would kindly help me, I'd like to sit
in the chair by the window, and Jenny, please would you
give me my dressing gown? It's hanging on the door behind
you.'

Once settled, he gave them the awful news.

'As I think you both know, I had a slight heart attack, for
which I am being treated --- successfully, I am told. I seldom
saw my doctor before this happened, but now he tells me

that I have cancer of the pancreas. He says this is treatable, but I have decided that any operation would be better carried out in Switzerland, where my brother lives.   Obviously, we hope for a successful conclusion but, if worst comes to worst, I would want my wife to be in a place more settled than this present-day Nigeria. So my brother has submitted the necessary papers for us to apply for Swiss residence. We fulfil the financial requirements and I propose to transfer the registration of my companies there if we are approved, so that should strengthen our case.

So, first of all – you Peter. Whaat I now have to say applies also to Jane, but affects you more. I have decided that the advertisements featuring her and your sister should cease. As I understand it, this would be happening anyway, since Jumoke became engaged to be married. That is why I made you the offer of buying shares, which I am delighted you have accepted.   I am sorry this had to be done, because I enjoyed seeing how well you and your staff produced them. Do you have any questions? By the way, no sympathy please. Let this continue to be a business meeting.'

'OK, if that is what you want, Jacob,' Peter said, 'although you must know how we both feel. Am I right in thinking that your son Saul will be taking over from you?'

'Yes, the shop will cease trading and he and his family will move here. My French chemist has returned home and there will be no new perfumes, but my son's factory continues to manufacture the *Mama Beauty* soap and cosmetics.'

'And the news for you, Jenny, is that my thoughts of retiring to Lancashire are abandoned. I propose to keep my investment in the Harrison business but those proposals for my nephew and me to develop the Daisy Hill site will not proceed.'

Jenny was taking notice of what Jacob had been telling them, but doubted whether she could take such a dispassionate view as Peter had. Already there were tears in her eyes, which Jacob had noticed. To her surprise, he said, 'So now, Peter, if you would be so kind, I want you to leave us for a little while and let me talk to Jane. Please ask Hepzibah if she would come and join us.'

In later years Jenny would come to regard this conversation as the turning point in her life.

*

Not having met Mrs Masoor before, she was surprised to be hugged and kissed on the cheek. Hepzibah opened a cupboard and drew out a plaid rug to place over her husband's legs, though the room was far from cold.

'Thank you, my dear', he said and turned to Jenny. 'Now, Jane, please sit with my wife on the sofa. I asked Peter to leave us because what I have to say to you is a very personal matter. Hepzibah and I have talked it over and I have relied on her opinion. Please hear everything I have to say before you respond.'

He took a sip of water. 'My nephew Nicolas is dear to us and we are aware that you, too, have become fond of him. But we are also aware that, emotionally, he is somewhat immature. He is a good-looking young man, as I'm sure you will agree. However, I have have been close to him since he was a young boy, and have seen that he has learned to use this attraction in what I can only describe as an irresponsible manner. You are now a mature and beautiful young lady. If Nicolas wanted to choose a partner with whom to spend the rest of his life, we cannot imagine anyone we would prefer.

In the short time I have known you, I have come to admire you. So it is with a sad heart that I am going to suggest that you dispel any thoughts of marriage to him. Perhaps at present he considers that you are the one for him, but we doubt he will ever be able to avoid benefiting from the advantages that his charm gives him. I hope you are not offended by what we suggest?'

Having just been described as 'mature', she now felt anything but! The tears she had been trying to hide now flowed freely. She felt a deep sense of gratitude for being told what she knew, in her heart of hearts, to be true. She felt the arms of Mrs Masoor around her. Just as the embrace of Harrie in that little park in Clitheroe had done, this gradually helped her to settle herself. Hepzibah went to her husband's bedside to bring a box of tissues.

When she had recovered, all Jenny could bring herself to say was, 'Thank you. Thank you *both*, so much.'

93

Peter said it may take a few days to have the whole portfolio copied, but Ranjit filled in the time for her. He was the ideal travel guide. They went to parts of Kano with which even he was not familiar. The huge open market was her highlight. There were stalls catering for every possible requirement. A whole section was devoted to providing for those travelling to other parts of Africa. Some women were loudly haggling over the price of British sovereigns and Maria Theresa thalers, which Ranjit explained were the African alternative to travellers cheques. At another stall men tried on false teeth, from racks of second-hand dentures.

The following day he took her to Kano Golf Club, of which he was a member. The 'greens' were 'browns'. He explained that keeping grass alive throughout the year in this climate was impossible, so sand was the alternative. A man with a rake and watering can was assigned to each 'brown.' After each group of players had finished putting, the sand would be levelled, compacted and watered. They had lunch at the club. She had become used to some of the local dishes cooked by Musa, but here was what could only be described as Nigerian gourmet.

He took her to the Indian quarter where, fortunately, her face did not appear to be familiar. His one concession to the privileged status of tour guide to a celebrity was to call for morning coffee at his club, where he proudly introduced her to a group of Sikh ladies, whom he knew he would find there. She was pleased to find they had no idea who she was. Ranjit was the 'celebrity' here. These ladies had such lovely coiffures that she decided to enquire where she might find a good hairdresser. Three of them recommended a salon within a short walk from the hotel, and one lady used the club telephone to make an appointment for her in the morning.

Jenny was pleased to be giving Ranjit some time off, but when she returned from the salon she found him back at the hotel, with news that Peter had phoned him at home last night to say that all her pictures had now been reproduced and that he was catching the afternoon flight to Okante. He asked Ranjit to apologise and say that he would send her an airletter as soon as he got home.

Now that she was ready to leave, she asked Ranjit if he would kindly take her to the BOAC office to book her return flight, but instead he took her to a firm called Compass

Travel. He knew that this agency handled all the Okantex business and would find the best connection to Manchester, rather than automatically putting her onto BEA. He was right. They found a flight which would take her home by KLM, with a connection at Schipol arriving at Manchester by six in the evening. She told them not to bother telling Harrisons about this, but the manager said it was essential under their contract that they do so. It occurred to her that a commission was involved, so she did not object. Before she left the office she drafted a telegram which they agreed to send to her Mum, saying when she would be home.

A sizeable amount of her 'trapped' Nigerian currency had gone and she was pleased that Ranjit had been able to share spending it. It was a sad parting. He was always been in the background. Now she realised he had been pivotal to all she had achieved.

94

When she emerged from Customs the last person she expected to see was Harrie, who gave her a big kiss and said, 'Don't bother with a trolley, I'll take the heavy case. We need to rush, I'm in the one-hour section, it's very near --- there's ten minutes left. We'll talk on the drive home.'

She set off at a pace Jenny could not match. They checked out from the car park with only a few minutes in hand.

Jenny recalled the first day Harrie picked her up and how little she had said. Now her friend hardly stopped talking and brought her up to date with what had happened while she had been away.

'Geoffrey told me when you would be arriving. I phoned your Mum this morning to say I would pick you up. I said I would deliver you to Bright Street. There is *such* a lot to tell you, darling. Everything is going right for me.'

The workmen had finished and the house was ready, but Harrie continued to 'house-sit'. Clarice had spent a few nights there, but she was using her spare time to supervise work on the Old Smithy.

'OK, now here's something you won't believe. Are you sitting comfortably? It's all down to my dear brother.'

'Go on --- or am I supposed to guess.'

'Never in a million years will you guess. You see, Mummy has been to *Okante* a couple of times and she told Geoffrey how well I was looking after the house and handling the workmen, so he took the opportunity to help me. He told her I wanted to go into a business partnership with a friend. I had been afraid to tell her because it would involve my leaving home.'

'Does she know about Clarice?'

'She knows we are 'pals' and, of course, she approves of her because she's posh. Anyway, to cut this beautiful story short, Mum thinks it is great news, her daughter having a proper job at last!'

'What about your Dad.'

'Geoffrey says he's aware Clarice and I are more than 'pals' but he's all in favour. Don't I have a lovely brother, Jenny?'

'You certainly have.'

'He came round here to see me, by the way. Did you know he has thought of buying a house here? I think he's too late though, they won't get planning permission for more. But there's more good news for you. He has got you a telephone connection,'

'So, I can ring and thank him.'

'You can thank him in person; that's the other thing I have to tell you. You're invited to dinner on Friday week. It's his birthday. He said he's keen for you to come and I *insist* you do. So there!'

'Who will be there? Will I fit in?'

'Course you will. It's just me and him, Mummy and Daddy. Oh, and probably my great-cousin Pommy --- she's quite a fan of yours. Geoffrey suggested it might be a good idea if you stayed the night, like you did last time. Mummy agreed, so Roger's room will be ready for you. Shall I tell them you will come?'

'OK then. Please thank them very much, I look forward to it. I'll get him a present. Any suggestions?'

'Don't do that, a card will do. We gave up buying birthday presents; after all, there's a limited amount of stuff anyone needs. Do you still have that lovely shantung dress with the short skirt?'

'Yes, I haven't worn it since the night I first stayed over.'

'I remember him loving it. Wear that and it will be your birthday treat for him. And don't forget to bring a change of

383

clothes this time. I have your riding gear. We can have a ride on the Sunday morning.'

They were now nearing Colesclough.

'I was feeling tired when we set off', Jenny said, 'but you've really wakened me up with all this news. Thanks so much.'

'Come to Gorsedale Close tomorrow as soon as you're ready. You'll have a lovely surprise. It's gorgeous. I'll open the garage doors so you can drive Wuzily straight in. My Mini will be there, but it's wide enough for three Wuzilies. I have been using the single room overlooking the garden. I've aired the bed in the biggest room, where I guessed you would want to sleep. By the way, I've met lots of nice people while I walked round the estate. When you have settled in why don't we give a party and I can introduce you?'

As they drove up Bright Street she said, 'I won't come in. Your Mum will be wanting to hear all about your visit. You can tell me tomorrow.'

Having helped Jenny in with her luggage she got in and turned the car round. Then she stopped. A brilliant idea had struck her.

I'll get them to take another walk. That should do the trick.

95

Fortunately she had not fixed a time to arrive at Gorsedale Close because it was almost ten o'clock before she woke. Her Mum had left for work.

It was close on lunchtime when she arrived. As she entered her house she saw just how brilliant Mrs Harrison's designs for the decor had been. Harrie noticed her reaction.

'Isn't Mummy clever? We knew you would love it. But do you mind if we do the unpacking later? The sun has just come out and I'm hungry. Let's walk down to that nice restaurant in Bank Street. I've got lots of food in for you, so *you* will be cooking dinner.'

She was glad her friend would be in the house tonight. Once she was on her own she would, no doubt, feel lonely, but she should be thankful a widow of her age was able to begin independent life in such comfort. That was the first time she had acknowledged the word 'widow'. It evoked memories of the confrontation with that dreadful van Vleet woman. Would she ever be 'merry' again?

When it came time for bed, she kissed Harrie goodnight and opened the door of her luxurious bedroom. After climbing into the double bed she closed her eyes and waited for sleep to come. But it would not. She turned on her side and tried to think of something happy, something which might clear her mind. Eventually her thoughts turned to the man she now loved.

In the dream that followed he lay beside her.

*

A few trips in the car brought down everything she needed, mainly clothes. She had already installed the household items Harrie would require, and made a list of what she had forgotten. These could wait.

People had noticed she was taking up residence and several women came to ask if they could help, most bearing gifts. All were invited in because this was a good way of establishing herself in the estate. Most did, indeed, lend a hand, though few stayed long. She had more cakes than she could eat and more chutney than she would ever use. She would drive to Broadholme chapel manse next week; the Mothers' Union would be happy.

Of course, she knew these visitors came to have a look round the house. Many said how they wished they hadn't kept the company's décor. Almost all had husbands out at work, most of them in Manchester. These women were, no doubt, more lonely than she would be. When she told one of them that her mother lived in Colesclough, she replied, 'Lucky old you. Both our families live in Prestbury--- you won't need to look round for a baby-sitter, will you?'

Saturday's visit to The Little Lodge was uppermost in her mind. But before then she needed to have a shopping spree. She found the listed kitchen utensils in Woolworth's and, as always, picked up much else that a tour of this shop always brought to mind. Then she crossed the road. She could never resist going into a shoe shop, and bought a pair of flatties to take with her. The Ball Brothers manager carried her Pye radio to the car and assured her the television set would be installed tomorrow afternoon. When she got home she took a good look in the mirror and decided that the Kano haircut still looked fine, so phoned to make an appointment just for a wash and set on Thursday.

On return from the salon she selected what she intended to wear and put it in the double-bed room. To arrive in, she opted for the Terylene trouser suit she wore on the plane. The shantung frock to change into, of course, as requested by Harrie. Then she got out a pair of jeans, a shirt and her

Fair Isle jumper, hoping he may ask her to go for a walk again. Along with her shoes, all this would easily fit into the smaller of her Samsonite cases.

What she must do now is to stop her heart from pounding.

96

Harrie had suggested she get there before three o'clock but there was heavy football traffic and it took over two hours to reach the junction into Whalley Road. Normally she would have driven straight to the house, but she found a place where she could pull off the road and took a few deep breaths.

Halfway down the drive of The Little Lodge she received the usual welcome. The two dogs ran up and chased Wuzily, giving the loudest barks they could summon, even after she had parked alongside the MG. She had rather hoped he might not be here yet, so that she could settle herself before meeting him. As soon as she opened the car door the barking ceased and Nemo was threatening to come in. He obediently responded to her loud 'SIT' and she walked along to ring the bell. But Harrie had heard her and was waiting with the door open.

'Go away!' she commanded, and they did.

'Sorry I'm a bit late, Harrie. There must be a football match in Blackburn.'

'Yes, it's what they call a Derby game. Daddy has taken Geoffrey. It's Rovers against Burnley. I'll fetch your case, you go in and join Pommy. We are in the conservatory.'

Mrs Hattersley got up to give her a hug. 'What a lovely suit, where did you find that?'

'I bought it in Kendals to wear on the plane.'

'Oh yes, we all want to hear about that. Let Alice know you are here, she's in the kitchen.'

Mrs Harrison was talking to the cook, Mrs Foster. The atmosphere was not charged, as it was the last time Jenny had seen them together, when Jacob and Nico visited; in fact they were laughing.

'Oh, there you are my dear.' She kissed her and addressed Mrs Foster, 'Well that all sounds lovely, Beatrice. I will make sure we are all dressed and ready to sit down by seven-thirty. I wonder if you would bring us some tea and biscuits. Have some yourself. We will be in the conservatory. Just four of us, the men are still at the football. Come along Jane, I hope you are prepared for some girl talk.'

It turned out they were already well-briefed on what she had told Harrie about her visit to Nigeria, so it was not long before Alice took over. Before then she had to field a difficult question, from Pommy.

'Did you see that gorgeous nephew of Mr Masoor's? Nicolas, is it?'

'Yes that's right. He left Nigeria when the Okante project was established.'

'What a pity. I was reading a copy of *Hello!* at my hairdressers a week ago. They had a feature about him breaking up with that foreign woman. Do you and he keep in touch?'

Loyally, Harrie intervened. ' Don't be so nosy, darling. But I can tell you ---the answer is 'no'.

After that, the 'girl talk' resolved itself into listening to her mother telling Jenny all about the wedding of Roger and Mabel, with illustrations from *Lancashire Life* and *Tatler*. She was pleased to be told that Pommy would also be staying the night.

By the time she heard the front door open she was quite ready. She could now face him without looking like a simpering schoolgirl. Even Harrie was not aware how deeply she loved Geoffrey.

*

Mr Harrison came up to shake hands. 'Welcome, Jane. I know I am going to get into trouble saying this, but you look beautiful.' He wore a broad smile.

'You are very kind. That cheerful face tells me that Blackburn won'.

'No, they lost. I support Burnley. That miserable looking chap behind me follows the Rovers.'

Geoffrey did seem sad, but when she looked into those 'bedroom eyes' they were shining.   With no hesitation he came to kiss her cheeks. This was going to be a lovely weekend.

'Now everybody', Alice said, 'it's coming up to six o'clock. I know you probably think this is early, but I want us all to go up and dress.'

'Must we, Mum?' Geoffrey said, 'Can't Dad and I wear lounge suits.'

'No dear. I know you are the birthday boy but I want us to keep up our standards. I am sure you can both remember how to tie a bow tie. I'm sure Jane has brought a lovely dress to show us.' Everyone set off up the stairs.

She was only halfway through getting ready when there was a knock on the door. Harrie was already dressed, in a nice blue trouser suit. Jenny commented on her choice.

'Thanks. Clarice bought me this. I thought you might help me with my hair, but I also want to make sure you come down last. What I will do is wait until everyone is down, then say I will go up to see how you are getting on.'

'No. I'm not happy with that.'

'Please, just for my sake. I want you to stun them all.'

'All right, then.'

She felt embarrassed as she walked down, but when she looked at the reaction of the only person who mattered, she was grateful to Harrie.

'My word,' Alice said, 'you look like a fashion model. That's lovely. Now Harold, off you go.'

Her husband returned carrying two bottles of Taittinger. 'Help me, son.'

They were each given a flute of champagne, except Roger. Harold said, 'No speech, you will be glad to hear. I just want us all to raise our glasses to the man who has been at my right-hand during the most promising stage in our company's history.'

'Happy birthday, Geoffrey', they all said.

While nibbles were being consumed and glasses refilled, Harold took her aside.

'This is probably not a time to be mentioning business, but earlier this week Geoffrey had a telephone call from Nicolas Masoor. He told him about his uncle's serious illness and that there would be changes to Jacob's plans. Surprisingly, he said you had seen his uncle very recently and would be able to explain the position better than he could do, over the phone. I have undertaken to drive Pomona home early in the morning, so I would be most grateful if you could have a chat with Geoffrey before you go on your ride with Harriet.'

'I would be happy to do so,' she said, with more sincerity than her host could realise.

When they entered the dining room she saw that a leaf had been taken out of the table. There was no 'seating precedence'. Alice put the younger three together on one side, so Jenny sat between Harrie and Geoffrey.

It was a lovely meal, but had you asked her afterwards what she had eaten she would probably not have been able to tell you --- she was in a happy daze.

Another two bottles of champagne were drunk with the meal. When Mrs Foster wheeled in the coffee trolley, Harold asked her to take it through to the sitting room. Bottles of liqueur were set out on one of the sideboards. However, on the lower tier of the trolley was an iced birthday cake, wine glasses and a bottle of Riesling. Harold carried these to a glass-topped table and poured six glasses of the wine. There was only one candle on the cake.

He lit it and said to Geoffrey, 'Your Mum said you wouldn't have the puff to blow out twenty-eight. So come on. I told her that next year I want it to be *us* coming to see you and your wife.'

After Jenny was given her piece of cake she took it to the sofa where Harrie was seated. Harrie suggested that they put off their ride until next week. She didn't say why. A date was fixed.

She found the rest of the evening something of an anti-climax. Harrie brought in a roulette board and they spent around half an hour playing, using Monopoly money. Then, about half-past ten, Pommy asked if anyone wanted to play whist. It was Geoffrey who said what she had been waiting to hear.

'OK folks, thanks for a lovely birthday party, but I suggest we call it a day. Pommy and Dad have to be off early tomorrow, and Jenny and I need to have an important talk . . .'

'Oh yes?' Pommy interjected.

'. . . an important *business* talk. So, goodnight everyone., see you at breakfast.'

392

As Jenny reached the foot of the stairs he took her aside, Pommy was helping herself to a nightcap and Harrie had not yet gone up, so they were being watched.

It was a whispered conversation. 'I checked the local TV news before you came down tonight. It's going to be a fine, sunny day tomorrow. Rather than us sitting in the library, it might be nice to take the dogs out like we did last time. And we could talk along the way.'

'I would love that.'

Instead of a kiss on the cheek, he hugged her. Which was nicer.

'Remember to wrap up well. Nightie night.'

97

She was last to come down for breakfast. Mr Harrison and his cousin had left. Alice explained that one of Pomona's sons and his wife were coming up to see her and they were to attend Matins. She sent her love and hoped they would meet again soon. Harrie was feeding the horses. Geoffrey was choosing his breakfast at the sideboard. He wore corduroys and a check shirt.

'Sorry I'm late, Alice,' she said. 'I forgot to set the alarm and slept like a log'.

'Don't worry,' she replied. 'I got up to early to see Harold and Pomona off and Harriet had to go to the stables. I hope

393

you don't need to rush home after you and Geoffrey get back from your walk. Can you stay for luncheon.'

'I will, thank you.'

While they ate they only talked about yesterday. Then he said, 'Don't rush. I'll have another coffee and then I'm going up to put a jumper on.'

'Give me twenty minutes and I'll be down.'

It was just after ten o'clock when they reached Sabden bridge. She could hear the bells of St Mary's church ringing the Catholic faithful to Mass. They encountered only one fisherman as they walked beside Sabden brook. He said, 'How do, Geoffrey?' as they passed. When they got to the path up the hill they let the dogs off the leash.

'OK, I think it's best if I begin by telling you how much Nico told *me*. Then I'd be glad if you could fill me in about what else Mr Masoor said. I don't mean anything personal of course, just what you think affects the company.'

Fortunately, he already knew about Mr Masoor's two ill-nesses, the move to Switzerland, his son taking over and the development of Daisy Hill not proceeding. The part of the story Nico said she would be in a better position to report concerned Jacob's holding of Harrison shares.

'He assured me he has no intention of disposing of any Harrison shares,' she said. 'As you must realise, these must be one of his minor investments.'

'Yes, of course. But what Dad and I are worried about, Jane, is what happens when the old man goes. What if he leaves any shares to his daughter, Sykes's wife? I can't recall her name.'

'Janna,'

'Yes, that's right. By the way, Dad has changed his mind about having Plantagenet on the board. He's discovered they talk the same language.'

'But in a different accent,' she said.

He laughed. 'God forbid, but if anything were to happen to dear Pommy and her family wanted to sell, we might find ourselves outvoted.'

'I'm sorry, Geoffrey. Please don't blame the messenger, that's all I can tell you.'

That was not strictly true. She had not mentioned that she was now confirmed as *Mama Beauty* and would soon become an even richer young woman. That was a secret she hoped to share with him one day.

'Let's walk up to that viewpoint again, so we can sit down. And it might be a good idea to put the leads back on the dogs, I have two important things to tell you.'

Her mind raced back to something Mr Harrison said yesterday --- "*and your wife.*"

When they got to the viewpoint he said, 'Let's leash the dogs to that other bench. We may be here for some time.

As she tried to restrain Nemo she prepared for her dream to be shattered.

But this was not the first 'Important thing.'

Once the dogs had been secured, he said, 'You are only the third person to know this, but Dad agrees with me you are to be trusted. I may be going to Africa for a short while --- but not to Nigeria. Since the Okante project was on the drawing board I have been in regular touch with Crown Agents. They supervise the distribution of UK aid funds to approved projects like ours.

  A few weeks ago they phoned Dad to ask if he would go down to see them and I went with him. The woman I normally contact at Crown Agents said two more countries are interested in having a cotton mill. The Overseas Development Corporation has recommended that Harrisons should submit proposals. I've been back twice since then. One is not even a member of the Commonwealth.'

He appeared to have finished. 'That's wonderful news, Geoffrey, but I'm not sure why I need to know.'

'I can't name these countries but I may soon be looking for someone to help me brush up my French. This person may also be asked to accompany me on my visits.'

'Oh, now I understand why you are telling me this. I already have the answer. Yes please, I would be delighted.'

He stood up and walked to the barrier as if they were now going to admire the view of Pendle. She wondered whether to join him but he had already turned round. He leaned against an ash tree, with the sun behind him. She could not interpret the look on his face. She steeled herself for what was to come.

There followed what seemed like a long pause.

'Now for the second thing I want to tell you. Please hear me out before you say anything.'

She nodded.

'I thought Dad gave the game away when he made the toast yesterday but you didn't look pleased. I love you, Jane, always have, from that first time I saw you in the mill. When I managed to have that dance with you at the Astoria I realised I wanted you to be my wife, but I was too late. I told Dad about this while we were in the car yesterday. He said he knew, ever since we went together to your wedding. Dad said, "For God's sake, do something about it before you go off to Africa. You mustn't loose her."

Het has known for ages, of course. We decided not to tell Mum, in case you say no. All I want you to do is think it over while I am away, but let me ask now.'

'Will you marry me, Jane?'

'Of course I will, you silly man. Haven't you noticed that I'm crazy about you.'

She got up and they met halfway. At last they were kissing. The dogs made a high-pitched sound she had never heard before.

Eventually he said, 'Do you think those two approve?'

'Doggish isn't one of my best languages but I thought I heard, "*About time too.*"

'Shall we go down and tell them?

'Let's. But there is just one favour I must ask of you, Geof-frey.'

He looked worried again,

'What's that, darling.'

'Please call me Jenny.'

Printed in Great Britain
by Amazon